I0525990

Sometimes In Shadow

WALTON MENDELSON

SOMETIMES IN SHADOW

One Off Press
2003

The opening lines of the *vr'trk* page 165 are from *1962 Aperture 10:4,* by Frederick Sommer. They are quoted with his permission.

ISBN 1-9747340-2-0
Printed in the United States of America
One-Off Press, fall 2003
www.oneoffpress.com

Printed by:
BookSurge, LLC
www.booksurge.com
1-866-308-6235
orders@booksurge.com

Sometimes In Shadow

To Louise for putting up with Jake's extended stay. To the memories of Fred, Frances, Lorna, and David. To Brent, who Evil took, I miss you and Jane. To friends who understood. And to Evil and your thugs, I'll drink a shot of single malt—I know you now, such small and petty creatures.

PROLOGUE

Peter Adams heard someone screaming, as the paramedics strapped him to the gurney. He tore at the restraints, pressing pink welts into his arms and legs. They dropped the gurney twice before sliding it securely into the ambulance.

The Emergency Room doctor gave him a sedative. For six hours, he slept. His wife waited patiently by his bed for him to wake. So did the policeman who had questions to ask.

"Mrs. Adams," the policeman said. It sounded to her as though he had said *atoms*.

She considered correcting him, but it seemed petty with her husband lying there.

"Mrs. Adams, has your husband ever had something like this happen before?"

"Peter?"

"Yes." He waited with his stubby yellow pencil—its eraser was worn and slippery black—poised carefully over the form on his clipboard.

"He's a vice president with BP. Does he look like someone given to fits?"

"I have to ask."

"Something must have scared him, why can't you find out what?"

"We're doing that too, but I need to know about him."

***

Mornings were getting colder and darker. White crystal patches of frost in the grass sparkled in the wash of the street lamps. The air carried in it the smell of winter; it was not from the red and yellow leaves carpeting the ground, but a quality of the air itself. And it was a feeling.

Running the dogs in the early morning hours was invigorating. On good mornings, Peter felt as if he could do twenty miles. His longest runs were never more than ten. He worried about his ankle. The warm-up exercises helped. It had been a year since he had last hurt himself, but still, he worried. After the third mile, it got easier as the mantra-like rhythm and repetition of each echoed stride absorbed his attention. His ten-mile run took him two and a half miles from his house to the gray, mud-filled lakes, five miles around them, and two and a half miles back.

The Shakers had built the lakes, which once provided water for farms and power to perform a variety of tasks, from grinding grain to cutting wood. The farms were long gone. Throughout the five-mile long park were a few half-buried stone buildings, several dams, and a broken, stone footbridge: the only reminders that the Shakers had been there. The halfway mark for his run was the lane that wound through the woods at the eastern end of Horseshoe Lake.

The dogs got skittish. It had happened before; they would act strangely, as though brushed by something primal. He found it unnerving. It made him feel that the wind was alive; that gods walked amongst men. That feeling would pass; years of schooling and cultural imprinting kept him from sensing their presence—primitive man's privileged condition. He yelled at the dogs, and gave their leashes a sharp tug. They sat down, shaking.

Peter looked around. In the early morning light, he saw

the black on black shape of things. Eddies of cold air carried a whiff of something—the slightest hint—but almost before he realized it was there, it was gone. He tied the leashes around a sapling and started to walk into the woods. The wind picked up behind him.

He was drawn to the old, stone, pavilion that sat on the tongue of land that cleft the lake. He saw its columns of weathered stone and the piers next to the steps that ran down to the water. He was almost there when he stepped on something soft and yielding. His foot slipped. As he fell, his first thought was that he had hurt his ankle again. He tried instinctively to break his fall. When he hit, his hand plunged into the cold, sticky-raw, disassembled guts of a large animal. The sudden stench rose to fill the world. He scrambled mindlessly through the viscera and dismembered parts.

He ran.

The police chiefs of Shaker Heights, Cleveland Heights, and Cleveland met to discuss the incident. This was the fifth time since the beginning of the year that they had found something like this. After the third incident, they brought in an expert on black magic and cults. The official stories, buried in the local papers, mentioned nothing of cults and Satanism; instead, these were the acts of drug-crazed kids from the inner city, who were out casing prospective targets in wealthy suburbs. Most people never read the articles.

The actual police report told a different story. These were the acts of people, maybe young, driven by a belief in Satan. It was a common pattern. The occult expert had seen it across the country. Usually it went no further than stray cats and dogs. These groups, or covens, would last a few years. Members were, after all, people with jobs and families. Jobs changed, children went to college, families moved, and the covens broke up. Rarely the violence went beyond animals. In every case, the police found a personal agenda, not Satanic, which powered human sacrifices. It was too early; there was too little evidence to know what direction this group would take.

This incident was the worst. They had found the bodies of thirteen dogs.

ONE

Bonnie Winslow had never been to The Bookstall. She thought it was empty when she first walked in. She did not see the alcove from the doorway.

The Bookstall was at the bottom of the marble stairs, on the right at the south end of The Arcade. It was small for a bookstore. There was a makeshift office in the little alcove under the stairs, two steps up from the level of the store. It smelled like bookstores used to smell. The walls were lined with leather bound books of burgundy, ocher, dark green, black, and a variety of grays, their titles embossed in red, or gold, or silver. In the alcove, in a small, stained cardboard box under the table, which also served as a desk, were cans of saddle soap, neat's-foot oil, and carnauba wax.

There were three rows of wooden, sectional bookcases, the kind with glass fronts that lift up and slide out of the way. No two sections matched, although age and bad lighting obscured these differences.

Between the rows were display tables heaped high with remaindered books, the only concession to contemporary writing in the store. Few of those books were bestsellers; rather, they represented the eclectic interests of the store's owner.

There was a single set of shelves, in the corner facing the alcove, which remained locked. In it were books whose design, binding, and printing epitomized the art of book making.

The Bookstall was not what Bonnie had expected.

Conspicuous through their absence were self-help and science fiction books—although there was a first edition of H.G. Wells' *Door in the Wall,* illustrated with photographs by Alvin Langdon Coburn—murder mysteries, romance novels, personal psychology books and paperbacks.

Jacob Krajczynski owned The Bookstall. The Bookstall's door always remained closed. It was glass with *The Bookstall* hand lettered across it in Baskerville; each letter was black with a thin, gold shadow. He usually sat at the table in the alcove, reading or polishing books. People who knew him called him Jake. He preferred that.

The Bookstall did not do much walk-in business. The store's regular clientele usually came in only to pick up books that they had on order; the store was, however, a wonderful place to browse. Sometimes, The Bookstall was closed during regular business hours.

Jake was an odd-looking man. His mother was Chinese-American; his father was Polish. He was five feet eight inches tall and weighed two hundred and twenty pounds. Some people thought he was in his late fifties, others thought he was in his mid-forties. He seldom shaved, just enough to keep from having a full beard. His face was creased. Most people remembered his eyes. In spite of their Chinese shape, they were blue; some days they were dark blue, other days they were light and watery. They were always intense.

Most people did not know to look to the side of the marble stairs; it was easy to miss The Bookstall. Jake liked it that way. Usually those who stumbled in expected something else. "Go there," he would mumble when people complained that he did not carry the kind of books that B. Dalton's stocked.

Bonnie went there twice. The first time was just after lunch. She looked around, focusing on the remainders. She bought a book about identifying edible mushrooms. Jake stared at her as he made change. He had an odd habit of squinting with one eye when he stared. It made her nervous.

Just before closing at six-thirty, although closing was any time Jake wanted, Bonnie came back to the store.

"Mr. Krajczynski?" She was looking up at him, holding out in front of her the book she had purchased earlier.

"I suppose you want to return the book. I didn't think you wanted it."

"How'd you know? It's just that—"

"You're worried about something, and want to ask for my help." He chuckled. "I'm not exactly what you thought I'd be."

It was Bonnie's turn to stare. She thought he had read her mind. It startled her.

Jake got up from his table and walked to the door. He locked it. He had an odd gait. For a moment she puzzled over it; she could not have defined it. Maybe, given his rotund build, it was that his step seemed light, not sprightly or springy. There was something different; the word that came to her mind was *light*.

Jake returned to the table. He pulled a chair out from behind him, which he placed next to his. Then he rummaged through the oil-stained cardboard box under the table. He pulled out a glass and a bottle of Scotch. The bottle was square, corked and sealed with black wax. The numbered label bore the name and title *Michael Couveur, export agent,* in brown script. He held the glass upside down and tapped it. "Clean," he said, as he poured some Scotch into it. He gave it to her. He poured some into the silver mug, which had been sitting on his papers.

"Please," he said, pointing to the chair.

"This sounds silly," she said, holding the glass close to her lips, hiding behind its thin edge. The words poured out. "I'm not sure I should've come to you. It's my son. Someone recommended that I come see you. It started a year ago. He's, or I think, no—"

"You're going too fast. Have a sip of Scotch and take a deep breath." He looked into her eyes with his odd stare. Her breathing slowed; she felt calmed. "Just relax. Take your time. Our introduction has been one-sided, you know my name, but I don't know yours."

Bonnie offered her hand. "Bonnie Winslow. I'm sorry. It's just that I almost thought that you'd have known my name. You did seem to know why I was here before I said anything."

"An observation; I'm not omniscient." Jake drank from his mug. He never looked away from her. "Your story?"

"It started a year ago. My son, Martin, he turned seventeen last month, began acting strangely. At first, you know, I thought it was just his age, but it's gotten worse. His old friends will not have anything to do with him. His new friends are bad. They scare me." She paused and sighed as though she had already unburdened herself of a lot.

"Why'd you come to me?"

"I started attending church. I talked with my priest, Father McNamara. He recommended that I see you. I asked why, but he said it would be best if I found out for myself. What did he mean?"

Jake laughed. He could imagine Mac struggling to describe him to her.

"He's a good friend. We have worked together often. As to your question, I have certain skills that in some circumstances can be . . . helpful. Tell me more."

She felt comfortable with him. It was like being with an old friend. She talked, and he asked questions.

A bell sounded.

"The Arcade is closing in fifteen minutes," he said.

Bonnie looked at her watch. "It's almost nine. I hadn't realized how late—"

"Don't worry; there wasn't anything on TV anyway."

"I should have been home at least an hour ago." She fussed with her purse. "May I use your phone? I need a cab."

"I'll drive you. You'd be lucky if a cab showed up in forty minutes, even if it didn't screw up the address. Come on, we can finish our chat while I close."

It took ten minutes for Jake to get ready. The glass fronts of each bookshelf had to be closed.

"Cockroaches," he said.

"What?" Bonnie asked, looking around for them.

"No. I meant I close the fronts to help keep them out. They always go for the old books. It's the glue."

He fussed over the stacks of books on the tables, straightening them, and moving a few from one pile to another. Occasionally he held one for a minute, thumbing through it. "Looks good," he would mumble. It was more of a ritual than a chore.

Jake got his car, a 1978 two-tone, green and cream, VW van, while Bonnie waited in front of The Arcade.

As she climbed in, he could not help noticing that she was an attractive woman. Her stylish light brown hair flattered her boyish features. She dressed conservatively, yet with a sense of style that was fresh and youthful.

They made small talk on the way to her house. He already knew a lot about her. She had two children, Martin, seventeen, and Julia, nineteen. Julia attended Oberlin College, majoring in music. Bonnie had been a widow for three years. Her husband, Robert, had been a successful lawyer at Jones

5

Day. He had died of a heart attack when he was forty-two. His life insurance left Bonnie enough money that she did not need to work, although she did volunteer work with the Red Cross several times a week.

And Martin's friends sounded bad. She had been right in coming to him.

TWO

Jake had driven by her house before, and recognized it. It was just off North Park Boulevard on the northeast side of Horseshoe Lake. In any other neighborhood, it would have been a mansion. It was brick and stucco, with leaded windows. The house stretched across the wide yard, from the drive lined with elms that formed a canopy over it, to the dogwoods and Japanese yew that bordered the other side of the house.

"Martin is home," Bonnie said. "That's his light on."

"Good. I'll get to meet him. Might as well do it now." Jake started to unbuckle his seat belt.

"Jake, maybe we could do this tomorrow. Or—"

"Tonight. I'm here, and there's no extra charge," Jake laughed.

"It's late. I just don't think that we—"

"Bonnie, no day is a good day for some things. If you want my help, if you trust Father McNamara, then let me meet him. Now." There was the edge of command in Jake's voice that she had not heard before.

She took a deep breath. "Okay," she whispered. "Let's go. I just hope he's not in one of his moods."

In the foyer, Jake stopped to open the two doors, on one side was a small half-bath and on the other a large cloak closet. Inside, the house sprawled, from the living room to the left; down a hallway to the right were a library, dining room, and family room on one side, and the kitchen opposite.

The house felt comfortable to Jake, in spite of its size. Most of the furniture was antique, simple, functional, family pieces. Above the fireplace in the living room hung a remarkable portrait of Bonnie's great, great . . . great-grandfather on her mother's side, painted in 1721. Her family had settled in Jamestown, Virginia, in 1617.

Bonnie went upstairs.

"Martin?" She tapped on his door. "Martin, may I come in?" There was no answer.

Bonnie opened the door.

"Christ!" Martin said, tossing his headphones onto the floor. "What?"

"Honey, there's someone I want you to meet."

"I'm busy," he said, flipping an empty CD case across the room onto his bed. "Tomorrow."

"He's here specially to see you."

"I said I don't want to see your asshole friend."

"You don't talk to people—"

Martin put his headphones back on.

Bonnie spun around to go downstairs, to tell Jake that Martin would not come down. Jake was standing behind her. She had not heard him follow her up the stairs.

He moved past Bonnie, pushing her back into the hallway and closing the door. Martin was tall, several inches taller than Jake was, and thin. He wore his long, light brown hair in a ponytail. There was a small diamond earring in his left ear. His tight black jeans and black tee shirt were the uniform of his age.

Martin scowled as he yanked his headphones off again. He mumbled something Jake could not make out, although the meaning was clear.

Jake smiled. "The door is closed. Say it."

"Who the fuck are you, fat man?"

"My name's Jake."

"Then, fuck you, Mr. Jake."

"That's it?" Jake taunted.

"*It?*" Martin asked, feeling challenged and embarrassed. "You mother fucking son of a bitch," Martin yelled. He threw his schoolbooks at Jake.

Jake grinned.

"Shit! Fuck! Dammit!" Martin grabbed anything near him: pens, books, CD's, papers, and threw them.

Jake never moved out of the way. He matched his breathing to Martin's. "Tired?"

They locked eyes.

"Shit. Damn," Martin tried to yell. The words sounded soft, hollow, and meaningless. He reached for things to throw that weren't there, and he fought to keep from crying in front Jake.

With every breath, Martin calmed a little more. Downstairs, Bonnie heard the tantrum, then the silence. She wondered who Jake was.

Jake joined her in the kitchen. "I smell coffee."

She poured him a cup.

"He'll sleep well tonight and tomorrow. Let him stay home from school."

"What happened?" Bonnie asked. "What about him?"

"Martin needed sleep more than I need information. If you don't mind, I'd like to stay here for a couple days. You have the room. I want to be here when he wakes up."

"What did you do to him?"

"I made some adjustments."

"I want to see him."

"Let him be. He'll sleep, peacefully, as long as—"

Bonnie ran from the kitchen. She went up to Martin's room. It was a mess, but he was asleep on the bed. Jake had covered him with a blanket. She leaned over him, adjusted the blanket, and gave him a kiss on his cheek.

"Okay?" Jake asked when Bonnie returned to the kitchen.

"Yes. What did you do?"

Jake ignored her question. "You were right; his friends are bad. They will feel my presence, and they won't like it. His friends won't want to give him up. Martin will need protection."

"He'll need protection from what? Now you are scaring me. If he's in danger, why don't I just call the police?"

Jake couldn't help recalling his initiation.

"Protection from what?" he had asked his Master. "Ghosts and goblins? I'm not the ignorant son of an ignorant farmer willing to do anything to get into a monastery. I don't need to be taught what's real and what isn't."

"What do you know?" his Master asked, as he tied Jake to the tree. "I'll be back in the morning. Whether you perform the Rite of Summoning or not, you will spend the night tied to this tree. You will be tested regardless of what you do." Chemmg Tse Lu turned, and walked silently into the dark.

"Protection from what?" Jake asked, as he calmed himself through ritual breathing. He had a feeling that it could be a long night.

Bonnie was staring at him. "Are you all right?"

"I'm fine. I was just thinking of a time when I asked the same question. It's late, but I need to explain some things to you."

Jake explained his theory of individual realities: the accommodations children make while growing up and trying to conform versus the oppression of society's constructed reality.

"Would Father McNamara approve of—"

"Yes. We've talked about it often. He knows my opinions," Jake smiled and poured some cream into his coffee, "all too well."

He talked about Good and Evil. He denied the Biblical heaven and hell. "There's no Devil waiting with outstretched hooves to steal your soul. It's worse. The Beast is Man."

Bonnie started to make the sign of the cross. She stopped and scratched her forehead, embarrassed at her fear.

"It's Jung's racial memory gone berserk. The Beast is a colony: the sum of many individuals. It feeds on chaos. There are people who attract evil; they give it dimension and direction. This collective evil posits in them. Such an individual becomes The Beast, whose driving force is to create and feed on fear, violence, rage, and destruction: the manifestations of chaos."

Jake paused. He poured another cup of coffee. Before he finished with it, it was more cream and sugar than coffee. There was a twinkle in his eye.

"Every generation has a few who don't see what others do. They may become artists, or mystics, or they may squelch their sensitivities and try to adapt—there is a lot of pressure to conform. Out of each few thousand who have this extended vision, a few find their way to mysticism, and a few of them have special abilities. If they are lucky, they find a Master who recognizes those skills and can give them focus. I am such a person."

The night of initiation was longer than Jake had thought it would be. It was cold; the top of a mountain was not where he wanted to be. It started to rain at about one o'clock. At first, he had to concentrate on producing body heat; Chemmg Tse Lu called it dumo.

He would die of exposure if he failed. The rain turned to snow. He took pride in his ability to stay warm; his underpants were not much protection.

He decided to chant the Rite, summoning up the demons of the world and commanding them to devour his body. It's silly, *he thought,* but I can tell Chemmg I did it.

Jake was tied to one of the few trees at the edge of the timberline; there he was exposed to the elements. At first, he was afraid of lightning, which seemed to crash all around him. Jake's fear died as he realized that if he were hit by the lightning, it would all be over very quickly. That would be fate.

He had just started the chant when there was another crack of lightning. In that flash, his life was shattered. He felt everything drain out of him. For the smallest part of a second, time enough to burn itself into his memory, he saw Evil grinning at him. There was no question of continuing with the ritual. He was in a fight to stay alive. The ropes that bound him, that held him captive to that tree, saved his life. They kept him from running in blind terror. They also reminded him that the face of Evil was within himself. The battle waged was invisible to the world. The fight took over an hour.

Jake laughed. The coffee was too sweet. He never could get it right.

"What?" Bonnie asked, startled by his laugh.

"I'm sorry. I've fought so many battles. It's not funny, but I've had to learn everything the hard way. Looking back, I can see why my Master used to laugh at me. I fought hard to stay blind."

Jake looked at the kitchen clock. "It's late. Go to bed. I'll sleep down here. I'll be okay."

"I've got a guest room."

"No, I don't want to be any trouble."

"It's made up. Please, I feel—"

Jake laughed. "Go on up, or we'll be arguing till dawn."

"At least let me get you a pillow and some blankets."

Jake sipped the last drop of coffee from his cup. "No, thank you. Go to bed."

Bonnie went upstairs. Even as she closed her door, she thought she could hear Jake's laugh coming from the kitchen. It was soothing. *Everything* will *work out,* she thought as she fell asleep.

THREE

Bonnie woke up at six-thirty. She got dressed and went downstairs. From the landing, she heard Jake snoring. Hearing it, she whispered to herself that she was glad her husband hadn't snored like that; it would have broken up a beautiful romance. At the foot of the stairs, she stuck her head around the corner to look into the living room where Jake had fallen asleep. She burst out laughing. He was not on the sofa as she had expected. He was sprawled on the floor, one arm wrapped around the leg of her coffee table. His hair was as disheveled as his shirt, and his right front pants pocket stuck out like a mocking, coated tongue. She ducked back, hoping he had not seen her.

"I'm up," he said.

"I'm sorry." She walked into the living room, her hand over her mouth, trying to stop herself from laughing. "Really . . . I am."

Bonnie was struck by Jake's eyes; they were bright, clear and sparkling.

Jake sat, laughing. Then, as if pulled straight up by a rope around his chest, he stood. He neither leaned forward nor held onto anything—he simply stood. It happened so quickly that Bonnie was not sure that she had seen it. Later that day, when she was alone, she tried to stand up as he had. It was impossible. Jake walked past her toward the downstairs bathroom, stuffing himself back into order.

Bonnie and Jake stayed in the house all day while Martin slept. At first, Bonnie wanted to go out. Then the phone calls started, calls for Martin. After the first few, which were about an hour apart, the phone rang every ten or fifteen minutes. Each time, a young male voice asked for Martin. By mid-afternoon, the calls turned abusive.

"I couldn't talk you into disconnecting the phone?" Jake asked. They were in the family room, where, for forty minutes, Jake had kept Bonnie company while she rode her exercise bike. "You've managed to get me to answer your phone every time."

Bonnie stopped pedaling. "I'm sorry. I'd hate to unplug it, but—"

"Just kidding. Anyway, I figure you'll get off that damnable thing soon." He squinted at her. "I don't think this much exercise can be good for you."

Bonnie wiped her face and arms with her towel. "Are the calls really bad?"

"Yes. I'll keep getting the phone."

"You said—"

"And I also said I was kidding. Now, go shower. If things escalate, I want you dressed and near me before it gets dark."

"Then let's leave." Bonnie suggested. "Take Martin and go someplace else."

"I'd like Martin to get as much sleep as possible. He needs time and rest to get back in touch with his soul—for want of a better word."

"Jake, if it's this bad, why not call the police?"

"You're right, I should."

While Bonnie showered, Jake called the police. He told them he had seen some suspicious young boys running around the neighborhood. They said they would schedule a drive-by. Jake knew it would not stop anything, but it could slow things down. They didn't say it to Jake, but they were worried. Bonnie's house was less than a quarter mile from where they had found thirteen dismembered dogs three days before. Complaints from Bonnie's neighborhood were taken seriously.

***

Chemmg Tse Lu was seventy-nine when he came to the United States. He was part of a large community of people who had fled Tibet during the 1959 revolution. His Master, Ka, who claimed to be a descendant, on his mother's side, of the great Milarepa, had wanted him to leave for some time.

People were born with diverse skills. Chemmg Tse Lu was a warrior, though not in the secular sense. He never took up arms against the Chinese. His battle was bigger; he fought Evil. He needed to find and recruit disciples in the West. The East was no longer able to fight alone.

In the late sixties, Jake left Chicago for California. He was not a hippie, but the allure of the West Coast was strong. In Los Angeles he found a house not far from the ocean. He rented the basement; the owner lived upstairs. One day a friend of the owner came to visit. His name was Bing. He had driven down from San Francisco for a week's vacation. He practiced Tai Chi four to five hours a day on the beach. Unlike the common, daily exercises that millions practice throughout the world, it had gone farther.

Jake watched him work out. Bing was oblivious to the audience. He was holding his hand palm out, fingers slightly bent. He pushed it away from his chest, the movement aimed inadvertently at Jake. Even at fifty feet, Jake felt the pressure, like being hit in the chest with a missed football.

A week later, Jake moved to San Francisco.

Jake studied Tai Chi for a year with Dr. Pak, Bing's Master. Jake was the janitor and handyman at Dr. Pak's dojo, in return for room, board, and lessons. He was the most diligent of Pak's students, but far from the best. When the other students weren't around, Pak would laugh at him, teasing and goading. The laugh argued of talents misapplied.

Pak sent Jake out for groceries; they were going to have a visitor for dinner. It was evening when Jake returned. Pak was playing Go with a plainly dressed, dark-skinned man, introduced to Jake as Chemmg Tse Lu. The game was in the first third of play. The four corners and sides were claimed. White and black were engaged in a struggle along the left side. It looked to Jake as though Pak, playing black, was winning.

Jake played Pak every day. He took a thirteen stone handicap and usually lost. The few times he had won, he felt Pak had thrown the game.

Within twenty minutes, black was in a position to capture a large group of white stones along the upper edge of the board. Chemmg smiled as Pak put the black stone he had been holding back into the red-brown, cherry bowl of slate stones on the floor next to him. Pak bowed, conceding the game, and laughed as they cleared the board.

"But . . . Dr. Pak would have captured—"

"Sometimes you must lose a battle to win the war," Chemmg said. These were the first words Jake heard from Chemmg, said with almost no trace of an accent.

Jake cooked dinner. He prepared three of Pak's favorites: vegetarian stir-fried crab meat, bean sauce noodles, and the salad—seasoned, parboiled asparagus called dragon whiskers.

"You are joining us, of course," Chemmg said to Jake, as he was serving them.

Jake looked uneasily at Dr. Pak. "Usually I—"

"Yes," Pak said, "it would please us."

Jake returned to the kitchen to get his plate.

"On your way back, there is a bottle of special plum wine in my bag," Chemmg said. "Could you get it?"

Throughout dinner, the two older men spoke Chinese, English, and Japanese. They said Jake's name often, looked at him, and laughed. Jake felt honored to be eating with them, but he was very uncomfortable.

After dinner, they went for a walk. Chemmg asked Jake questions. Pak practiced pushing out with his open palms, as Jake had seen Bing do on the beach a year earlier. An empty, green, wine bottle shattered under the absent-minded pressure. Chemmg laughed. "As long as I have known you," he said to Pak, "you have been a show-off."

The next morning Chemmg was meditating when Jake got up. Jake asked him if he wanted a cup of tea.

"Yes, in a few minutes. First, sit. We must talk."

Jake sat on the floor opposite Chemmg.

"You are like a fish ready to spawn, but trapped in the wrong river. Pak and I have talked about it. I would like you to study with me. I cannot promise that you will ever learn feats of physical prowess. I can promise that you will find a challenge like no other. Pak has recommended you over all his other pupils for this, and he is right. Will you join me?"

"I came here to learn Tai Chi. I'm not the best, but it's what I want and like."

Chemmg's childlike smile threatened to connect his ears; his eyes twinkled. Jake thought he was quivering beneath his robe. "You are one of the worst I have ever seen to be so dedicated to the physical arts."

Jake's eyes teared; he jumped to his feet. He had taken an instant liking to Chemmg. Now he wanted to turn away from

Chemmg, to put a wall between them. Jake's reaction was all that Chemmg could take; Chemmg burst out laughing.

Jake was shocked. He stared at Chemmg in anger, and Chemmg stared back. Jake never knew at what point the laughter stopped. He felt a gentle massaging and pressure on the nerve centers in his solar plexus, in the base of his head, and in his mind. His anger and hurt disappeared, but were not forgotten. Chemmg could have removed them as though they had not been felt, but that would not have served his purpose. Jake relaxed.

Years later, when Jake had mastered the technique, he looked back at those moments. Chemmg's control had been subtle, strong and thorough, but without bruising or tearing. What amazed Jake was how Chemmg had been able to exercise that control while leaving so many of Jake's feelings intact.

"You have potentials that are different from the physical world you have your heart set on. You are rare, Jacob Krajczynski." Chemmg paused. For a second time, Jake was shocked. It was not that Chemmg had no trouble pronouncing his name that shocked him, but that he had known it at all. Jake never used his surname. "We'll work together, and there is never enough time. Get your things, and we will go."

Jake felt a hand on his shoulder. He turned and looked at Dr. Pak. A narrow strip of morning sun from the open window grazed his ear and ran down his right shoulder and chest. "Go. You are in the care of the most talented man I know. This is your destiny."

They drove in Jake's car. Chemmg explained briefly the problem of Good and Evil. Jake glanced at Chemmg, "If Evil works through people—people who commit crimes in order to create chaos—why not call the police? Here at least, the police and the courts function fairly well to remove such people from the streets."

***

The police would slow them down, but not stop them. It would be dark soon. Jake had checked on Martin. Martin was in a deep sleep.

Bonnie made sandwiches for dinner, and they split a beer. Jake was telling Russian jokes. The shriek of a cat broke the spell. Jake put his sandwich down. He had checked the doors a few minutes earlier. He had assured Bonnie that they would be safe, but he was nervous. He knew he would be okay once something happened, once he could gauge his opponent. Until then, he worried.

Something broke a window in the family room. It was a rock. He picked it up, tossing it from hand to hand as if it were too hot to hold.

They're suckering me away from Bonnie, he thought. "Bonnie, come in here," he yelled.

"What?" She asked, setting her plate down on the desk next to her exercise bike.

A second rock came through a window in the living room, at the opposite end of the house.

It's not Bonnie, he realized, it's Martin. "Quick!"

Jake nearly knocked her over as he dashed out of the room and down the hall. "Come on!"

They ran to Martin's room. A young man, dressed in black, held Martin's arm, and was leading him to the open window. As the door slammed open, the man let go of Martin and pulled out a knife. He lunged at Jake. Jake jumped back, out of the young man's reach, pressing Bonnie against the doorjamb.

The man turned back to Martin.

Jake tackled him, pushing him away from Martin. The man fell across the bed, leveraging his legs free of Jake's grip. He spun to the floor and faced Jake with a jackal grin; his knife slicing down at Jake's face. Jake struggled to find a foothold amongst the slippery CD's, papers, and books while keeping clear of the blade. For a second, the man glanced away, looking for Martin. Jake got to his feet. He parried the next swipe, and ignoring the threat of an attack from the man's other hand, he reached around and touched the back of the man's neck. A quick shift of his fingers and Jake located the nerve cluster. He pressed, and the man collapsed—dead on the floor.

Bonnie was hugging Martin, standing between him and the man on the floor. Martin's face was wet with tears.

"He'll be all right," Jake said to Bonnie.

Jake looked out the window; whoever else had been out there was gone. He led them downstairs, and called the police. They would have a car and an ambulance there in five minutes. Jake called Father McNamara.

"Mac, this is Jake. I'm with Bonnie and Martin Winslow."

"Are they all right?"

"They're safe."

"What's happened?"

"I don't have time to talk now. The police are on their way; I've had to stop someone. We'll—"

"One of Martin's friends?"

"Yes. We'll be tied up for several hours. Take your time, but come over. Also, they'll need to sleep at your place." A light from the driveway shone through the window. "I'll see you in a while. The police are here." He hung up.

FOUR

The police were there for three hours. They interviewed each one of them, and photographs were taken. Martin's room was dusted for fingerprints. Several officers were outside looking for evidence; they would come back in the morning, when there was light.

Martin identified the body. "His name's Richard Todd. What happened? Why—"

Jake was upstairs, talking with one of the police officers. Bonnie sat next to Martin on the sofa while a policeman interviewed him.

"How do you know him?" the policeman asked.

"We met in school."

"Where?"

"Heights High. Mom?" He turned to Bonnie. "What's happened? What was Rick doing here? Who's the fat guy?"

Bonnie started to brush a lock of Martin's hair out of his face. She caught herself, and pressed a damp, balled Kleenex to her eyes.

"Officer," she looked up at the policeman, "Martin has had a tough time the last few weeks. You can see he doesn't know or remember much about any of this. Can we continue this later?"

The officer looked through his notes. "Sure. If we need more, later is fine."

The police were just leaving when Father McNamara

arrived. There was something old-fashioned, comforting and right, about a priest being there. "Mrs. Winslow, are you okay?"

"Yes, Father. Jake is in the kitchen with Martin. He said that he'd fix Martin something to eat. If you're hungry, I'm sure—"

"I may have recommended you get help from Jake, but I didn't suggest that you eat his cooking. I have."

Jake and Martin came into the living room. Each held a plate. "Spanish omelets," Jake said with a smile, "my specialty."

Mac laughed. He knew Jake's idea of a Spanish omelet was a fried egg on toast, dusted with garlic powder, salt and pepper, and covered with ketchup. Floating in the ketchup were a few green peas. Jake had made it for Mac—once.

"The peas make it really good," Jake claimed. Everyone, even Martin, laughed.

This was the best Mac had seen Martin, and it was obvious that Martin liked Jake. *Jake can work miracles,* Mac thought. He watched the three of them. It was hard to tell someone had been killed in this house earlier.

"How do you two know each other?" Bonnie asked.

***

Mac had been stateside for a day. He had hitched a ride down the coast from Fort Ord. Mac was hungry when they stopped for gas. His ride went on, and Mac went into the cafe. He was halfway through his hamburger when he heard two men taunting a young private, who, by his appearance and comportment, was just out of boot camp. The two men had ridden in on motorcycles, a few minutes earlier.

"Hey soldier boy, kill any babies? . . . Like them Asian

girls? . . . Maybe you like the little boys better. . . ." They laughed, and pushed the soldier back and forth between them. "Hey soldier boy. . . ."

Mac stood up. He knew it wouldn't be a fair fight, even if he got into it, but they could kill the young soldier.

"Leave 'em alone," he said.

The soldier looked at Mac; from the uniform, he recognized Mac as a Marine chaplain. "Father, don't. Call—"

"Ah, Father." One of the two men pulled off his chain belt and began swinging it. "Yes, join us. We are truly sinners."

Mac whispered a quick prayer and walked toward the men. He had taken three steps, when the man who had been sitting a few seats down from him at the counter stood up blocking his way. Mac reached out to push the man aside. His hand barely touched the man's back when he found himself falling into the counter. The man walked up to the bikers. "You heard the chaplain, let him go."

They shoved the young soldier to the side, onto a small corner stage. He landed with a crash in a beat-up, metallic red and silver drum kit, sending two brass cymbals and the snare drum rattling across the empty hardwood dance floor.

As the chain swung at him, the man turned, hit the chain arm away and grabbed the biker's lower jaw. They pirouetted; the man used the limp, scuffed, leather-clad figure to block the second biker's attack. They locked eyes.

"Don't," the man whispered, as arresting as any drill instructor Mac remembered from basic training. "You two get out of here."

The stand-off lasted for what seemed like a full minute. The biker walked over to his friend and helped him outside.

Mac broke the silence. "Thanks. Let me buy you a cup of coffee. My name's Mac, short for McNamara, Tim McNamara."

"Jake." They shook hands. "Just Jake."

***

". . . We've been friends ever since. Eight years ago, I heard there was a bookstore for sale. Jake was living in Portland, but I knew he wanted a change. He drove in, looked at the place, and bought—"

"You want some ice cream?" Martin interrupted.

"How can I refuse?" Jake said, following Martin down the hall.

"And you two work together?" Bonnie asked Mac. "What does that mean?"

"You've seen Jake. This is what he does."

"This happens to other people?"

"Not exactly like this. But yes."

"You mean he . . . kills people?" Bonnie asked.

"Sometimes that happens. But didn't you see Martin? When was the last time you saw him laugh and carry on like that?"

"It's been so long," Bonnie paused, trying to remember, "years maybe."

"Well, that's also what Jake does."

Jake and Martin returned from the kitchen. They were laughing, and both had chocolate sauce on their shirts.

"What a mess!" Bonnie said.

"We cleaned up the kitchen," Martin said. "Okay?"

Jake looked at his watch. "Now, you've all got to go. Take what you need for a night or two. You'll go with Mac. I'm staying here. I'll talk with you later."

"I don't understand." Bonnie said. "I—"

"Jake's right," Mac said, taking Bonnie's arm. "We should go."

The house felt empty when they had left. Jake walked around, getting a feel for what had happened. He knew that someone would be back. Just as Jake was trying to give features to his opponent, he too would be trying to figure out who Jake was. Jake turned out the lights, and sat down on the floor in the corner of the living room.

There was a hint of light coming through the trees. Outside the window facing the backyard, a twig broke.

The window slid open; a black clad figure climbed through. The intruder did not see Jake. He moved toward the stairs. He was a young man, in his late teens. He was confident, with the confidence of youth, not of experience or of skill. Jake sensed that he was there to reconnoiter.

The boy will be easy, Jake thought as he watched the figure move through the hall. *I'll get him on his way back.* Jake wanted the boy to see the house, to see where his comrade was killed, to see how easily it had happened. After a chat, Jake would let him go, let him report back. *Good PR,* he thought.

The young man stood confused in Martin's room. There was no sign of a life and death struggle, just expected clutter. Rick had been the best of them; he had even liked to break into houses while their owners were entertaining. Rick had taken chances that none of the rest would, and he had been a good fighter. He would not have been taken so easily; more things should have been broken in the struggle.

The young man knew there was nothing more to learn from the room; he went back downstairs. As he turned to enter the living room, he was suddenly unable to move. He had no idea what had happened. Later, when he tried to describe it, all he could recall was the shadow of a man, sitting in the opposite corner. He thought the shadow's eyes had glowed.

The boy's mind was easy to work, too easy. It took Jake a

few seconds to discover why: someone else had been working on his mind, adjusting nerve centers so that control would be quicker and easier. There were also blocks, crude but effective.

"What is your name?" Jake asked.

"Ed Forbs," the young man replied in a whisper.

"Why are you here?"

"We . . . I wanted to know what happened."

"Do you know the name of the fellow who died?"

"Errrr . . . Riiiii . . ." There was a block.

"Who else is in your group?"

"No one . . . nobody."

"Who is behind your group?"

Ed's body began to stiffen. Jake probed deeper; there was another block. He started to remove it. He watched, stunned, as Ed fell sideways to the floor, his face locked in a sardonic grin. He had set off a trigger—designed to keep out someone with his talents. Even in the dim light of dawn, Jake could see that the boy was turning blue. Pink froth dribbled from his mouth. He heard a choking, gurgling sound coming from Ed's chest. The boy's muscles contracted against each other; his right arm cracked as it bent behind his back. Ed writhed in a horrid, tetanal dance, his body arched, and his legs and arms twisted.

Jake knew that the boy would die if he didn't breathe soon. He was frightened—he didn't want the boy to die—he didn't want another death on his conscience.

Jake cradled Ed's body. He worked, nerve center by nerve center, to relax muscle groups, first the chest. It took over an hour to normalize Ed. Once Jake was confident that Ed could live on his own, he began to make adjustments. Subtlety was not a concern. The mere fact that Jake had saved Ed's life would tell his opponent too much. Jake wanted to give the young man a chance to rest and recover. Ed may have been bad, but he wasn't evil.

Jake carried Ed to the VW, and drove him to the hospital. It took a while to get him checked in. Hospital bureaucracy was not set up to handle the act of a Good Samaritan.

Jake wondered as he walked back to his van. Ed would be relatively safe; the hospital could deal with another seizure, if one occurred. He had no idea who else was involved in this. He would check out Ed; the police might know something. There was one thing Jake knew for a certainty: whoever was behind this little gang was tough and ruthless.

FIVE

Mac drove Bonnie and Martin to St. Boniface. The rectory was large, and more than able to accommodate them. They had the two guest rooms overlooking the courtyard. By the time they had unpacked, Mac had to get ready for early Mass. Martin went to sleep. Bonnie was restless; she said she wanted to help Mrs. Meyernik, the housekeeper, with breakfast.

St. Boniface was a small, blue-collar, church built in 1924, in the heart of the steel mill housing, just to the south of the Flats. It was at the end of Jay Street, which ran to the edge of the bluff above the Cuyahoga River. It was an odd building, designed to look like a Gothic cathedral in miniature. What made it strange was that it was rough, red brick, with undersized, stocky buttresses that were out of place and comical. Heavy wire mesh covered the stained glass windows.

All the houses of the immediate neighborhood were kept up in even rows with alternating squares of green grass and strips of gray concrete. It was a tight, prideful community of Slavic families. The men had worked the mills for three generations, silently carrying the scars.

Bonnie quickly discovered that she couldn't help Mrs. Meyernik, other than to stay out of her way, while she made pastries.

"How long has Father McNamara been the priest here?" Bonnie felt awkward calling him Mac.

"Ten years, I'd say." Mrs. Meyernik wiped her hand on her apron. "It wasn't easy then."

"When he was first assigned here?"

"He's Scots-Irish, you know." She waited for Bonnie to nod her acknowledgment. "Well, this neighborhood's Slavic. Irish live a few miles west. They beat him up a few times, and sent him to the hospital once. No one knew who did it, and he never said."

"He's a priest!"

"He said it was kids out for trouble, but there was talk. Back then, a lot of jobs left when the mills cut production. He fought the steel companies, the banks, and the city to hold the neighborhood together.

"Could you get the door?" She interrupted herself to put the tray in the oven. "Thanks. Now, the Father is a hero. Today, he's so well liked that if he told the parish to vote Republican, they would." She laughed. "That makes him almost a saint."

The rectory was made of the same red brick as the church. The interior was European. All the rooms—wood paneled, dark with painted graining—were shadowed and priestly somber. Each room, other than the kitchen, had a worn area rug over pecan stained, oak floors. Mrs. Meyernik kept the house neat. Mac had brought people to the rectory before; "Sanctuary, Mrs. Meyernik, sanctuary," he would tell her.

In the front, along the street side, was a wall, eight feet high that ran between the house and the church. It was red brick, topped with shards of roofing tile. Opposite the wall, about forty feet away, was the hallway that connected the rectory with the church. In the front corner of the courtyard, under three hawthorn trees, was a small shrine to St. Boniface and a goldfish pond that the priest before Mac had installed.

After Mass, Mac joined Bonnie and Mrs. Meyernik for

breakfast. "Bonnie, I never asked you, why'd you start coming to St. Boniface? We aren't around the corner for you."

"My grandparents lived two streets over. We used to take the bus here on Sundays. The whole family would go to Mass with Father Zednik."

"People still talk about him," Mac said.

"He meant well," Mrs. Meyernik confided, "but it took a while to get to know him."

"He scared me," Bonnie went on. "He was always so serious. I think he was the reason I stopped going to church. When I had a choice, in college, I imagined that all priests were like him. You're not. Anyway, after Mass we'd go to my grandparents'. They died about fifteen years ago."

"What was their name? I've been here a long time."

"Semczyszyn."

Mrs. Meyernik shook her head. "No."

"We always had stuffed cabbage and dumplings. If it was warm, we'd eat outside. They would serve us wine, even my sister and me. That would get mom mad; she and grandma would argue about the old ways and what mom thought were the right, American, ways. My grandfather would pour us more wine, and wink at us. I think he liked to see them fight.

"Anyway, a year ago when I felt that I needed the Church, it was sort of easy for me to come here."

Mac and Bonnie never noticed when Mrs. Meyernik said, "Chores," and left the room.

Bonnie told him about college, meeting her husband Robert, their marriage, and her daughter Julia; she told him everything, except about Martin. Mac listened, occasionally asking a question or two. When Mrs. Meyernik came back to clear the table, they went into the front sitting room. In stark contrast to the rest of the house and its furnishings, there was a stereo system and rows and rows of records that added color to the room.

Bonnie walked over to look at the records. Starting at the upper left shelf, she went through them.

"I've been going to the orchestra every week for years. We started going during George Szell's last two years. And I don't recognize one title, not one."

Mac knew she was confused. "Early music. I love it. If you look down there," Mac pointed to the lower shelf, "you'll see I do have a fair amount of Bach, Handle, Vivaldi, and even some Mozart."

"There has been music written since then, you know."

"Of course, of course. Here," Mac knelt down to pull out a record. "Beethoven, the *Ninth*, on original instruments."

Bonnie grinned, "Charles Ives? Igor Stravinsky? The Beatles? The Rolling Stones?"

"Never heard of 'em. You're making them up."

They both laughed. Mrs. Meyernik heard them from the kitchen. She smiled. "It's good to hear laughter," she heard herself say aloud. She had just finished putting the breakfast dishes away when she heard the opening strains of *L'Orfeo*. She didn't know the title; in fact, she had never heard it before. All Father McNamara's music sounded alike to her. She had laundry to do in the basement.

Mac played the disc jockey, with bits of this and bits of that. Bonnie liked it, and that was all the encouragement he needed. They were listening to *The Vespers of 1610*. "Performed under the direction of David Munrow," Mac said, as though that meant something special. He found himself wishing that Jake would keep busy for a while, and stay away.

***

Jake drove to his apartment on Euclid Heights Boulevard, a couple miles from Bonnie's house. It was large and old, and a private showplace for his obsession with collecting.

Two little boys were playing in the back when Jake parked his van. They ran to meet him. "Can we come up?" they asked.

"Only if your mother says it's okay," Jake said, although he hoped she would say no.

"Mom, can we?"

Mrs. Rapoport leaned over the metal rail of her back landing, "Jake?"

"Ten minutes," Jake conceded. "I'm tired."

"You heard Jake. Ten minutes, then I want you back down."

They ran up ahead of Jake. Inside, they knew what they could and could not touch.

On the enclosed porch, just in front of a Norfolk pine that blocked what little direct sunlight could get in, was a Hemiodemagnitizer, circa 1923. This was the first of four medical machines that he had fixed. The carved mahogany cabinet—the size of a large console television on legs—contained dials and gauges, with a switch marked *Diagnosis/Treatment.*

"I'm the doctor," one of the boys said, running to the Hemiodemagnitizer first.

"You were doctor last time."

Jake brought in a chair from the dining room. "Okay, doctor, you can stand on this."

"Jake?" the other whined.

"Take turns."

The other boy sat on the floor and put his arm on a small box, attached to the Hemiodemagnitizer by an electrical cord.

"Jake, where's the dagno—"

"Diagnosis. Here." Jake flipped the switch. The machine flickered and hummed.

There were thirty dials and gauges, divided into five rows. The dials were set to null out the gauges. This would determine the various intensities of the "healing color rays of yellow, green, red, blue, or white. Generated by magnetically energizing exotic subterranean mineral crystals. . . ." In the treatment mode, the Color Ray Emanator was attached, and the practitioner shined the colored lights onto the patient. The instructions gave eight pages of detailed warnings about the misuse of the equipment, but neglected to say exactly which ailments, if any, the machine could diagnose. The man who sold it to him couldn't locate the Color Ray Emanator; Jake talked him down on the price.

In his repair room, originally one of the two bedrooms, Jake had several more medical machines. He did not know exactly what he had, and wouldn't until he found the time to restore them. Most of them he had bought from a man near Pittsburgh, who was cleaning out the barn on a farm he had just inherited.

Across from the Hemiodemagnitizer was a cabinet, filled with old cameras, four trumpets, two clarinets, and one trombone. On the porch was also one of five barber chairs in the apartment; it had red velvet upholstery. The other four were in the living room. All of them were rechromed and reupholstered; two had brown leather seats and two had green velvet.

"Time's up," Jake said to the boys. "I promised your mother."

"Will you let us pick a song?" the doctor boy asked.

Jake gave them two dimes. "Okay, one song each. Then that's it."

On either side of the fireplace was a jukebox. Both were Wurlitzers, and both worked. It had taken Jake three years to fix them and to stock them with vintage records. There were two remote units—the kind found along counters in diners, chrome boxes with metal levers at the top and pages of selections. One was in the kitchen, the other in the bathroom.

When Mac visited, he was most impressed by the collections of little things, kept in stacks of glass covered boxes: lacquered pens, engraved straight razors, polished metal keyhole escutcheons, dental tools, metal machinist's rules, buttons—one each for brass, silver, leather, and bone—mouthpieces for large brass instruments, combs, and a collection of butterflies and moths. Jake had been told that the butterflies and moths had come from an eccentric collector and novelist who had lived in up-state New York. Jake never fell for stories like that, but the collection was nonetheless beautiful.

Mac once asked him if there was one special piece, one that Jake would keep over all the rest. Jake walked to the mantel and picked up a small eight by ten black frame. He handed it to Mac. It was the yellowed program for a weightlifting competition, the Nationals held in 1957. The type was red and blue. Across the bottom was a signature, written in blue ink with a fountain pen, "Norb Schemansky."

Mac knew Jake's love for weightlifting competitions, especially local meets. Jake had dragged Mac to enough of them over the years. Yet with everything in the apartment, and the enthusiasm Jake had for each new purchase, the program seemed an unlikely prize. Mac laughed.

Jake grabbed the frame back. He stared at Mac, not with his odd, one-eyed squint, but with a look of pain and hurt, a look that Mac never wanted to see again.

"You can say what you will about all the rest, but never, *ever,* laugh at this."

It took Mac two years to find the right time to ask Jake about the program. They were on their way to Connecticut for business. Jake managed to take a detour to the New England Weight Lifting Regionals, held in Springfield, Massachusetts. They had just finished watching what Jake said was a near perfect lift. Mac still could not understand. He had lifted in college, not to compete—Cincinnati didn't have a weightlifting team—just to stay fit. Mac was impressed with the heavyweight lifters, *Who wouldn't be?* he thought. *But this was perfect?*

"What did he lift?" Mac asked. "One hundred forty five kilos, so what?"

"Mac, you'll never see it. It's not just how much, but how you make the lift. I could tell that he was at his limit. Yet he had the guts to attempt that in competition. Not only did he make the lift, he also executed it beautifully, with style and finesse. Of all people, you should understand style and finesse." Jake laughed; their tastes were polar opposites.

After ten minutes of Jake trying to explain things to Mac, Mac asked about the program. "Jake, tell me something. I don't mean any disrespect by this. What's so special about the program you keep on the mantel? The one I—"

"I know which one. In the world of sports today, it is comparatively easy for someone with talent and drive to be successful in many sports. A champion can endorse almost anything. For money and recognition, it's almost easy to work out hard. In weightlifting? Never. Even now, there is no money, no glory, and no recognition. These guys do it for the love of the sport—I'm not talking about body builders or power lifters—"

"Gigolos! I know, I've heard all this before. What is it about Schemansky?"

"Okay, Schemansky competed in the late forties, fifties, and mid-sixties. He's still around, I see him—"

"Jake?"

"I'm getting there. He was a crane operator. In his off time, he worked out by himself: no drugs, no glory, and no money. He was U.S. Senior Champion six times from '48 to '65, and brought home medals from three Olympics. So what happened at home? The papers called him names, insulted him, and insulted lifting. If you want a hero, it's Schemansky."

***

Jake took the boys back down to Mrs. Rapoport, and then he called the police. He told them that he had a run in with Ed Forbs at Bonnie Winslow's house. Forbs was in the hospital.

"Jake, we've had his name in the system for a few years. He's a bad apple. We can't touch him. You know his father is Judge Forbs," the officer reminded him.

Jake knew who Judge Forbs was. He had retired from the bench a few years ago. He was *the* Ohio Democratic Party, behind the scenes. For years, there had been rumors about his corruption, but nothing ever came of them. He was untouchable. Forbs was a power broker.

"The Judge looks after his kid. He won't like your interference. Jake, you may be in over your head on this one."

Jake thought for a second or two. "Yeah, good thing I can swim."

SIX

Judge Forbs arrived at the hospital at ten. He parked his dark green Jaguar in the doctor's lot. Ed was in room 412. They had just brought him up to his room, and a nurse was helping him get settled when the Judge walked in.

The Judge epitomized the trappings of wealth and power. His shoes were handmade for him by two brothers in Lucca, Italy. He wore silk suits, designed for him in New York, and made in Kuala Lumpur by a Thai tailor. The New York shop also had a standing order from him for twenty-one shirts a year. Each shirt was identical: white linen, with French cuffs, a high collar with long pointed tips, no pocket, and no buttons. The Judge always used separate studs that matched his cuff links. His ties, mostly regimental stripes, were made in London. He never wore handkerchiefs.

Although the first thing anyone saw when they met the Judge was his clothing, he worked hard to keep in shape. In the old European manner, he went to the barber everyday, after his early morning workout at the Racket Club.

Ed looked up as his father walked in. Ed's face showed no reaction; he didn't know what to expect.

"I understand you've had quite an ordeal," the Judge said as he sat down, taking off his black, calfskin gloves. "I'm his father," he said to the nurse, "I'll take care of him. Please, leave us."

"I'm okay," Ed said to them, hoping she wouldn't leave, and answering the question his father wouldn't ask.

"What can you tell me?" The Judge asked Ed as the door swished closed behind the nurse.

"Here?" Ed knew that it didn't matter where. His father could read him like an open book. *Maybe he can read my mind,* he thought.

"You failed."

"There was a man there. In the dark, his eyes seemed to glow. What was I—"

The Judge began to probe. Someone had set off his trap; that didn't bother him as much as the fact that the same someone had been able to keep Ed alive. Once the muscles had begun to lock, the controlling nerve centers should have burned out, flooded by an excess of acetylcholine. The man who had brought in Ed had a name, Jacob Krajczynski. The Judge thought about his options: he could have Krajczynski put out of business, have him arrested for any of a number of charges, or have him killed. Whatever he decided, he first wanted to meet this man, to see who would challenge his authority.

"You failed," the Judge said.

"Honest, I tried. I was careful," Ed begged futilely, "I was really careful."

"You know I can't ignore this." He started to tweak Ed's sciatic nerve. He felt resistance. There was a block. It had to have been Krajczynski. *We will meet,* the Judge thought. "You stay here for a while," he said to Ed. "I'll send the car when the doctors release you."

The Judge put his gloves and coat back on quietly. *Too quietly,* Ed thought, recognizing his father's anger.

***

Jake collected a few shirts, socks, and underwear. He'd be fine for a couple of days. He knew Mrs. Meyernik would take care of it if he forgot anything.

Mac and Bonnie were in the front room listening to music when Jake got there. "I thought you'd be napping," Jake said. "It was a long night."

Bonnie laughed, "Mac's educating me on the classics."

"Careful, at twelve hours a day, there are four months of nonstop music here. He wouldn't hesitate to play it all, if he thought he had a captive listener."

"Jake, how'd things go?" Mac asked as he sipped a cup of coffee. "You look beat."

"Mrs. Meyernik!" Jake shouted toward the kitchen. "If that's coffee you've given the good Father, please, a cup for me." Turning back to Mac, "I am tired. We had a visitor."

Mrs. Meyernik had heard. She brought him a mug of coffee on a tray with sugar and cream. She knew that for Jake there was some mystery as to what proportions of each were required. It was easier to let Jake do it. The coffee was ready by the time he had finished telling them what had happened. "Perfect," he smiled, "must be that we're in God's house."

"Jake, whoever did this, whoever *could* do this, he'll come after you. He'll be tough."

***

Jake had been with Chemmg Tse Lu for six years when Chemmg told him that it was time to be tested. "There is a Tong boss in San Francisco who is evil. Normally, I tolerate the Tong; they may do a lot of harm, but they also do some good things. On the other hand, this one is evil. You and I will go there. I want you to stop him. He'll be tough."

They left in the morning; it was a two-hour bus ride to San Francisco. They stayed with Dr. Pak. After a warm reunion, Jake and Chemmg went out to have a glimpse of the boss. They found him in a small, run-down restaurant at the very edge of China Town; out of the way for most tourists.

Chemmg ordered tea and *tza heh tao*—fried sweetened walnuts. He had few vices, but his sweet tooth was one of them. While they were eating, he coached Jake. "Just probe. Nothing more. Remember, no matter who you are against, always assume that he is very good. Do not provoke anything here; this is not the place for a fight. Just try to get the measure of him."

Jake felt some confidence having Chemmg next to him. However, he knew that Chemmg would not interfere if something went wrong, not until things were almost too far gone. He probed gently. The Tong boss never moved, but there was resistance. Jake didn't push deep. It was obvious to Jake that the man had felt the intrusion. After a moment, the Tong boss turned to look for the waiter. He used the move to examine the room. They were the only other people there. Chemmg Tse Lu was the logical candidate, but Jake could tell the man knew it wasn't Chemmg, and the man never considered Jake. The confusion could be useful, Jake thought.

After the Tong had left, Chemmg toasted Jake. "He'll be tough. But for now you have the advantage."

***

Mac was laughing at Jake.

"What?" Jake asked, trying to look innocent, but knowing what had happened.

Mac explained to Bonnie, "Our dear Jake has an odd habit. Just when you think you need his attention most, like now, he goes on vacation."

"I've seen it," Bonnie said.

Jake grinned, "I know. You were saying that whoever he is, he'll be tough. Vacation, ha!"

The phone rang. Mrs. Meyernik answered it. She walked into the living room. "Jake, it's for you."

Jake took the call on the kitchen phone. "Hello?"

"Mr. Krajczynski—"

"Please, it's Jake, just Jake."

"Mr. Krajczynski, this is Judge Forbs. I would like to thank you for helping my son Edward this morning."

"It was nothing. I happened to be there when your son needed help." Jake didn't know whether the Judge knew that his son had broken into a house, or that he had been involved in something worse. "It's a long story. I'm just glad he's okay."

"I would like to meet such a remarkable man; I would like to thank you in person. Could we meet for lunch? Let's say one o'clock at Sammy's."

"I'll be there," Jake replied without hesitating.

The Judge hung up.

"Who was that?" Mac asked.

"The kid's father, Judge Forbs."

"How'd he find you here?"

"I don't know. It's something I intend to find out at lunch. We're meeting at Sammy's. Do you have a tie I can borrow?"

SEVEN

Mac had been through this sort of thing before. Mrs. Meyernik kept a small wardrobe for Jake: a Harris Tweed sport coat, two sweaters, several pairs of slacks, a shirt, and a tie. These were all items that Jake had left one place or another; Mac had collected them. Mrs. Meyernik kept them in the closet in the front guest room; the one they held for Jake.

They all fussed over him, clean shirt, jacket, and combed hair. Bonnie suggested he shave, but Jake wouldn't hear of it. After a few minutes, she stepped back and watched the show. Getting Jake ready for his lunch with Judge Forbs reminded her of getting a four-year-old dressed for a birthday party.

As they shoved Jake through the door, Bonnie turned to Mac, "Is he like this all the time?"

"Mostly. Some days are harder than others."

"He's like a little kid."

Mac understood her concern. "Never underestimate his skills. Jake is quite able to take care of himself. This little show is his way of acting out, of getting past what has happened, and what he fears may happen. He will never look or dress like Fred Astaire; no matter what we do. That's not Jake; although, I think he likes the attention. Mrs. Meyernik is great with him."

"It's just—one minute he's so competent, so much beyond us, and then he's like this."

"You haven't seen anything yet. I've warned you about his cooking, although every once in a while he manages something brilliant." Mac laughed. "Then there's his apartment; just traveling with him is an adventure. All things considered, he's the most remarkable man you and I are ever likely to meet. But don't try to explain him to anyone; no one will understand."

Bonnie was having trouble keeping her eyes open. Mac suggested she take a nap; Mrs. Meyernik would watch after both Martin and Bonnie. Mac had parish duties that could not be put off. Bonnie gave in. She didn't want to leave Mac; she felt safe with him, and liked his company.

She smiled as she fell asleep.

It took Jake a while to find a good parking place. He didn't trust parking attendants with his van. He had never eaten at Sammy's before. It had a reputation for good food, but it was pricey. The restaurant was on the second floor, above their market. The maître d' led Jake to the Judge's table by the window, overlooking the Flats.

"Sir?" The maître d' said quietly to the man behind the *Wall Street Journal.* The maître d' glanced at Jake, straightened his back, and bending stiffly at his waist, leaned into the paper again. "Sir?"

"Ah, Andrew, thank you." In one continuous motion, the Judge folded the paper into an eighth its open size, set it beside his crystal glass of seltzer, and stood. "Mr. Krajczynski, please."

Jake hesitated—*Krajczynski*—the Judge had pronounced it correctly, with the same inflection that his father had used. Jake could hear his father explaining to a new acquaintance, "Krajczynski, you pronouncing it just as it is sounding. Kra—jczyn—ski." Even in Cleveland with its large Polish community, he seldom heard it pronounced right.

"Mr. Krajczynski?"

"Sorry." Jake sat down. "You caught me off guard."

"Off guard?"

"My name. You said it correctly."

Their conversation was the dance of strangers, never getting too close, and always skirting the question: what happens after the dance?

"Mr. Krajczynski, as I said on the phone, you are quite a remarkable man."

"Please, Judge, it's Jake, just Jake. And I was lucky to have been there."

"But you were there." The Judge sipped his seltzer water. "That's the point."

"It's a long story. I was just glad to have been able to do what little I—"

"Little? Oh, no. The doctors said that considering what happened to Edward, he owes his life to you."

"Basic first aid."

"He had a seizure. He couldn't breathe, and he was tearing himself apart. Whatever you did was hardly basic or first aid."

"Please, Judge, it's done. It's good to know that Ed will be okay. I am curious though, I know I signed in at the hospital, but how did you find me at St. Boniface?"

"No mystery." The Judge smiled. "I—"

"Gentlemen, may I take your orders?" The waiter interrupted them.

"Of course. Jake?"

Jake opened the menu. The entrees read like a list of hunt club awards.

"Jake?"

The descriptions teased more than informed; Jake got lost in them.

"While he's looking, I would like the blackened fish, with swordfish, if it's fresh, no potato and your special vinaigrette on the salad. Jake, ready?"

Jake shook his head. "Ah . . . no, I'm—"

"If I may, make that two of the swordfish," the Judge looked at Jake, "and he'll have the potatoes Lyonnaise. Also, we'll have a bottle of the house Zinfandel."

Jake was impressed. The food was good, although the servings seemed a little small.

"Judge," Jake asked while the waiter cleared the table, "did Ed ever mention Martin Winslow?" He watched for a reaction.

"No. Is he a friend of Edward's?"

"I suppose." Jake had wondered if the Judge had known more about what had happened the night before. Now it looked as though he would have to go back to Ed to find out anything more. "I was just curious."

After lunch, they had coffee. Jake was distracted; he was struggling with the cream and sugar. The Judge sensed the opening and struck. It was not intended to be lethal, merely to test him. Jake knew he had been careless, but there wasn't time to worry about it. Lethal or not, he couldn't afford to let the Judge get the upper hand.

The waiter glanced over at the table. He saw the two men quietly staring at each other for a moment between sips of coffee. Nothing showed the strength of the struggle—like fencing, lightning quick thrusts, parries and feints.

Jake stopped the Judge's attack; it would take more than a distraction to trap him. Nevertheless, the Judge was powerful.

Judge Forbs nodded, and stood up to leave. "Mr. Krajcynski this has been most informative. We will meet again I am sure. Please," he put his hand on Jake's shoulder, "stay and finish your coffee, you've worked hard on it."

***

The Tong boss was waiting for them. He gave a slight bow and addressed Chemmg Tse Lu, "You have business with me?"

Chemmg smiled. Jake wondered if there was another lesson here. "No, it's my young friend."

Jake felt as if he were sliding on ice. One minute he was safe in his obscurity, the next he was exposed. He could just make out the cracking sound of ice breaking under foot, as his emotions were checked by a slap to his arm. Reflexively, he had blocked a blow to his head; he was on guard.

This time Jake probed deeply. He reeled, overwhelmed by a dark, overpowering, psychic stench. For all his training, he was unprepared for it.

The older man got past Jake's defenses, and clamped his gnarled tobacco stained fingers around the back of Jake's neck. Jake felt his arms begin to relax. He broke from the man's grip, and restored the intramuscular connections. Jake locked eyes with the man. He matched his breathing. He concentrated.

The older man was surprised. They were too far apart for him to physically break off the attack. It was Jake's turn to take advantage of a loss of attention. The man would stop breathing soon and pass out. Chemmg nodded—Jake had to finish it.

Jake caught the unconscious man as he fell. He pressed a spot between the shoulder blades and one at the base of the neck, and the man died. It was painless, quick, and left no signs.

Together, Chemmg and Jake carried the man to a bench

in the garden at the side of the restaurant. They placed him there; he looked as if he had fallen asleep amongst the cherry trees. "You have done well, and I grieve at the taking of a life. But you have learned two things: never relax your attention, and your enemy will kill you if you don't kill him."

***

The waiter was shaking Jake's shoulder, "Hey, you okay? Sir? You want anything?"

Jake looked up at him. "No. Sorry. I was just thinking. I'll finish my coffee."

At the rectory, they talked. Mrs. Meyernik produced a bottle of Jameson's Black Label and two glasses. It wasn't as good as Jake's Scotch, but it came close.

"He's strong. He's confident, and he won't scare. He'll be tough, but he's a bully."

"A bully?" Mac asked.

"You remember the Regionals we went to a few months ago? There was that one guy, he'd been a power lifter—wanted to get into the real world. He made his lift and won in his weight class. He did it on his strength, no finesse, no skill, just raw power. That's Judge Forbs. He would break my neck if I let him. So I can't give him that chance."

Mac looked worried. "What about Martin and Bonnie?"

"I don't know. I think he'll be more concerned with me. After all, I've challenged him. They should be okay here."

"Do you have a plan?"

"Only to take a nap. Let's talk about it after I get a couple hours sleep. You'll be here?"

"I've got a lot of paper work to do. I'll be in the living room."

Jake slept for two hours. It was dusk when he woke. He

went down to find Mac. From the dining room, Jake heard him talking angrily to someone in the courtyard. He went out to help.

There were two boys, dressed in black, cornered in the courtyard. One of them had fallen into the pond. The noise was what had alerted Mac. On the ground between them was a hinged, pole ladder. Extended, it was long enough to reach the second floor guest rooms.

The boy who had fallen into the pond turned and started to climb the hawthorn to get over the wall. The other boy attacked Mac. It was a short fight. Mac wasn't bothered by his lack of subtlety. He threw a punch to the kid's jaw. The boy went down. Mac saw Jake standing in the doorway. "That's the way to do it!" He grinned at Jake. "None of your oriental yubi wazi crap."

"You missed one," Jake said, pointing to the wall where the other boy had just been. "I'll call the police."

When the boy came to, he wouldn't talk. Mac and Jake sat with him until the police showed up ten minutes later. The police got Mac's statement and took the boy away.

Mac told Mrs. Meyernik that the kid was probably from nearby, looking for something to steal. He didn't tell her about the ladder he and Jake had hidden behind the flowers along the wall; he didn't tell her about the second boy. She went back into the kitchen to work on dinner; it was almost ready.

"Jake, wasn't that close?"

"Yes. I was just thinking we might want to move, though I don't think he'll try anything again tonight. We can get Bonnie and Martin out tomorrow. What do you think of Roy's? He's not so far that we can't get there in an hour, but far enough to be safely away from the Judge."

Mac thought a bit. Roy had helped them before. Mac

liked him. He lived in a small house, about three miles east of Kent, Ohio. "Sure. That would put my mind at ease."

Mrs. Meyernik came out of the kitchen. "Dinner is ready, if one of you would wake Bonnie and Martin."

With Martin, Bonnie, Mac, Jake, and Mrs. Meyernik the table was full. Mrs. Meyernik was a good, although eccentric cook. She had prepared palacsinta filled with calves' brains, with a hint of onion and parsley, and Transylvanian cabbage stew, made with pork, brisket of beef, bacon, and a healthy dose of caraway. Mac had discovered a Bulgarian vineyard, Trakia. Their Cabernet Sauvignon was a good table wine, inexpensive, mellow, round and dry.

Mrs. Meyernik tried not to tell them what the palacsinta filling was. She had learned that she could cook almost anything for most people, provided she didn't tell them what it was. Sometimes, if there was company, Jake liked to pry the ingredients out of her. With Martin on Jake's side, she held out for only a few minutes.

"Mrs. Meyernik, this is by far your best. So, you'll tell me what's in it?" Jake asked.

Mrs. Meyernik looked at Mac and Bonnie for support. The game was obvious, and they were laughing too hard to say anything.

"Jake?" she pleaded.

"Yeah," Martin joined in. "I'll bet it's—"

Jake clamped his hand over Martin's mouth. "Now, Mrs. Meyernik, before you set off young Martin's vivid imagination, you'll tell us?"

"Calves' brains," she whispered.

"Mac, quiet please, I couldn't hear. What did you say?" Jake let go of Martin. "Did you hear?"

"No," Martin said.

"You're impossible, Jacob Krajczynski. Impossible." Mrs. Meyernik had turned as red as the wine with embarrassment. It was a game—all in good fun—she knew that. However, she couldn't help playing the goat. "Calves' brains," she said, slapping her napkin onto the table. "Okay?"

The look of horror on Martin's face was too much, even she burst out laughing.

After dinner, Jake set things up with his friend in Kent. Bonnie and Martin would be welcome. Roy would be home all day.

Everyone was asleep when Jake left his room and went into the courtyard. He had lied to Mac; he *was* concerned that the Judge would try something.

Jake had been sitting in the corner behind the pond for an hour when he heard someone walking along the wall on the street side. He sensed that the prowler was debating climbing over. Jake gently reached out, making mental contact. The thought came to the young man, dressed in black, that he shouldn't be so scared. He saw himself breaking into the rectory—everyone was asleep. There would be something, maps, papers, or notes. He would find out what was going on. Maybe, yes, maybe he could even get Martin. The Judge would be proud of him.

As the figure jumped down from the wall, just missing the pond, he froze. Jake had controlled him perfectly. It took ten minutes to prepare the young man. Jake needed to know what was going on, who was involved, and what the Judge's plans were. He needed a spy.

It was nearly two o'clock when the young man climbed back over the wall. *The Judge will be pleased,* he thought. *The priest and the fat man had been awake, sitting in the dining room. I heard it all. They talked about their plans. They never suspected I was outside listening. I was by the French doors between the dining room and the courtyard. They had talked for almost an hour. I heard it all. . . .*

Jake smiled as he watched the boy clamber up the wall. Now, he could go back to his room and sleep.

EIGHT

Chemmg Tse Lu was born in 1890. His father was an indentured farmer. Tibetan life was harsh; for one born in poverty, comfort, much less nobility, was a lottery not to be won in this turn of the wheel. In spite of the large number of monasteries—which stood as oases amidst the desert of lives for whom even hope was often denied—the odds of gaining entrance were slight.

In a world of ignorant, superstitious, fearful people, the boy Chemmg stood out. He accepted the rituals of Tibetan Buddhism. Unlike the rest of his family, he tried to hear and understand what was being said. His joy in finding understanding, even over little things, was uncontrollable. Chemmg's face fought hard to retain the appearance of solemnity, but laughter would win out. His father had no idea what to do. He was humiliated that his eldest son was apparently crazy. He wanted to hit him, to make him quiet, but that would draw even more attention. Each time, he prayed that if he got through this, he would see that it never happened again. He prayed that whatever spirits possessed Chemmg would leave him.

The Abbot of the local monastery heard about Chemmg, the little boy who laughed with joy during the reading of the Sutras. Every month, the Abbot had to pass judgment over children who would be neophytes in his Order. He knew that the monastic world required several types of people, being religious didn't guarantee the success of a monastery. It needed laborers, whose faith was required to keep them working; it needed bureaucrats, who could keep accounts and deal with the minutia of institutional life; it needed scholars who could interpret the words of the Buddhasvittas, the Sutras, and the Vows of the Middle Way. Beyond them, beyond the monastic world, was the mystic, the true engine of the Yellow Hat Buddhists. The Abbot had known well two mystics; both had laughed.

The Abbot knew that Chemmg's family needed the boy's help, but also that they would take great pride if their son were selected to enter the monastery. He knew this, not because he knew the family, but because all poor families were alike. Chemmg was brought to the Abbot's quarters by two yellow-clad mendicants.

It had never occurred to Chemmg that he could be a part of this world. He had friends whose fathers had tried to get them into the monastery. Chemmg's father had thought about it even though he needed the help in the fields, but he was always deterred by Chemmg's laughter. He feared the insult of having Chemmg rejected because of his possession. The whole town would know.

"Why do you laugh?" The Abbot asked the young Chemmg, looking down from his carved, red and gold chair. Chemmg was silent, held spellbound in the phantasmal light of a hundred flickering butter lamps. Carved, brightly colored grotesques—demons and gods—grinning and snarling, stood guard around the room. The brocade patterns in the sooty silk wall hangings fluttered in and out of focus. The Abbot repeated his question. "Why do you laugh?"

Chemmg trembled.

"Aren't you the boy who laughs?" The Abbot asked, beginning to suspect they had made a mistake.

Chemmg's eyes drooped a second. When they opened, he stood straighter, his face radiant, and he smiled at the Abbot as though they were equals.

"Why do I laugh? I laugh because I see through the illusion of self. Because all around me I see people desire what isn't, and overlook what is."

The young boy's transformation startled the Abbot. "But why laugh?"

"Because life is funny."

"Is winter funny? Is cold funny? Or death? You can leave, if you think such things are mere amusement."

"They are real . . . to the body." Chemmg laughed. "In spite of all you must know about reality and illusion, don't you use the bridge to cross the chasm? Is the chasm real, or not?"

"You are a boy playing games with words," the Abbot said, although he suspected otherwise. "I am hardly convinced."

"I can tell you a secret," Chemmg said.

"What?"

"Your name."

"My name?" the Abbot whispered. He looked down at his robes and adjusted several folds.

Chemmg waited.

In the silence, the Abbot was hoping that Chemmg was no more than a prankish, uncultured boy.

Just a boy, he convinced himself.

Chemmg caught his eye and held it. "The Abbot's name . . . it's Kyaing."

The Abbot gasped. Kyaing was his lay-name. He had not heard it spoken or even thought it, for sixty years.

"Who told you that?"

"Who here would know?"

The Abbot suddenly understood. "And what was your name? Do you remember?" he asked.

A wind blew through the room, rippling the silks, and briefly damping the flames.

Chemmg shook under the stare of the Abbot. "I don't know why I laugh." He started to leave, to turn and run. Then he stopped. "For me there's pain. I see my family hungry and cold. I wonder why am I? Am I who I think?"

"Please, stay. We must talk. I think you would be more comfortable sitting."

They talked for several hours. In spite of the Abbot's discovery, Chemmg was nonetheless an illiterate, ignorant, eight-year-old boy. At the end of the talk, the Abbot sent his personal secretary to the boy's family, to tell them that Chemmg was accepted, on probation, into the monastery. The Abbot knew that probation was unnecessary, but rules need following and discipline must be preserved. He knew too, that in spite of his best efforts to make this a normal entrance, it would be difficult for Chemmg. A five or ten minute interview with the Abbot was as much as most neophytes ever got. This special attention would single him out.

But Chemmg went from dirt floors, mud walls, and the smell of burning dung, to relative splendor. He didn't care that his quarters were, as they were for all just gaining entrance, the poorest in the entire complex. As he fell asleep that first night, it was as though a window opened and he was able to look out on the entire world with eyes no longer blinded by superstition. Blissfully, he didn't know how much he had to learn and how hard it would be to overcome his ignorance.

***

Over coffee, they talked. Jake explained that Bonnie and Martin were going to Kent. They would be safer there. Jake did not mention the early morning visitor. He didn't tell them that he was worried. "The hard part will be to get away unseen. Any ideas?"

"Mrs. Meyernik usually goes shopping in the morning. The parish car is in the garage. Bonnie and Martin can hide in the back. I will have Father Little from St. Ignatius pick them up from the parking lot at the market. He knows the car. They can remain hidden until he feels it's safe. If Mrs. Meyernik can find two empty spaces in the lot, he'll pull in next to her. . . ."

They ate one of Mrs. Meyernik's breakfasts, enough food to hold even Jake for hours. Mac made arrangements with Father Little. After cleaning up, Mrs. Meyernik was ready to go, and so were Bonnie and Martin.

Two boys in a dark red Camero followed Mrs. Meyernik as she drove to the West Side Market. From his guest room, Jake saw the red car pull out. Mac's plan was sound. He just hoped they wouldn't have any bad luck. Jake got a sweater from the closet, and went back downstairs.

"They were followed."

"You knew they would be. Luckily, we can depend on Father Little. You know he's one of your admirers?"

"I've never met him, have I?"

"No. Every time I set something up, you had some weightlifting match or antique show that got in the way."

"Love me, love my eccentricities. I'm not trying to avoid the good Father. From what you've told me, I'm looking forward to making his acquaintance." Jake was fussing with his coffee. Father Little taught chemistry. Maybe he could help Jake with his coffee problem. Jake's theory was that the pH of the water and of the beans varied enough to upset the way in which cream reacted with the coffee. He didn't think that sugar varied much. But he did wonder whether there was a standard degree of sweetness for sugar. *Yes,* he thought, *Father Little will see the problem immediately.*

"He'll call us when he has gotten Bonnie and Martin back to St. Ignatius."

***

Chemmg was asleep. He had worked hard that day. His Master, Ka, always gave him more than was possible. They had been staying in a small hut, a two-day climb from his village. In spite of the work, he savored every minute.

In his dream, Chemmg was running, trying to keep his footing on the rocky trail that ran along a steep gorge. A large, orange and black tiger was loping after him. Chemmg stopped; hesitating to jump over a three-foot section of the trail that had washed away. Close behind, he could hear the tiger approaching.

A figure jumped down from the edge of the cliff above him. Its robes billowed as it floated down. It was Ka. He stood before Chemmg, blocking the trail.

"Quick, we must run. There's a tiger. It's after me."

Ka laughed at him.

"It's not funny. We'll be killed."

"Calm, we're safe."

"No, we have to run."

They both stood, each urging the other to do what he didn't want to do. The tiger appeared around a turn in the trail, a few feet from Chemmg. It stopped, its ears back, and it stared at him. Only its tail moved, flicking back and forth. "Master, please," Chemmg begged.

Ka held out his hand, pointing to the tiger. "Watch!"

The tiger blurred, pulsating; colors swirled. Chemmg was suddenly conscious of the stillness of the air and the dry heat of the sun. Even the ever present flies had vanished. In that instant, the tiger became a parrot, green with a bright yellow head. It flew high in the air, spiraling around Chemmg, and lighted on Ka's outstretched arm. In reds and blues, its tail feathers fanned out. It nibbled at Ka's sleeve. Then it cocked its head at Chemmg. "*Tat tvam asi*," it squawked.

It flew to Chemmg and landed on his shoulder. Its sharp talons pierced his robe and dug into his skin. It side-stepped closer to his ear, and picked at it with its dry, warm tongue. Chemmg reached up to move it off his shoulder. It pushed off and flew into the air.

"*Tat tvam asi. Tat tvam asi*," it shrieked in a flurry of bright feathers that blocked the sun in front of Chemmg's eyes.

Ka laughed.

In the morning, Chemmg woke with the dream fresh in his mind. Unlike other dreams that faded with the brightening of day, this dream remained strong and real. Chemmg made tea. He offered the first cup to Ka, as he had every morning for the last four years. Ka stretched out his arm to take the cup; he laughed, "*Tat tvam asi . . . tat tvam asi*."

Chemmg dropped the cup. "How did you know?"

"So you thought that you knew almost as much as I? You would become the young Master? What do you know? The parrot told you. Didn't it?"

Chemmg spent the day sitting on a rock along the bank of the river, ignoring his daily chores and his exercises, and drowning his senses in the sound of the torrent rushing toward the flat farmlands miles away. Ka let him be. This was a hard lesson: to discover that even your dreams were open to some.

At dusk, Ka sat down next to Chemmg. The air was cooling, but the rocks were still warm from the sun. "Of the lessons you've learned, with all the effort you've made, today you begin a new study."

"I've never heard of anyone do such things."

"It's rare, but it is done, as you have seen." Ka touched Chemmg's hand, "And you are even rarer, Chemmg Tse Lu. It is dreamsharing, and it is your destiny to learn this and more.

"As I can enter your dreams, someday you will enter mine. I will pay a price for giving you these skills." Ka laughed. It was a natural thing. He had done it to his Master, he to his, and so on. He stopped smiling. "And you will learn that dreamsharing can be deadly."

***

Mrs. Meyernik turned into the parking lot slowly. She wanted to be sure that Father Little could find her. She recognized him as he pulled in behind her. Together, they drove around looking for two adjacent parking spaces.

Except for dry goods and cleaning aids, she did all her grocery shopping at the West Side Market. It was an acre of half-covered stalls, only partially indoors, with vendors of ethnic foods, meat, fish, and fresh produce. Its atmosphere was a bouquet of smells, impossible to dissect until one came to know each offering of each stall. There were dozens of kinds of sausages: smoked, spicy, sweet, hot, bitter, salty, fatty, or lean. Every nationality had its own ways to make them: more pork, more beef, some with garlic, some without, some with caraway, paprika, or green peppercorns. Two stalls specialized in organ meats. In the middle of the market was a bakery. On Wednesdays, they had potato salt-rising bread with its slightly sour smell. They also had herb breads, marble breads, Italian and French breads. On Saturdays, very early, they had fresh Russian black bread. Mrs. Meyernik bought it for Mac; he liked it toasted with butter and fresh sour cream.

There had been talk of doing away with the Market. The Flats had proven to be a gold mine, and developers saw the Market as an ideal location for luxury condominiums. The community rallied, getting it declared an historical landmark.

Mrs. Meyernik caught a glimpse of the two boys in the red car, the same car that had followed her. They were waiting on the street, in front of the parking lot entrance. "Father Little will take care of things," she said to herself as she walked into the Market, her empty, blue paisley, cloth shopping bag hanging from her arm and her black leather pocketbook in her hand.

Father Little had seen the red car pull up as Mrs. Meyernik drove into the lot. He saw that from where it was, neither the passenger nor the driver could see between the cars. He got out, went into the Market, and bought some cheese from the booth next to the door. After a few minutes, he took his package and walked back. He tapped on the window of Mrs. Meyernik's car. He looked up at the clock on the building across the street. He made a show of setting his watch, while Bonnie and Martin changed cars. He drove away; the two boys were unaware that anything had occurred.

From his office in St. Ignatius he called Mac. "Mac they're okay. I've got them settled. They can stay here as long as you think necessary."

NINE

Jake went to The Bookstall. Deliveries were held for him at the Health Emporium, the health food store next to The Bookstall. The two women who owned it were helpful, although he was an enigma to them. They gave him sound advice on running a business for success: he should understand his market niche, develop a business plan—"One that accommodates your style of management, of course"—and set goals, promote the store—"You know what happens if you don't promote: nothing"—hire an assistant—"Who could keep the store open when you can't be there"—and so on. . . .

Jake would listen with rapt attention, soaking in the nuances of their savvy business sense. Sometimes, he would catch himself beginning to think that he should try some of it. Then he would walk back to The Bookstall. Sitting at his desk, fussing over a cup of coffee, he'd look around. "Why do I want anything else?" he would ask himself.

There were special orders that he had to take care of. He wasn't worried about losing customers, but these were the obligations of promises made. He had the time, and he thought the nonchalance would throw off the Judge.

While Jake was away taking care of business, Mac arranged for Bonnie and Martin to stay with their friend Roy in Kent. Jake had introduced them several years ago. They got along well. Roy insisted that it was their strong Gaelic heritage.

"Roy? This is Mac. I need a favor."

Roy laughed. "First Jake, now you. You only call when you need me."

"Have you ever tried to phone out? It'll work in that direction."

For several minutes, they traded insults and laughed.

"I'm sorry we never get together except for business," Mac said.

"We ought to set aside a night to get drunk. But who would put up with us?"

"We'll do it, but this isn't the time."

"Okay, Mac, you need my help. What is it?"

"Jake talked with you about Bonnie and Martin? He said you could put them up."

"Yeah."

"We got them away from here. They're safe at St. Ignatius. But I'm afraid that we're being watched. Could—"

"Listen, if I leave now, I can be there by five, or five-thirty. Why don't I pick them up?"

Mac chuckled. "I like asking favors of you; you always volunteer before I have to beg."

***

Ed Forbs had been home a day. The doctors said that he was healthy, but exhausted. The muscle rips and strains would take several weeks to mend. His right arm had been immobilized; they wanted to see how the elbow healed before doing any surgery. His father had been friendly, neither badgering nor abusive. Ed had a sense of foreboding. His father was never nice unless he had a reason. Ed could only sit around and wait.

It was funny, he thought. He hated his father yet he loved

him; he had a deadly fear of him, but he missed him when he wasn't around; he wanted to run away, but wanted another chance to prove himself. It had been like this since his mother died, when he was seven. She had died of a stroke while riding an elevator with his father at a legal convention in Dallas. During the first few years, Ed thought of her all the time; they had had a special relationship. In his teens, he stopped thinking of her—until now.

The Judge was going to be out late. He had said that he was meeting with *his boys*. "Some of them know how to handle themselves."

As Ed waited, he thought about all that had happened. In spite of his exhaustion, he felt lighter, more relaxed than he had been for a long time. When he thought of his father, his chest didn't constrict as much as it had just last week. He caught himself feeling a tinge of remorse over all the things that had happened in the last few years.

One night a week, sometimes two, the Judge met with his boys at The Camden House, a community services organization. In the community, people thought well of Judge Forbs, in part, due to his civic contributions. He donated money, time, and equipment for the boys. The Camden House wrestling team regularly won state and regional competitions. Last year, one of the boys was runner up for national high school wrestling champion in his weight class. The Judge had gotten him interested in wrestling a few years earlier. Everyone liked Judge Forbs.

During practice, he would counsel some of the boys. The President of Camden House was proud of the Judge's extra commitment to the children. They reported to him, "The old woman had gone shopping; she was gone a little over an hour at the market; she returned before noon; the priest had never left the rectory; the fat man had gone to his bookstore; he was there until two thirty, then he returned to the rectory; Mrs. Winslow and Martin had never left." As they talked, a couple of the boys noticed that the Judge's face was flushed. He was losing his patience.

***

Jake and Mac had decided to stay at the rectory that night. Roy called at around seven to say that he had picked up Bonnie and Martin from St. Ignatius. They had just gotten in, were safe, and no one had followed them. Jake and Mac planned to visit them the next evening.

After dinner, Mac tried to get Jake to listen to a new recording of Gesauldo madrigals.

"Jake, you'll like him. He was a sixteenth century Italian prince."

"He's been around four centuries," Jake mumbled, looking through the TV Guide.

"He murdered his wife and her lover—"

"There's a bantam weight match on."

"Come on. I've had this record on order for six months; it's out of print. I had to go to a second hand shop in New York. Jake, this is the first free minute—"

"You'll still have it later, when the fight's over."

Their argument was a ritual; nonetheless, it made Mrs. Meyernik uncomfortable: it sounded real. She took refuge in the basement with the laundry.

A little before one o'clock—the rectory was dark, except for a little counter light in the kitchen that Mrs. Meyernik insisted stay on—there was a crash of breaking glass. It woke everyone. Flames lit Jake's room. He saw pieces of a bottle among the window shards. Someone had thrown a Molotov cocktail. He grabbed the blanket and started to beat out the fire. He didn't hear Mac run downstairs to deal with the fire there.

Mrs. Meyernik called the fire department. By the time the fire truck arrived, the fire in Jake's room was out. It took five minutes to extinguish the fire downstairs. The damage to the rectory wasn't great, but they would have to sleep elsewhere. For Mac, the worst thing was that he had lost most of his record collection.

In all the running around, with half the neighbors outside, no one noticed the two young men, dressed in black, standing around the corner. They knew the Judge would be furious. Not only had the damage to the rectory been minimal, but also Martin and his mother were not there.

Mac saw to Mrs. Meyernik. Jake talked with the police. Lt. Dombrosky knew and respected Jake, and Jake trusted him.

"Lieutenant, I think I know who's behind this. But I'm not sure you'll like it."

"You and Father McNamara have always been straight with me. I may not like what you're going to tell me, but I guarantee I'll listen."

Jake took Dombrosky's arm, and led him a few steps away from the rest. Jake knew him, but he didn't know or trust the other policemen; power like the Judge's was corrupting. "I'd bet on Judge Forbs."

"Oh, come on." He looked around as if he were embarrassed to be seen with Jake. "Christ, Jake! Here, that would be like suggesting the Pope's queer. No. No, I can't even whisper that to anyone."

Jake outlined the story. "You can check with Cleveland Heights and with the hospital."

"Jake, the Captain's on the board of directors for Camden House; his son goes there. Even if you're right, if you had a photo of Forbs holding the matches, I'd never get support from the Captain. It would be my ass."

"I hear you. Can you do anything off the record?"

"The Captain takes incidents like this seriously. He's scared of anything that might look like his precinct's falling apart. He'll be watching this one. I'll have to keep him happy—happy as a pig in shit." Dombrosky laughed. "But, I'll see what I can do. You'll be around?"

"I'll either be at my apartment or with Mrs. Winslow and her son. I'll call you. We can go for a beer."

As Jake walked to his car, he wondered what was so important that the Judge would put forth this much effort. He could see that there was something personal between them, because he had interfered with the Judge's son. The entire matter started over Martin. What did Martin know? What was it about him?

Jake knew that Lt. Dombrosky was right. A man with Judge Forbs' reputation would not fall easily. Even if they couldn't help much, Jake had to go to the police. Taking on people like the Judge was what Jake did, and it was always outside the law. He tried to see that the police were not his enemies, even if they couldn't be his allies.

Mac and Mrs. Meyernik would stay with parishioners; Jake drove forty minutes, across town, to his apartment. By the time he got there, he wasn't tired. It was too late to play music, so he decided to work on the Ultrasonic Neoplasmectometer. He had found it in a junk shop in Winston-Salem, North Carolina. A doctor had used it for several years; what belief in Jesus couldn't cure, he would, at least until the warrant for his arrest was issued. Two and a half million dollars in a Bahamian bank helped to make his exile bearable. This was the newest medical machine Jake had. It was digital, ". . . making use of the latest computer technology. . . ." The doctor's brochure said. Other than digital read-outs and blinking lights, nothing happened. Most of the electronic components were removed and the baby blue, enameled metal cabinet left outside in the rain.

**

Three years earlier, Chemmg Tse Lu had visited Jake. It was the last time Jake saw him; he died a month later. Chemmg brought with him, as a gift for Jake, a teapot with three, small, mismatched cups. The pot was large for ceremonial use, and small for what Jake would have considered normal. It looked to have been unglazed terra cotta, but a hundred and twenty years of use had stained it a dark, almost glossy, brownish black. It was round and squat, with the worn image of a dragon on one side. The handle had been replaced many times. He had gotten it from Ka, and it was old then. Chemmg had used it daily for fifty years.

"If I did not know you as I do, I would think you are insane," Chemmg said as he walked through the apartment. He walked slowly, due to his desire to see everything, not because of his age. It took him an hour and a half.

He didn't care for the barber chairs, the juke boxes, musical instruments, or cameras. Chemmg was captivated by the little collections of things. In the dining room, safely snuggled into the corner away from danger, was a large, glass bell jar, thirty inches tall and sixteen inches in diameter. Inside was a collection of twenty-three stuffed song birds: an iridescent blue-black indigo bunting, a scarlet tanager, two summer tanagers—both rosy-red males, a yellow, black and red Louisiana tanager, a Baltimore oriole, and a golden oriole from Europe—it was the only bird in the collection with a label. The rest of the birds were unidentifiable. Jake was sure that they were from Asia.

Where he could, Chemmg would open cabinet doors or box lids and hold each item, as though each piece could unlock life's mystery, or least Jake's. Each button, comb, and tool . . . everything was a treasure. Jake tried to talk to him, but Chemmg was oblivious.

Jake went into the kitchen to finish the chili. He thought Chemmg would like it; he had made it vegetarian. When Chemmg was through looking around, he found Jake, "Still trying to cook?"

After dinner, they reminisced. There was a lot to talk about, they had stayed in touch, but they had not seen each other for five years. There was too much the two wanted to say. Finally, there was silence, each taking comfort in the other's company. Chemmg looked at Jake. "You have never disappointed me. In fact," he paused to make a theatrical display of looking around at Jake's possessions, "you continue to amaze me.

"I grew up in poverty, where to have nothing was already a lot. I took vows of poverty, knowing the trap of desiring and ownership. Here you sit, surrounded not only by things your culture says you must have, but also by things of whose use even you have no idea. Rather than being destroyed by all of this, you are stronger now than ever.

"You know your destiny. And I know what you give up for it, in spite of all this."

Jake swiveled nervously in his chair. He couldn't help still feeling like a student next to Chemmg. He felt confused by Chemmg's gentle rebuke softened with praise.

"Don't let this go to your head, Master Krajczynski, but you are the best student I have ever had. My Master would be proud of me for this achievement. But I do have one regret, that you have not taken a disciple."

***

Jake decided to give up on the Ultrasonic Neoplasmectometer, and sleep. It haunted him that he had no disciple, not even a student.

TEN

The next evening, Mac drove out to visit Bonnie and Martin at Roy's house. Until the mid-sixties, Roy's house had been a chicken coop. As Kent State University grew, rental property became more profitable than farmland. The farms disappeared, as they built houses. The chicken coop was cleaned out, fumigated, painted, refurbished, and turned into two apartments. Roy rented the one farthest from the street.

The only thing that suggested its original design was that it was long and narrow, with low ceilings. Even in winter, it was surprisingly comfortable.

Roy wrote men's adventure novels. He was good at it. They were not great literature, but they were entertaining. His agent assured him that adventure novels sold better than the opaque, plotless exercise he had first wanted to write. He had started by ghosting a couple of thrillers. Someone else had developed a series: its characters, its style, and the basic direction of each story. After its success, the publisher hired ghostwriters to do the sequels. For the last two years, Roy had been working on his own series. He had just started his fourth book; he didn't want it written by anyone else.

Jake first met Roy at The Bookstall. They had an instant liking for each other; each was amazed at how eccentric the other was. Roy was one of the few customers who liked to browse. Whenever he ferreted out a good find, Jake said that he had overpriced the book. "These things happen, I get careless." Jake always gave him fifty percent off.

Jake liked Roy, but he had never read any of his books. "I won't read 'em, and I won't sell 'em." Mac thought they were great.

Roy was six feet four inches tall, and weighed just over two hundred and twenty-five pounds. He had the kind of bone structure that made him immensely strong, and he had the Gaelic temper to match. He owned, and rode, a pink Harley-Davidson. Over a beer, Mac once asked him why he had a pink motorcycle. Roy smiled, "Because I can."

Most mornings, he had coffee and a roll at Captain Brady's, a popular coffee house. In the corner, there was a cigar-store-Indian that Jake had been trying to buy for three years. At first, the owner wanted too much; now he claimed it was not for sale.

Some people thought that Roy was lazy, killing most of the mornings at Brady's. But he had a good ear, and his agent thought that there wasn't a writer around with as good a sense for dialogue. He picked up a lot over coffee.

He liked to threaten Jake. "I'm writing you into my new book, four scenes. Trouble is, if I say too much no one will believe the character. I'm not writing fantasy—just four scenes. Then you'll have to read it."

Mac arrived shortly after seven.

Roy lived alone, except for a regular and loyal following of women, who occasionally stayed with him, in what seemed to Mac like a rotation.

"Angelica is in the kitchen getting some pizza," Roy said to Mac, "and I've got a bottle of Old Bushmill's. Who wants a shot?"

Bonnie passed; beer went better with pizza. Martin asked

for some. Roy agreed. "This is a special occasion. It's only social."

"No. I don't want to be unsociable, but I don't want Martin to drink."

Martin protested. "Come on, I've had whiskey before. I'm not going anywhere; I'm not driving. Just one shot."

"No."

"Mom, come on."

"No."

"Roy said I could. Father McNamara is having a drink. Why can't—"

"No. That's final."

"You drink. What is wrong with it? I'm seventeen. I'm not a kid."

"No!"

Tears welled in Martin's eyes. This was so unreasonable to him. How could she treat him this way, like a kid, in front of everyone? "Fuck you!" he shouted as he slammed the door on his way outside.

Roy apologized. "I shouldn't have encouraged him."

Bonnie was embarrassed. "No, it's just that he's seventeen. That's a tough age."

Mac followed Martin out. Martin hadn't gone far; he didn't know where to go. Mac remembered being a teenager. "Martin?"

Martin made a show of moving away from Mac, a step or two.

"Martin, listen to me." He put his hand on Martin's shoulder, and turned him around. "I'm going to talk to you as Mac, not Father McNamara. Okay?"

Martin didn't want to answer; he was fighting back his tears. His throat choked.

"Okay?"

"Yeah, fine," Martin whispered.

"Let's take a walk to the corner and back."

It was dark, but the streetlights provided enough light to see the sidewalk. They walked, hands in pockets. Martin scuffed the fall leaves with his feet. Mac remained silent.

They stopped at the corner. "Father McNa—"

"Mac."

"Mac, why can't she understand I'm a grown up, you know? I mean, seventeen, that's grown up. What's wrong with a drink?"

Mac didn't answer.

"Can't she remember being seventeen? Doesn't she understand?"

By tacit consent, they started walking again.

"Martin, you've had a rough year. Your mother cares very much for you—I know you know that—she's worried."

"Yeah, but what's wrong with a drink? One drink. Roy said it was okay."

"That's not the point. When I was your age—and I don't want to sound like every other adult, but it's hard not to—I had the same arguments with my father. You left out some of the best points: in some cultures you'd be a father by seventeen, you'd have been married four years, and there have been kings younger than you. In a few months, you could be in the army, and if you were old enough to be in the army—what's a few months? You know them, but they're not the issue."

"Yeah, but I'm not a kid." Martin felt he couldn't give it up.

"I guess I do sound like an adult. Listen; be angry, that's a part of growing up. It's normal to complain about this to your friends. It will seem unfair even when you're older, have children, and are doing the same things to them. That's life. Never doubt your mother's love. She came to me for help because of you. It wasn't easy. She's holding together while people are trying to harm you and her. She loves you very much, and she doesn't want to lose you. And maybe this small feeling of control is all she's got at the moment. Let her kept it."

Mac stopped. He could hear himself saying all the things he didn't want to say, at least not this way. He wanted to get through to Martin; he wasn't doing well. "If I can talk your mother into it, would you settle for a beer?"

"Yeah."

Mac heard him sob.

***

Jake spent the day on the phone. He had a network of people who were also sensitive to the patterns of Evil. He was the warrior, but they provided the reconnaissance. He needed to know how far things went, and whether there could be someone above the Judge. During his last visit, Chemmg had wondered about such things.

"At the end of my life, you have made me question so much of what I have learned," Chemmg said. "I hope that in the next, I will remember them and maybe an answer or two, while I am young. We have talked about Evil. We have dedicated ourselves to fight it. Perhaps we don't know what it is.

"We have taken—what may seem to many—an atheistic stance. We have had to, if we are to fight. But I wonder. We see patterns that repeat themselves. Why does Evil work the way it does? Is it that men are so linked that they give it common direction? Or, on the other hand, is there something behind us? Are we puppets in some universal duel between Good and Evil?"

Jake had similar conversations with Mac. Where Chemmg questioned, Mac clung to dogma, "Evil is the negation of perfection, it presupposes Good, and is opposed to Good."

"That's a clean way to say nothing," Jake said to Mac.

"Yes, if that is it. But from there, we can say Evil, though it does exist, it exists as non-being. And it can only act on a being whose nature is naturally good."

"Mac, what is it we keep running up against?"

"Evil, certainly, but it isn't a being and it isn't total."

"You've seen it. It's almost killed you. And you talk about it like it's part of a cake recipe."

"No, it makes sense. If it was absolute, and it is the negation of Good, then it would bring about the total denial of its every subject and would, ultimately, destroy itself for lack of something to affect."

"That's it," Jake said. "That is exactly what it tries to do, to destroy everything, and we are here to oppose that."

It was hard not to talk about Evil, but it always sounded to Jake like a college freshman philosophy discussion. Fortunately, he did not have to know how to define it in order to be able to stand against it.

That night, Jake drove to Kent. He was looking forward to a drink with Roy and Mac. He liked to set them up against each other, and then watch the sparks. It was all in fun, but what fun.

There was a residue of tension when he got there. They had finished the first pizza. Angelica brought out a second one. Jake gladly accepted a whiskey with it. Martin, he noticed, was drinking a beer. Mac saw Jake's glance toward Martin; when he caught Jake's eye, he gave him a wink.

"How's the book coming?" Jake knew that Roy could talk about it for hours. Within minutes, they were all offering better story lines to Roy. They would rewrite it for him, given half a chance. Roy worked hard to hold onto his original story. Within half an hour, the room was alive.

By one-thirty, they had run out of new ideas for Roy, and some of their suggestions were beginning to make sense to him.

"We've got to go," Jake said, grabbing Mac's arm. "Come on."

Martin was asleep on the sofa in the living room. Roy covered him with an old, heavy, goose feather comforter. Bonnie shuffled into the small guest/storage room.

Standing in the doorway, Jake said to Roy, "Oh, I've got a good ending for you."

"Quick, it's getting cold."

"There was an earthquake, and they all died."

"Earthquake? I guess I—"

"Roy, think about it." Jake laughed. "Tomorrow."

Jake and Mac stopped at Mac's car.

"I've made some calls," Jake said. "It'll take a few days to learn anything. Can you get back out here tomorrow?"

"Other than a few business matters, and early Mass, I'm free."

"Good. You get back out here as early as you can. I have a few contacts to make; I'll get here when I can."

At six in the morning, Jake drove to the West Side. It took ten minutes of driving in circles to locate where the boy lived. He parked the car and sat for a while. He didn't know if he'd find out much. Given the Judge's patience, there was no telling if the boy would know anything. After all, his report to the Judge would have been bogus: Bonnie and Martin had been secreted away to Kent.

Jake made contact with the boy. It took several minutes; the boy came outside and got into the van. "What are the Judge's plans?"

"He's going to kidnap them."

"How? Does he know where they are?"

"He said something about the phones."

Jake had a sinking feeling, "When is he going to do this?"

"This morning."

Jake spent a moment on the boy—he couldn't just leave him without erasing traces of this contact—but he had to hurry. As soon as he finished, the boy went back into his house. Jake drove to the nearest pay phone. He called Roy. There was no answer. He called Mac; he hoped that the fire had not screwed up the phone. Mac got it on the fourth ring.

"This is Jake. Get back out to Roy's immediately."

"What happened?"

"There's no answer, I just tried. I think there may be trouble."

Mac got there twenty minutes after Jake. "My God! What's happened?" Jake was pacing the apartment. Roy was sitting on the sofa: his right eye was swollen closed, there was blood all over him, his nose was broken, and his lip was split. He was slouched down, holding his head in his hand. Angelica was trying to dab a chunk of pinkish gauze at his face.

Jake led Mac outside. "Roy feels terrible that he let this happen, but he never had a chance. The Judge was here, with some of his boys. They worked him over; Angie hid under the bed. They didn't bother her. He has three broken ribs, some internal bleeding—I've stopped that—and he lost two teeth. And—"

"Bonnie? Martin?"

"They've been kidnapped."

Jake looked at Mac; he was taking this hard. Jake thought he understood; they all had a good time the night before. Bonnie and Martin were good people; of course, Mac would feel as though he too, had let them down.

"Mac, stay here with Roy. When he feels a little more together, get him to the hospital. If Angie wants to stay with Roy, then that's probably best for him. I've got to find the Judge."

***

The day after Jake had killed the Tong Boss, after his elation had wound down, Chemmg brought up the confrontation. "You think it was easy. Risky, but easy. This time it was. Remember we came in, looked for the man, and although he confronted us, he was off guard.

"In Tibet, we were invaded by the Chinese. They had no special skills. They were men with guns. Leaders a thousand miles away ordered them into Tibet. What were we to do? I was sixty-two. I knew others with skills like mine—like ours. I thought we should do something. We were all agreed. I went to Ka. He was almost a hundred. We knew he wouldn't fight, but we wanted his blessing and his suggestions.

"I talked with him for hours. He said we were impotent to fight, and fools if we tried. I could tell that he was deeply torn in saying what he did, but he was telling the truth. We were no match for tens of thousands of bullets. Ka asked what we would do if the Chinese took hostages? What if they killed a hundred villagers for every Chinese we killed? Could we live with that? The Chinese had won against Chiang Kai-Shek, could we really expect to stop them?

"I was distraught. Suddenly he slapped the table, loudly. A single fly flew up, away from his hand. With a look of sorrow in his eyes, he picked up his hand. He had crushed three flies—they never had a chance.

"This is a lesson that hurt very much to learn. Imagine an entire nation. Someday you will have to learn the limits; we all learn this lesson differently."

***

Jake drove back. He steadied his breathing. He knew that the Judge had found his weakness. The Judge had no compassion, no sense of obligation or duty. He operated in a world void of constraint, except for appearances. Evil seemed to have the upper hand. It could strike anywhere. Jake was always putting out fires. It was hardest when the innocent were hurt.

He got back to his apartment. It took several calls to locate the Judge.

"This is Jacob Krajczynski."

"Ah, Jake, it's a pleasure. I suppose you would like to meet?"

"Are Mrs. Winslow and Martin all right?"

"For now, of course. What do you take me for?"

"If you want me, we can meet. Let them go. Why bring them any harm? What have they done?"

"Yes, I would like to meet. You perhaps got the better of me last time, but that was a child's game." The Judge paused. Jake could imagine him sitting, phone in hand, smiling. "As to why, that I doubt you will ever know."

"When and where?"

"Jake, you shouldn't be so impetuous. Why not be my guest for lunch? What are you in the mood for? You liked lunch at Sammy's. Let's meet there in an hour, a quarter to one."

Jake meditated for twenty minutes. He had let the Judge excite him. He couldn't afford to be careless.

ELEVEN

The maître d' stopped Jake. He had no tie and no jacket, but he had a choice: the restaurant maintained a small wardrobe. The only jacket that was large enough was a bright green plaid—the ties were worse. He felt silly; he would stand out more wearing their jacket and tie than he would in shirtsleeves. He was preoccupied; the fuss over his clothing flustered him.

The Judge noticed the commotion, and signaled the waiter. The waiter delivered his message to the maître d'. The maître d' escorted Jake to the table, without proper attire.

"I've taken the liberty to order. You had trouble last time."

Jake nodded.

"My son, Edward, is doing well. His right arm may require surgery. Otherwise, he's fine. You got him through a tough time. I'm sure he wants to thank you himself, but you know kids, their manners aren't always exactly polished. So, I'll take the opportunity to thank you for him."

"What about Mrs. Winslow and her son?"

"Why don't we eat first, before we discuss . . . business? It would be rude to keep you from enjoying lunch. I know you don't get here often. . . . Do you read? Well, of course you must, you run a bookstore. Have you ever read any gothic horror books?"

Jake knew that for the time being it was the Judge's game. "No, I haven't. I don't read much contemporary work."

"That's a shame. Many are good. They do a fair job describing Evil, although I don't always agree with the story lines, but such is the license of writers. There is usually too much emphasis on horror, although the two are often found together. I think they are best when they deal with myth or Good versus Evil.

"I think that we've lost something today, limiting ourselves to only one god; doesn't it make more sense that if there were one there could be two or three, or more? Certainly, I would go so far as to say that Evil is a—ah, here's lunch." The Judge sat back while the waiter rearranged the table. "I think you'll like the trout. Fish is good for you. You should probably watch your weight; it looks as though it could get way out of hand."

His comment made Jake angry; the fish smelled good, and he knew he should watch his weight.

"Anyway, I was talking about the Gods. There is more than one. They are hurt that we, their creations, have forgotten them. What insolence! Do you think that they created Evil? Or do you think that there is a God of Evil? I don't mean the Christian Devil, that's a whitewash job. They will destroy us all, and everything around us, if we don't give them their due: Good and Evil.

"So here we sit, enjoying our lunches. Do you like the fish? I can't seem to engage you in conversation. Why?"

Jake steadied his breathing and kept his attention on his lunch. *It's your game, but I don't have to play by your rules,* he thought, ignoring what the Judge was saying.

After the waiter cleared the table, Jake ordered cheesecake. It was phony; no more than fluffed up gelatin. The Judge saw his expression. "Well, we live in changing times, even here."

Jake turned his attention to his coffee. There were two

kinds of sugar, white and natural. He had tried natural sugar once. It threw everything out of kilter. He wasn't going to make that mistake again.

"Pass the. . . ."

TWELVE

The Judge opened his eyes, letting in the blazing rush of sunlight. It hurt. He squeezed them closed, pushing out the pain. There was a flat, anonymous ache, which took awhile to find. He probed with his fingers and found a large, bleeding gash in the back of his head. He sat up, turning away from the sun. Slowly, he opened his eyes again. On the ground was a jagged rock, red-brown from the drying blood on it.

The landscape startled Judge Forbs. He was sprawled near the top of a hill. There was nothing anywhere, no houses, no roads, no people, and no trees—nothing. The ground was rocky and covered with tall, rough, yellow grass, and cactus. He willed himself to his feet, and shook the cramps out of his muscles. He walked to the top of the hill.

The land rolled in all directions, a blinding sea of yellow. In the distance, thirty miles west, was a range of snow-capped mountains. The hill wasn't high enough for him to see what lay elsewhere.

"Jaaaake!" he yelled. Again, and again, "Jaaaake!" Over and over, until his voice grew horse.

No one answered. He was alone in this forsaken land.

He drew in a breath, slowly calming himself. "I'm early," he said, "that's all; Jake hasn't come yet." He stood stiffly to meet an unseen challenge. "So, I have the advantage, Mr. Krajczynski. I'm here first and it's my move."

The sun was hot. He would be okay, of course; this was his world and his dream. He willed the sun cooler. Nothing happened. *Maybe,* he thought, picking at the clotted blood, and restarting the bleeding, *I'm still disoriented.* He willed himself cooler.

"Ah," he sighed as he felt his body temperature drop a little. "This one, Mr. Krajczynski, you'll lose."

He decided to walk to the mountains where there was water, and he would have the advantage of the high ground.

The back of his throat was dry. He was beginning to feel too warm again. His ears hurt, and his skin prickled. For now, the easiest thing was to shut out these discomforts. He knew there would be time to reshape the dreamscape, time to prepare for Jake. The Judge smiled—thinking of Jake's reception—as he kept walking west. Other than the sun, it would not be a difficult walk, twelve hours at the most. He would get to the mountains just after dark.

There were no animals. At least, he didn't see any, nothing except bees and flies. He wondered about that. Why would he bring flies into his world? Why, in fact, was he walking thirty miles? He willed himself there.

Nothing happened except that he became more aware of his discomfort. "Damn sun!"

"I am the Judge, I'm in control." He repeated to himself. He brought his breathing and heart rate into rhythm. In a trance, the Judge walked straight for the mountains, unaware of his surroundings.

The sunset was beautiful. The sky along the eastern horizon was already indigo turning black, but overhead plumes of lavender and crimson brushed the night sky, escaping, as if they could, from the now hidden sun. Gold, orange, and turquoise bands squeezed out along the ragged mountain silhouette. Late evening clouds, like stage curtains, pressed in on the sky's colorful stripes, pushing them back into the rocks and finally over the horizon. Bashful stars rushed to fill the emptiness.

The Judge never saw any of this. He didn't feel the swirl of damp, cold, night air streaming out of the mountain crannies, where during the day it hid. He didn't see the night creatures, rising reborn to stalk the land looking for prey. In those moments between day and night, he could have discerned the discrete odors of desert life: the desert sage, round and full with a hint of earthiness, the cactus, sharp and acrid. The grasses had no obvious odor, but within the clumps, sheltered from the sun, were tiny white flowers that had a sweet, almond-orange scent. The scurrying animals smelled of oils, musk, and dirt.

The Judge missed it all as he climbed through the rocks towards the highlands.

Shortly after sunrise, he stopped at a small mountain lake. He allowed himself to come out of his trance. Following animal tracks in the soft, moist dirt, he pushed his way through the waist high, green grasses and reeds. He was thirsty, and the smell of water drew him. At the water's edge was a clear patch of moss-covered ground, under a dogwood. He knelt. Cupping his hand, he scooped out some water. It tasted acidic, and burned his lips. He spit it out.

He looked around. He saw tracks leading to and from the water; it should have been safe to drink. He leaned over to look in, to see if there were fish. What he saw made him retch. His reflection showed the horror of his face. It was swollen and blotchy, yellow and red; his ears were cracked, and each helix was greenish-blue with yellow pustules; large boils had formed around his neck, above his collar. He held his hands close to his face. They stunk; their backs were swollen, cracked and oozing.

Anywhere the sun had touched him he was rotting. In stunned disbelief, he realized that he was allergic to the sun. This world would kill him, long before Jake ever showed up.

He ran in terror from the pond, away from the sun, and into the rocks—searching. His clothes and hands were torn, and he was bruised and bleeding by the time he saw the cave. The Judge crawled into the cool, damp, blackness. Relief flushed through him, and he slept.

He woke, days later, his body exhausted in its effort to recover. He felt his hands, face, neck and ears; the excrescences had reduced in size. He had dreamt. He had seen a black figure, wandering the lands, punishing those who opposed him. The Judge knew that he would become that black figure. It was only a matter of time until it was safe to go out, when he could change the sun, and put things right. He smiled, maybe what would be healthy for him, would be harmful for Jake. He liked that idea a lot; it had a delightful irony to it.

The Judge found that he could not simply will a suit of black. He experimented with a variety of materials, things he could shape into armor. Nothing worked. Then one morning, after another dream about the black figure, he realized that he had misunderstood the dream. It was not a suit of armor he was wearing; it was his skin.

Once he had the idea, it was easier; he would transform his skin into a hard, black, impenetrable shell. He overcame his nausea for the water. In the early morning light, he went out to collect his catch from traps he set the night before. He ate and drank as much as he could; he knew he would need all of his strength.

During the daylight hours, he either slept or meditated on what he was to become. He probed his cells, discovering what each gene did. He experimented on individual cells. It took a month to regain his strength and to figure out how he could do it. It would hurt.

He made a frame in the back of the cave, nine feet high. The frame he braced so that it could not shift or fall. He collected reeds and wove them into rope. He made two loops that he tied to the upper crosspiece. Naked, he meditated for several hours. His excitement and anticipation abated.

He was ready. He grabbed the top of the frame and swung his feet up and through the loops. Once locked in he let go; thus suspended, upside-down, he became the pupa.

Long before the transformation began, he entered into a trance, deeper than he had ever gone. He had to go beyond the pain, below the nerves, into the genetic material of life. He needed a chrysalis: a temporary shelter within which he would perform the metamorphosis. If that worked, if he could secrete the scabious material that would protect him, he knew he would succeed. In order to do that, he had to be past knowing or even caring.

He knew that if in this dreamscape the sun could kill him, he had to accept that this transformation could also. In surviving, however, he would gain knowledge that would be of inestimable value anywhere.

Had he been aware, had he the luxury of extra energy or breath, he would have screamed. Every cell hurt with the exertion. A scab formed over his body, not from one end to the other, but all over at one time. Starting as clear, sticky ooze, it darkened as it hardened and oxidized. Once it set, the actual metamorphosis began. Cell by cell, from his toes to the top of his head, he made the genetic changes that would set things into motion.

He hung inside that cave for half a year. Through the cold winter months, what would have been shelter for any number

97

of animals remained empty except for him. Something in his presence scared them away.

He had come to the land in late summer; he awoke to it in spring. Every minute muscle group had to be worked, slowly at first; then the large muscles; circulation; respiration; everything brought back to normal levels. When the Judge opened his eyes, he saw below him piles of pinkish-red scales, the slough that had been his chrysalis. He raised his arms; they were black and muscular. He pulled himself up, unhooked his feet, and lowered himself to the ground.

Into the Toth Mountains, impervious to the cold and the sun, walked death. Death was what he had become. At a cellular level, he had known his pain and it never left. At that level, all he wanted was revenge. The Judge didn't kill outright; that would not have served his purpose. No, he caught things; he didn't care what, and worked on them, playing with their genes, watching what happened. The animals could not shut off the pain. They all died—some took longer than others did.

By summer, he was able to change animals into what he wanted without their dying right away. He kept at it. Besides feeding off the pain and death, he had a goal: to create life forms to his whim, out of pieces of other living things. By fall, leaving a wake of death behind him, he ventured out, exploring the land.

As he walked, he created his Changelings and left them to live or die as they would, for he had succeeded in discovering how to mold life to his desire. He made things in the mountains, in the swamps, and in the plains. He didn't walk the desert. Perhaps he could have, but he carried a fear of it.

He was self-absorbed, but over the next year he began to feel uneasiness. He couldn't understand it. It crawled into his dreams and from there into his consciousness. He felt a need to be on guard. As he sat looking out towards the desert, he saw in his mind a harpy. He knew he could do that. Therefore, he did. His creature was a black, filthy bird, with a small hairless head, part bird, and part humanoid. Its body was covered with scales; a small bony hand grew from each scapula. It could not talk, so from the bee he took the genetic material that controlled their dance. His second harpy danced for him.

He created a band of harpies. They would be his spies, flying around him, reporting about anything that approached. They were not smart, but given their simple task they could be effective.

Occasionally, he saw people, but they ran from him. Tales about him spread through the inhabited lands. People thought that they could avoid him, that they could run from him. It made him laugh. *Avoid me?* he thought. *Never. I'll be back for you when I want.*

For another year, he wandered. His Changelings thrived. He was getting better at creating. As his pain had never left him, so he made sure that pain never left them. People began to leave the areas he had seeded. He took pleasure in their terror. This part of the world was good to him, but he never crossed the desert.

One day he felt a tremor that seemed to shake the world. It startled him. In the back of his mind, a thought started to take root, but he could not grasp it. Something pulled at him, something from the south. So he ran. He ran as fast as his harpies could fly. He felt the warmth in his muscles, and felt good about running south. With quiet and speed he passed through villages and farms. He leapt chasms and swam rivers and lakes.

It was almost noon when he arrived at the waterfall. He

felt that he had reached his goal. He stopped and walked around cautiously. It frustrated him that he still could not remember what he was seeking. He looked over the edge at the pool below; in the sand lay a man, larger than most, and strangely dressed. Another tremor shook the ground. He watched as the man stood up. The man looked around, then up towards him. He ducked back from the edge, afraid.

He crept towards the edge again, hiding in the underbrush. There, unseen, he watched. Another man appeared; he felt an energy that made him uncomfortable, yet curiosity held him captive. *If I could only remember,* he thought.

For the first time, he saw something that disturbed him greatly. He saw the second man throw a black stick into one of his Changelings. The wound was mortal. *How?* He wondered. He felt no loss over the death, except that it had taken time to create the creature, so that was time lost. He felt fear and was challenged by these men. He knew that he held the answer deep in his mind.

With the speed of an evil thought, he ran north to his camp.

The Judge got back after nightfall. He had heard people call their name for him, *Vritrk.* He felt fear and resignation from them, all except the two by the water. They were the key to his ending the frustration. The harder he tried the further it slipped away.

He called his harpies. He described the two men to them, they were to find and follow the two men. One was to return to him with information. He sent them off. During the night, he had a dream. He saw that strange, heavy man; they were together; the heavy man opposed him. In his heart, he knew they were enemies. The heavy man flew at him. The Judge woke up.

He heard himself scream, "Jaaaake!" He remembered.

In his waking, he had a plan. They were after him; therefore, they would come to him. He would wait and prepare. His harpies would keep him posted. He had all the advantages. There was regret; he felt sorry that it would be over so quickly for his enemy. If he were lucky, he could capture Jake alive, then he would work on him, in pieces, keeping Jake's mind aware, watching as his own body turned into more of the Judge's Changelings.

The Judge liked the sound of *Vritrk*; it was a good name; he took it for himself. He created more Changelings, who did his bidding. They built a throne.

Made of polished black stone, *Vritrk's* throne stood in the center of a black disk at the top of a crag rock in the Toth Mountains. From it, he had an unobstructed view of the n'Geent Desert with the L'zotk capping the horizon like a black scab. He could just make out barges on the Zot River. Whichever direction they came from, he could watch their approach.

The throne sat on a stepped dais, five feet above the floor. Around the edges of the disk, fifty feet from side to side, were supporting columns, twenty feet high, for the massive black stone roof. Except at dawn, no sunlight ever touched the throne. When he wasn't working on his Changelings, he sat there, surveying his world.

Vritrk felt no impatience. He knew he had control; he had time to prepare. And he knew who his enemy was; in that knowledge, he knew he would win.

THIRTEEN

The ground shook. A deep rumbling filled the air as trees swayed and rocks fell. Jake was lying by the water, a deep pond at the base of a waterfall. When it subsided, he knelt by the edge and looked into the clear, cool water. He recognized his reflection the second before he disturbed the surface with his hand as he splashed his face. A little of the water trickled into his mouth, he liked the taste.

A chill passed through the air as a shadow crossed over his on the ground. He looked up to the top of the precipice. For a second he saw a black, muscular figure, which retreated out of sight beyond the edge.

Jake heard birds singing in the trees. They got louder as the shock of the earthquake wore off. He laughed at the cacophony around him. Standing in the sun, he was sweaty, and he was hungry. At least, he thought, he could take advantage of where he was, and take a swim. He felt like a child as he waded into the water.

He was swimming in circles about fifty feet from the shoreline. With a start he saw that a man was standing next to his clothes, poking at them with a stick. Jake yelled to him. "Hello. Careful with them. They're all I have."

The man held his hand over his brow to shield out the sun, and searched the water for the voice. Jake swam towards the shore with a slow, clumsy, over-head stroke, slapping the water. With the sun behind him, Jake could easily see the man. He was young, maybe twenty-five, lean and wiry, with wavy blonde hair. He was wearing a coarse, ivory colored cloth robe that came down to the ground. In his right hand was a stick; no, a staff, long and black, with bands of silver inlaid around the upper half in an intricate Celtic-like pattern. The top was capped in ivory; the bottom had a silver tip. Whatever its purpose, it was beautiful.

Jake was fifteen feet away; the water was shallow enough that it was difficult to swim. He started to stand up. The man's face distorted. With a look of horror, the man raised his arm to throw the staff at Jake. Jake prepared to parry it.

The staff missed his shoulder by several feet. "You missed," he started to yell, when he heard a splash behind him. He pivoted. The staff had transfixed a slimy greenish arm, extending out of the water six feet behind him. The arm twitched. Its texture was like a giant slug, with folds of translucent skin hanging from it. Above the staff was a three-fingered hand, each finger ending in a two inch, bone white claw. What was at the other end of the arm, below the water, he did not want to know. The wounded arm oozed, and an evil stench filled the air.

Jake reached for the staff to retrieve it.

"No! Stop! Don't touch—"

Jake saw no reason not to get the staff for the man. "No sense in you getting wet," he said as he pulled the staff free. The arm slapped the water and sunk in a viscous, yellow-green cloud.

Jake shivered at the sight and waded to shore.

The staff was odd. It looked to be ebony. At an inch and a quarter in diameter and five feet long, it should have had some weight, but it did not. It was feather-light. His hand tingled; he felt good holding the staff. It felt almost alive.

Jake handed it to the man. "Thanks. You seem to have saved my life. My name is Jake."

"Who are you? How did you do that?" The young man's eyes locked on Jake in disbelief.

"Do what?"

"Only a priest, with a special calling, can hold the Staff. There are two of us." The man's voice dropped to a whisper. "It should have killed you."

Jake laughed as he put on his pants; he felt ten pounds lighter. "What was that?"

"I don't know. There have been many strange things happening. Odd things that no one understands. I've been sent out to learn what I can about the Change." His eyes narrowed, he gripped the staff tighter, and he took a step back from Jake. "Who are you?"

"My name's Jake. You just saved my life. Where I'm from and what I'm doing here, I'm not too sure of. If what I think is correct, you'd find it an even greater mystery." Jake matched his breathing to the priest's breathing. He touched the man's mind, gently; he did not want to startle him. When he had made contact, he opened his mind to the priest, enough to allow him to see Jake's world. The melding lasted a minute.

"You are an enemy of the man you call the Judge?" The priest's voice was low, each word separated from the others with the struggle to master his thoughts.

"Yes. I don't know how much you understand, because I'm not sure what I know. This is not what I expected. I mean, it is, in some ways, but not in others. Your world is complete, beyond my imagining. It's complete, with a history and a tradition. I'm confused . . . I'm also hungry. May I tag along with you?"

The priest had been looking at Jake, spellbound. He had to shake himself to answer. "I must go back to the temple.

It will take two days. We can eat along the way; there are a number of villages where we will be welcome."

"And along the way, what do I call you?"

"I'm sorry. My name is d'Solteen. I just thought you knew . . . after seeing your world."

"Now, priest d'Solteen, you can return the favor and show me yours."

Jake finished buttoning his shirt as they walked into the forest on a small, well-used path. The lushness impressed him. It was more jungle than forest. There were tall, majestic, palm-like trees. Amongst them was a variety of plants. All had waxy, deep green leaves, waving gently on long stalks. Some of the leaves had other colors, stripes of violet, blue, or yellow. Patches of sunlight dappled the jungle floor. What struck Jake more was the odor; it was a rich, earthy, musty, bouquet, which stopped just short of cloying. It was a variegated odor, changing as Jake walked, smells getting stronger and weaker as if competing for attention. All the while, the birdsong filled the air.

They walked in silence. Both wanted to talk, but neither was willing to intrude on the other. The path led along the base of a precipice that seemed to run for miles in a north-south direction. Occasionally, Jake saw bones, or the body of an animal, along the base of the rocks. After three quarters of an hour—Jake figured they had walked two and a half miles—the path forked. The right leg continued along the base; the left leg turned east. They went east.

Jake was beginning to think that he'd have to settle for being hungry when they came to a clearing at the top of a hill. Below them, maybe half a mile, was a small, orderly village of thatch-roofed houses. The bouquet had changed slightly; he could make out the odor of food cooking. "I was just thinking that eating was an illusion."

D'Solteen turned to him. "These are good people. They will welcome us, and you will get your meal." He paused, unsure if he was about to overstep his place, "Although, from the look of you, I don't think you need it."

Jake laughed.

FOURTEEN

Jake and d'Solteen covered the half mile through the terraced fields in fifteen minutes. They had to follow worn, meandering footpaths that defined each plot, and led the way through the maze and down the hillside.

"It's beautiful," Jake said.

"Efficient too. The farmers work a variety of crops at a time. No one crop blocks the sun of another."

"What do they grow?"

"Grains and vegetables. They have worked out the rotation over a thousand years. It saves the soil, and allows them to grow more."

Jake counted his paces along several plots. "One family is going to eat better than the other. The smallest, there, can't be more than twenty square feet, and this one could be four hundred."

"The farm is communal."

"How long is a growing season?"

"Below the Singren Rim it's—"

"Singren?"

"It's a five thousand foot rise in the land that divides the Arrit Mountains in the north from the low lands, stretching from the ocean at Arrit Gateway, inland about eight days. It runs—"

"Stop. Sorry I asked, without a map I'm lost. The growing season?"

"Nine months."

"I smell food." Jake grinned. "We could walk a little faster."

D'Solteen shook his head. He liked this strange man. He had never seen anyone quite so big, taller, yes, but none of the neeZeen people ever got heavy. And he had the power to hold a Staff, yet he was unaware of where he was. If he could believe his own mind, he had seen the strange man's world, smelled its smells, and tasted some of its food. How was that possible? He could sense that the man was good. Molezeen will be happy: here is the third.

They were fifty yards from the first house, when a dozen children ran out to meet them. "I hope you like children," d'Solteen said. "They're always happy to—"

He never had a chance to finish the sentence. The children's shouts drowned him out. They knew him, and were clearly excited by his visit. But they became silent when they stood next to Jake. No one moved. D'Solteen watched as one little girl, daringly reached out to pat Jake's stomach. She was hesitant, as though she were testing to see if a kitchen pan were hot. She giggled and patted him again.

Jake roared with laughter. It was like a signal. The littlest ones jumped at him. He had no choice but to catch them. The others pulled at his arms and his shirt.

By the time they got to the center of the village, everyone had gathered to see this strange man—covered with giggling children—waddle into town with the priest. It took a while to tear the children away. Jake did little to help; he loved children.

They were led to the largest building. It was thatched, like all the rest, but it had only one large room. Two men brought out dishes of food, one after the other, as though they were feeding a dozen, not two. D'Solteen motioned Jake to start. Jake didn't let anyone down. He ate more food than they had ever seen any man eat at one time.

"I've . . . shown . . . you . . . something of my world." Jake forced himself to slow down eating. "But what of yours? What is the Change? Tell me about your staff."

"You ask a lot. I am not sure how much I want to tell you, not here. Let's talk later, on the trail."

Jake agreed, and reached for the last of what he thought was curried fish. D'Solteen laughed. "We may have trouble keeping you well fed."

A wave of tittering swept through the invisible audience.

Three village women bowed before the priest and sat next to him. Jake tried to follow their conversation, but they discussed matters of local commerce. He gave up, and looked around; to the right of the doorway were the children. He got up and walked over.

Spellbound, they watched Jake pull a coin from his pocket. "Have you ever seen anything like this?" he asked holding a silver dollar in his right hand. As one of the children reached for it, he walked it across his fingers, making it disappear under his hand, only to reappear on the opposite side to walk across the tops of his fingers again. Over and over he did this. The children laughed and squealed. It had taken Jake two years to master this simple trick, and he always carried the silver dollar since then. The unprofessional grin on his face showed that he would have spent a lifetime to learn it for a moment like this one.

Jake looked over his audience, one face at a time. They were beautiful children: tan skin; straight brown or black hair—one girl had curls; white, perfectly shaped teeth; well-toned muscular bodies, the kind seen on active, healthy children; they all had almond shaped eyes. What struck him most was their spiritual health. These were children, innocent without being naive, simple but not stupid, alive with the joy of life.

"This is from a world far, far from here. It's magic."

"Where?" one of them asked.

"There." He pointed up. "Beyond the sun." He had no idea if he was right, but it impressed them.

Jake held up his right hand, the silver dollar between his thumb and index finger. He turned to the little girl, the one with the curls. "What's your name?"

"Jasin."

"Mine is Jake. I am going to make this disappear. Whisper my name."

He passed his left hand over his right.

"Jake," she whispered.

Jake opened both hands. The coin had disappeared. The children swarmed; hands searched his pockets; felt his hands and pried apart his fingers; they made him stand up. No one could find the coin.

"Jasin, what's that in your ear?"

She reached for her ears—fingers searching—although never having seen anything like this, she had no idea what she could be looking for. "What?"

"In your ear?"

Jake stretched out his hand and lightly brushed her left ear. There, shining brightly in the sun was the errant coin. Jake flipped it high in the air.

The whole village cheered when he caught it. He marveled at the scene. Here, in a land beyond his imagining, a land haunted by real magic, simple slight of hand could be so exciting.

D'Solteen put his hand on Jake's shoulder. "We must leave. We have a long way to go before nightfall."

Jake stood up. The little girl—still touching her ear, hoping that something more would happen—had tears in her eyes. His hand was open and empty as he reached over to her. He tugged at one of the folds of her simple dress. The coin fell to the ground. She grinned.

"It seems to like you." He picked it up, and handed it to her. "It's yours."

Before Jake could leave, each child gave him a hug. They had fallen in love with the strange, fat, man.

D'Solteen and Jake walked in silence. The trail went east, towards the river, and then followed it all the way to Zot'qrt, the capital. The river reflected blue, deep and clear. It was busy with boat traffic, like schools of darting, giant, water bugs. There were wood barges, heaped high with grain or produce. They had ropes running to the footpath, where animals that looked to Jake like mules pulled them. There were large boats, something like Chinese junks. Most prominent were dozens of lateen-rigged boats, used by the fishermen.

"You have quite a way with children," d'Solteen said after an hour.

"I've always liked a good audience. These were the best. Back home there are children who live in my building. They like to come up to my apartment. It's sort of a child's museum of odds and ends. They love it. Now and again, I'll take the time to learn a new trick. But they're smart kids. They don't want to appear less than savvy to the real world. Therefore, when I do a trick, I often get lots of moans. I know they like it, but they can't show it as much as these kids." Jake stopped and stared at the boats. "Yes, I like children. Somewhere, as we grow up, we lose that quality that made us children. I don't mean the physical; I've seen five-year-olds who are old. What is it? Where does it go to?"

The priest looked into Jake's eyes. "I don't think you've ever lost it."

"Maybe not. But now I need some answers, enough about children. You were going to talk to me."

"You've seen a creature of the Change. There are more, I can't tell you what. They are always different, and always deadly."

"It wasn't far from the village."

"I know. That's why I didn't want to talk about it there. I think they're pretty safe. But where would they go? For now they are best not knowing."

"How long has this been going on?"

"We think about four years. It started with reports of a creeping darkness in the far north."

"Has there ever been anything like this before?"

"There are stories—we were told them as children—about a time before history, when Evil first came into the world. The Gods fought Evil and won, but they did not destroy it. The second time a great war took place, men fought for the Gods, who had been tricked by Evil. Lazz, who was given immortality by the God's for his help, led them. Evil was cast into the Void. We think that it's happening again. Evil is back.

"Our High Priest is a remarkable man. That's where we're going, to meet him. He realized that this Change was real and would destroy the world if we couldn't fight it. It's not a war to be fought by the world; if it were to get that far, Evil would surely win. No. Molezeen, he's our High Priest, he says that this is a war to be fought by a few, against a few.

"Two years ago he found the Staves of Li—there are three. This is one of them. He holds one. The third lies waiting. We never knew if we would find someone who could hold the third. Now we have." He touched Jake's arm to confirm his statement.

"We'll see," Jake said uneasily. "Are they magic?"

"Maybe. In the *Koth'seen,* we are told they are alive. But I don't know how that could be. We don't know much about what the Staves can do, nor how they can help us fight, except as you saw earlier. The legend says that originally there were fifteen. Since the first Change, twelve are lost. What can we do with only three?"

The question dampened Jake's desire to talk. He was being consumed with this world's problems. He felt that they were up against something too big for three men armed with pieces of wood.

Night was beginning to fall. They walked on until they saw a campfire. "We'll share the warmth with the bargemen."

There were five men gathered around the fire. They were the crew of one of the barges. The fire was big and warm; grills had been set up where they were preparing dinner. One of the men looked around. "Who's there?"

"A priest and his friend. May we join your camp?"

They were welcomed. The bargemen had plenty of food to share. In return, d'Solteen entertained them with stories about pirates, until the fire burned down.

Early in the morning, Jake woke. He heard something being dragged through the leaves. In the flickering light of the embers, he saw for the second time a creature of the Change. Standing no more than four feet tall—its face, head, and back covered with an excrescence of bumps and pustules—it held the neck of one of the bargemen. From the angle of the head, Jake knew the man was dead. He was being dragged off into the woods. Jake jumped to his feet, and grabbed the first thing he could: d'Solteen's Staff.

"Stop!" Jake yelled. He pointed the Staff at the creature. Jake remembered nothing of what happened after that. He was aware that the monster lay dead, ten feet in front of him, and the air was full of an evil stench.

Jake stood, rooted to that site. No one moved. It was a moment that none would ever forget. D'Solteen walked over to Jake, and reached out for the Staff. As his fingers touched it, it felt cold to him; he removed his hand. For the moment, it was no longer his Staff.

Jake's eyes unglazed as he recognized the priest. "What happened?" he whispered.

"You don't know?" D'Solteen led Jake away from the fire. In reverent tones, he described to Jake what he had done.

As Jake pointed the Staff at the creature, the silver tip began to glow; its light covered the area for two hundred feet in all directions. The creature turned to face Jake, dropping the body.

Behind it, in the fringe of the light, were two more creatures, feeding off a second body, sucking on it, their faces covered with blood.

The remaining three bargemen and d'Solteen sat motionless. They were unable to move—not from fear—but as if waiting to be carried off.

Then in one horrible, nightmarish leap, the closest creature propelled itself into the air in an arc that would have ended at Jake.

Jake followed the creature with the silver tip. In a deep, resonant voice, his eyes fixed on the monster, he said, "No."

A bolt of blue lightning struck the creature; its body shook. Yellow-green, fetid drool dripped from its mouth. Its eyes opened wide; it groaned. In that moment, it died; momentum carried it over the fire.

Jake turned to the two feeding creatures. They never

stopped eating. Two bolts from the Staff broke the air and hit them. They fell, smoking and throbbing. Their bodies began to dissolve.

"How did you do that?" d'Solteen asked, knowing that he would not get an answer.

"I do remember one thing," Jake said. "It must have been just as the first creature died. I felt the creature. It was confused. It had been created without a past and without a future. Its only purpose was to frighten and kill. You can not create life, even as awful as that, without creating something of a soul. It felt . . . relief, I think. Relief that it no longer would have to do the bidding of another; it would no longer have to live without a past. It knew its future: the end to its private torment."

Jake and the priest returned to the camp. The men had begun to dig a grave for the creatures. The bodies of their two friends would be returned to their families. The men kept their distance from Jake, and avoided his eyes. Jake was now someone who, although he had killed the beasts and saved their lives, was to be feared. D'Solteen helped break up the camp. He thanked them for their hospitality. The barge captain asked if d'Solteen would say the Rite of the Dead, and give them his benediction.

It took another hour for them to get the barge under way. Jake waited for d'Solteen to finish. "Now what?"

"Now we continue as we were. Nothing has changed, has it?"

Jake looked around him. That one moment *had* changed something. He had become aware of their vulnerability. He had also lost something, something he couldn't quite put his finger on: his past was more of a memory; the present was becoming more real.

"No, nothing has changed."

FIFTEEN

The rest of their trip was uneventful, except that people stared at Jake. Now he wasn't just oddly dressed and big, but he had a reputation. Word of his feats preceded them from barge to barge, with the spead of the dawn breaking along the Zot River. Jake was unusually quiet.

"You soared through the air, transformed into a purple and yellow dragon. The flames of the volcano were spewing from your mouth. Around and around you flew, fighting the transformed Arrit Giant, taller than anyone has ever seen. The fight lasted hours. You were wounded, poisoned cuts that would have killed an ordinary man instantly. What a fight! You killed the monster with thunderbolts, stolen from q'Tondrd, the God of Fire and Lightning. By the Gods, what a battle!"

Jake stared at d'Solteen. "Are you—"

"Now wait, don't get me wrong, I wasn't there, but my brother-in-law has a cousin, whose best friend was one of the bargemen. It's true, as I stand here."

D'Solteen tried to hold a straight face, but Jake's puzzled look was more than he could take. His face was wet with tears and his laugh seemed to echo off the hills miles away. "Jake, I'm kidding."

"Sometimes," Jake grinned sheepishly, "it takes a while."

They stood laughing for several minutes. "Thanks. I needed to hear what really happened," Jake said. "I'm not so sure about the flames of the volcano though. You're exaggerating."

They got into Zot'qrt after nightfall. D'Solteen got rooms in an anonymous, run-down inn, near the North Gate.

"This is the best you can do?" Jake worried. They had passed several attractive inns, which d'Solteen had rejected.

"In your world, don't men intrigue?"

"Of course. It's only—"

"And here too. My journey was secret." D'Solteen looked around. "Molezeen's interests are also secret."

"Surely there is something better than this, yet discrete?"

"Have faith, please." D'Solteen grinned.

"What should I have expected from a priest?" Jake mumbled as they pushed their way through the crowd by the door.

After they checked in, d'Solteen sent word to Molezeen, in code, that they would meet with the High Priest later.

The great room was loud, dark, and smelly. It was cloaked in the dirt of hundreds of years of use. Jake wondered if it had looked any different the day the doors first opened. Standing at the thick, wood bar, they ordered dinner and drink. He put his hand on the rounded edge. He was startled; it felt as though it were coated with plastic. Plastic? Then he understood: generations of oil and grease, rubbed and polished through daily use. Jake wanted to wipe his hand clean, but didn't want anyone to see. He put his hand in his pocket.

They took their drinks and waited for a table to open up. "They will bring us dinner when we get a table," d'Solteen explained.

As Jake's eyes grew accustomed to the low, yellow light, he looked around. There were twenty tables, some for two and some sat ten. The tallow colored walls were covered with drawings. He was just about through with his examination when he saw it in the corner. It was wood, five feet long, two and a half feet wide, and a foot deep; standing on four legs. One man was leaning over the end; another stood next to him, looking on. D'Solteen watched as Jake's smile grew. Jake knew a gem when he saw it. "I love it," he said as he handed d'Solteen his mug and walked away. "I never—"

It was a mechanical, wooden, pinball machine.

"Why not?" Jake thought. He walked around it, looking at it from every angle. The man who was playing, and obviously losing to his companion, decided to blame Jake. The man turned to face him. "Snowsnake," he snarled.

Jake ignored him.

"Hey, fat man, I called you a snowsnake."

Jake could have cared less what he was called. He wasn't sure what he would do with a pinball machine, but he felt an overwhelming desire to have it. The bottom and back were open. Jake crawled on the floor to watch the mechanism. By means of a counter-balance in the back, which had to be set periodically, momentum was imparted to various sets of gears and pulleys. The cork-covered paddles were energized by means of a coil spring and an anchor escapement, activated by a single button on the side of the machine. The ball was made of laminated hardwoods. It rolled down a dark, shiny shoot. The paddles propelled it back up the sloping table, to careen off pins, rings, and automatic paddles. It functioned exactly like a metal, glass, and plastic, electric pinball machine. It didn't have a theme, nor did it have flashing lights; although there were counters, flags, and bells. Jake wondered if it had a tilt mechanism.

The player was drunk. Jake never looked, as the man drew his knife. D'Solteen watched, unable to do anything in the crowded room. The man's hand drove down towards Jake's back, the knife blade catching the lantern light. Jake's right arm blocked the man's knife hand. Jake stood. As he did, he moved his hand, grabbing the man's wrist, and twisting it. The knife fell to the floor. The man tried to kick. Jake continued to twist. The man slumped. Jake let go and turned to the man's companion, who was considering how to get involved.

"Don't," Jake said in a quiet but commanding voice.

The man looked down at his friend. "I told you not to drink so much. Let's go." As they left the inn, Jake turned to look for d'Solteen.

"Do you usually attract so much trouble?" d'Solteen asked, handing him his wine.

"It's magnificent. I would never have imagined it possible."

"What? Batter? You wouldn't have found it at those fancy inns you wanted to stay at."

"Batter? Are they all like this?"

"Sort of." D'Solteen pointed. "That's our table. They're cleaning it. What's so interesting about a game?"

Jake sat down and drank some wine. It had the body and fullness of a Cabernet Sauvignon. Jake stared at the mug, then at d'Solteen. "It's good."

"The place might look filthy, but that doesn't mean that it has to have bad wine."

They ordered a pitcher; dinner was every bit as good as the wine. Jake tried to explain the mystique of pinball to d'Solteen.

After dinner, they went to their rooms. D'Solteen had taken three, one for each of them, and one that they could use as a sitting room. The sitting room was the inn's best: a large bed, three wood chairs, a bench, a table and a fireplace. With another pitcher of wine, they waited for the High Priest.

***

D'Solteen looked forward to seeing Molezeen. He was excited about having discovered Jake, but he felt bad that they had to meet here instead of at Molezeen's quarters. *Damn temple priests,* he thought. He and High Priest Molezeen had talked about it often.

"You have dedicated forty years of your life to the Middle Path," d'Solteen said to Molezeen a few days before he last left the capital. "You live and teach with integrity, with dignity of means. You respect those around you. Now in an unprecedented time of danger, intrigue and politics threaten to destroy man every bit as much as Evil. How do you put up with it?"

"You ask me that? I think you, of all people, should know best." Molezeen's voice was gentle; he was careful not to sound as though this were a rebuke. "But isn't that man? Don't we carry the seeds of both our redemption and our damnation? Some say it's our culture. That is too easy. It's the very shape and hue of our souls."

D'Solteen was still mystified. "I know enough history about the High Priests to know their corruption, their hypocrisy, and their duplicity. Yet, the very people who were party to and benefited from that corruption selected you. I know you. You walk above the mire. How? Why?"

"You have heard me say it before. This is the Gods' way. We are at war with Evil. The power of Good has seen that I'm in a place to help and direct our side of the fight."

Molezeen poured two mugs of *troan*—the sweet, winter beer of the Arrit people—from a barrel he kept hidden in his quarters.

123

"The Gods put you here?" d'Solteen asked.

"This is a conversation that should remain between us. It wouldn't do for the High Priest to say some of this. But I don't know the difference between Good and God. I don't know if this is an entity or a power, and I don't know where it resides: in man, in the earth, in the universe?"

"But your devotion to the Gods?" d'Solteen asked. "The teachings of the priesthood?"

"That I don't know, nor have I seen the object of my devotion. That I question accepted theology, that I refuse to give over to ritual my moral responsibility, none of this makes me any less a believer. My belief is constantly being reforged by the events of my life.

"Between us, I must say that belief must flex and stretch, it must be challenged and must challenge in return—it may not be nurturing and sheltering—but this is belief that is ultimately right. To be an automaton, what do you get then, when you really need strength?"

"What of the war against Evil?" d'Solteen asked as he got them each another mug of *troan*. He knew Molezeen was worried about his upcoming trip, or he would have said something about a second round of *troan*—he hoarded it like a miser's gold.

"I don't know. I think that we will find our way one step at a time. Am I blinded by arrogance? I hope not. But I do know we must discover for ourselves how the fight is to go. No one is going to tell us."

***

It was a while before they heard the knock. They had gotten sleepy with the wine and food and the heat of the fire. The knock grew louder before d'Solteen went to the door and opened it a crack.

"It is I," said a man in the hallway.

D'Solteen stood back. A tall man, covered in a simple, dark blue, cape—his face hidden in the deep, pointed, cowl—walked in. Without looking at Jake, he walked to the fire. He stood warming himself as he awkwardly untied his cape with his left hand. When he had flung the cape to one of the chairs, Jake saw that in his right hand was a Staff, identical to d'Solteen's. The man turned to Jake, and gave a nod of acknowledgment.

D'Solteen looked embarrassed. "Forgive me. Molezeen, this is someone you should meet, ah . . . Jake. Just Jake. Jake this is High Priest Molezeen."

They pulled the chairs around the fire, poured a third cup of wine and talked. D'Solteen spent a few minutes describing things that had happened before he and Jake had met. Then, in detail, he told of their adventure. Molezeen listened, quietly, showing little excitement.

Jake was enthralled by the story. D'Solteen told it carefully and faithfully, with no exaggeration. However, he told it with the enthusiasm that comes from years of story telling. It was to Jake almost as though he were hearing it for the first time.

Molezeen stood up at its end. He walked to the fireplace, and casually picked up his Staff. He called Jake's name, and tossed it to him. Deftly, Jake caught it. Molezeen grinned, and walked over to Jake. "I had to see. I meant no disrespect."

Jake stood to hand back the Staff. Molezeen took it from him. "D'Solteen was right." He gave Jake a hug. "Yes, now we are three." Molezeen turned to d'Solteen. "Could you get us another pitcher of wine?"

He waited until d'Solteen had left. "Jake, please, what can you tell me about this black figure above the waterfall?"

"I can't say much. I was disoriented, and it happened

quickly. But if I can trust my memory, it stood about your height, maybe a little taller. Its physique was tight and muscular. It was unclothed, and it was without gender; although I would have said it was male. And it was black, as black as your Staff. As I caught a glimpse of it, I remember thinking that it moved too quietly."

Molezeen had been staring into the fire. He turned to Jake. "Can you do to me what you did to d'Solteen? Show me your world?"

"Yes."

"Now."

Jake started to make contact with the High Priest. He paused—what would he see a dream, a fantasy, or reality?

Molezeen sensed Jake's uncertainty. "Go on. Don't worry, it's important."

Jake opened his mind. He intuitively trusted Molezeen. He let Molezeen see as much as he wanted.

Jake had no idea how long they had been. D'Solteen was sitting, silently, in the corner, sipping a cup of wine. Molezeen looked gaunt and pale.

"You are an enemy of the man you call the Judge?"

"Yes."

"We, the people of the neeZeen lands, have a different standard than where you come from, although not so different from yours. We are people, neither good nor bad, just people. Most of us believe that we must serve the problem; that is, we must try to understand and yield to what we come to know. In understanding comes the path. It is not an easy way. How do you teach people to recognize that which is never the same?"

D'Solteen knelt on the stone hearth to put a log on the fire.

"Anathema to us is what you would call command, the

ordering of things to fit a preconceived pattern. Behavior like this shows a wanton, selfish, disregard for nature. We are not perfect. There are people who take advantage of others, who behave in antisocial ways, who disregard nature. Because of our beliefs, one of the most distasteful responsibilities, which usually falls on the circuit priest, is to *vr'trk*. It is both a noun and a verb."

Jake looked confused. He tried to pronounce the word. Molezeen smiled. "No, you must give an aspiration between the syllables, and the second has a click."

Jake tried again; it sounded more like a sneeze than a word. "What does it mean?"

"Let me say first, that many have seen that black man. He is spawned of Evil. He does its bidding. We call him *Vritrk*. Do you understand? Do you know why you're here and why we need your help?"

Jake felt a shiver; he wasn't sure of the answer, and he knew he didn't want to hear it.

"*Vritrk* is a child of the Change. *Vritrk* is the father of the Changelings; he is death. *Vritrk* and *vr'trk* are the same word. *Vr'trk* means to make a decision against another. *Vritrk* is the person giving judgment."

An ember fell from the grate. It hit the hearth with a small burst of sparks. There was a hiss from the back log. Jake looked into the flames. He didn't hear himself as he said it, "The Judge."

In spite of having realized that the Judge was here, a part of the Change, he slept well. He took comfort in his new understanding. Molezeen would be a good ally, as would d'Solteen. He couldn't know how things would work out. In the telling, they seemed ill equipped and too few to fight *Vritrk* and his Changelings. But he took solace in his new found camaraderie.

When he woke, he found that d'Solteen had ordered breakfast for them in the sitting room.

"I like your High Priest."

"Yes, I thought you would."

"Now what?"

"Well, after we eat, we'll leave here and go south. We have to meet some others, and then wait for Molezeen. Then, I don't know."

Jake was working on his fourth piece of smoked fish. Fish, cheese, and watered wine made a good breakfast.

"When you finish, I've something for you."

Jake wiped his hands. "Okay." Then he laughed, because he knew his eating amazed d'Solteen; he added, "For now."

D'Solteen brought in a long, narrow, wooden box from the other room. He handed it to Jake. "It was delivered early this morning. It's from Molezeen."

Jake took the box and sat down by the fire. He opened it. In it were several robes and a heavy, cowled, dark blue cape. As Jake took them out, the cape felt stiff. He looked inside, strapped into a deep, narrow pocket was a Staff. It looked very much like Molezeen's and d'Solteen's.

D'Solteen smiled. "That's the third."

SIXTEEN

Molezeen spent hours in his suite playing the *tarrid*, the music doubling and tripling itself off the bare stone walls. Before the Gods graced him, he had been a trained musician. In private moments, he preferred the contemporary, romantic style to the *katteqattice* school he had been brought up in, although it infected his playing. *Katteqattice* was the most introspective of the three traditional schools of *tarrid* playing and the best suited to Molezeen's temperament. Tondeseen, Molezeen's teacher for many years, considered Molezeen the best practitioner of *katteqattice tarrid* playing.

Molezeen wore his salt and pepper hair long and pulled back. He had a short, well-trimmed beard. With piercing dark blue eyes, a straight nose, a high forehead—suggesting his Arrit Mountain ancestry—and standing well over six feet, he was a commanding figure. With the base of the *tarrid* held between his knees, it looked small when he played it.

Molezeen was twenty-seven when the Gods graced his life and he entered the priesthood. Like so much in the world, the priesthood was rife with politics. Molezeen had risen through the ranks to become High Priest, unscathed and almost oblivious to political intrigue. Even his opponents acknowledged his genius, some called it cunning. They believed he was able to anticipate those entanglements that trapped most men of power; and in that awareness, he wound his way through. Molezeen knew differently. He believed in the sanctity of the priesthood, in the salvation he accepted for his belief. "It is, simply, and truly, the way of the Gods."

These were troubled times. He knew that the wrongness of things would have happened regardless of who held the mantle of High Priest; nonetheless, he felt some guilt, wondering if he had failed in some way. He would snatch precious minutes to play, taking succor in his music. Soan, his secretary and a young priest of twenty-three, was proud of Molezeen; secretly, he would bring people to stand in the hallway outside Molezeen's chamber door, to hear the High Priest play.

Molezeen knew, as well as anything could be known, that he had to live with the dignity becoming his office, never to do less. People looked to him for his wisdom. "The wisdom of the Gods," he would remind them.

A few years earlier, they first noticed the Change. Reports came in that desert-land had begun to spread in areas south of The Line of Rolines. At the edge of the desert there was a creeping darkness—some called it a void—like cloud-shadow on barren land, spreading ever southward. No one knew what was in that darkness. Any life that could, fled before it, and nothing voluntarily went into it. Strange mutations began to appear, pained and deadly, and seeded throughout the land, except the n'Geent, which remained free from the monsters.

Molezeen's advisers were unanimous: ignore the desert; ignore the void; ignore the mutations—these were hysterical fantasies. A year later, Molezeen disappeared for almost three months.

***

Molezeen, his secretary Soan, and Jho, a warrior-priest, rode north. They left at night, Molezeen dressed as a traveling musician and the other two as pilgrims. When the guards at the city gates were questioned the next day, they remembered nothing that could have helped the search.

Molezeen knew that he had to disappear. If he had approached his advisers, they would have made it state business. It would have taken no less than a month to mount the trip. He would have with him a retinue of a hundred. The logistics of such a legion moving north would have created its own universe of problems. Molezeen would never have learned a thing.

The disguise was not a theatrical device. He had left home when he was sixteen to live the life of a *tarridseen*, an itinerant musician. For others, it was a hard life; for him, it was like a dream. Certainly he had ridden at night through cold winter rain, went days without a meal, and had been cheated by a greedy innkeeper or two, but he had been well known and well liked, and it was the life he wanted.

Molezeen was brilliant in several ways. His technique was flawless and virtuosic. He had an uncanny memory for melody and harmony. Having heard a song once, he could replay it years later. Tondeseen said that Molezeen's real genius was in being able to combine elements of various styles of music, to change melodies and harmonies—in ways so subtle that most never knew they had changed—so that the classics took on a new life.

Molezeen had grown up in n'Jaspinth, a day's ride south of the capital. In his years of roaming, he spent most of his time in the Arrit Mountains. He had felt his spiritual awakening there. In total, he spent five years in and around Alinge. The library of Alinge had hired him to map the toon'Arrit ruins, the trails and roads. He had taken on the commission at the request of his spiritual mentor, T'sngeen.

To meet with T'sngeen, if he were still alive, was the goal of their secret journey. Their trip to Arrit Gateway took five days. They rode hard, taking little time for rest. Once through Arrit Gateway, they slowed, taking three weeks to make the four-day ride to Alinge. To play the part of the *tarridseen* meant to be a *tarridseen*. Molezeen played for their keep.

Each town along the way had at least one inn. Molezeen counted on his memory to make their going easier. Most inns were passed down from mother to daughter or daughter-in-law, as was the custom in the lands north of the Singren Rim. In every town, save one, d'Lante, he knew the women who owned each inn. They were flattered that one of such musical skills remembered them. No one knew that he had become the High Priest whose office represented to them the soft, needful South. It hadn't been kept a secret; it was that the High Priest was unimportant to them. The circuit priests cared for, and watched over them, not the Southern bureaucracy. Of the forty years past, he said that he had been traveling the South, but he wanted to live his last years in the Arrit Mountains where he had spent his youth.

He played a few days in each town, hoping that word of him would travel ahead. It made his disguise more impenetrable and, he hoped, their task a little easier.

In Valo'q, on their sixth day traveling above the Rim, they encountered the only problem they were to have before getting to Alinge. The Mouth of the Swan, the only inn in Valo'q, was named after a bird common in the Southern Hemisphere. In the Arrit Mountains it was almost a mythical creature. A young musician was already staying there. Valo'q was not big enough to support two musicians, unless the first one was willing to share, which he was not. As was the custom, Molezeen challenged the other to a contest. The younger musician accepted.

They were to play, one against the other, at dusk. As the one challenged, the young musician had the option to go first or not. Having never heard his opponent play, the accepted wisdom would have been to play second. The youth, blinded by ego, decided to play first.

"Jho," Soan whispered, "let's get Molezeen away."

"Why?"

"He'll lose. He's good, but this other guy is great, I mean, just listen. He's—"

"No. See it through."

"But—"

"Have faith, little priest, and be quiet."

The inn was crowded; nothing like this had happened for many years. The youth had become almost a permanent resident of Valo'q. He played for an hour, holding his audience captive. Later, they all said that he had played better than any had ever heard him play.

Molezeen was delayed while lanterns were lit and two boys stoked the fire with huge logs. The lanterns' yellow parchment shields dulled the whiteness of their flames. The yellowish light gave the great room a warm and friendly cast. There was no space left, even to stand. It was possible that the entire town had turned out for the contest. While Molezeen set up and tuned his *tarrid*, the room was abuzz with people placing wagers. Although they were willing to give the old man a chance, they thought that chance was slight.

In parts of the world like those north of the Singren Rim, losing a duel meant not only losing a job and a place to sleep. For an itinerant musician, it was a prideful loss that meant going without shelter through the often lethal weather of the Arrit Mountains until a new town welcomed him. Word of his defeat would become his traveling companion; dogging him wherever he stopped and making him fair game for other challenges. It was easier to share or walk away than to be the loser.

Molezeen finished tuning. He sat calmly, waiting for the room to quiet. Softly, without any show, he played an arpeggio, the opening chord of a classic *katteqattice* hymn. He played it again with more space between the notes; it was as if he were playing the silences. The chord slowly transformed into a hymn-form, which was a series of improvised variations, each based on a note of the arpeggio, making an epic cycle. Molezeen's playing held his listeners spellbound. He based his first improvisation on the younger musician's major theme.

There was magic in his playing. The seventh and eighth variations were virtuosic, intended solely for the young musician, who was the only one there who could have appreciated and understood exactly what Molezeen was capable of doing.

There were five more variations before Molezeen stopped playing. When there was no more music, the great room remained silent except for the popping and hissing of pitch burning in the fireplace. After some time, the silence was broken by one, shared, breath, and the room filled with clicking, the form of applause reserved by the mountain folk for that which was truly exceptional.

The young man left the inn, defeated. Later that night, he came back. He broke silently into Molezeen's room, and crept towards the sleeping figure. He walked with such care that it took five minutes to traverse the fifteen feet between them. He was skilled in areas other than music. His knife was out as he stooped to kill Molezeen. In the darkness of the room, Molezeen opened his eyes. The young man could see them staring up at him. He froze, not from having been discovered, nor out of fear. He was held motionless, as if pierced through his soul by Molezeen's stare.

Tears puddled involuntarily in the youth's eyes, and the night winds seemed to gather about the inn. Molezeen whispered. "We know each other as would a father and son, though we are not. There is more in you than this wanton act you would commit. You will leave here. In the spring, you will come to me, the High Priest, in the capital. You will dedicate yourself to me, the priesthood, and the world that so desperately needs help. Tonight will be forgotten. Now, leave as you came."

Molezeen closed his eyes.

The young man stood still for several minutes, unable to move. When he felt in control, he slipped out of the inn and out of town.

The next morning, Molezeen told his story to Soan. "You must promise to keep this secret."

"But he tried to kill—"

"We need him in this time of desperation. Would you have me call a *vr'trk*?"

"For attempted murder? Yes."

"Regardless of the judgment, we would lose what little time we have left to learn what is going on, and we would lose help we need."

"A small price," Soan pressed. "You knew I'd feel this way, why tell me at all?"

Molezeen smiled, "Because when he comes to Zot'qrt, he'll need to be trained and I want you to oversee it."

"Me? But he's—"

"He's to be a priest. Nothing be served by his undoing."

At midday, on the fourth day of the Eighth Half Moon,

Molezeen, Soan, and Jho rode into Alinge. They stabled their horses, and took rooms at the Black Stream Inn, opposite the Indigo Temple.

SEVENTEEN

By all accounts, T'sngeen was 107 years old. Although he performed his religious duties as head of the Indigo Temple, he found himself spending most of his time in bed. When younger priests marveled at his age, T'sngeen would say, "I am waiting." On the fourth day of the Eighth Half Moon, his waiting was over.

The Indigo Temple was the best known and most awe inspiring north of the Singren Rim. It took up several blocks at the center of Alinge. For over five hundred years, it was both temple and university. West of Arrit Gateway, and north of the Singren Rim, it was the advocate for education, culture, and law. Its buildings were made of bluish-black granite cut from the mountains north of Alinge by the people of Dorn. Boiling water from an underground fissure was ducted to the temple and run through internal stone aqueducts, gently heating the floors. In the summer months, the water was diverted from the temple. Beautiful tapestries hung in the corridors and the temple proper; most depicted the myths of the toon'Arrit, much to the distress of many of the High Priests in Zot'qrt. During T'sngeen's tenure, the temple was home to thirty-one priests, with an additional staff of eleven. At all times, they kept six cells available for visiting circuit priests.

T'sngeen's cell was that of a simple monk. As head of the temple, he was entitled to more comfortable quarters. He said that he had spent so much of his life living in that very cell;

he couldn't bring himself to move. It was seven by thirteen feet. He owned nothing. There were two stools, a wooden cot, a desk, and a wrought iron brazier, the only concession to his age. The temple had a small, but adequate library with offices adjacent to it, which he used. He had no need for more than his simple cell.

Just before dinner, Molezeen went to the temple. Had the priests known his true name, or had he been dressed in his official robes, they would have been stunned. They attributed T'sngeen's stories about having known Molezeen years earlier as the fantasies of an old man. What they saw instead was an itinerant musician of some repute paying a visit to the old priest.

Molezeen and T'sngeen embraced. In the privacy of the priest's cell, they shared the *Chi'* Ceremony.

> *". . . and Gods who watch our earthly span,*
> *we sing your praise that all will know,*
> *and not forget your names and deeds."*

T'sngeen finished the first part of the ceremony and poured some tea into two cups. Molezeen continued.

> *"I must recall those names and deeds,*
> *to let me know what path to take,*
> *to let me know what's right and wrong."*

Each drank a sip of tea and sat in silent prayer.

"We share our dreams and prayers," T'sngeen said, holding his cup out to Molezeen.

"We share our dreams and prayers," Molezeen replied in a whisper, taking T'sngeen's cup and replacing it with his.

They drank from each other's cup, symbolically exchanging their supplications as insurance against selfish prayer.

"Thank you, old friend. It has been a long time since I have celebrated *Chi'* with such grace."

"Surely the High Priest can find others to celebrate with in Zot'qrt?" T'sngeen teased; he knew the truth of the southern temple and the bureaucracy it engendered.

Molezeen embraced T'sngeen. "I have missed you."

"So tell me. I am old," he winked, "and could die before you start your tale."

"Even though we may be soft in the south, we aren't deaf. We have heard the stories of the Void and of Evil's spawn, *Vritrk*. I was told to ignore them as the ravings of mad men, but I feel Its touch. It's real."

"I knew you would come to me. Where else could you turn?"

"It's been so many years. My duties as High Priest have made me a bad disciple, I could have written, or sent you word. I didn't even know if you were alive. I should—"

"I've known of your career and the consumption of time that it demands. I take pleasure in my memories of you, even in an occasional retelling to some of the younger priests. They laugh at me behind my back, thinking that I've lost my mind and make things up. After all, how could a simple priest in an out of the way place like Alinge have known the great Molezeen? Let them think that; such is the fun of youth."

"I don't want them making you an object of derision."

"We celebrate the student, not the teacher. And the secrecy of your visit is more important than the ego of an old man. Anyway, what is sent forth returns; I remember laughing at some of my teachers when I was young."

"So do I," Molezeen whispered.

"I've given much thought to the Change. It's closer to us than to you in the South . . . I've been rereading the *Koth'seen* and the *nQert'seen*."

"Children's stories."

"They're the most recent story of the coming of Evil. I think they are true. The tale of Lazz—"

"You'd have me follow nGin, the prankster God?" Molezeen joked. "He led Lazz on a merry chase around the world, what? A hundred and fifty years, before Lazz confronted Evil." Molezeen laughed. "I doubt we have the time."

"No. But Lazz used the Staves of Li to fight Evil, so can you."

"But they're just fable. Even if they existed, where would I find—"

"Here." It was T'sngeen's turn to laugh. "Three of them are here, in the library."

"You're serious, aren't you? You believe—"

"Lazz found Li's Staves, fifteen were alive. He lost one in the ocean, leaving fourteen. After the battle of nQert, they disappeared. Three turned up at the library of Alinge four hundred years ago, in a collection of toon'Arrit artifacts."

"I know the library well; you had me work there. I never saw them."

"No, you wouldn't have. You saw the public collection. In the basement, there is more. Most of the things in the basement are junk. In the vault, however, are three staves. I think they're three of Li's Staves."

"Supposing they are, how can they help?" Molezeen asked.

"You'd ask me that, when these are just children's stories?" T'sngeen laughed. "I don't know. But I think that you should get them."

"As Molezeen, that won't be hard."

"You must do it secretly. Whatever their value, whatever they can do, you will receive nothing but ridicule if you're known to have them; you'd be the believer in nursery stories, impotent to lead as the High Priest you are. But I'm sure they are the key."

"You want me to steal them?"

"Well, yes."

"I don't recall your having a larcenous streak."

"No, but in times measured dangerous, one takes dangerous measures. If I'm right, you could be in great danger. There is a story, which is all but forgotten now. According to it, many years ago the Staves were on public display. A young boy tried to pick up one of them. He must have gotten it out of the display rack because they found it next to his body. He was dead; his hands were charred black. The man who found him also died. When he tried to move the Staff, it killed him. The curator was lucky. He knew, or guessed, that the Staves could be moved with wood as an insulator. They were taken to the basement, and sealed in a vault. They have never been seen since."

"Why do you think that I can hold them, or should I use wood?"

"If you have to use wood, you won't succeed. The story also says that each Staff weighs as much as a man or more, except to those who are special, who can wield a Staff of Li. If it's true and you're not destined to be a Staff wielder, you could move them, but never all three, never secretly, and not back to the capital. I think it makes sense that someone alive today should be able to hold and wield them. Why not you, the High Priest?"

"Why not I?" Molezeen asked. "You know as well as I that being the High Priest is more political then religious."

"But I know you. You're not political. You're being here demonstrates that. You stand out, amongst the last twenty or so High Priests as the only religious one. So, I ask, why not you?"

T'sngeen knew a lot about the library, and he used his authority to get Molezeen an appointment. Once Molezeen located the Staves, they would plan how to sneak them out. Molezeen, with his two companions, would be shown around.

The curator gave them a warning as he led them down into the basement. "There are a lot of invaluable and fragile things down here. Many of them have yet to be cataloged. Normally, we would not let anyone go down alone, but T'sngeen's request was most specific. Please, however, respect our rules. Look, but do not touch. Of course you may open drawers and cabinet doors, but leave the contents alone." He didn't know about the Staves of Li; he didn't know T'sngeen's story about the removal of the Staves from public display.

Molezeen, Soan, and Jho carried lanterns.

"I'll be back for you—" The curator stopped to sneeze. "Sorry, it's the dust. I'll get you at closing."

Molezeen watched him shuffle back up the stairs in the flickering light. The curator sneezed several more times before he reached the ground floor. Although he would never have admitted it, he was afraid of the basement.

For a few minutes, the three stood motionless, looking at the subterranean world. The basement was a labyrinth of corridors radiating out from the central and largest room. The vaulted stone ceiling, twenty-five feet above them, was supported by two rows of three, fluted, stone columns, which divided the room into twelve large bays. There were ten hallways leading from the room.

They had three hours.

T'sngeen's description had been vague. He had remembered being told that the vault was in the north-western most room. Beyond the central room, things were so divided over hundreds of years that what should have been an easy search took an hour. The vault was the last room; sealed from the rest by a large set of bookshelves. It took another half hour to move enough of the books and shelves that they could gain access. Soan stood guard against the curator's early return, while Jho and Molezeen entered the vault.

The room smelled of stale air cluttered with boxes and shelves, the accumulated debris of several hundred years of archaeological exploration.

"Don't touch anything that you can't recognize, and nothing that could be one of the Staves." Molezeen ordered Jho.

"And if you can't touch them, your life would be the greater loss—"

Molezeen's stare silenced Jho.

Almost at the end of their last hour, Molezeen found them at the back of a low shelf, farthest from the door, under a few discarded rags. By accident, Molezeen had brushed one of them, which, when it moved, revealed the pointed silver tip of a Staff. He called Jho over with his lantern. Carefully, Molezeen started to lift off the rags.

The warning bell rang. They had thirty minutes before the curator came for them. Molezeen felt desperate, it would take them at least that much time to put everything back. Without thinking, he ripped the rags away and grabbed the three Staves. The blood drained from Jho's face, as he watched Molezeen recklessly pick up the Staves.

Molezeen fell back against the shelves. Jho moved towards him.

"Stay . . . away," Molezeen said, struggling to find his words amidst the sudden colors and feelings that swept over him and battled for his attention. He was dizzy, and his hands tingled. He put the Staves down. His vertigo disappeared and his thoughts came back to him. "I'll be all right. Let's straighten up and I'll get these out of here."

They had the shelves back and the books in place when they heard the curator calling for them as he slowly came down the stairs.

Molezeen took a deep breath and picked up the Staves. "By the Gods," he whispered to himself, "let me get these out of here." His hands tingled, but the dizziness was milder. He tucked them under his robes; it was awkward, but he could hold them at his side with the ends behind his neck, hidden by the folds of his cowl. "Do they show?"

Jho and Soan held up their lanterns. "No," Soan said, "but try not to be so stiff."

Molezeen thought it odd; the Staves were featherweight. Although almost too long to be hidden, they were no problem to hold. His mind blurred as they followed the curator out.

At the top of the stairs, the curator turned to Molezeen. "I've heard about your musical skills from T'sngeen. Would you and your companions join me for a drink? I'm something of an authority on *katteqattice*, you know. Perhaps we could exchange theories. . . ."

Molezeen could not follow what the curator was saying. The Staves called to him, begging for his attention in the warm colors of spring wildflowers. He stared at the curator.

The curator talked on and on, unaware of Molezeen's distraction, but Soan knew. "I hope you won't take offense, but we're late for a meeting with Abbot T'sngeen," Soan said. "Perhaps, if you're free, tomorrow would be better."

They set up an appointment.

Soan and Jho escorted Molezeen to the temple. After they saw him in, they went back to their rooms. Molezeen was feeling almost normal by the time he got to T'sngeen's cell.

"We had a problem; it took too much time to find the Staves. I had no choice but to simply take them with me." Molezeen pulled up his robe and removed the Staves. "And they aren't lethal."

"Put them down on my bed, at the foot."

Molezeen placed them on the bed. It creaked, the right leg broke; the bed collapsed under the weight. T'sngeen picked up a stool and tried to push the Staves. Molezeen watched as T'sngeen shook with the effort.

"But they are light. I—"

"Should I touch them to prove the rest of the legend?" T'sngeen asked.

Molezeen pushed him away, picked up the Staves and stood them against the wall. "No, I'm a believer. Now what?"

"I think that you've got to find the old ones. You need to know more about their Gods and Evil's second coming. And," T'sngeen paused to look at his protégée, "they need to know about you."

T'sngeen leaned back in his chair. "Could you make me some tea?" While Molezeen fussed with the kettle and the brazier, T'sngeen went on. "You know where to look. Find them. Have I said that I am proud of you?"

"No," Molezeen said.

"I am."

T'sngeen fell silent until Molezeen started to pour the boiling water.

"It's been hard to hang on. No one will look in on me until morning." He reached out and touched one of the Staves, and collapsed in his chair.

"T'sngeen, if you need someone to stay the night with you," Molezeen turned with the pot of tea in his hand. "I can."

"T'sngeen," he whispered, "are you all right?" He knew the answer, T'sngeen was dead, and his fingers were black and smoking.

For forty years, Molezeen had known T'sngeen. They had been close; even apart he took courage in their friendship. That had just ended. Molezeen picked up the Staves and tucked them under his robe again. He paused in the doorway, "Goodbye my friend. I pray you find comfort in The Distant World." He closed the heavy wood door behind him.

The walk back to the Black Stream Inn should have been long and lonely. It wasn't. He felt joy that T'sngeen had been able to give so much and to die when he wanted. The Staves seemed to resonate and amplify that joy. T'sngeen would live on in his heart. "What more could one man give another?" He wondered aloud.

He went to their rooms. Soan and Jho looked worried when they heard the story. A search for them would be launched. They had paid for a week at the Inn. They left what they could afford to leave in the rooms, making it look as though they would be back. They got their horses and rode west out of Alinge.

EIGHTEEN

Molezeen carried the three Staves of Li carefully. He assumed that as long as he held them, as light as they were for him, the horse would not feel any increase in weight. That was easy to test. What he would not test was whether a Staff would kill his horse if it touched him; if it didn't, could the horse carry the Staves alone?

They had ridden for an hour. It was a dark, moonless, night. The stars were bright, but not enough to allow them to ride faster than a walk. Without clouds, the night air had dropped to freezing. Soan, city born, was not comfortable. Riding was not something he did voluntarily. For him, night had always been a time for study, not exercise.

Molezeen and Jho rode with feelings of nostalgia. They each had grown up riding, and each had spent many years in the Arrit.

Ahead of them, by another half hour's ride was their first decision. The seeq't Inn was located at a divide in the road. They could stay there, or they could go north, south, or west.

"Let's stay," Soan said.

"What do you think?" Jho deferred to Molezeen.

"The weather is favorable; I think we should ride as long as we can. But that still leaves the question of where we ride to?"

"You said that T'sngeen told you to search for the old ones. Doesn't that suggest that we avoid inns and cities?" Jho asked.

Soan groaned.

"You're not making our little priest happy. He dreams of soft, warm, beds and good food. But you're right. There is a small bypass just before the seeq't. It's a footpath; we'll have to walk the horses. From there, we have a two or three-hour ride to one of the most magnificent of the toon'Arrit ruins. We can stay there. Forty years ago, there were signs that people still used them for ceremonies. I never met any; I thought they were crazy, and they avoided strangers. Now, we'll have to find them."

It took them longer to get to the ruins than Molezeen had expected. The path around the inn had not been used enough to keep it clear. But they were able to get around without being seen or heard. The main trail was well used; however, they missed the branch that led up the mountain to the ruins. When Molezeen realized that they had gone too far, they backtracked. Jho found the fork.

Soan couldn't believe that they were on a trail at all.

It took an hour, weaving through the trees, to get to the first clearing. From there, they could see the silhouette of the stone walls against the night sky.

"The toon'Arrit called it Jzynth,'" Molezeen said, as they rode through what remained of the main gate. "It means 'high meadow.'"

The clicks of their horses' hooves on the old, cobblestone streets resounded through the ruins, grating against the weight of a thousand years of abandoned tranquility. Most of the buildings, houses, shops, inns, and meeting places stood in outline of their original form, roofless piles of rock. Square holes in the walls marked the places where massive wood beams had once supported upper floors or roofs. The wood had long ago rotted and the dust blown away with the memories of

Jzynth. A few of the tall, three to six story temples were still intact, as if their maintenance and use had never stopped.

"In the morning, we'll explore. I remember that some of the buildings had basements that were still accessible. We'll scout out a place where we can take shelter. We've been lucky; we could get snowed in."

They found a place where they could huddle, safe from the cold wind, and slept for an hour or two. They did not hear the footsteps in the ruins, just ten feet from them.

When they woke, the sun was already warming the air. Birds were singing. It was an Arrit summer day, unseasonably perfect—a gift from the Gods. Jho and Soan went out to collect firewood and to look for water. Even in ruin, Jzynth was magnificent. They found six tree lined boulevards, parallel to each other, running in a north-south direction. Perhaps as many as fifty of the original trees still stood in the parks, with trunks ten feet in diameter and towering one hundred to one hundred and fifty feet. Most impressive to them was the now dry system of stone canals that criss-crossed the city, connecting eight park lakes, which, Molezeen later told them, were used exclusively for recreation.

Throughout the downfall, the stonework represented a puzzle maker's delight. No two pieces were alike. Although the smallest pieces were hand size, many were the size of a man, weighing hundreds of pounds. They interlocked in a devious pattern. What looked like mortar was merely chinking to keep plants from taking hold. But where a fallen tree or collapsed roof had pushed out a wall—breaking away the chinking—vines and saplings had taken root, giving those sections the look of brocade.

Alone at their campsite, Molezeen unwrapped the Staves. At first glance all three were the same: five feet long, an inch and a quarter in diameter at the top, tapering to half an inch above the silver tip at the bottom. Each was capped with ivory, and each was decorated in intricate, interweaving bands of silver. It was in those patterns that they differed one from the other; although it took him several minutes to discern those subtleties. They were also more than black. They were the darkest things he had ever seen. They captivated him. *They feel*, he thought searching to define it, *almost*— But his thought vanished in the mesmerizing, seemingly changing, patterns.

Jho and Soan were coming back when they saw a dozen men gathered around their campsite.

Soan started forward. "Who the—"

Jho clamped his hand over Soan's mouth, and pulled him back around a wall. "Quiet," he whispered.

Jho pointed to a way around the men that would keep them hidden. Soan nodded his agreement. They climbed to the top of the wall behind Molezeen, where they could listen, unseen.

An old, wrinkled man sat on his heels four feet in front of Molezeen. Behind him were eleven more. All were clad in cloth, leather, and fur. They resembled one to the other in their disparity. They were all old men. Their faces locked in a common expression of religious awe. "The old ones," Soan whispered.

The man closest to Molezeen spoke. "You have the Staves of Li."

Molezeen nodded.

"You can hold them. Who are you?"

Molezeen answered in a voice developed over years of training, the voice he used in giving benediction, but kept low. Without understanding what was going on, he sensed that to these men this was a moment only dreamt of before.

"I am Molezeen, High Priest, from the capital, Zot'qrt. I have come to the land of my ancestors, the toon'Arrit, to seek help. The world is threatened by the Change. My advisers speak of retreat; they are cowards before the Evil. I must fight, but I do not know how. I took these Staves, the Staves of Li, from the Library in Alinge. My teacher, T'sngeen of the Indigo Temple, told me to ride into the hills and seek advice from those whose service to the Gods of the toon'Arrit still keeps them alive." Molezeen paused. He assessed his listeners. "I need your help."

The old man in front of him gave a slight bow of understanding and recognition. "Most think we're crazy old men. We, too, have sometimes thought that. We hold to Gods who seem to have forsaken the world. We are awed this day. You have brought the Staves of Li. How can we help you?"

"That is just it. I can hold them; T'sngeen foresaw that. I have seen that they have the power to kill if touched by others. Unfortunately, that is all I know. I read as a child, as we all have, the *Koth'seen* and the *nQert'seen*, but—"

"The tales of Lazz are true." The old man interrupted. "And can help you."

"I was young, and captivated by nGin's jests and Lazz's adventures. What I remember can't be of much help." The old ones nodded. They seemed to like the High Priest who came to them without the arrogance of the South. "I need to know the stories of the toon'Arrit. I was raised south of the Singren. I heard little as I grew up. Please, tell me."

Jho and Soan climbed down the wall, and with the others, gathered about the two men sitting on either side of the Staves. They sat in a circle, sheltered from the cool, mountain air by the ruined walls of a city long forgotten. The old man spoke until nightfall. He told of the birth of the Gods, of their loves, their hates, their quarrels. He told of their discovery of immortality. He told of man's creation. He spoke of Li, the hermit god, who created the Staves, and of their magic. He whispered of the first Change, three thousand years ago, of Evil and its threat to man and to the Gods. His voice rose as he declared their victory over Evil and described the golden years of the toon'Arrit. He spoke with sadness of man's hubris after Evil's second defeat a thousand years ago, for in that pride lay the seeds of the death of the toon'Arrit. The Gods, all but forgotten, left the land. The Sacred Mountains were emptied of their magic. Man moved south, and found new gods.

When he finished it was almost dark. The old man stood. "Come," he said, and walked into the darkness of the ruins. The other old men followed.

"Do you really think they can help?" Soan asked.

"If we loose them, standing here talking, we'll never know," Molezeen said, grabbing his horse's reins, and following after.

The old ones had their camp on the other side of the ruins. While they ate in the flickering light of the cook fire, the old ones' leader talked to Molezeen. "You have so little time to learn what most of us have spent years learning. I can only hope that you will remember well what you hear. I am not crazy. I know that some of our tales are the creations of men like us, sitting around campfires trying to tell stories better than the last time. I also know that much of what I will tell you is true. Only you, a High Priest and Holder of the Staves, will be able to know which is which."

Molezeen, Jho, and Soan stayed there a week. They listened to the stories that Molezeen hoped would help defeat *Vritrk*. Years later, he would say that although the magic and stories of the toon'Arrit had saved the world, man would forget them again. If the time came when Evil once more laid his dreadful hand on the world, man would have to rediscover how to fight. Molezeen did not want the tales to become merely an anthology of children's stories illustrated with cute drawings. He felt strongly that the toon'Arrit were deserving of more than that.

It was the night of the first of the Ninth Half Moon; the old man had a bigger than usual meal prepared. "In honor of the new month," he said.

They ate well. In that week, all had become friends. The old men of the mountains had seen the proof that their years of struggle had not been in vain. Molezeen, Soan, and Jho had come to know something of the old ways, something precious.

"Tell us of your Faith," the old man asked Molezeen.

"But it may be *that* Faith that has led to this Change. I—"

"How often do we share camp with the High Priest from the South?" The old man smiled. "It's a small request."

Molezeen spoke with an eloquence befitting his title. He talked until late in the night, trying to give a balanced, and yet favorable, impression of a religion that these men held in contempt. He stopped when he felt he had said enough. "It is late. This is a good time to leave some tales untold."

"You speak well," the old man said. "I see in you a place for the Gods of the toon'Arrit and the old ways. We are pleased."

They broke up to go to sleep. Molezeen said to the old man, "I am honored to have been able to speak to you. I hope you will ask me again."

The old one patted Molezeen's arm in silent reply.

In the morning, Jho was the first up. He nudged Molezeen. "They've gone."

Molezeen sat up. "Gone? How could they just leave without one of us hearing them? Why?"

Every trace was gone: no campfires, no food, nothing. They split up, and systematically went through the ruins. The sun was directly overhead when they met again. They had found no trace; it was as though the old ones had never been.

"We must leave. Now. This is a sign that there is no more to for us to learn in the Arrit Mountains. The weather will turn soon." Molezeen drew a map in the dirt, showing the lands north of the Singren Rim. "If we get separated, this is how we must get back." They would go south. The trail was unmarked, like what they had taken to get to Jzynth. "Anything else will add too many days and treacherous mountain passes."

They mounted their horses. As they rode out, through the gate and across the large clearing that surrounded Jzynth's walls, Jho thought he felt something in the cold, fall air, something fetid and foreboding. It was fleeting. He pulled up his collar, placed his left hand comfortably around the hilt of his sword, and gave his horse a gentle kick.

The ruins had lost their warmth.

NINETEEN

Snow fell in the afternoon.

Throughout the Arrit Mountains, there was a system of hostels and inns, organized a little less than a day's ride apart. Even the ruins were spaced a day apart from each other. One was always within a half-day's ride of help or shelter, except when it rained or snowed. Then the trails became treacherous and the traveling slow.

They had not had time when they left Alinge to equip themselves for serious late fall travel. The trail they were on was unused; even in good weather it held special dangers. But Molezeen was correct in choosing it. It dropped over six thousand feet in the first half-day; by the time they would reach Tyl they would be traveling at almost the same altitude as the Singren Plains. The weather at that level was much milder than what they would have encountered had they doubled back through Arrit Gateway.

At halfday, they reached the only stretch of trail about which Molezeen was truly anxious. The descent from Jzynth followed a tributary of the T'ng. A half-day before it leveled off, it went through a gorge, a mile long, with sheer, vertical walls. A fragile trail was cut into the western face. Forty years before, when Molezeen was mapping the trails, it had been precarious; now, he had no idea what its condition was.

It started to snow half an hour before they got there.

They were on foot, walking the horses; Jho was in the

lead. He stopped them just before the gorge, and tied his horse to the stump of a mountain oak. "Stay with the horses," he said to Soan.

Jho and Molezeen walked ahead to assess the trail, which took a sharp turn to the left just before the narrows. The stone path was barely six feet wide, at its widest, and several, long stretches had collapsed into the gorge leaving less than three feet extending from the wall. The trail's hard, flat surface was glazed with ice. Molezeen and Jho walked slowly, hugging the wall. "Leading the horses will be difficult; I'm scared. The ice is bad and only getting worse." Jho yelled back to Molezeen.

"Our options are limited," Molezeen mumbled through his cowl, watching Jho's ghostlike figure disappear in the falling snow.

For half an hour, they struggled on. "The Gods!" Jho yelled.

Molezeen hurried to catch up. "Are you all right?"

Jho was sitting on a large, black rock, in the middle of the trail. "We're doomed." His words were flat, each weighted down with the falling snow.

Molezeen knelt next to Jho, catching his breath. "We can move this." Molezeen felt around the rock, confident that they could.

"No. Keep going."

Molezeen climbed around the back of the rock and past Jho. Twenty feet beyond was a rockslide. Tons of sharp, jagged rock, ten feet high, blocked the trail. Molezeen understood. It would have been dangerous work to clear it without the storm, but with the snow and ice, it was a deadly task. He climbed carefully up the pile, praying to see that it extended only a few yards. Through the blowing snow, he recognized the end of the gorge trail, a hundred feet ahead. Half of that distance was covered with the rockslide.

Molezeen sat next to Jho. "I heard stories while I was exploring. Before this cut, the old trail made a loop around the mountain behind us, rejoining this route about an hour down from here. It added a full day to the trip south, so they cut this stretch. Can you find it, the loop trail?"

"If it's there, I can. But I can't work miracles; that's supposed to be your provenance."

They backtracked on foot behind Jho. In the storm, it took two hours. What even Molezeen would have passed over as a small streambed in the rocks, Jho recognized as an old trail. For hundreds of years, only the mountain animals had used it.

When night fell, they had gone less than a mile. They shared the silent fear that what would have been a long day, had now become many days, due to snow and disuse. If it was passable at all.

They had no choice. If they stopped, they would freeze to death. No matter how difficult it was, they had to go on. Molezeen's knees ached. The cold and the climbing were crippling him. He took one of the Staves to use as a walking stick. It helped.

The temperature kept dropping. Molezeen's hands were numbing. He caught himself thinking that they would be dead by morning. "No!" he said aloud, but to himself. "No, you won't win." He remembered one of the stories about the Staves; how they saved the lives of Lazz's warriors caught in a blizzard. He concentrated his will, and repeated, "We are warm. We are warm. We are warm. . . ."

In the dark, shrouded in falling snow, his optic nerve sensed flashes of color. He wasn't sure when he realized that his hands burned with renewed circulation. Soan, who had stoically tolerated the cold, screamed with the pain of warmth. Jho stopped. "What is happening?"

Jho and Soan turned to face Molezeen. They felt the warmth; it was coming from the Staff in Molezeen's hand.

"Are you doing that? How?"

Molezeen shrugged his shoulders. They gathered around him. The cold of the night melted away. They shared hard bread and several mugs of sweet, syrupy, *troan*.

"I don't want to be the one to spoil the mood," Jho said after a second sip. "But, I don't think we're doing much better than a quarter mile an hour. We'll run out of food even if we don't freeze."

"If I can get the Staff to make heat, what about light?" Molezeen asked.

"Try," Jho said.

Molezeen tried. After a few minutes, a faint glow came from the top of the Staff. It was enough to allow them to see Molezeen's face. His effort made it look as though he had stomach cramps. In spite of their predicament, Soan and Jho laughed.

It took Molezeen an hour to learn to produce heat and light. If he tried to talk, he would lose one or the other, or both. The effort was exhausting, but they were able to make almost normal time along the trail. By dawn, he felt that there was a knack to it; for a few seconds here and a minute there, he could relax and keep the light and heat.

In the early gray of morning, Jho pointed to a black hole in the side of the mountain.

"A cave?" Soan asked.

"Yes. We've got to rest," Jho said, leading them off the trail.

The cave was perfect. It took a sharp turn twenty feet in, making a storm-break. "There's plenty of room," Jho said, looking around in the light from Molezeen's Staff. "And it's dry."

Jho collected firewood; Soan saw to the horses. Molezeen sat down with his Staff. At the edge of his consciousness, he felt alarm. He was exhausted, and couldn't make it out. He watched the activity around him.

Suddenly it hit him, Soan was about to unsaddle Molezeen's horse. "Stop! Soan stop!"

Soan froze, his right hand inches from the other two Staves. Molezeen had his answer about the horse; it could survive contact with the Staves. Sometime during the night, he must have tied them to the saddle, but he did not think that Soan would survive. "The Staves—don't touch them."

Molezeen pushed himself to his feet and went over to his horse. He took the Staves. "We are blessed," he said to Soan.

"You can rest," Jho said to Molezeen when the fire was going. "This will keep us warm. I'll tend to it."

Molezeen laid the Staff down, and fell asleep immediately.

"He must be exhausted," Soan said.

"Small wonder after his effort to keep us alive. You too, little priest, need to sleep."

For twenty-four hours, they slept. When the fire died, Jho got up to tend it. Molezeen and Soan never woke. The next day, they woke to the sound of birds. The storm had passed. They melted snow in a large cooking can and added a cup of *troan*.

"I think I am developing a taste for this," Soan said, pouring himself a second cup.

Jho and Molezeen laughed. "A few weeks in the Arrit," Molezeen said, "and even our city-born Soan, has lost some of his soft ways."

Soan blushed, and Jho gave him a wink.

Although snow covered, the trail was easy for Jho to follow. The snow was fresh and full of air, it hadn't begun to collapse and thicken as it melted. The air was still. The sun felt hot in the cold air. They had ridden for half of a day, when they got to a steaming, bubbling lake.

"By A'toon, that's awful." Soan gasped, and pulled his heavy, brown, wool cowl across his sun burned face.

"That mountain must be a volcano. Sulfur vents under the lake would explain the smell and the bubbling," Jho suggested.

"Hold tight," Molezeen said, pulling hard at his horse's reins. "The horses don't like this."

For a distance of three or four paces in from the water line, the ground was snowless, and it was the only way around the lake. The horses made slurping noises as they pulled free their hooves from the sticky mud. Nothing grew from it.

"I don't think it's volcanic, this is new," Molezeen whispered to Jho. "The mud hasn't always been so unwelcoming, look at all the dead trees and bushes. They were alive once, not too long ago."

"Let's get out of here," Soan pleaded from behind his cowl.

The trail led along the edge of the steaming lake on the north side. It was slippery and muddy, and their journey on it an hour long. They were within sight of the far end when Soan's horse shrieked. Its rear legs were sinking into the muck.

As it kicked and struggled, Soan fell off onto his back. He crawled to the safety of the snow-covered rocks. Molezeen jumped from his horse and tried to get near the terrified animal, but its front legs were kicking out blindly. Its eyes rolled madly, and foam dripped from its gnashing jaws. Carefully, afraid of being caught in the mud, Molezeen worked his way closer to the rear legs. The horse was not sinking. It was being pulled into the ground.

In the cone of mud around each leg, wet, brown fingers had wrapped themselves around the horse's shanks. In a rage, Molezeen struck the muddy hand with the Staff. "No!" he screamed.

Cold blue light streaked up out of the mud. A spray of hot, sticky mud splashed through the air. The horse's left leg was free. He struck again, closer to the right leg. More mud splashed, and the horse was freed. They heard a groaning sound. Molezeen moved to higher ground, next to Soan. The mud heaved and tore as if it were alive and had been mortally wounded. A noxious, yellow-green cloud oozed out of the ground, spreading towards them.

Jho tied Molezeen's horse to a branch and rode after Soan's.

"I don't think you should ride him," Jho said to Soan, as he led the skittish, limping horse back.

"None of us should ride. We'll have to lead them through the rocks. Thank the Gods, it's not far."

At the end, just past the water, where they picked up the main trail, they stopped. Jho looked at Soan's horse. It had calmed down, but it limp was worse. Most of the hair was gone where it had been held around its fetlocks, and the skin was dotted with yellow blisters. "I've never seen anything like this," Jho said.

"Can you help?" Molezeen asked.

"I can treat the pain, but I don't know about the infection. There's already an odor."

Jho handed Soan the reins. "Keep him calm." Soan looked confused. "Talk to him. For all he's carried you, it's not much to ask."

Jho walked into the woods. Molezeen heard him mumble something about city-born.

Half an hour later, Jho had the wounds wrapped with compresses of herbs and fresh water. Soan took turns riding double with them.

They arrived in the ruins, which Molezeen called Tyl, after dark. What should have taken one day from Jzynth, had taken three. Fortunately, the worst was over. Because of the change in altitude, most of the snow had melted, except what had lain in shadow. They found shelter among the broken walls, and set up camp.

In the morning, as they were packing, Molezeen found a gold bracelet next to his bedroll. He was puzzled that he had not seen it in the Staff's light when he had spread out his sleeping roll.

"Did either of you see this last night?" he asked, holding it out to them.

"Put it on," Soan said.

"No. It's not mine," Molezeen said, starting to put the bracelet back on the ground.

"It's no one's if it's not yours," Jho said. "Go ahead, put it on."

Reluctantly, Molezeen slipped it around his left wrist.

"Looks good on you," Soan said.

"Keep it," Jho said. "If anyone lost it, they've been dead a thousand years. Anyway, Soan's right, it looks good on you."

Molezeen always dressed simply, avoiding all jewelry except that required by his office. "Well, all right, it does look good," he said, turning his hand around, making the sunlight sparkle from it.

In the center was a crudely polished stone, the color of his eyes, deep blue. Inscriptions covered the gold band, written in the forgotten language of the toon'Arrit.

"When we get back, I'll send it to the library in Alinge

for their collection," he said, polishing it with the sleeve of his robe. "Maybe they have someone who can translate what it says."

As they rode away from Tyl, they never saw the raggedy old man or his smile, as he watched them from the ruins of the city gate.

They felt better as they rode. The weather was mild and the trail was easier to follow. In two days, they got to Ren, a real town, a little less than a day from the Singren Rim. The local blacksmith, who owned the best stable, according to the innkeeper, looked at Soan's horse.

He removed the bandages. "The Gods! What done that?" He backed away from the odor.

"We were attacked by a Changeling," Molezeen said. He knew no further explanation was necessary.

"I've never seen anything like this. The doctor, for our city and Rim Edge is away. He's due in the day after tomorrow."

"We haven't the time. How much for a new horse?"

"Not in trade?" The smithy cast a sorrowful look at the horse as if his day had darkened.

"No. We'll pay, and we'll pay for you to keep this horse and the doctor's fees."

Molezeen and the smithy bargained over the price while Soan and Jho carried their things to the Sage Inn, where they took two rooms.

Each of them bathed. Soan went right to bed. Jho and Molezeen took a light snack before sleeping.

"Our little priest looks more rested than I've seen him in weeks," Molezeen said.

"Of course," Jho said, "he hasn't seen a bed for almost two weeks."

They slept late into the morning. The beds were a

comforting change from the hard, cold ground. Even Jho found it difficult to get up. By the time they came down, people had begun to gather in the great room. They ate breakfast at the bar to be out of the way.

"It's strange to see so many here at this time of day," Jho said to the innkeeper.

"Our priest came in last night; he must do *vr'trk*." The man lowered his head as he said it and touched his right eye with his little finger.

Jho also looked down and touched his right eye. The last High Priest who officially accepted the gesture—it was called *g'lt*—had died two hundred years before. The Middle Path had changed over the years, adapting to the dynamics of a developing civilization. In the South, *g'lt* was considered superstition. But people brought up in rural areas, and in the North, still did it. Molezeen had too much respect for other people's beliefs to say anything, and never would he have criticized it before Jho.

The circuit priest sat in the far corner, his patched cape thrown carelessly over his chair. He could have been many years Molezeen's elder, his face etched with a hundred snows and thousands of miles. Like all circuit priests, he rode from town to town, performing what duties or obligations were required of him. It was a hard life, and took a rugged, fiercely independent man. Molezeen had known many during his *tarridseen* days. Since becoming High Priest, he had often wished that these men could have been his advisers, and not the soft, intriguing lot to which he seemed tied.

It was hard not to eavesdrop. This was an important moment. It was conducted with great solemnity. The priest spoke the opening lines of the *vr'trk*,

*"Every judgment is a last judgment,
or the triumph of death.
We remember: law is not elegant,
and life is not just. . . ."*

Molezeen was humbled by the priest's delivery. For most, the opening was a formality, recited by rote. For these people it held full and ripe meaning, and from this priest it was being spoken as if for the first time.

A man had dammed a stream to better care for his livestock. He hadn't considered those who lived downstream. He hadn't totally blocked off the water, but it was enough to cause irreparable damage. Small animals were the first affected. They either left in search of more water or died. Their main food source was insects; Linsz grubs lived on the roots of the lowland oaks. Without anything to keep them in check, the grubs destroyed most of the trees. Erosion from the summer rains and spring runoffs ruined as much as twenty square miles of grazing and farmland. It had taken seven years for the damage to occur.

Had he consulted the local experts or his neighbors, he would have been advised against the dam, and alternative plans considered. He had been selfish. He had caused damage. Today, he stood *vr'trk*.

Confronted with the sequence of events, the man could hardly deny the casual relationship. His only defense was that the dam had been built on his property; he had not completely stopped the stream; and he had never thought such a thing could happen. By noon, everyone who wanted to speak had.

The priest sat pensively, a lifetime of training and experience being brought to focus in this vr'trk. Finally, he signaled that he was ready. And he spoke,

"The debt of guilt,

consider its finality;
Recognize the priorities,
exempt the family;
vr'trk fails personal consideration;
Determine the garnishment of payment. . . ."

The room stayed silent; no one moved. It seemed that no one breathed. The priest pronounced that the man was to deed his property to his children; he was not responsible enough to be a landowner. He was also to remove the dam and replant the entirety of the damaged lands, by his efforts alone. A moan passed through the room. In spite of the damage done because of the man's selfishness, everyone felt the severity of the *vr'trk*.

The room emptied. Alone, the priest walked to the bar and ordered a pint of *troan*.

"Please, let me," Molezeen said.

"That's kind," the old man said as the innkeeper placed a mug in front of him. "Thanks."

Molezeen slapped a silver coin down on the counter. The priest's smile turned to shock; he stared at the gold bracelet on Molezeen's wrist. Tears came to his eyes. He reached his hand out, not for the mug of *troan*, but to touch the bracelet.

"You?"

Molezeen had no idea what the man meant.

He repeated his question. "You?"

Molezeen knew that something bothered the circuit priest. He opened the clasp of his cape and pulled out his pendant, the symbol of High Priesthood. He knew the old man would keep his secret.

The priest nodded, and took a long swallow of *troan*, emptying the mug. "My name is Kendt. I've traveled these mountains for sixty-three years as circuit priest. I've heard the old stories, and I've seen the coming of Evil. I had all but given up hope: it seemed that the neeZeen weren't to live through this Change, that no one could save us. But here you are."

"I'm the High Priest, but does that make me man's savior?"

"No. You are to be the savior, who happens to be a priest."

TWENTY

The way south from Dorn was difficult.

Dorn was at the end of the trail, and it was too small to have much traffic. The town survived because its men were skilled at cutting stone.

They would send out surveyors to determine the best source of stone for a particular job. Cutting rock and hauling it weeks through the mountains was too destructive, and too expensive.

The Dorner men were a guild. They only worked together. If they quoted on a job, and if they got it, which they always did, they left Dorn. The new quarry set up temporary housing. There they stayed until the job was completed. Even amongst the Arrit Mountain peoples, Dorners were the most independent and rugged.

Kendt made Dorn one of his regular stops on his circuit. He tried to get there once every other half moon. He was twenty-five when he first went there; everyone ignored him. He was given room and board at the inn, but that was all. For six years, he came there, and for six years, no one spoke to him.

Dorn was perched precariously on the side of the mountain. Split wood walks led from one to another of the fifty log and stone buildings, which were terraced into the steep woods an hour's walk from the timberline. Kendt arrived, for his thirtieth visit, during the Fourth Half Moon. Millions of unopened buds gave a faint haze of color to the bare wintered trees. The sun felt hot on his face as he paused to guess how long before the leaves came out. *Twelve days*, he thought. He was usually very close, but he wouldn't know this year, he never stayed in Dorn longer than a few days. A prickling on his neck, just above the fold of his collar where the sun had found some pale skin, caught his fleeting attention long enough for him to adjust his robe. The spring runoffs were early that year.

He was a few minutes out of town when he heard a scream. He jumped from his horse and ran through the trees, a hundred yards down the mountainside. Hanging onto a rock in the middle of the river was a boy. Kendt threw off his robe and waded in. The water felt colder than ice; he knew he couldn't survive more than a few minutes. He fought his instinct to turn back.

Kendt got to the boy, who was barely out of the water, his arms purple against the wet black rock he hugged. Looking over his shoulder at Kendt, the boy's Dorner pride wouldn't let him ask for help, but his eyes begged.

"You're going to have to grab on to me, boy," Kendt yelled. He wedged his right hand into a small crack to steady himself.

The boy turned too fast, and began to slide off the side of the rock away from Kendt.

"Don't move I'll come around."

Kendt's feet slipped out from under him and he went under. He felt something crack in his wrist and his skin tore, but his hand stayed anchored to the rock. He fought for a footing and pulled himself back up.

"Boy, I can't get around." Kendt coughed.

The boy tried again. He moved slowly.

"That's it. Put your arms around my neck." Kendt reached out with his free hand. "Come on, I'll catch you."

The boy hesitated, scared of that second between the rock and Kendt.

"Hurry!"

The boy pushed himself off the rock and onto Kendt. His fingers dug into Kendt's back.

Kendt worked his hand free from the crevice. The white foam around him turned pink as he struggled to keep from losing his fragile balance carrying the boy back. He used the current to guide him into rocks—stage by stage—until he got to shore, two hundred feet below where he had started.

Kendt carried the boy to his robe, wrapped him in it, and put on a spare robe from his bag. He had never been so cold in his life. The short ride into Dorn lasted beyond consciousness. He didn't remember riding into Dorn; nor carrying the boy to the inn; nor handing him to the owner.

He woke in his usual room, a mug of hot *troan* on the table next to him. His right arm was in a splint, and his hand and wrist were bandaged. He had to reach awkwardly across his chest with his left hand for the *troan*. He winced as he leaned against his bad hand, but he had the mug. The *troan* warmed him.

They had pulled the curtains back from his windows and tucked them into wrought iron loops on the wall. He could see down the mountain through the trees. "Twelve days," he thought as he fell back asleep.

The next day, he went downstairs. He was hungry. The owner brought him a platter of lamb stew. While he ate, the regulars made small talk with him; he had never heard so much as a "hello" before. No one ever said anything about saving the boy's life, not even the boy, it was not their way.

***

The way south from Dorn was difficult.

Kendt had ridden a half-day from Dorn when he felt the pain in his head. It was worse than it had ever been. He was midway between Dorn and the seeq't Inn. The weather had turned, and he knew he couldn't last another half-day. To the west were ruins that offered closer shelter. "I'm getting too old for this," he thought, as he turned his horse off the trail.

He lost consciousness after a half-hour of struggling through the rocky woods. His body, used to being in the saddle, hung on. Kendt never saw the old man who led the horse to the ruins another hour away.

Eight men, old ones, cared for him. It was two days before he regained consciousness.

Kendt stared in disbelief at the men. He had seen them at a distance, or seen men like them. But he hadn't realized how old they were. In the evening light, just before dark, they seemed as old as the ruins themselves.

"Where am I?" he asked.

No one heard. He repeated himself. Nothing.

He tried to stand; his body wouldn't move.

The man who was tending the fire turned towards him, and saw that Kendt was awake.

"Please don't try to move. You can't. We found you almost dead, an hour from here. You have a growth in your brain. If you recover, you will surely have this happen again. We can help."

Kendt blinked both his eyes; it was all he could do to acknowledge the old man.

"Do you know the snowsnake?"

Kendt's eyes opened, his pupils dilated with fear. He had seen what a snowsnake could do—one didn't live in the Arrit Mountains and not see it. The snowsnake was a winter creature, a warm-blooded, reptile-like animal that hibernated in the summer months. It burrowed through the snow and ice—making beautiful tunnels—seeking its prey. It was evil white, almost translucent. Its venom caused the victim's blood to solidify. At its leisure, the snowsnake would feed on the victim through a small hole, consuming the innards.

Stories said that in the cold winter air, the victim's mind remained alert for days, as the snowsnake fed. No one knew; no one ever survived the bite.

"Yes, I see you do. The venom of the snowsnake has remarkable qualities. In very small doses, it can halt or reverse a growth like yours. For you it would be life. But—" The old man turned back to the campfire and filled a mug with something from the cooking can. He sipped from the mug as he talked. "There's a catch. Even in small doses it can kill, it stops the heart. If the dose is small enough, your heart will start again; if not, you die. I don't think you have a choice, but it's up to you. Are you willing?"

Kendt thought about his life. It had been full; sixty years he had been a circuit priest. If he were to die now, or live, it would make little difference, to him or to the world. It was the Gods' will.

The old man crouched, rocking on his heels, a foot from Kendt's face. Kendt could smell the hot *troan* on his breath. The old one was staring at him, with watery gray eyes. He recognized Kendt's fatalism. He leaned closer. "Circuit priest, you're not to die. The world has need of you. . . ."

The old one talked of the toon'Arrit, of their Gods, of Evil; he talked of man's victory and the defeat of the Gods by man's pride. ". . . And today, you're needed to help defeat this Evil."

Kendt understood. Not all, but enough to know that he had no choice.

"You understand. Good." The old man held out a crystal flask. It was small, an inch and a half wide, about three quarters of an inch thick, and two inches tall. It was polished amethyst, and looked like the kind of perfume bottle used by Southern city women. He pulled out the stopper; affixed to it was a slender, gold spoon, not much bigger than a pin. He removed it and allowed all the liquid to drip back into the flask. "That's the amount, the residue on the spoon, never any more."

He took another mug, filled it with liquid from the cooking can, and swirled the spoon in it. "You must drink this quickly before you lose consciousness and can't."

Another man held Kendt's head up. Together they helped him drink. It burned his throat. He tried to turn away from it. The inside of his bones grew cold and numb. The world darkened. There was a sudden deep rushing sound. He felt his mind implode, collapsing in on itself. He turned inside out, flayed within his clothes. Sensitive, exposed nerve endings ached at any touch. Bright flashing lights of red, yellow and blue blinded him. Kendt fought to stay alive. He was not breathing; he could not breathe with the weight of a mountain pressing against his chest. He wanted to scream. He fought to force his lungs open, to take in air. He had to live . . . he had to.

When he was aware that he was alive, it was morning. Kendt tentatively moved his hand. He touched his face. He looked around. The toon'Arrit had built magnificent cities; even in ruin, he felt their genius. It was beautiful. The old man was tending the fire.

"Thank you." Kendt heard his own voice.

The man turned. "We knew you'd live. It's good to hear you."

As they ate, Kendt took stock of himself. He had not felt this good for years. Everything looked brighter. He felt as if a film had lifted. He was alive. He was excited.

"Circuit priest, we've searched for you for a long time. We kept missing you in your travels. Our time is limited. A coming Evil threatens to make that time even less. We must teach you. There's much you must know."

The old man talked more of Evil and Good. He talked of man's weaknesses. He explained why the Gods couldn't fight.

"Am I to be the sav—"

"No. You must find him and convince him of his destiny. You must be there for him if he weakens. You will be his strength, in life and in death."

***

The Sage Inn suddenly felt emptier. "Savior," Molezeen whispered. Jho and Soan were stunned. Molezeen stared into the circuit priest's amber colored eyes. This was not one of his temple court's smarmy sycophants. No. There was no hidden agenda in these eyes. They were frighteningly honest. Saddened with the unasked for burdens given over to him by the needy; sorrowed because he was looking on the man who would carry the biggest burden in the fight against Evil.

"Yes, savior," Kendt said, touching the bracelet as confirmation.

"Would you come with me?" Molezeen asked.

"Yes; you who can give benediction to others, who would give it to you? You will need my counsel."

They rode south; they were four. Kendt, in spite of his years, rode well; he set them to a faster pace than they were riding at before he joined them.

At halfday, they had reached Rim Edge. They bought tickets for the lift. Because it was fall, they only had to wait an hour for their turn.

Most commerce between the South and the lands above the Singren Rim took place through the Arrit Gateway, where the Rim was merely a slight hill and the ascent into the mountains gradual. West, along the Rim, there was no other easy way up onto the Plain, except too far west and north, near the Line of Rolines. The two places where people could get up from the South to the Plains were Greatfalls and Rim Edge. These elaborate lifts of stone and wood were created centuries ago. There were trails, but only people on foot, usually the poor, used them. In recent years, it had become a popular sport to race up the trails at Greatfalls and Rim Edge. Ten races took place each year. Hundreds would turn out for them. The poor, who were suddenly unable to use the trails, now had free passage to the lifts.

Four polished granite tracks, set in an incline against the precipice, allowed two lifts to operate. The weight of one balanced against the other; one went up as the other descended. Three miles of heavy rope coiled in one big loop. At the top and the bottom, the cable doubled around massive blocks, turned by waterwheels through an elaborate system of pulleys and gears.

There were two towns, an upper and a lower, at each lift. In the summer, the wait for the lift could be as much as four days. The inns did a thriving business. The competition was so stiff that it was natural for some of the inns to look for ways to distinguish themselves. Some became resorts, offering the best food and service. Families booked rooms a year ahead, to spend a week at Rim Edge or Greatfalls, even in the dead of winter.

Molezeen did not intend to spend time there. The lift could accommodate all of them, in fact, there was quite a bit of room unused. The ride down took half an hour. The view was spectacular. Due south, across a corner of the n'Geent Desert, they could make out a dark scar just below the horizon: L'zotk Gorge, a ragged, dry canyon, a mile deep in parts, two days long and a half-day wide. Farther south, a faint green line on the horizon was the Southern Farmlands. Soan thought that if he ever had a family it would be fun to come back for a week or two. One wanted to share this place with others.

Their trek south from there took eight days. They had to go east and rejoin the Coast Road. On the thirteenth day of the Tenth Half Moon, they arrived within the walls of Zot'qrt. Soan, Jho, and Kendt took rooms at an inn near the North Gate. Molezeen returned to his quarters in the temple as though he had never left. Under his great cloak, he smuggled in the three Staves of Li. People scurried around, his sudden arrival having caused an unusual commotion.

Earlier that week, the Senate had initiated a new election for High Priest. Political factions debated, back and forth. All came to naught with Molezeen's return. His advisers chided him. They tried to pry from him where he had gone and what he had done. Of that, he was silent. For two days, he allowed them the satisfaction of taking him to task. Then he stopped it.

"By law, I am High Priest until my death, or my resignation. Therefore, it shall be. You will need my body to prove my death. As you all sit here and haggle over the price of victuals and whose sleeve gets lined, the world is threatened by the Change.

"You would have me ignore it. 'Such matters are the fantasies of the ignorant,' you tell me. To this, I would suggest that you ride out yourselves, to see this fantasy first hand. You will not, and I do not want you to. In your way, you make the government run, and it must continue.

"If I should leave again, you will do your jobs and not fight and plot; I will return. Now go. I have work to do."

After they had left, he sent word to Soan to return to the temple. He met with the others later.

**

On a small farm, not far from n'Jaspinth, he brought them together. He did not have an army; he had a band. Foremost were the three who each held a Staff of Li: himself, d'Solteen, and Jake. Molezeen had not wanted to include Soan; he was young, city-born, and ill trained for their task—as if any of them were well-trained—but Soan had been persuasive. "After all," Soan had argued, "I went with you into the Arrit Mountains two years ago. You trusted me then." Jho the warrior, in a day when wars were unheard of, was an anachronism; but in ten years of service with Molezeen he had proven his worth as he had his loyalty. There was also Kendt, the old circuit priest; he had knowledge and understanding of the toon'Arrit ways. They were a band of six.

Llo, a cousin of Molezeen's, owned the farm. There was a main house with five out buildings. The architecture not only varied from building to building, but the house itself was a textbook of styles. Llo explained that over the years, as the family expanded, so did the house. Front to back, each addition reflected what was popular with that generation.

She lived in the main house with her seventeen-year-old brother Stel, and a cook.

"Where is everyone else?" Jake asked Llo while she was showing them around.

"Who? The field workers? They won't be back until harvest time."

"No. Your family. The house is pretty empty."

Llo turned to adjust the curtains next to her, to hide from Jake's question. It was a good question, she had grown up asking her mother it often enough. "The world has changed," she whispered her mother's answer.

She turned back to Jake.

"I'm sorry, I was rude to ask," Jake said.

"You weren't rude." Llo walked to a bookcase and pulled out a large, black leather portfolio, tied closed with a leather thong, "This is my family album. Would you like to see?"

They gathered around the table in front of the window, with Llo in the middle. She untied the portfolio and opened it. One by one, she placed a color drawing or watercolor on the table. "This was my great-great-great grandmother on my father's side, Tolen . . . this was my grandfather's second cousin Jhen. . . ."

"But what happened to the family?" Jake asked.

"Four hundred years ago, the family worked the farm. But in the last hundred years, the world has changed, as my mother used to say to me."

"It must have changed a lot," Jake said waving his hand around. "You could open a hotel here."

Llo pinched Jake's arm. "That's a good idea." She laughed.

"What did change?" Soan asked.

"The cities. They lure people away. They offer comforts we don't have, and in return they paint out your souls. You forget the land. Today, I hire our labor."

"Hey, what about me?" Stel asked. "I work."

"Yes, Stel works, but he is only one. The farm is more profitable this way, but . . . I do miss family."

The band stayed in one of two bunkhouses, awaiting Molezeen's arrival from Zot'qrt, where he was attending to matters of business. Llo had invited them to stay in the main house. Kendt said that unless there was no other room, it wasn't proper. Had it been harvest time there would have been no room at all.

From the first day they were there, d'Solteen found miraculous reasons to see Llo. They were the same age, and had taken to each other at first sight. Jake, Kendt, and Jho bet on d'Solteen. When would he next contrive to be alone with her? What would he say had needed doing? How long would he be gone? Even d'Solteen laughed about it. They all did, except Soan. In spite of the time that they had been together with Molezeen, Soan seemed to distrust d'Solteen with every fiber of his being, although it was not mutual.

Jake cornered d'Solteen once. "Tell me. Soan would as soon see you dead as not. Why?"

"He has his reasons. And, from his point of view, he's right; but, in fact, he has no reason to distrust or fear me."

"Come on, you can tell—"

"No. I'll only say he's right."

That was all Jake could find out. Otherwise, they all got along well. For their part, the neeZeeners liked Jake. He was the object of a lot of humor for them, but humor with a very big dose of respect.

By the end of their first day there, it was obvious that d'Solteen was interested in Llo. Her brother had an older friend who imagined himself the object of Llo's affections. He became madly jealous. After a week, he was plotting against d'Solteen. He made Stel his unwitting accomplice.

"Let's surprise him, give him a scare. D'Solteen goes riding everyday. Right?"

"Yeah."

"We'll ride out after him."

Something told Stel that there might be more, "That's it? We'll just scare him?"

"Yeah, like we did Kol last spring. Remember his face?"

They laughed; it had been funny seeing Kol fall off his horse when it reared in surprise. He landed in the mud and couldn't get up without getting muddier. Even Kol could laugh about it now.

"Sure. He rides twice a day. No one goes with him in the morning. Meet me at first light."

The next morning when d'Solteen got up, Jake was awake and snooping around. "Hey, want to ride?" d'Solteen asked.

Caught off guard, Jake didn't have a witty reply, "I'm going to have to get used to it. Why not?"

They went to the barn to pick out two horses. Jake had explored much of the farm, but had never gone into the out buildings. He was impressed with the barn. It was a split-level structure, built on a hillside. The walls were a foot and a half thick and made of stucco. There were shutters, for storms, and double bifold windows. D'Solteen explained that the buildings in the South had to be able to withstand the spring hurricanes, which came inland below Zot'qrt. Inside, the barn looked like a Shaker house to Jake. Everything was stored in floor to ceiling cabinets and lockers. The woodwork was simple and graceful. Mixed woods of carefully matched or contrasted grains and colors were used throughout: dark, light, red, brown, and blonde. The barn was swept clean twice a day.

D'Solteen watched the horses closely, looking at their reactions to Jake, as they walked along the stables. A gray stallion with a mahogany star on his chest shook its head and walked towards them. "Go ahead, scratch his head," he told Jake.

Jake hesitated.

"Go on."

Before Jake could do much more than touch the horse's

neck, it pushed up against Jake's shoulder, and nibbled at his shirt.

D'Solteen stared at them. "You have a friend." It was more a question than a statement.

"What?" Jake asked. "So, he likes me."

"He's a stallion. He shouldn't be taking to you like this."

"I'm a likable guy." Jake hugged the horse, taking some pride in d'Solteen's disbelief. "We're buddies."

"I can see. Let's get him saddled."

Jake couldn't do much except watch.

"Is this typical?" Jake asked d'Solteen as he fought with Jake's horse to put its bridle on.

"Stallions are usually aggressive, like this. I am surprised by the way he likes you."

"I meant the farm, and this barn, and all."

"Fairly. Although, I'd say that you'll likely not find much better."

"How old is it?"

"Llo said the farm was four hundred years old, didn't she?"

"Yes, but I thought she was exaggerating."

"She probably was. It's more likely closer to five hundred. It wouldn't be uncommon for a farm this size."

D'Solteen rode more slowly than usual, to accommodate Jake, who would never be a horseman. Although, he was learning, and his horse was remarkably patient.

They had ridden out an hour from the farm. The countryside had become hilly, wooded, and rocky. Small white blossoms spotted the green bushes on either side of the trail.

"You know, I've turned down your invitations to ride before, but if I say no again, remind me of this. It's beautiful. And I think I'm getting the hang of steering a horse."

"If you like this, you should see the Arrit Mountains, in the summer of course. . . ."

Jake felt danger. He looked around, but couldn't see anything. The horses were fine; d'Solteen was describing the mountains.

There was a crashing sound: the sound of horses charging through the underbrush. Jake's horse bucked, catapulting him through the air. D'Solteen kept his horse just under control.

Two riders reined in their horses just in front of them. One was Stel, who was laughing at the surprise they had caused. The other was his friend, who had a knife in his hand.

Stel stopped laughing, shocked at seeing the knife. "What are you doing?" Stel asked.

"I thought he was alone," the other said, seeing Jake lying on the ground.

"Hey, let's go; we got 'em—but it's not as funny as before."

"Shut up. Watch the fat man." Turning to d'Solteen, "I challenge you," he spit the words out.

Jake was startled, he had not seen this kind of violence among the neeZeen.

D'Solteen had his left hand on his Staff. He was tempted to use it, but it reminded him of his obligation to Molezeen, which was deeper than knives or staves or the challenge of a jealous pup. "I can't take it up."

"Then, having challenged you, I'll kill you." He threw his knife. D'Solteen tried to duck, but holding the Staff and trying to calm his horse gave him little room. The knife hit him in the shoulder.

Jake jumped to his feet. "Stop!" The shout gave him a momentary advantage. Jake stepped to Stel's friend and grabbed his wrist.

"The Gods!" The young man screamed and pulled at Jake's hand.

The horse turned and the man slid towards Jake, anchored by Jake's grip. Jake held him a second around the shoulders, pinching a nerve cluster at the base of the man's neck. He let him go and the man fell from the horse, his right foot twisted up in the air, caught in the stirrup.

Jake turned to d'Solteen. The knife had severed an artery; blood covered his riding tunic. Jake helped him off his horse.

"I'm fine," d'Solteen said weakly.

Jake worked quickly. He put him to sleep, and then pulled out the knife. Stel was dumbfounded to see the bleeding stop suddenly. Jake tore his shirt, making a bandage and a sling. He tied a compress over the wound, and then tied the arm so that it wouldn't move too much. "He'll be okay."

Looking at Stel, he sensed Stel's innocence and his guilt. "I could make you feel better, to forget your part in this. I know you did it in jest, but your friend did not. This is a lesson you should carry with you. You're better than this, and better than him." Jake pointed to Stel's friend. "Help him up, and take him back. He'll be like that until I return. Put him in my room and stay with him."

D'Solteen started to come out of the sleep, and would tear open Jake's work. If he were to heal in time for their quest, he needed to be still now. Jake matched his breathing to d'Solteen's. He entered his mind to shut-off those nerve centers that would disturb his rest. He saw a glimmer of a memory; a young musician, insulted and hurt because of his pride. The young man had been about to kill an older man, a *tarridseen*, out of jealousy. That young man had stopped in time, before he did something that could not be undone.

It answered a lot.

***

Llo nursed d'Solteen. Jake had done a lot to help the healing, but Llo's love was one thing he could not match. For two weeks, d'Solteen did not have to dream up excuses.

"Explain something to me," Jake asked Kendt the afternoon he had brought d'Solteen back. "You hold *vr'trks . . . vr'trks.*" Jake repeated the word, trying to get it right. "Why won't d'Solteen ask for one against this boy? There's no question the attack was wrong, and there's no question as to fault."

They were walking along the pasture where the horses exercised. Kendt stopped, and leaned against the top rail of the fence.

"Yes, there's no question. Asking for a *vr'trk* is d'Solteen's prerogative. But he won't."

"But he could have been killed."

"True. But you said it, everyone knows what happened, and the young man will carry that everywhere he goes, for the rest of his life. D'Solteen would feel some guilt at requesting a *vr'trk*, and thereby bringing down yet more burdens for the young man to carry. That is why there are so few. A man of conscience, even if wronged, would rather seek understanding before retribution."

"But—"

"What is the price of that injury?" Kendt squeezed Jake's shoulder. "What price would you levy?"

The question burned Jake's conscience. He saw in the circuit priest's eyes the burden carried by a lifetime of having to answer that question.

Jake started riding everyday. The gray stallion was his for as long as he wanted, a gift from Llo. He was feeling healthier than he had in years. At dinner, he found himself stopping at thirds. He would sit back and pat his stomach. "You can laugh, go ahead, but I am losing weight. Look, there's still food on the table."

"But who helps clear the table? Where do the scraps go? You don't fool us," Jho said, grinning slyly.

Of course, it was true that Jake had become quite friendly with the cook.

Stel hung around them, trying to do them favors, and, being seventeen, getting underfoot. Jake was pleased to see that he had no contact with his friend since the incident with d'Solteen.

Molezeen came to the house at the end of their third week. After dinner, he went to his room. He had just finished unpacking when d'Solteen came to visit.

"May I have a few minutes?"

"Of course. How's the shoulder? You've had the best care possible." Molezeen smiled; it would have been impossible for Llo and d'Solteen to hide their love.

"Thanks for asking. It's fine." He made a show of moving his arm around, while he shuffled about.

"D'Solteen, please, sit down. You're making me nervous. Obviously, you've something on your mind."

"Yes. Sorry. I've pledged myself to you and to our fight. But, I . . . I'm in love with Llo. Wait, before you say anything, let me explain.

"I'd like, if I return after it's all over, to marry Llo. I know that as the eldest woman in the family she is free to make that decision, but I'd do nothing without your blessing as my mentor, my friend, member of this family, and as High Priest."

"What of the priesthood?"

"Llo doesn't want to leave the farm. I'd live and work here, of course. Perhaps I could be the local priest."

"No. You would not be asked to leave the priesthood, and you would always have its status, rights, and obligations, but I would ask that you not practice. Whatever your life is to be, make that commitment. And whatever you choose, you have my blessing."

D'Solteen stood up to leave. "Thank you."

"Oh, there is one more request." Molezeen was smiling, "Don't forget your music; you're quite gifted. Sleep well."

The band of six left on the third day of the Fifth Half Moon. They rode north-west to bypass Zot'qrt. Their pace was deliberate.

No one saw the rider, following at a quarter hour's distance.

TWENTY-ONE

Their plan was tfo ride along the Zot, retracing Jake and d'Solteen's earlier trip. From all that Molezeen had learned, *Vritrk* was somewhere in the Toth. They would find a way up into the mountains near the waterfall.

The night before they left, Molezeen spent a few hours with Kendt. They were fond of one another, and would have been friends even without the Evil. For two hours they sat, silent, watching and tending the fire in the sitting room. Llo tiptoed around, trying not to disturb them. She could have run her cattle through the room without disturbing them; they were deeply lost in reverie.

Kendt called Llo. "Could you bring us a couple large mugs of warmed *troan*? Thank you."

When the men had first met, at Ren, Kendt had insisted that if he were to travel south he wanted a full keg of *troan* for himself. "There're times when there's nothing like it. The South, so civilized, so sophisticated, but what do they drink? Sheep piss."

Molezeen had bought a packhorse to accommodate Kendt. "It's a small price for saving the world," he told Soan as he counted out a handful of silver coins from their coin bag. "Of course, a mug of *troan* is one of the great pleasures."

Llo brought the *troan*. She couldn't stand the thick, sweet, winter beer. "I don't know how you can drink this. It's bad enough cool, but heated!" She put the tray down on the heavy, polished wood table in front of the fireplace. "And you, cousin, you have absolutely no excuse. You were born here in the South, raised in a good family. I assume you were taught good manners. But maybe not. My aunt was always a little odd."

Molezeen and Kendt laughed.

"I wish we had known each other before all of this," Molezeen said, kneeling on the hearth, reorganizing the burning logs.

"Does it matter? We are here today, bound together in a common goal. We have had today and will have tomorrow together."

"I know. But you haven't spent years of your life surrounded by mealy-mouthed bureaucrats masquerading as priests."

"No, and you haven't ridden three days through the snow and sleet to get to a dirty, small town where someone has asked for *vr'trk*, for something that could have been resolved easily, years before."

"I know, and I'm sorry for your burden."

"Have you ever been to Dorn? . . . No? . . . Well, Dorners are a strange people. I have great admiration for them, but they represent the other side of the problem. They have never had a *vr'trk*, not in a thousand years.

"They pay a price for that, for their fierce independence. In what to the rest of the world appears to be the height of bad manners, their way is to either work everything out or to hold everything in, usually the latter. It's a paradox.

"I must have stopped there thirty times before anyone spoke to me. However, in all the years since, wherever I've gone, I've never felt such community. Except with the old ones."

"We've never talked about it. Was it they who told you of me?"

"Yes and no." Kendt paused, looking into his mug. "I've gone dry. Llo, could you bring more *troan?*"

She brought in a pitcher.

"Llo, I hope that you don't think that I'm so ill mannered that I order you, my host, around."

She smiled; she liked this rough old man. "No, you're my guest." She gave him a little kiss on the cheek.

"Careful, d'Solteen could find himself with another rival." Kendt took Llo's hand in his for a moment.

"Careful? I would be a winner either way." Llo laughed. "My only question is how much help would you be during the spring calving?"

"Now I see how your family has managed such a large farm. . . . Molezeen, you'll say nothing to help me?"

"Old men like us should be careful when it comes to matters of the heart." Molezeen laughed.

"I've got to get up early, some of us have chores in the morning," Llo said. She gave them each a kiss and left the room.

Kendt turned back to Molezeen. "A remarkable family, High Priest."

"Llo's side is the more interesting. But you were about to tell me about the old ones."

"Yes . . . they saved my life. They said that I had to find you, although, after years of looking, I had all but given up. They didn't describe you, not physically. But they said that I'd recognize you. That bracelet . . . a gift from them? It was a clue. It made me stop and look at you. Then I knew."

"What are we supposed to do?"

"That I don't know. They told me stories. They said that my value to you, to our defeat of Evil, was that I could synthesize from the stories and tales what you would need to understand at the moment. I would be your support."

"So, do we just go riding?"

"Yes. I think we'll figure out what we must, or react as things happen. I feel that our victory may lie in our spirit and souls more than our prowess."

"We have the Staves."

"But what makes you able to hold them? Surely, it's not physical strength. It is your spirit. You, Jake, and d'Solteen are soulful people. And you will gain strength from the rest."

"What do you think of our band?"

"I'm impressed. Their loyalty to you, and to each other, is remarkable."

"I'm afraid that Soan may never accept d'Solteen," Molezeen said.

"You're too close to them to see. Soan feels a great distrust for d'Solteen. I don't know why, and please don't tell me. But that wariness is good, it keeps us a little more alert. And I think that the time will come, when d'Solteen has proved himself to Soan, that they'll become close."

Bathed in the dancing light of the fire, they finished their *troan*. As they bid each other good night, each felt the closeness that usually comes with the rediscovering of a lifelong friend.

***

Dark rain clouds rolled and gathered about his crag lair. All day, a gray veil obscured the sun. As it set below the mountains, the day grew darker and more ominous. The winds had started around noon; by dusk, they had become gale force, and they were cold and wet.

Vritrk sat on his throne. His heart sang with the coming storm. He looked out into the vast darkness. It was his world.

The lightning started at day's end. Massive blue-white bolts crashed around him. In the blinding light, he could see his Changelings running in terror. He smiled—terror gave him great satisfaction. The Changelings had never grown up; they had no idea of shelter; they had no past; they had no future. There was for them only the present and that had gone feral.

Vritrk sat. He breathed in the power of the storm. He basked in the fear. He had forgotten that his Changelings had a purpose to him, forgotten that he had an enemy in the distance. The deliciousness of the moment consumed him.

At first, he didn't hear it. Below the thunder, in tones whose frequencies were slow and deliberate, to be felt more than heard, were undertones that suggested a greater malevolence. The thunder repeated itself, in variations of a sepulchral melody. His discomfort crept slowly into awareness. It took several hours for him to realize that he had become tense.

Through the unabated storm, he struggled to understand why. Towards dawn, he gave up. Unable to detect the laughter in the thunder, he decided to sleep.

***

Jake saw the large, ugly, black birds. They circled through the clouds, high above the band. He felt their purpose.

He stopped his horse next to Molezeen, and pointed his Staff into the air. "Have you seen them?"

"What do you think?"

"They're his. Probably keeping tabs on us," Jake said.

"Should we do something?" Molezeen asked.

Kendt was squinting through cupped hands, trying to follow their slow, distant circles.

"If we stop them, he'll just send more. Let them be. One way or another, we'll meet *Vritrk.*"

Jho rode two hundred yards ahead. The rest of the band rode in a pack, uneasy about being watched.

Soan was the first to notice that they had picked up a friend, a fawn and white mastiff. It kept to the trees on their right. When they stopped for lunch, it settled down about twenty paces away.

Jake tore off a piece of dried, smoked beef. He whistled to the dog. It stood up and walked a few steps towards them. Before reaching them it shook its head and laid down. Neither whistling nor cajoling could get it to budge. "Some mascot you are," Jake said, eating the beef himself and turning away from the dog.

Molezeen nudged Jho. "You're right. He does have a way with animals."

D'Solteen whistled, holding out a piece of bread. The dog stood up and took a few steps. "There, there! Did you see that? He knows who's a friend."

When it laid down again, they all laughed. Jho entered the game. "You've all got it wrong. Do you respond to a whistle or a name? He needs a name."

It took a mug of watered *troan* each to decide on a name. While it lay dreamily with its massive head between its paws on the ground, they debated its gender, which no one had noticed. They argued over its character, its age, and its loyalty. They told dog stories, imparting to the mastiff their special memories—all except Kendt. Molezeen turned to him. "You don't have a story?"

"No, I never had a dog. I never liked them much. But don't worry about me," Kendt replied. "Having a mascot is a good idea." There was too much noise for Molezeen to hear Kendt's lack of conviction.

They agreed on Dusty. Jho took three steps away from the rest, crouched down, and called to him.

"Dusty. Come here Dusty."

It stood up and started to walk to Jho, who clapped and urged it on. "That a way, yeah, come on. Good Dusty." Dusty lay down in front of Jho. He reached out to pet the dog. Dusty rolled over and sprawled on his back. Jho rubbed his stomach; when he stopped, the dog jumped up and licked his face, knocking Jho over. Dusty shook and danced, too excited, too happy, to be able to calm himself.

Dusty, who was male, was hungry. They took turns offering him food. They felt good having him along; they had forgotten the harpies.

As they rode on, Dusty kept good care of his flock. He took turns running along side of each of them. At dusk as they searched out a good campsite near the river, Dusty disappeared into the woods. When they were set up, they heard a rustling in the underbrush near them. Jho and Jake stood, alerted. Into the light of the fire, trotted Dusty, a large, freshly killed rabbit in his mouth. Jho laughed. "For want of the right name, we could be eating cold jerky."

Jho took the rabbit and dressed it. Soan made a stew. They ate well. By the flickering light, they took turns playing fetch with Dusty.

Sometime in the early hours of the morning, Jake felt someone shaking him awake. Strong, capable, hands clasped his mouth and held him still. "Quiet, don't move," Kendt whispered in his ear.

Jake nodded.

"Don't ask questions. Take your Staff and kill the dog."

Jake hesitated. "Dusty?"

"Now." Kendt's whisper was commanding; this was not the time to question the old man.

Staff in hand, Jake stood. With all his skill, he moved

towards the dog, his step so light that he seemed to float. There was no sound.

Dusty lay against Jho, his head across Jho's leg. Jake looked down. For a second, he opened his mind to them; he felt Jho's childlike love for Dusty, comforted by their closeness. In that instant, as he drove the Staff down into Dusty, Dusty woke. That first look of love and trust turned vile and froze.

Dusty howled as the Staff pierced his heart. His eyes glazed over in death, as his body convulsed for several minutes.

Jho looked up at Jake. With tears in his eyes, he stroked Dusty's head. "Why?"

The entire band was awake, staring at Jake, who was still holding the Staff. The silence deafened him. "I, I—" He tried to find an answer, but couldn't.

Kendt walked into the center of the camp. "I told Jake to kill the dog." They stared at the old circuit priest. "Look." He pointed at the dog.

Even in the faint light, they could see that Dusty's blood was not red. There was a yellow-green discharge around the wound. Jake pulled the Staff out. There was a groan, a death rattle, and the fluid began to ooze more quickly. It volatilized, forming a cloud around the dead dog. As it spread, they smelled it. Soan and d'Solteen ran into the woods to vomit.

Jho rolled out of the way and jumped to his feet. "What is this?" He asked, fighting his need to gag.

"That is one of the Changelings." Kendt turned away from them and whispered. "*Vritrk* has developed a cunning that we never anticipated."

"How did you know?" Molezeen asked.

"I'm not sure that it was any one thing. Why would a healthy, good-tempered dog be out alone? I may not like dogs very much, but you all seemed too infatuated with it. It didn't smell right to me . . . and I had a dream."

"Why ask me to kill it?" Jake asked, feeling relieved, yet a little used.

"No offense, but that's what you do better and more easily than any of us." Kendt felt saddened to have to say it so bluntly; he liked Jake.

They buried the dog, although it had already decomposed into a shapeless pile of fur and gelatin.

They drank cold *troan* as they got ready to ride. While they worked, they discussed the Changeling. Their quest had taken an ominous turn; *Vritrk* had upped the ante.

They had all mounted when Jake turned to Molezeen, "Let me say the obvious," Jake looked at Jho, "it seems that I'm to be a fighter here. Why don't I ride point with Jho."

Molezeen, disheartened by how few they were, knew they could not afford to lose anyone. He looked at Kendt, then back to Jake, and nodded his approval.

"Also, we're being followed," Jake said.

"What?" asked Soan, still shaken by the Changeling. "The Gods, what next?"

"Not what. Who. I think we have to make a decision," Jake said.

Jho stopped looking around. "What decision?"

"Do we want a seventh?" Jake asked.

"Who?" Molezeen asked, impatient with Jake.

"Your cousin!"

"Llo!" Molezeen said. "D'Solteen you'll have to convince her to go back. We can't be worrying about her safety. She has no place here."

Jake looked at Molezeen with confusion. "No, not Llo, Stel."

TWENTY-TWO

Molezeen spurred his horse. He rode back down the road, away from the band. Around the first bend sat Stel, mounted and waiting.

"How can you?" Molezeen shouted, reining his horse in.

"Cousin, I thought—"

"You've endangered yourself and the others. This isn't some schoolboy adventure. This is real and it's deadly."

"I just thought, I mean, you could use help."

"You're a boy. Your sister must be beside herself not knowing where you are. Go home."

"I left a note. She'll be fine."

"And there's the farm. It needs your help. Please, go."

"It's not the harvest yet. I'll be back in time to help."

"Why am I arguing with you? Go, just go."

Stel fought back the tears, but his rage slipped through. "Damn you. Damn you all! I'm not a boy. I hope he wins." He turned his horse, and galloped away.

Molezeen had not wanted to hurt the boy, but anger and rage were a better alternative to being killed. He rode back to the band.

Stel, however, hadn't gone far. As his rage blew over, he let the tears come. He stopped his horse. "Damn them. Damn him." He wiped his eyes. "They'll see, they need me. They'll see."

Stel stopped, and waited to follow them at a greater distance.

"He went home?" Jake asked as Molezeen rode up.

"Yes. I told him to go. He's hurt and angry, but he'll get over it. Anyway, it's best for all of us. What could he do to help?"

Jake and Jho rode point, but not as far away from the rest as Jho had been the day before. They needed to feel each other's presence.

"Old man, what more is there?" Molezeen asked Kendt.

Kendt didn't have an answer.

They were blind to the beauty around them. Large arcading elms filtered the early summer sun, the dirt road dappled in its yellow light. The trees had been planted one hundred fifty years earlier, when the road was reworked after severe spring storms had washed it out. Long stretches of its banks were lined with stone, and campsites were permanently installed at a few hours distance from each other. The road paralleled the barge path, twenty to a hundred feet in from the river.

The bargemen had a language of their own. It was part song and part chant, full of colorful expressions, as happens when occupations segregate workers from normal social intercourse. They advised each other about upstream or downstream conditions; they gave each other their ferriage charges and upcoming bridge or lock fees; they discussed the women they knew at this inn or that. Their talk wafted up to the road, inlaid with birdsong. This was the season for mating and nesting.

The band rode on; they were not so much oblivious to their surroundings as they were unsettled. Dusty had shaken their sense of the rightness of things.

At halfday, they stopped for lunch. "Look at us," Kendt chided them, "a fine bunch. Scared of our own shadows. It would make the old ones laugh." He poured himself a full mug of *troan*, and sat down on the log next to Molezeen.

"The old ones tell the story of Abbid, the blind singer. He was young and handsome. He had curly brown hair, brown eyes, and a square jaw. His voice, they say, could sing high with the birds or deep with the thunder. His songs could transport people to far away times and distant places. He sang of the power of beauty, the Gods, and of love, and of battles with Evil. His songs were magic, the magic of the toon'Arrit. Those who heard him never forgot his spell."

"Abbid? Wasn't there an Abbid who wrote the *nQert'seen?*" Molezeen interrupted.

"Yes, he was the same person, and he probably wrote the *Koth'seen*, even though that's unattributed. But this is a story from his youth.

"He wasn't always blind. He had sight until he was almost twenty. His beauty fetched him many girlfriends—I imagine not unlike our d'Solteen a few years ago. One day, he was showing off, riding too fast along the mountain trails near his home. He fell and hit his head. It was several days before he regained consciousness. In spite of all the doctor did, he was blind.

"For many months, he lay in his bed, in a darkness that buried even his soul. Unwilling to go out or have people over, his friends forgot him; no one visited. Except one, a girl he had never given a thought to, the girl who brought him his meals. She was a plain, simple girl, who had grown up helping her family and never had the time for play or friends. She hadn't a chance before, although she had dreamt of his kiss every night, from when she was but thirteen. She brought him his meals and cared for him every day, for all those black months.

"'They've killed me. Worse, they've left me to wither, to

play my dying over and over in the darkness of my mind. Some Godly jest, I owe them less than nothing.' He would yell.

"She held his hand. 'No. Don't blame the Gods.' Silently she prayed, 'Forgive him. He's lost so much, so quickly. Give him time.'

"Then he would turn on her. 'Don't blame them,' you say. Look what they've done to me, and you want me to like them?'

"Everyday he railed, some days worse. And she prayed for him, never losing her faith.

"On the good days, she coaxed him. 'Sing for me. Please. Just a little song. Or a poem. You're so good.'

"Tears ran down his face, and he tried to push her away. She wiped his cheeks, and held his hand, 'Please?' she asked, but he would not sing.

"Hardest on her was when he would complain that his girl friends had forgotten him. He would name them, and whisper secrets about them, and about intimacies shared. Perhaps he'd have stopped if he could have seen the pain in her eyes, or felt the tears burning her cheeks. He didn't, and she was good at pretending it didn't matter to her.

"He wouldn't bathe, and he ate very little. He became obsessed about all that he had lost. And, of course, he didn't know what he had. One day before she came, he decided to kill himself. On all fours, he crawled out, and down the trail that lead to a great chasm nearby. She discovered his absence and searched for him. She found him, about to jump.

"She yelled, 'Stop! Don't!'

"'Why?' he asked. 'Why shouldn't I end this joke?'

"She argued, 'You have your whole life yet to live.'

"'As what?' he asked. 'A blind man, a beggar? nGin's jest?'

"'Your music. You're so good. You haven't lost that.'

"'You haven't heard me sing since it happened. I can't. I won't. Anyway, who cares any more? I'm as forgotten as last year's good weather.'

"She was standing next to him by then. She grabbed his arm and locked it in hers. 'Then I'll jump with you.'

"He was horrified and took a step back from the edge, pulling her to safety. 'The Gods! I won't.'

"She touched his face. Then she took his hand and gently placed it on her wet cheek. 'Together we'll die.'

"'No,' he said. 'Why would you want to die?'

"'Do you want to know why, Abbid? Because I love you. And I want to be with you for the rest of my life, however long or short that might be.' She pulled at his arm, towards the chasm. 'Come.'

"He resisted, and then he knew. He had to go on living. He realized that he had been so preoccupied with his problems that he hadn't taken stock of what was around him. That night they got married and together they traveled the Arrit Mountains for over sixty years. His singing and writing was more magical than ever.

"The old ones keep this memory alive because we all get so obsessed that we become blind to the beauty of the world around us. It's only in seeing and sharing that beauty that we are able to keep the real darkness at bay."

Molezeen smiled. "Thank you, my friend. You are right. We are alive. And we're well. That's our boon."

The band packed up and continued their ride northwest. They talked, not a lot, but *Vritrk's* spell had been broken.

Towards nightfall they stopped. Jake and Jho turned to rejoin the others. Jake caught a shadow down the road. "Molezeen, I thought you sent Stel on his way?"

Molezeen turned, but it was too late to make out one shadow from another. "I'll—"

"Let me," Jake said.

Jake's gray horse broke into a canter as they disappeared into the shadows.

About three hundred yards down the road, he found him, his horse tied to a mountain oak. He was unwrapping some smoked beef.

"You're not going to try to send me back too?"

"No. I wondered if you'd join us." Jake got off his horse. He sat down next to Stel; he groaned.

"Sore?"

"Yeah, I've never ridden until a few weeks ago. I'm sore in places. How are you?" Jake asked.

"I'm fine, I grew up riding. I—"

"No. How are you? I know you ride."

"I guess I'm fine. Why would my cousin want to chase me away? I mean, you're not an army; you need help."

"Molezeen's worried about you."

"He doesn't have to yell at me like I'm a little kid. I'm grown up. I am."

"I know. As we get older, we forget how quickly we ourselves grew up."

"I can help."

"I know. Suppose I take you back to camp. I'll take your side, but, and I mean this, don't say anything about fighting along side us, even if Molezeen brings it up, drop it. 'Cause it's obviously a sore point—sorer than I am," Jake said, rubbing his backside.

Stel laughed. "All right, but—"

"No but's. None. If you argue with him over any of this, you'll be on your own. I'll have nothing to do with you."

They rode back. The others had tied up the horses and built a fire. Jake and Stel dismounted and saw to their horses. Molezeen walked over. Stel grinned. "Cousin, I—"

Jake gave Stel a sharp jab in the ribs, knocking the wind out of him. "Molezeen, we had a talk. It's okay. You don't want to send Stel back, or have him out there alone. He'd make an effective hostage against us. *Vritrk* must know about him." Jake looked at Stel and winked.

Molezeen shrugged; it made sense that Stel could be used against them. "Why fight it? Fine."

Excited, Stel ran around the horses to Molezeen. "You'll be—" He looked at Jake who was squinting back at him with that look of his that made one rethink things. "Thank you, cousin. I'll take care of our horses."

Jake thought Stel would be okay, at least until there was trouble.

TWENTY-THREE

Stel took Jake's advice to heart. In the morning, he insisted that he saddle the horses for them. Jake was pleased to see him working.

"I've come to like this stuff," Jake said to Molezeen as they sipped warm *troan*. "We don't have anything like it."

"What do you drink?" Molezeen had some idea, from having shared Jake's mind, but he had little understanding.

"Nothing like this. We have lots of different beers, some of the English beers come close to *troan's* body, but they aren't sweet. Some Trappist beers have something of the sweetness, but not the body. In the Medieval times, people drank mead, that's fermented honey and water. We have Medieval dinners around Christmas; everyone dresses in robes; people walk around playing the lute, and recorders, and there are jugglers; we eat out of wood bowls or on big, flat slices of bread, and worse, put honey in beer. Now stout, there is a drink, thick, dark and bitter; the English just order a pint. They drink it at room temperature. It separates the men from the boys. French beer, on the other hand, tends to be—" Jake stopped mid-sentence. They were all staring at him. No one had any idea what he was saying. Jake grinned. "Sorry, back home we drink dish water."

Stel had picked up several saddlebags. Laughing with the rest, he swung them over his shoulder. Kendt's had not been packed well, nor tied shut. Some of Kendt's things fell to the ground; there were purple shards of broken crystal where something had hit a rock. Stel stooped to pick them up.

"Stop!" Kendt bellowed.

They all turned. Stel froze, his hand inches from the crystal.

"Don't touch that! Get up and back a way."

Stel moved. Kendt walked over, crouched down, and surveyed the damage. Molezeen started to say something to Stel. Kendt stopped him. "No, it's my fault. I'm old enough to know how to pack a bag. There was no reason for Stel to have done anything differently. He was helping." Kendt looked at Stel with understanding and forgiveness, but there was sadness in his eyes.

"What is it?" Molezeen asked.

"Get me the camp shovel." They watched as he dug a hole. He brushed everything that had fallen out of his bag into the hole. He buried the rock and the contaminated dirt. He gathered a few small rocks and put them in, and then he filled the hole and stamped on it.

Kendt sat down, stooped and weary.

"Are you all right?" Molezeen asked.

"I have to go north. I'm sorry."

Molezeen poured some *troan* into Kendt's mug. "Why?" He asked, handing Kendt the mug.

"I have a growth inside my head. The old ones found me, more dead than alive. They saved my life, and gave me something that reduces its size. I am fine for a while. But when it starts to grow again, when I feel it, I have to give myself more. That's what broke, a vial of the medicine."

"Surely, we've something in the South that would work?"

"No. Only in the north. It's—"

"What? What is it?"

"Snowsnake venom," Kendt whispered.

"A'toon!" Jho said, and touched his eye.

Molezeen looked at Kendt. "We'll go with you. You're one of us. We're friends. Anyway, where we meet *Vritrk* doesn't matter so much does it?"

Kendt smiled. "Thanks."

They were a few hours past the trail to the L'zotk Gorge. The quickest way into the Arrit would be to go north between the n'Geent and the L'zotk; they could pick up the trail to Rim Edge in a day and a half. Although Molezeen was angry with Stel, he thought to himself that this might be for the best. *Vritrk* was in the Toth, probably watching their approach. He was prepared for them. But if they went into the Arrit, they might just draw him away from the land he knew best. That could make the odds a little better.

Jake and Stel rode next to Jho. "What's a snowsnake?" Jake asked.

"It's an awful thing; it lives in the Arrit Mountains," Stel said.

"That's it, 'awful'?"

"I'll tell you," Jho said, and then he lowered his head and touched his eye in *g'lt*. "I saw a body once. It had been killed by a snowsnake. Molezeen and I were riding during a beautiful spring thaw. The trees were beginning to bud. We found the horse first. It had slipped, looked like it had broken its leg, then it fell off the trail into a crevasse. About ten minutes farther, we found him. Must have been a terrible storm and he had taken shelter between two large rocks. His body was perfectly preserved. He looked awake, sitting upright, but his eyes! He was frozen with a look of such terror. I've never seen anything like that; it still haunts my dreams. Molezeen said that we should move the body, and give it a proper burial. It weighed little more than the clothes on it. We turned it around. In the back was a hole. The snake had eaten out the insides.

"He could have lived—or at least his mind could have lived—for days. Conscious of his fate, conscious of the pain, but unable to move at all; waiting for death to stop his awareness."

"And that's where we're going? The Arrit Mountains?" Jake asked. He patted his horse's neck. "Don't slip," he whispered.

"We should be fine. They hibernate during the warm months. I've never heard of anything good coming from one of them, but I guess you never know." Jho touched his eye again. "The old ones, huh?"

They got to the ferry just before halfday. It took them across to where they could pick up the trail northeast to the L'zotk. To their right were the rich farmlands above Zot'qrt. To the left, a little less than a day's ride was the southern edge of the n'Geent.

Jho reminisced. "It's beautiful along the North Rim of the L'zotk. My parents, when they got married, came here to celebrate. In their generation, it was the thing to do. Although newlyweds don't frequent it so much anymore, it always draws people, year round. I've been here four times."

"My father was going to bring me here," Stel said. "When I was twelve. But he took sick and died."

"He was a good man," Molezeen said. "I liked him. He's missed."

"We were going to come this time of year, too."

"This is a good time," Jho went on, "it's not too hot, and the colors are the best. If we want to push our ride a little, there's a wonderful inn. It has great food and the best view. Of course, we can camp almost anywhere, and there are dozens of sites along the way."

By unanimous consent, they decided that if they felt like more riding, the inn sounded good.

Stel was excited. "We were going to hike the gorge. We had maps and father had worked out our trail and everything. Wait until I get back and tell everyone about this. This is great. Boy, will we have fun. . . ."

Stel kept talking about it, until he got his first glimpse, then he, like everyone else, fell silent.

Molezeen whispered to Jake and d'Solteen that the first people to live in the plains south of the Singren Rim considered the L'zotk sacred. Sacred or not, it held an energy that could not be ignored.

As the sun moved across the sky, the colors of the canyon changed, purples and blues gave way to golds, reds, and yellows. Flecks of schist in the rock gave a specular, twinkling quality to the scene. The trail divided frequently: one followed out along the edge; the other was straighter and shorter. The edge trail didn't look too much longer, so they took it.

At dusk, they stopped to decide about going on or camping.

"I was here, many years ago," Jho said. "I stayed at a lodge maybe an hour or two on. They had a cook . . . well, I had a game platter of organ meats, served in courses. The liver was lightly fried in butter with a—"

"Stop," Jake protested. His appetite had been tested by too many meals of smoked beef. "No more."

"We're convinced," Molezeen said. "Speaking for Jake, let's ride on."

It was dark when they got there. Attendants took their horses and their bags. The band went inside the magnificent log and stone structure. The center room was open to the roof, with a massive central fireplace. The floor was polished slate.

The first floor divided into three sections: a bar, a restaurant, and a lounge; at the back of the lounge was the sign-in desk. The second floor held thirty rooms. There were only a few rooms available when they arrived.

Most guests booked rooms for a week at a time, and there was a comfortable system of carriages to bring people in or take them back to the main cities.

Although dinner was better than Jho had suggested it would be, it was breakfast that left them breathless. It was held on the large, covered, stone verandah. Whether by design or accident, the verandah was unique. Even in the windiest of storms, the air around the tables remained absolutely still, and rain and snow never came in. It was as if the clearest of glass, without a hint of reflection or distortion, enclosed it. They ate a great breakfast, while sheltered from the elements, and the view, which encompassed the entire length of the gorge, was almost unbelievable.

During the meal, they saw people, children and adults, walk to the low wall that ran along the outer edge, and surreptitiously reach out, as though they thought what they saw was an immense stage set, and they could touch the other side.

No one wanted to go when Molezeen announced that it was time to leave. Day's end would bring them to the trail along the T'ng that would take them, in another day, to Rim Edge.

As they rode, Jho tried to recall all that he had been told about the L'zotk. At the northeastern end, there were ruins of stone houses built into the very walls of the gorge. They predated even the toon'Arrit. A few hundred years before, scholars had tried to determine how the people lived and who they were. After a generation of work, it was decided that it would be a greater harm to dig up more than to know less. All study stopped, and everything was put back to its original condition. Hundreds of years later, the gorge dwellers still remained a mystery.

Stel tried to stay out of everyone's way. He rode up with Jake, his benefactor. After halfday, d'Solteen joined them; he missed Llo and asked Stel to tell him about her, her childhood, her parents, and her early boyfriends. It was a good diversion for Stel.

While Stel and d'Solteen talked, Jake joined Kendt. He sensed that the old priest was in some pain. Jake liked him and wanted to help, but he suddenly felt awkward; he wondered about the ethics of his occasional interference. A wave of pain settled the question. He matched his breathing with the priest's, and gently entered his mind, seeking out the pain centers that could be adjusted. He worked slowly. "For once," he thought, "I have time."

Jake was also careful to preserve Kendt's privacy. This was a proud man who wouldn't suffer intrusion. Jake took almost a half hour. The tension in Kendt's chest eased; his breathing slowed and became deeper, more normal. Jake broke contact. He was pleased that he had alleviated the pain. It would come back, he knew, and he wished he could have done more.

They found a good campsite on the bank of the T'ng. It was early. They could have ridden another hour, but it would have gained them little. Stel took care of the horses. Jho and Soan built a fire and prepared dinner. They took a lot of razzing; dinner the night before had been too good. Over a second mug of warmed *troan*, d'Solteen regaled them with his account of meeting Jake and their adventures. Although they all knew what had happened, this time d'Solteen embellished the story, lingering over Jake's quirkiness. They all laughed, and Jake laughed the hardest.

When the fire had begun to burn down, they turned in. Kendt placed his bedding next to Jake's. Kendt whispered to Jake. "Thank you. You were very kind to help me this afternoon. I hope that I can return that kindness."

Jake was startled that the old priest had known of his interference. As he lay wondering, it occurred to him that these were quite remarkable people, and that he erred if he underestimated them.

He slept well.

TWENTY FOUR

Above Rim Edge, in Ren, they parted company.

"I must do this alone. Wait for me here. I'll return in a week." Kendt rode off leading a pack horse. He was taking the trail north, parallel to the T'ng on the west bank. The band took rooms at the Sage Inn, and waited.

Kendt worried about his search as he rode. If he had to get venom, this was as good a time as any, better than winter, he knew, because the snowsnakes would be hibernating. The old ones had said he would be safe, if he were careful, but fear haunted him nonetheless.

The first night, Kendt stayed at a hostel. They were scattered throughout the Arrit. It was unclear who, if anyone, owned the hostels. They ran on a volunteer system. If travelers needed shelter, but couldn't afford to pay in food or money, they gave a few days time, cleaning and cooking. There was always food, and the company was good. The hostels attracted three kinds of people: young, poor, and those who now had money but who had made use of the hostels in their poorer, or earlier, years. Fledgling entertainers used them to hone their skills. Among the neeZeen, the camaraderie of the hostels was legend. As long as people's stories told of them, they would continue to be run in this fashion.

On the second day, he took an old, unused, trail to the first of a series of minor toon'Arrit ruins that ran west and north of the T'ng. Digging around for snowsnakes was so crazy that people might try to stop him, thinking they were doing him a service.

By day's end, he arrived at the ruins, an acre of collapsed, half-buried, brown stone walls, in a copse of birches above a small waterfall. He smelled a cook fire. "The old ones," he thought. He smiled, longing for their companionship, if only for a few hours.

Kendt tied his horses and walked around a wall to the campfire. "Hello. I'm—" He was confused. This was not an old one, but a young man. "Eh, my name is Kendt, may I share your fire?"

The man was startled, but quickly composed himself. "Please, sit down. My name's Tesn'. I have rabbit here. I was about to cook it. Would you join me?"

"That's a fine offer. I'll pour you a mug of *troan* and I've got some good bread and cheese left; better to share it than have it go bad."

They ate and talked. It was hard not to like the young man. He was handsome; Kendt was sure that he broke the girls' hearts everywhere he went. Tesn' was average height, but thin and muscular, which made Kendt think of him as tall. His eyes were emerald. "An unusual color," Kendt commented.

"So I've been told. My mother's family all have this color. She told me it meant good fortune, but I don't know if one should believe in such things."

"My curiosity is getting the best of me. You are a long way from anywhere. Why?"

"My father raises and breaks horses. He wants me to join him. I'm of age now, you know. He doesn't want me to just say yes. I'm to take the summer, travel, and see the world."

"What do you think?"

"It's only been a few weeks. I don't know."

"You're lucky to have such understanding parents."

"My father's a fine man. He has ambition, but he doesn't want to force me into anything. I know he'd like my help, and I'm sure that I'll give it. But he remembers being young, so he wants me to come to him of my own will."

"You have my best wishes."

"You're a priest?"

"Yes. I am a circuit priest."

"I don't know of any villages along this trail. Where are you going?" he asked Kendt.

Kendt hesitated; his search would sound insane to anyone. It would be easier to lie. Yet the boy inspired trust. "You may think me crazy, but I'm looking for . . . for a snowsnake. Its venom has certain properties that are medicinal, which I need."

Tesn' made the sign of *g'lt*. "How? Aren't they dangerous even now?"

"Yes, they're hibernating, but with a little care I should be safe."

"You've done this before?"

Kendt took a long swallow of *troan*. "Actually, no. But I've been told how it's done, by the old ones."

"I see. I hope that you don't mind if I travel on before you start looking. The thought of them, well, it's—"

"I understand. I'm not looking forward to the task, but I have to do it."

They turned in. Kendt dreamt of his boyhood, so many years distant.

He saw his father, the day he left to go to the seminary. It was the day after his sixteenth birthday.

They were standing next to the corral, watching their sixteen horses, a sign of success in the North Country, prance in the warm, spring sun.

His father had been getting the plow ready for a long day in the fields, when Kendt came out from the house, dragging his overstuffed backpack. His father's face was wet with tears, but he tried to act as if this were a day like any other.

"Got to get the fields turned as far as the stream by week's end or we'll be late for the rain."

"Father—"

"Remember when we were late four years ago? It took—"

"Father, I've got to go."

Kendt's father looked up from the leather traces. "Kendt." He wiped his face. "Be careful. That pack isn't new, the seams won't last." He tried to laugh, but the tears made him turn away and hide his face. "I'll miss you."

They hugged.

"I love you, my son."

Kendt waved towards the house where his mother stood on the porch, watching in tears.

It was the last time he ever saw his father; he died in an avalanche the following spring, not long before Kendt returned for summer break. In his dream, Kendt knew that, and wanted to warn him, and to say, "I love you," but the words stuck in his throat. The more he tried the harder it became. This was his last chance. He had to tell him. His dream merely allowed him to stand, mute and frustrated, while the wind picked up the smell of the horses, of the hay stored in the barn, and of the damp earth, already turned in the field. It was so normal, except he could not do anything but walk away, taking the trail south. At the edge of the clearing, he turned to wave. His mother had come out, and was hugging his father. His father waved back. Only then did the words come. "I love you."

It was light when Kendt woke; the words whispered in the air, "I love you."

He looked around. Tesn' was tending the fire, heating water, and getting breakfast ready. He was looking down at Kendt, smiling. "Ah, you're awake," Tesn' said. "I'll have something to drink in a few minutes. Are you hungry? I have some cereal I can make up."

Kendt felt oddly embarrassed. He stretched and turned, hiding the flush that had crept up his neck. His dream had already begun to fade. "Could I decide on the cereal after I'm awake?"

They drank warm, watered *troan*. Kendt decided against eating. He packed quickly. He felt sad in their leave taking, and didn't want to delay.

"Tesn', you have my blessing. May you find what you are looking for, and may that be a decision that you will find comfort in for all your years to come."

Kendt rode north. He knew there could be snowsnakes anywhere, but it would be easier to ride until he saw tunnels, instead of crawling through the brush. It was just after halfday when he saw the two holes. He tied the horses and got out all the things he needed. The old ones had told him that the snowsnake tunnels looped, the snake lying at one end. Although hibernating, it would wake, its lethalness no less diminished by its sluggishness.

If the snake faced out, the light would slow it, giving Kendt a better chance to hook it behind its head. If it came out backwards, it would be all the way out before the light hit its eyes. Then, it would be angry, and it could move more quickly.

Kendt collected some dry leaves and tinder. He lit a small fire. Then he tore off a corner of his shirt. Wrapping it around a stick, he held the cloth in the fire long enough to make it smolder. He put the stick into one of the holes for a second.

He had a fifty percent chance of guessing right. If he had the wrong hole, the snake would back out. He heard the old ones warning repeatedly in his mind: ". . . if that happens, don't let it get all the way out. . . ."

Only the pain in his head kept him there. He put the smoking stick back into the tunnel several more times. Then he stood, waiting for the snake to come out the other end, a forked stick in his hand. He heard himself chuckle over a morbid joke. "Heads or tails?"

His palms were wet and his heart pounded so loudly that he knew that it would scare off the snake. He wondered if the snake might not come through the smoke, and out the other end, three feet away. It was foolish, but could it?

A minute later, he saw the white head below the stick. He waited until the head was out six inches. The old ones had told him not to kill the snake. The venom was a combination of two fluids, one from its poison gland, the other some of its digestive juice. Alive, the snake did the mixing correctly.

He fixed the head to the ground. Carefully, he leaned down and grabbed the snake behind the head. For the briefest second, it stared up at Kendt with white and black, translucent eyes. "By A'toon you're ugly." It hissed and wiggled in his hand. "And Evil, if ever I've seen it."

He held it facing away. The old one had also said, "I have been told that the snake can spit its poison . . . with deadly accuracy."

The snake was heavy, fifteen pounds of muscle; even slowed by the heat, it squirmed enough to test Kendt's mettle to its limit.

Kendt took the crystal bottle he had waiting, held it under one of the upper fangs of the snake, and pushed up into the gums. A drop of deadly fluid glistened at the end of the pale white fang. The drop got bigger, but did not want to let go. He waited, afraid that he would fatigue and drop the snake. It took several minutes for the first big drop to fall into the bottle. Alternating from one fang to the other, for thirty minutes, he kept at it. He had a dram.

Then he realized that the old ones had not told him what to do with the snake afterwards. Would it come after him? How fast could it travel in the heat? Did it have more poison? His arm had cramped. He calmed himself. Carefully, he put the crystal bottle on the ground and capped it. Then he put it into his saddlebags. Walking back to the edge of the woods, making sure that nothing was under foot, he flung the snake away from him, and ran back to the horses. He climbed on as fast as he could and rode south. His heart soared. "Yeah!" he screamed like a schoolboy. "I did it!"

He looked forward to day's end. He would be at the same ruins where he had spent the previous night. The ruins were cold and empty. "Silly," he thought, "why should Tesn' have stayed here." He felt foolish for his feelings.

By week's end he was back at Ren.

TWENTY-FIVE

Kendt was welcomed back like a long-lost friend. Sitting around a table in the bar at the Sage Inn, where Kendt had first met Molezeen, d'Solteen asked what they all wanted to know. "Did you find a . . . snowsnake?"

Kendt smiled; it was hard for him not to. It had been one thing to talk about it, but quite another to swallow one's fear and do it. He reached into the saddlebag next to him on the floor, and palmed the crystal vial. He leaned forward, savoring the moment. "Yes," he whispered, and opened his hand on the table. Every eye fell on the vial. They were breathless in the sight of such a marvel.

"I did it." Kendt broke the spell.

They laughed, and cheered. In a way, they saw Kendt's search as symbolic of their own and Kendt's success portending theirs.

"Tell us," Stel said, putting two full pitchers of *troan* on the table.

"You can know something, but to actually do it! Well, the old ones had told me what to look for and how to go about it. But to have to face that horror?"

Kendt turned the white crystal vial around on the table as a sculptor might his latest maquette before a group of admirers.

"They are even more fearful than in your darkest imaginings. And to be fixed by the eye of a snowsnake, ah, that's something you wouldn't wish on anyone. . . ."

Kendt talked for an hour. He described the hunt in the greatest detail, for this was the thing that legends grew from.

It was dark when he finished. They ordered dinner, and Molezeen told them his plan.

"There's a trail, used by hunters, that goes along the Rim's edge. I say we follow it west. That will take us towards the Toth. We'll make sure we've enough provisions tomorrow, and then we'll set out." Molezeen paused, and looked around at his band. They stared at him expecting more. Molezeen tried to find something, "I . . . think . . ."

"This trail, where do we find it? Here?" Jho interrupted, getting Molezeen off the spot. "I've never been west of the T'ng."

"We'll pick it up in Rim Edge. It's an easy trail, used by hunters and traders."

"Do you really think that we'll find *Vritrk*?" This was the first time Stel had said his name. They looked at him as if he had gone too far. "You know. I mean, we'll kill him when we meet him. I can't wait; it'll be—"

"Stel!" Molezeen was red in the face.

"What? That's why we're—"

"Enough–now!"

Stel jumped to his feet, knocking his chair over. He ran out the door into the cold night. No one went after him.

In the morning, they checked their provisions, bought a few items, and left Ren. It was a half-day back to Rim Edge. "We should keep going. There's shelter less than another easy half-day," Molezeen said.

The trail west was well worn. It was not hard to find. It wound through a pine forest that extended four days along the Singren Rim. Icy mountain streams scarred the forest floor, terminating in misty cascades at the rim's edge. The smell of pine and the cool moist air was invigorating. Deer, startled by their passing, broke the silence, but not the spell of the woods.

At dusk, they spotted a lean-to. Families and tourists did not travel the Western Plain, so there was no need of inns or hostels. Kendt explained that centuries ago, a *vr'trk* had been handed down to two brothers; no one remembered their misconduct, or their names. Their judgment was to build the lean-tos that dotted the trails along the Rim.

They were all the same: fifteen feet deep by twenty-two feet wide, the peak about ten feet high. They were made of log, with a raised floor, eighteen inches above the ground. There was a four-foot overhang along the front. Heavy cabinets had been built-in to hold food; people would leave excess supplies in them, and they had to be secure enough to keep out wild life. The floors lay covered with pine boughs and needles. A stone fireplace in front could provide needed heat that made them usable all year. Each lean-to was near a stream.

As they approached, they smelled smoke. "There are two horses tied up in front," Jho said. The custom was to share the lean-to with anyone. They tied their horses. Molezeen was the first to approach.

"Hello, may we join you?" Molezeen added sheepishly, "We are seven."

"Of course, there's plenty of room, 'though I can't feed you all."

Kendt recognized the voice; it was Tesn'. "Hello. I hadn't expected to run into you again."

Molezeen looked at Kendt.

"Remember I said that I shared a campsite in the ruins. Well, this is the young man. Molezeen, this is Tesn'. Tesn' this is Molezeen. I'll let everyone else handle his own introductions."

225

They had settled in, and dinner was under way when Kendt sat down next to Tesn'. "I thought you'd be halfway to the Southern farmlands by now."

"That was my intention, but I've had a lot of time to think about it. I miss my father. I decided that if what I was going to do was to work for him, why not now? I'll have time to go places; I'm young."

"Where does your family live?" Molezeen asked.

"About three days west and two north. We have a horse ranch. My father wants me to stay and help run it. He also wants me to make that decision on my own. So I've been traveling, taking time alone to think; that's how I met Kendt. But, even though I haven't gotten very far, well, I think I know what I want."

Molezeen could not help thinking of Stel, running away from his obligations. *Why can't Stel be like Tesn'?* He thought.

They had a good meal. D'Solteen entertained them with stories about nGin and his Godly pranks, and about Lazz's many adventures. No one noticed that Stel was moodier than usual.

In the morning, Molezeen asked Tesn' about the trail west. "Does it lead directly into the Toth?"

"No. You'll have to cross a spur of the n'Geent. Then you pick up another trail."

"Is it a hard trail?"

Tesn' looked at Jho. "No. Especially with Jho. You'll have no trouble."

They were saddled and ready to ride. "If we're going the same way," Molezeen asked, "why don't you join us? The company's good."

"It would be pleasant, but I don't want to intrude.

Anyway, I'm not going as far as you. Thank you, but I'd just be in the way."

"Nonsense," Kendt said. "If we're traveling the same way, what would you have us do, avoid you?"

Tesn' looked at the band. With reluctance, he shrugged his shoulders. "Fine. Let me know if there's anything I can do. I feel like an intruder."

Tesn' rode next to Molezeen.

"That's a magnificent staff," Tesn' said reaching out idly to touch it as they rode.

"Stop! Don't touch this, or any of the Staves."

Tesn' looked hurt.

"Sorry, but they'll kill you. Only three of us can touch them or control them. To anyone else, they're lethal."

Tesn' was relieved, but distanced himself from Molezeen a little more, and he touched his eye in *g'lt*. "My father used to tell me stories about the magic of the ancients. He said that it died with them. All that remained were stories—these are theirs?"

"Yes."

Tesn' lowered his head and touched his right eye again. "Where do three men of magic go with such power?"

"Have you or your father seen anything odd in the last year or two?"

"Like what?"

"Evil, distorted things. Things that weren't before; and that should never be. Changelings."

"We haven't. But there was a man who came through to buy some horses last fall. He told us some stories. He said both the Toth and the Arrit are seeded with deadly things, nothing like he had ever seen. His stories were frightening. After he left, my father said that such stories were the workings of the over-active imaginations of city-born." Tesn' gasped at his own rudeness. "No offense meant, I didn't mean—"

"No offense taken." Molezeen smiled.

"Were the stories true?"

"Yes. There's Evil abroad. We're out to stop it."

Tesn' went white as snow. "Where?"

"You needn't worry about your family's ranch. From what we know, you're too far north and east of where we must go."

"I'm sorry if I appear, well, scared. It's just that the ranch is all I know, and my father, too. And I've decided to—"

"It's fine. We're traveling companions only; and of course, we neither expect your help nor want it, other than advising us on the trails."

Tesn' touched his eye again. "Thank you."

Stel, riding several lengths back from Molezeen and Tesn', snickered, "Yeah, chicken."

Jake heard. "Stel, don't. Tesn' is not part of this group. He has grown up differently from everyone else. It's not his battle."

"It's just that everyone seems to dote—"

"Drop it," Jake said.

At halfday, they stopped for lunch. Tesn' seemed ill at ease. Kendt sat next to him. "What's the problem?"

"It's just that you all are . . . magicians. I'm—"

"No, not at all. In fact, not a one of us is a magician. We are men, like you. We may have skills that are different from yours, but we're no less men."

"But the Staves?"

"Yes, well they *are* magic. But you're safe with us."

"What should I tell my father? I mean, can I tell him?"

"Why not? Except that he probably won't believe you."

Jho sat opposite Kendt and Tesn'. He couldn't help

staring. Tesn' reminded him of his first days in military camp and of Rol, his partner. His father had been a warrior; it was a family tradition. There was a training facility in the South, the only one left in all the neeZeen lands. They maintained the old ways.

Everyone was paired. It was called doth'nor. *Each pair did everything together. In the days of the Great Wars, if any one thing contributed to their victory, it was* doth'nor. *It built discipline; it created competition; it saved lives. Rol was his opposite: light complected with light hair, to his dark skin and hair, joking and mischievous to Jho's serious quiet nature. Jho loved Rol: that was the idea. Some of the young men became lovers. Jho had resisted, although Rol had wanted him. This was Jho's biggest regret in life.*

His squad was out on winter maneuvers; they were in the Arrit, along the coast. Each doth'nor *had a particular destination; each had to bushwhack through the woods, find a flag, and return it to their base camp.*

In the wilderness, two days north of Lantrent, Rol broke his leg. In the late afternoon, as the sun was casting a warm, flat light over the hills, they crossed small rapids, to set up camp on the other side. Rol was telling a story about how he had gotten in trouble for some childish pranks that had gotten out of hand. "It was as if nGin guided me. Everything went—"

Rol stepped on a rock that shifted under his weight. With a splash barely audible above the sound of the running water, he fell in. His leg wedged between two rocks. It snapped as the current grabbed him.

Jho turned to see why the story had stopped. He saw Rol, his head an inch or two below the foaming water, his eyes wide with fear and pain.

Jho dove in. Rol was drowning, in blind terror he thrashed wildly. Jho struggled to get Rol's head and chest out of the water without going under. Once out, he held him while Rol retched and gulped air.

"I've got to get your leg free."

"No!" Rol clung to Jho, knowing that it meant falling back into the black terror of the water. "Don't let go."

Jho dove down, and while trying to hold Rol up, he pulled at the rocks. Again and again he went under; Rol fought hard to resist the terror. Twice, Jho lost his grip and was carried downstream. Each time, he had to fight Rol to save him.

As darkness blanketed them, Jho finally freed Rol's leg. He carried him ashore, and wrapped him in both their bedrolls. Exhausted by the struggle and pain, Rol lost consciousness.

By the light of the campfire, Jho set the leg, and put it in a splint. Rol was unconscious until dawn. Through the night, Jho held him trying to keep him warm, praying to the Gods that Rol would survive.

In the morning, Rol was conscious, and Jho had a chance to look around. The terrain was too rugged for Jho to get Rol out by himself.

"Get help. If you leave the tent and some of the food, I'll be all right until you get back."

"I can't desert you like this," Jho pleaded, but he knew that Rol was right.

"The weather doesn't look like it will hold out for too long. Please. Leave."

Jho left. It should have taken a few days. But the weather turned worse by halfday, and Jho didn't get back with help for a week.

There was still some wood, dusted with snow, stacked by the cold remains of the campfire.

"Rol!" Jho yelled as they crossed the rapids.

The loose tent flap snapped back and forth in the wind.

Startled by the sound of men, a wolf that had just discovered Rol's body ran from the tent.

"Rol!"

The commander of the rescue team grabbed Jho. "It's too late. We'll take care of things."

"But—"

"Keep him back," the commander said to two of the men.

Rol had died from shock and exposure.

They carried his body back for a proper burial.

"I should have," Jho whispered.

"What?" Jake asked.

"Sorry, I was just thinking. It's nothing."

At dusk, they found a lean-to that had been built close to the Rim's edge. They sat around the fire and watched the sun set across the n'Geent. The fiery desert glowed with mineral colors in the orange-red light. The air was still, disturbed only by the gentle sound of evening birds hunting insects.

They sat in reflective silence until the only light was that of the moon and the fire. It got cold quickly on the Rim after the sun went down. Soan got up to put more wood on the fire and to get his bedding. The others stirred. D'Solteen looked at Molezeen. "The riding accumulates; I seem to be getting sorer."

"We're also getting older."

They laid out their bedding in the lean-to. Without having given it any thought, Jake and Molezeen settled on either side of Tesn', who went rigid.

"Are you all right?" Molezeen asked.

"Yes. Well . . . no. I'm scared of that," he said pointing to Molezeen's Staff. "I could roll over—"

"I'm sorry. It's become so much a part of me that I don't think about how it affects someone else." Molezeen stood up. "Here," he said to Jake, taking his Staff, also. He propped them up in the corner by the food cabinet. "They are not that far away if we need them," he mumbled.

D'Solteen slept by the end of the lean-to and kept his Staff next to him.

"Thanks. I'll sleep better," Tesn' said as Molezeen settled down.

No one heard Stel as he mumbled into his shirt, rolled up into a pillow. "Asshole; chicken-shit, asshole. Sucks up to them, and they buy it. . . ." Stel slept uneasily.

The others, older and more tired than Stel, were able to sleep deeply. When morning woke them, they all felt more refreshed than they had for weeks.

"I like this forest air. It's invigorating," Kendt said to no one in particular as he poured some *troan*.

The farther west they went, the trail became less obvious. Jho would have had no trouble following it, but because Tesn' had actually ridden it before, it was Tesn' who rode point. Jake and Stel rode at the back.

"You doing okay? You seem awfully down on Tesn'. Has he said something to you?"

"None of you see it. Even you! He's spoiled. I mean, you can all expect this or that from me. But he just whines a little and my cousin's all ready to do anything for him. What a baby."

"Stel, I think you're being unfair. Give him a chance, there's something about him that might surprise you."

"Yeah, stepping in horse shit is surprising too."

Jake squinted at him. "You know, I think you're jealous."

Stel kicked his horse, moving a little ahead of Jake. "Sure, that's it. I must be jealous of him."

TWENTY-SIX

In another hour or two, the trail splits," Tesn' explained to them when they stopped at halfday. "There's a lean-to there. I'll stay for the night then go on north. You keep going on the other path, and there is a lean-to two hours farther. It's a day to the divide. I think the trail follows along it—you can see the Toth from there. I've never ridden that far, but my father has. He said that it's not hard to find the trail over."

"If we're to part company soon, let me offer a toast. May your wishes be what you want, and may they be true to you," Molezeen said.

They drank to Tesn'.

It was mid-afternoon when they arrived at the fork in the trail. A giant fir, a hundred feet tall and five feet in diameter, had been struck by lightning. It lay across the shattered lean-to.

"I guess we weren't intended to part company yet," Molezeen said surveying the damage.

"No, please, go on, I'll be fine." Tesn' stopped, embarrassed by Molezeen's suggestion.

"We'll help set this right. We've enough hands, it's within our ability, and therefore it's our obligation."

They tied up their horses. Their supplies, equipment, even the Staves, they set aside. They had four or five hours of light.

With a small camp saw and two axes, they attacked the

tree and the lean-to. Kendt and Molezeen picked up broken branches. Jho, d'Solteen, Jake, and Stel took turns sawing and chopping. Soan used one of the horses to haul the logs away.

There was a lot to do; they didn't work quickly; they worked steadily.

D'Solteen crouched down by the fireplace, pulling some branches aside. "I don't know about this. We'll be cold tonight."

"I was taught masonry by my father. Maybe I can help," Tesn' said.

"Then our first task is to clear up around here."

Later that evening, Tesn' had not only fixed the fireplace, but also had a roaring fire going.

"Bravo!" Molezeen said, surprised at Tesn's success.

"Well, it may not last as long as it should; I didn't have good mortar."

"It's better than we could have hoped."

In spite of the fire, no one had much energy for cooking; dinner was quick and cold. Everyone was asleep minutes later.

Jho was the first up. He rebuilt the fire, and heated water. Tesn' took care of the horses. The rest were up within a half hour. Jake looked at his hands; he had several big blisters. "This will slow me down," he mumbled as he gingerly held his mug of warm *troan*.

After a quick breakfast, they were at work. The tree they cleared away just before halfday. At dusk, the work was done. The camp looked a little worse for the wear, but it was usable.

Tesn' volunteered to cook. Between their supplies and what was left in the cabinet, he managed a good dinner. As tired as they were, there was a feeling of celebration for a job well done. They could have ridden on—there was no legal obligation to do as much as they had—but it was unlikely that as many men would stop at that camp again. The repairs would have been a daunting task for one or two.

When they set out their bedding, Molezeen reminded Jake to put his Staff out of the way.

"Thanks, I simply can't get used to the idea of being so close to them," Tesn' said as he crawled into his bedding. "It'll be good to sleep."

There was a round of "amens." No one had the energy to stay awake.

While they were falling asleep, the wind picked up. "I'm glad we fixed the lean-to," Jake thought as he drifted off, "feels like quite a storm."

Clouds rolled in unseen. They hid the stars and the moon. The wind continued to quicken.

Around midnight, a cold rain started. Molezeen thought about getting up and looking after the fire, but his bedding was too warm. He fell back to sleep.

The thunder started an hour later. It rumbled, deep and resonant, as if laughing at their meager shelter. Lightning lit the sky, crashing between clouds. Jho pulled his bedding up around his shoulders. He hated early summer storms.

It was another hour before the dream started:

A childhood nightmare of an attacking monster, shared by them all. In their dream, they stood together to face the danger; through the rain and thunder it approached. They saw nothing. They heard things in the woods; it knocked over trees. They smelled it—the smell of decay. They gagged in its stench as it came closer. Suddenly, they knew that they had to run for safety. As is often the case in such dreams, they could not move. Rooted where they stood, they were helpless.

As the lighting crashed about the lean-to and the thunder roared, these men of destiny rolled and tossed in the throes of a primal nightmare.

The rain stopped. Cold drops of water dripped from the overhang of the lean-to, the leaves, and the tree limbs. Without the rain to cover the sound, one could hear each drop as it hit the ground. By the lean-to, they landed with a splash in the puddles and mud. In the forest, the drops fell on wet pine needles, almost silent, making a quiet thump. The dampness crept into the lean-to and through their bedding. They huddled deeper in the shelter, trying to escape.

No one knew who heard the laugh first, but within seconds of one another they were all awake and aware of it. It got louder. It pinned them to the floor. It was colder and damper than the air. It chilled their souls.

"What would you do? Where would you go?" It asked invisible in the dark.

It laughed.

In one blinding flash of lightning, he appeared, standing in front of the lean-to, blacker then the night, shining in the lightning flashes. Vritrk stood, his arms crossed, an arrogant smile on his face.

"This is delicious. You are all here. That's good. I don't want any of you to miss this." Vritrk paused and walked back and forth along the edge of the floor.

Jake tried to move, to reach out for his Staff that wasn't there. Like the rest he couldn't move, except his finger, which he could twitch a little.

"What are you trying to do?" Vritrk yelled at Jake. "Do you think your powers can work in my world?" He stepped on Jake's finger. "It is my world, I was here first."

Jake heard someone scream. He didn't know it was himself.

"Oh, poor Jake. You must feel awful, unable to move. For what? For that Staff you thoughtfully set away from you." He laughed. "Do you think it can help? Do you?"

Vritrk *stamped his foot down on Jake's hand again.* "Do you?"

"Yes." *Jake groaned.*

Lightning flashed. It hurt them, searing their eyes. No one could turn away.

"Let me get it for you," Vritrk *cooed.* "You shouldn't be without it, not tonight."

Vritrk *walked to the end of the lean-to and grabbed Jake's Staff.* "It isn't much, Jake. Just an old piece of wood." *He turned it around in his hand.* "Maybe I'll keep it when we're through; it'll make a nice walking stick. . . . Here, take it. Go on, you can move, I'll let you."

Jake tried. White pain burned through his arm as he got to his knees. He slumped over.

"Let me." Vritrk *reached down to help him.* "It's almost sad to see you like this. I had expected more."

Jake stood next to Vritrk. *Only now did he smell the pall of fear. It turned his stomach.*

"It is my world." Vritrk *smiled.*

Jake grabbed the Staff. It was heavy and cold. He lifted it up, pointing it towards Vritrk. "No! This is not your world. Damn you. Go to hell."

Vritrk *doubled over, but it was only a second before the laugh came. His laughter filled the world.*

Jake tried again. The Staff was dead in his hand.

Thunder crashed, hitting the air back hard into the lean-to. No one could breathe. The lightning struck the large fir next to the lean-to. A small fire sputtered in the tree where it had split open; in that light they saw that Vritrk *was gone.*

"Molezeen? Jho?" Jake asked.

"I'm . . . is—"

"Vritrk? He's gone?" Jake questioned.

Jho crawled out of his sleeping roll and built up the fire. It sparked and spit. In a few minutes, they were all up and sitting along the front of the lean-to.

Jake's hand throbbed, but nothing was broken, not even the skin. His Staff leaned against his shoulder.

They listened to the water dripping from the trees. It was cold and damp, but no longer ominous.

"He's gone," Molezeen said.

Kendt stood up and walked slowly around the lean-to. He poured a mug of cold *troan*. "Wasn't here."

"What?" Jake said still cradling his hurt hand. "You can't mean it."

"He was never here." Kendt stood in front of Jake, challenging him. "Never."

"Christ! My hand."

Kendt pulled Jake's hand out. "Look at it! All of you." Kendt flattened Jake's fingers. Jake started to yell with the pain, but it didn't come. Kendt turned Jake's hand in the flickering light. "Look."

One by one they did, and one by one they knew that it hadn't really been hurt.

"A dream," Kendt said.

Jake hugged his Staff. He could not feel its tingle. He squeezed it harder, trying to make it feel alive.

"My Staff?" Jake whispered, but no one answered. Jake carried it back to the wall and leaned it next to Molezeen's.

Despair hung like gray smoke over the campsite.

The clouds broke open in jagged black scars, and the moon shone through. Silver light sparkled off the wet leaves and off the puddles. Slowly, the sky cleared.

Behind the lean-to, in the east, light rimmed the horizon.

"No one to greet me?" The voice was rough and catchy as though the speaker had not spoken for a long time. "Not even a hello?"

Jake looked up at the tall black figure. "Go to hell," he mumbled.

They sat, eight figures, in a row in front of the fire, uncaring, unmoved, unmoving.

"This is something," *Vritrk* said. "A crusade. But look at you." He laughed. "I'm glad you are here Jake. Really, I am. I intend to save you. You will watch the rest die—no, I won't actually kill them. I'll turn them into some of my Changelings. You've seen them haven't you?"

Vritrk picked up the cooking can and swished around the warm *troan*. He smelled it. He stuck his finger into it, and licked it. "Mmmm," he said, and he drank it down in one voracious gulp.

"Do you know what I can do?" He wiped his mouth on the back of his hand. "I could change just the smallest part of you into anything I want . . . a ferret's head, feral, angry, rabid, growing from your shoulder, or arm . . . your hand a slippery slug or several more of your heads." *Vritrk* laughed. "You would watch yourself be turned into any variety of things, part by part. It would hurt. You could take that, couldn't you? . . . Imagine your body, no longer yours . . . but mine."

Vritrk talked on. He taunted them, as he walked around the campsite, but to no avail. Despair had gotten them first, and its grasp was stronger.

Stel sat shaking. He had never been so terrified in his life. He wanted to run; he knew that if he could get into the woods he'd have a chance. He tried to move his legs when *Vritrk* was looking at the others. They moved. "The Gods, it had been a dream," he whispered.

He had to wait for the right moment, but he knew it would come.

Stel listened to the voice of Evil. He heard its insults, its threats, and its obscenities. Then he started to think about his cousin and his quest, so hopelessly ended, almost before it had started.

They were helpless; they would not move. He could. He could run off into the woods, back to the Southern farmlands—to safety. Who would know what really had happened? He would be a hero, just for having survived.

Stel realized that this was Evil. They had all worked for this moment. This was Stel's chance to take a stand.

If he could not leave them, what could he do?

Jake felt something tweaking at the threads of the web of gloom that enshrouded them. *Resistance*, Jake thought. He was not sure why that was important, but he felt it was. *Who?* He started to probe the group. *It doesn't matter, we're*— Jake caught himself slipping further into the mire of despondence. *No. Who? Who is it?* He fought to gain control over his feelings and yet remain passive, to draw no attention to himself. Then he knew: *Stel.* Jake's heart sang the name.

Stel stayed as motionless as the rest, but he watched carefully. *Vritrk* walked all around, but he avoided the Staves. *He's afraid of them*, Stel thought. Stel knew that to pick up one meant suicide. Then he saw it. It was a long shot. If he could inch over, nearer to them, if *Vritrk* did not notice, he'd have a chance. When *Vritrk's* back was turned, Stel would stand against the wall. He'd push himself off and grab a Staff as he started to run. It would kill him, yes, but his momentum would carry him into *Vritrk*. If the Staff were to kill, if the power resided in it, Stel, in dying, would deal the deathblow.

If he couldn't kill *Vritrk*, then maybe the attack would

make *Vritrk* loosen his hold over everyone else. *I'm the only one who can help. The only one,* he thought.

He prepared himself: he saw Llo as he had the night before he left. He saw her with d'Solteen as wife and husband; she would be happy. He saw Molezeen, High Priest and victorious over Evil. He saw Jake back in his strange world. The neeZeen would sing of Stel's sacrifice; they would see that they had been wrong about him.

He readied himself.

It took almost ten minutes to slide back across the floor. *Vritrk* never noticed Stel. His attention was obsessively riveted on Jake and Molezeen; what attention remained he directed to d'Solteen and the others.

Vritrk turned his back to Stel.

Now. Stel thought.

"Judge?" Jake said loudly. "Is your fight with them or me?"

"Judge?" *Vritrk* repeated the word. He leaned against the far wall, his arms locked across his chest. "Judge?" he whispered to himself.

Stel grabbed the closest Staff as he leapt forward. His adrenaline pumped. With all his energy, in one last full-out effort, he drove the end of the Staff towards the black head.

Too late, *Vritrk* saw Stel out of the corner of his eye. He sneered at this youthful impudence. *In my world, you'd dare this?* He thought.

Stel felt something hit him—deep, in his soul—but his momentum propelled the point of the Staff. *Vritrk* started to turn his head as the metal tip pierced his left temple with a sound not unlike that of breaking crystal.

Vritrk shrieked.

The Staff impaled *Vritrk* against the wall; it quivered as

Vritrk writhed and his arms flailed. He tried hopelessly to get a purchase on the Staff. He desperately tried to pull it free.

It held fast.

In that instant, whatever had held the band there was released. Everyone was up. They moved away from the twisting body. And Evil died in front of them amidst distant thunderclaps.

Jake felt a passing shudder; he thought he had heard laughter—laughter that mocked their victory.

Moonlight filtered low through the trees over the horizon. A long night was ending.

Molezeen looked down at Stel, motionless on the ground. "He's dead?"

Jake was sitting cross-legged, holding Stel in his lap. "No. He's alive. I don't know how, but he is."

Molezeen got a couple of blankets to wrap around the limp body.

D'Solteen looked at him. "Who would've thought?"

Jho tended the fire. There would be another hour before the sun was up; they needed something to warm them.

They heard a crackling noise. The black figure hung motionless, no longer as cold or black as it had been. They watched as the shell began to break apart. Chunks fell and shattered, collected on the floor like dark slivers of broken mirror. The shell was hollow.

Soan was the first to notice the smell; the smell of the steamy lake, the smell they had encountered when Jake had killed Dusty, only worse. This was deeper, richer in its decay. It didn't come from the shards on the lean-to floor. Soan looked around, puzzled. The others noticed it, too. One by one, they saw him standing on the far side of the fire, pale, strangely puffy.

It was Tesn'. The fingers on his left hand were dripping off; they oozed and bubbled, turning translucent yellow-green. The smell was coming from him.

"Tesn' what is it? What can we do?" Kendt ran to him, but was unable or unwilling to touch him.

Tesn' looked at Kendt, and smiled. It was a malapert, arrogant and contemptuous smile.

"By A'toon! What are you?" Kendt cried, as he moved away.

Seeing Kendt's dismay, Tesn's face contorted back into a look of innocent sufferance. He held out his right hand, pleadingly. "Please. Help me. I need you, my friend. Help me," he whispered.

Kendt knelt in front of Tesn'. He fought with himself to take Tesn's hand. As he touched it—about to take it into his, to give comfort and succor—one of the yellowed fingers dripped into Kendt's hand. Kendt fell backwards, wildly brushing his hand in the mud.

Tesn' smiled. "My father was right about you all." Then he laughed, looking at each of them, one by one. In the cool morning light, they saw his face and arms blister and bubble. Rot dripped from him like fetid raindrops from the trees. "Do you really think you killed him?" he asked.

Those were his last words.

They watched, hypnotized by the degeneration. Tesn', who stood grinning at them, collapsed into his own waste. Their attention was so great that they forgot the odor.

When the sun was up, the deterioration was almost complete. Tesn' had become little more than a heap of throbbing, clabbered liquid. Although his face held its haughty shape, and still seemed aware as it fixed them in its stare.

His senses unable to block out anymore of the horror,

Molezeen retched. It was a signal. They collected their belongings, saddled the horses, and rode away.

No one looked back.

TWENTY-SEVEN

They rode in silence. Jake held Stel, to better work on him. The Staff had not hurt Stel; there wasn't time to worry why. The psychic blow from *Vritrk* had caused some damage, but Jake dealt easily with that. The real damage was what Stel had done to himself. Stel had prepared himself so completely for death—to be killed by the power of the Staff or *Vritrk*—his mind could barely accept life.

They rode all day and all night. They didn't stop until they got to Rim Edge. There in the lower town, they hired a barge to carry them to the Coast Road. Only then did they sleep. It was a three-day trip to the coast.

On the second day, they woke to the sound of bargemen chanting. Molezeen looked around. Birds sang and flitted through the air. Morning haze drifted from the river over the fields. He felt as if their adventure could have been a dream, like the haze melting in the warming sun. At the stern of the barge was a cook fire. The bargemen always kept something hot to drink. Molezeen got up.

He was looking around when he realized that he couldn't find Kendt. He woke Soan. "Have you seen Kendt?"

"Not since we fell asleep." Soan yawned. "But this is the first that I've gotten up. Is there something to drink?"

"Yes. Yes," Molezeen said, turning away to keep looking. He found the Captain, standing at the bow. "Excuse me. I'm looking for Kendt, the old circuit priest. Have you seen him?"

The Captain reached into the pocket of his smudged canvas apron, and pulled out a folded piece of paper. It had Molezeen's name on it. "He left while we were tied up last night. He asked that I give this to you in the morning. Is everything all right?"

"I don't know." Molezeen walked over to a barrel, sat down, and opened the letter.

Molezeen, High Priest and Friend,

As you read this, I should be many miles away. Please do not follow me. Read this and if you care for me let me be.

I should have died many years ago. I was given time; time to find you and time to go with you. I wouldn't trade that for anything. I have come to love you and all the others. Moreover, I am proud to have you all call me friend.

Nevertheless, I am not proud that I was taken in by Tesn'. I know his purpose, and he almost got away with it. I vouched for him. I let him get close to you. In that closeness, he got you to put aside the Staves. He drugged you, as he did me. I don't know how; blinding us with dreams of youth, of love, of things gone and of things to come, and finally of despair.

He led his creator, his father, to us.

And poor Stel. We all saw him as an unruly child. We relegated him to a world of petty, youthful folly; when it was Stel who was willing to sacrifice everything, his entire future, for us.

I am an old man. My time is over. I have lived to feel shame for my aged blindness. In that shame, I cannot continue, not in your company. So I say good-bye. Accept my love and admiration. Give my blessing to everyone.

Kendt

Molezeen wiped the tears from his cheeks. He would miss the old man. He wanted to stop the barge, to go ashore and ride after Kendt. But he knew that Kendt's dignity shouldn't have to suffer such interference.

The Captain stood next to Molezeen. "The old man asked that I give you this, after you'd read the letter." In his hand was a small leather pouch. Molezeen took it. Knowing what he would find in it, he opened it. Inside, was a tightly sealed, crystal bottle. Molezeen closed his hand around it, as if he were squeezing the will to live back into Kendt.

Jake saw Molezeen sitting, trembling in his robes. "How are you?" he asked. "It's Kendt, isn't it?"

"Yes. He blames himself for what we all did. This is his medicine." He held out the brown suede pouch. "He'll die without it."

Jake sat on the gunwale next to Molezeen. "He's lived a long life. A full one. I think I understand, although I don't agree. He doesn't want to be reminded with celebration and praise of what we all would do well to remember, that in the face of Evil, we're weak. I'm sorry that I could not have said good-bye."

"Would we have been strong enough to let him go?" Molezeen asked.

"Perhaps he knows us too well."

Molezeen put the pouch in his pocket, next to the letter. "How's Stel?"

"He'll be all right when he wakes."

"We're all grateful for your help. I don't think he'd have lived if you hadn't helped."

"No, but I wonder if there'd have been any need to help if I'd never come to your world," Jake said.

Molezeen left Jake staring down at the waves washing along the hull. He got a mug of warm *troan* for Stel, who had just opened his eyes.

"Stel? How are you?"

"Cousin, I'm fine. I don't remember much. There's a big hole in my memory. Are we all right? Did you do it?"

"Do it?"

"Yes. Did you kill . . ." Stel stopped, unwilling to say the name.

"Me? Stel, for all of my efforts, for the power of this band, it was you who killed *Vritrk*."

"How could I?"

Molezeen sat down with him. In detail, he described the events. Slowly, as Molezeen talked, Stel's memory returned in pieces. He knew that what Molezeen said was true. But the Stel that listened was no longer the Stel that had boasted, bluffed, and felt hurt at all the world's unfairness. He listened as though he were hearing someone else's story.

Throughout the day, they talked. A feeling of bereavement hung over them. They hadn't realized Kendt's contribution to the band until they had to face his loss. He had been their keystone, locking them together.

They arrived at T'ng'qrt noon the third day. After stabling their horses, they took rooms at the Sunbreak Inn. They bathed and rested. Their clothes were cleaned and dried. The inn offered all the luxuries they would have expected in the capital. They took a small, private room for dinner.

D'Solteen had arranged everything. The menu was set. Wood was stacked neatly next to the large fireplace, with a small fire already started. And the lamps had all been filled.

Instead of their accustomed *troan*, d'Solteen had ordered several pitchers of local wine. They drank a toast. "Please. To Kendt. I know that he accepted a lot of guilt over our adventure, but if there is guilt, we share it equally. In our victory, he should share. Let's remember him for the confidence he gave us, his companionship, his humor, and his sense of rightness. I drink to his memory. May I live to be worthy of it." D'Solteen drained his glass.

Molezeen poured more wine. "I don't want us to turn this into a drink fest. But I would like to formally apologize to Stel, and to accord him the honor he so much deserves." Molezeen bowed to Stel.

During dinner, they retold their story, trying to understand what had happened, and why. They laughed; they fell silent; and they each cried.

Molezeen wondered about Stel. "What was it that kept Stel from being trapped by *Vritrk?*"

"Didn't we all see in Tesn' our own youth? Did we not feel our losses? Did we not dream of what could have been?" Jho suggested, still unable, or unwilling, to shake himself of the raw memories of Rol.

"Maybe that's it. Maybe because Stel is still young, still a youth, he could not be trapped in longing. All he felt for Tesn' was rivalry."

Soan looked at Molezeen. "Yes, but surely he could feel despair, and that doesn't explain why he could hold the Staff."

They looked at Stel for an answer. "I don't know either," he said, feeling uncomfortable being the object of everyone's attention.

"Perhaps his innocence and his conviction were enough to overcome its danger," Molezeen suggested.

D'Solteen nodded. "And Stel's conviction and his resignation insulated him."

They discussed this, back and forth for the rest of dinner.

The waiters cleared the table and left the room. Jake stood up, as uncomfortable with the discussion as Stel seemed to be.

He walked to the stone fireplace. Next to it, leaning against the gray, polished rock mantel were the three black Staves of Li. The one that Stel had used, which had been Jake's, no longer had a bright, silver tip; it was mottled with purples and black where it had pierced *Vritrk's* skull. Jake had tried to polish it, but the discoloration was permanent. He picked it up.

"Stel!"

He tossed it.

Everyone gasped as Stel caught it.

"What hasn't occurred to any of you is that Stel's control over the Staff is no different than mine, or Molezeen's." Jake stood behind Stel, his hands rubbing Stel's shoulders. "He was invisible to *Vritrk*, who was blinded by his own arrogance. *Vritrk* was so ecstatic at the thought of his clever victory; he never thought an innocent—a boy—could defeat him. I think that the blow that he hit Stel with might have killed any of us, and yet Stel did not know he had power. Isn't it time to acknowledge another Staff wielder?"

Molezeen again bowed to Stel. "Jake is right. You do have power. Now I understand what my job is—what Kendt's was. I have tried to make the High Priesthood a position of honor, respect, and sanctity. I've gathered around me men who could contribute to that task, and I've found the next High Priest: my cousin Stel. If you'll accept it?"

Stel sat silent. This was almost too much for him. He was a kid. This could have been one of the prankster god's jokes, except that it was Molezeen, High Priest, not nGin, standing before him. He remembered the trip he never made with his father to the L'zotk. He remembered his friends back in n'Jaspinth, and thought about how much he had wanted to tell them about the adventure. His face flushed when he remembered his part in the attack on d'Solteen. He should not have to make such decisions, not now. Yet, he saw himself at that moment, trying to deny his destiny, all the while holding the Staff of Li that he had used to kill *Vritrk*. How could he dismiss his future? He nodded to Molezeen.

"Then we are gathered here to celebrate another great victory: the continuation of the soul in the priesthood through Stel. Although, with the defeat of *Vritrk*, we won't be in as much need for it."

"I wonder," Jake said, still standing behind Stel. "Did anyone else hear the thunder?" The room quieted. They all knew what he was saying. "The shell of Virtrk's body was empty, but remember Tesn's last words. I think that although we should celebrate, we should also pledge our support to Stel, who may be in greater need of it than we know."

Every one took a turn to toast the group, to toast Stel, and to pledge to fight Evil.

Molezeen turned to Jake. "My friend, I think you've lost weight. Could that be?"

They all laughed.

"Show us the magic you did for the children," Stel asked. "What d'Solteen saw."

Jake looked around. None of these men had seen his magic, except d'Solteen. They would be a great audience. Jake excused himself. "I'll need some things. Give me a few minutes." It took ten minutes and the help of six members of the inn's staff to find what he wanted. He stepped back into the room. He stalled. He tied several of the napkins in knots and juggled them. He told jokes, most of which the neeZeeners did not understand. They tried not to laugh even when they got the jokes.

"Don't think we're going to make this easy for you," d'Solteen yelled.

A waiter brought in a box, which he set down in front of Jake on the table. Jake sifted through it; he had enough, although none of it looked magical to anyone.

He started his patter. He told stories, made up magic words, and made things disappear. For two hours, he worked his spell. His hands were clumsy, blistered, and sore, but everything worked. He did card tricks with a neeZeen deck, thirty-seven cards, including the wild card. The cards were bigger than what he was used to, and they weren't slick. In the flickering lamplight, his fingers found their way, loosening up with practiced routines.

Within a few minutes, everyone had given in to the spirit of the night, and they laughed and cheered. Most of the inn's staff sneaked in to watch, including the innkeeper.

Jake let everyone try some of the tricks, pretending to show them the secret, but always leaving out something. He repeated everything. No one caught on to a trick.

It was midnight when he finished. Molezeen suggested one last drink before they turned in.

"Please, it's on the house," the innkeeper said, and he brought in his best liqueur and enough crystal glasses for everyone, including his staff.

Molezeen filled the glasses. They toasted Jake. He basked in their admiration. "I love a good audience," he said.

As they chatted, Jake emptied his glass. "Molezeen, please, could you pass the . . ."

TWENTY-EIGHT

". . . cream."

Jake blinked, startled by the light. It took a few seconds to recognize Sammy's Restaurant. "The cream?"

The Judge's right hand shook as he slid it across the table towards the cream pitcher. He could not tell when he was touching it, and knocked it over. He looked embarrassed. Their waiter came over with a new pitcher of cream and several napkins.

"Thank you. We're fine," Jake said, not wishing to have to deal with someone else. "I'll clean this up."

He looked at the Judge. *He's had a stroke,* he thought. The Judge's right eye drooped. Under his white hair at his left temple was a bright red splotch; there was a hint of moisture, a slight drop of saliva, coalescing at the right corner of his mouth; and his right hand was palsied.

"Judge, do you know me?"

The Judge tried to smile; it was lopsided. His head shook.

"Who am I?"

He struggled to find the words, as though they were in a fog. "Y. . . y . . . r" Tears welled in his eyes as he made the effort to remember something he knew he couldn't.

"My name is Jake." He paused, looking carefully at the Judge's face. "Do you remember Mrs. Winslow and her son Martin? Do you remember where they are?"

The Judge sat motionless except for the shake. There was no sign of recognition. Jake probed, but he knew it was hopeless; most of the Judge's recent memories were gone.

Jake motioned to the maître d'. "Call 911. The Judge has had a stroke. Also, I'll take the check."

Jake sat with the Judge, waiting for the ambulance. "You'll be fine. . . . You've had a stroke." Jake gently wiped the Judge's mouth with a napkin. "The ambulance is on the way. . . ."

Jake tried to help the paramedics.

"We'll take it from here sir."

"He's had a stroke. He's—"

"We know. Now please, we'll take good care of him."

Jake sat back down, and watched the paramedics put the Judge onto their gurney, and wheel him out.

The maître d'—now ever so polite—tried to refuse payment for lunch. Jake would not hear of it. He left the money, and went out to his car.

He walked slowly. He felt fine, but he was slightly disoriented from the change in reality. He found his VW around the corner in a public lot. He drove to Kent.

Mac had left a note for Jake on Roy's door. Mac was waiting for Jake at the hospital. Jake fumbled through the bag of maps in his van looking for the Kent street guide. It took him a while to locate the hospital.

Jake found Mac sitting in the emergency room lounge area.

"How's Roy?" Jake asked.

"He'll be okay. Angelica is with him now. The doctor taped his chest and gave him some Tylenol. They're checking him for other internal damage. The doctor is impressed. You must have done a great job on him. He said that the external damage indicates far greater trauma, but it's not there. I'm sorry, I'm just going on. What have you found out? I heard that something happened to the Judge."

"How did you hear that?"

"There was a little news blurb on the TV. Did you—"

"Later. What I did not find out was where Bonnie and Martin are. I've got to poke around. Why don't you see that Roy and Angie get home. Then come by my apartment. If I'm not there, wait. I shouldn't be long."

Jake left Mac, and drove back to Cleveland. He had to talk with some of the Judge's boys. From what Lt. Dombrosky had said, the first place to check would be Camden House.

It took Jake a half-hour of driving around to find it. He knew it was off the park in Tremont, but the area had become chic. The buildings refurbished and painted. Mercedes and BMW's were parked along streets that Jake remembered being lined with junkers. His sense of the tarnished landmarks was confused by their shining.

At Camden House, it was easy to recognize the Judge's boys. They reacted to him because they knew who he was. But they were at loose ends; they had heard about the Judge's illness, and his control was over.

Of the four boys, Jake singled out the tallest as their leader. "You know who I am?"

"Yeah."

"Then you must know that I'm looking for Mrs. Winslow and Martin. Where are they?"

"I don't know 'em."

"What about the rest of you?" Jake asked.

They shook their heads.

Jake's patience was running thin. He made little effort at subtlety. He marched through their leader's mind. "Where are they?"

"He had them driven to Pennsylvania."

"Where?"

"I don't know. He had someone with us. I didn't know him. He took them."

Jake was angry. He had lost the trail. He released the boy. "If any of you hear anything, call me. There's an answering machine on my home phone."

Jake drove around for a while, trying to get his bearings. "Ed Forbs," Jake said aloud. "Why not?"

He drove to the Judge's house in Bratenahl. It was one those few magnificent houses along the lake. Although his was one of the smallest, it was still fifteen rooms, on two and a half acres.

The house had been built for one of the Cleveland steel magnates, designed by an architectural firm out of Ithaca, New York. Something had happened to the original owners. No one ever found out exactly what, although there was a story of an illegitimate child, and rumors of two wives. The house was sold to a prominent trial attorney who had a dock and a boathouse put in. During prohibition, he ran whiskey in from Canada, sixty miles across Lake Erie, in a twenty-two foot Hacker. The boathouse was torn down during the fifties, but the stairs and dock were left.

Several sections of the fleur-de-lis topped wrought iron fence had rusted loose from their anchors in the stone and brick columns along the street side of the estate. They hung askew, like besotted watchmen. Jake smiled, seeing that the Judge had allowed the disrepair that acted as a counterpoise to his otherwise fastidious character. The serpentine brick drive was three hundred feet long, winding through a small forest that shielded the house from the street. The house looked like a small French chateau, of stucco and stone, with leaded windows. The drive ended at the carriage house, which was a miniature of the main house. Jake wondered what it would be like to live in that space—let alone the house—as he walked to the door. "Probably fill it up pretty quick," he thought.

He rang the bell. It took several minutes for someone to get the door. It was Ed.

"How are you?" Jake asked.

"I'm fine. Do I know you? I—"

"I'm Jake. I took you to the hospital." Jake offered his hand.

"Sorry, I know what you did, thank you. But I never got a look at you, at least not that I remember." Ed shook Jake's hand. "Come in, but my father's not here."

"I know. He's . . . in the hospital."

"What happened?"

"He had a stroke. I don't know where they took him, but I'm sure they'll call you. Actually, I came to talk to you."

Ed led Jake into the library. For a minute or two, Jake's love of books got the better of him. He browsed the shelves.

"Can I get you something?"

"What? Oh, it's hard not to be impressed. Do they get read?"

"Some. My father used to collect. That is, when I was kid. He doesn't use this room much."

"Ed, what can you tell me about Mrs. Winslow and Martin?" Jake asked, pulling out a leather bound edition of *Morte d'Arthur.* "Where are they?"

"I don't know, really, I don't."

"One of the boys at Camden House said Pennsylvania. What does that mean?"

"My father has some colleagues there, people who do him favors."

Jake rifled through the pages. He stopped at each steel engraving, printed on heavier paper and protected by a thin sheet of glassine. He closed the book and slid his fingers over the waxed, maroon leather. "Come on, Ed. Who? Where?"

"All I know, is they're near Pittsburgh. That's it."

Jake sensed that Ed was being honest.

Mac's car was out front when Jake got back to the apartment. He parked his green and cream-colored van in back, in the garage. For a minute, he was distracted, rubbing his hand along the rust spots. Were they were bigger than yesterday? Soon they'd connect and . . . he didn't want to spend the money, but he knew the van wouldn't last if he didn't get it fixed up. "Mac!" Jake remembered.

He ran up the back stairs into the kitchen. Mac was in the living room.

"I've been here about twenty minutes," Mac yelled when he heard the kitchen door slam shut. "I poured you a Scotch. It's on the table."

He had pulled a chair in from the dining room—he always felt funny sitting in a barber chair. Jake paced.

"Did you find out where they are?"

"They're probably in Pittsburgh."

"It's not much. Is it enough?"

"I hope so."

Mac looked too worried. "Are you going to be okay?" Jake asked.

"Oh, yeah. I'm fine. I'm just worried about them. What happened to the Judge?"

"It's a long story. We met for lunch. We dreamshared. But it was more than anything I've ever experienced, more complete."

Mac was staring at Jake, waiting for more. "Like what?"

"It was a world, with a history, a tradition, a culture. It was very, very real . . . and it wasn't . . . a dream. I'm not sure I want to talk about it until I've had more time."

"Okay, but what about the Judge?"

Jake stopped by the front door. He had a collection of walking sticks in a green, tarnished, brass umbrella stand, with angry griffins embossed on it, in the corner. Mindlessly, he picked out a thin, cherry stick, with a scrimshaw handle. He sat down in one of the red leather barber chairs, and rolled it between his fingers while sipping his Scotch.

"The Judge?" Jake mused. "Well he had the pointed end of a very dangerous staff pushed through his temple."

"And here?"

"Here, he had a stroke. Unfortunately, it destroyed much of his memory. I doubt that he even remembers who Bonnie is. He barely recognized me."

Jake kept spinning the stick, as if he were weaving his thoughts. Something slowly began to take shape. "You're more worried about this than I've ever seen you."

"Come on Jake, Mrs. Winslow—"

Jake was squinting at Mac with one eye, "Mrs. Winslow?"

"Okay, Bonnie, and Martin. We lost them. They should have been safe. I'm worried for them."

"You're in love!" Jake grinned.

"I'm a priest."

"You're a man first. And, you're in love. Have you thought about this?"

Mac sighed. He had tried to deny his feelings—to bury them—but if Jake knew. . . . "Jake I've thought about it. What do you think? Do you know what this means?"

"Yes, I do. I think I—"

"I have to make a choice, don't I? If we find her; don't I? I have seen myself as a priest all my life. It's what I do, and what I am. How do I just turn my back on that? Or is this just a test of my strength?"

"Come off it." Jake lightly tapped the cane on floor, punctuating his thoughts. "Your vows of celibacy, you know where they came from: they aren't religious, they grew out of economic concerns and the problems of nepotism. They hang on as extra baggage. I know how seriously you take them, in spite of their foolishness." Jake stopped; a dull spot on the ivory had caught his attention. He wiped the side of his nose with his index finger, and used the oils to polish the ivory.

"But this isn't a test of your faith. It's a test of your religion's ability to be compassionate." Jake held the ivory closer, examining its sheen in the lamplight. He stared over it at Mac. "And it is that which has failed you."

"Jake, it's not that simple."

"Actually, it is. But you're too close to see it now."

"If you don't need me, at least for a while, I want to go pray."

"Certainly. Come back when you're through."

Mac drove to the Carmelite Monastery. It would be closed, but the Mother Superior would let him in. The chapel was plain and white, with black metal grills along one wall, about twelve feet off the floor. The cloistered sisters could attend Mass from there, unseen.

Mac had gone there now and again. Its simplicity made him feel closer to God. As he knelt in prayer, he heard in his mind the opening strains of Schutz's *Resurrection*, "Die Auferstehung unsers Herren Jesu Christi. . . ."

He never felt the tears wetting his face as he prayed.

TWENTY-NINE

Jake took the call shortly after nine.

"Mr. Kry . . . Jake?"

"Yes. Ed?"

"Yeah. I just remembered something. Stuff is coming back to me. I'm remembering things, since my father's stroke. He said to someone, I think one of the men who took Mrs. Winslow and Martin, he was on the phone, that if they didn't hear from my father in a week, they . . . were to take care of them."

"Take care of them?"

"You know . . . kill them."

"That's it?"

"Yeah. I've tried to think if there was more, but I can only remember that."

Mac came back at around ten. "Jake, you were right. I just wish it were easier for me."

Jake was working on a large tumbler of Scotch. "Jake, you okay?"

"Mac sit down. We got a problem."

Mac sat in the barber chair opposite Jake. "What happened?"

"The clock is running. I got a call from Ed Forbs. With his father's influence gone, things have been coming back to him. He remembered that the Judge gave instructions to the men who took Bonnie and Martin. They are to be killed in a week if their captors don't hear from the Judge."

"God in Heaven! What do we do?"

"That's all Ed said, and I believe him. Knowing that they might be in Pittsburgh, that's a help."

"You sound as if you really believe that, sitting there working on a pint of Scotch."

"Okay, okay. After the call from Ed, I called Bobbie in Pittsburgh. He'll start a search. He said he'd call first thing in the morning. So we wait."

It was a long night. Neither Mac nor Jake needed an alarm to get up. They were both in the kitchen by six, drinking coffee.

The call came at a quarter of seven. "Jake? Bobbie. I didn't wake you did I?"

"No, we've been up—feels like I never slept—Mac's here, too. What do you have?"

"Actually, not much, but I think I will. We have located someone with ties to the Judge. I'm going out this morning to talk to him. Why don't you get over here? If you leave now, I could wait for you."

"We can be there in three hours. See you then."

Jake hung up and poured a little more coffee. "Want to drive to Pittsburgh?"

"They found them?"

"No, but Bobbie has a lead."

They finished their coffee. Within ten minutes, they were in Jake's VW.

"I think we're being followed," Mac said.

Jake fiddled with his rear view mirror. "The blue car?"

Mac was looking out his window into the passenger side mirror. "Yes."

"Let's see." Jake took the next turn, down Mornington Lane. He drove back toward his apartment. The blue car was following them. Through a gap in the traffic, he got across the boulevard. He cut up onto the common drive behind the apartment building, then down an alley to Mayfield. "It'll take us twenty minutes longer to get there, but we've lost them."

"Shouldn't we drive something less conspicuous?"

Jake laughed. "And give up all this luxury? Never."

Mac kept his eye out for anyone who might be following them, but it looked as though they were in the clear.

"Well, what did you decide last night?"

"Jake, you're right. I do love Bonnie. When we find them, I'm going to ask her to marry me."

"And the priesthood?"

"If what I'm doing with my life is helping people, I can help even if I'm not a priest."

"Are you sure?"

"Are you trying to dissuade me? Yes, I'm sure. I went to the Carmelites last night. After I prayed, I talked with the Mother Superior. Maybe because there's been so much trouble in the Church with women, I don't know, but she was very perceptive and understanding. We talked—she reminds me a little of you—anyway, yes, I'm sure. Maybe this is something that's been growing inside me for a while—a dissatisfaction with the Church—even before Bonnie. But my love for her has brought everything to a head."

"You have my fullest support. And if you need a job . . . The Bookstall can always use a full-time clerk."

They exited at Sharpsburg. They were a few blocks away from Bobbie's house, stopped at a traffic light. "The parking is terrible 'round here," Jake said. "If you see anything, yell, we'll take it . . . Ah, there."

Jake aimed for a space on the other side of the intersection. As Jake took the key out of the ignition, Mac saw that they were in front of an antique store. "Jake, no. Come on; this isn't the time."

"Hey, I promise, just a quick once through."

"I should've known you'd pull something like this," Mac said locking the door. "I'm going in with you. If you get into one of your shopping moods, I'm going to deck you on the spot."

The store had just opened. Mac walked in reluctantly, but not Jake. This was his world. Jake had been to so many antique stores that it was as if he knew what it had and where. He avoided the china and bottles. He looked under tables and behind shelves. He was determined.

"Jake, come on," Mac said looking at his watch.

"In a minute, in a minute."

"You said that fifteen minutes ago."

Jake let out a whoop. "Here, here." Calling to the clerk, "How much?"

The clerk, a young woman with long red hair, wore a dark blue corduroy skirt and jacket. *Probably the owner's daughter,* Jake thought. She walked toward them. "Isn't there a price on it?" she asked.

"No."

She knelt down, and crawled under the table next to Jake. There, behind a painted wood chest, under an Amish quilt, was a large, horn-shaped device. At its open end, were six colored lights; the other end narrowed to a bracket, with a bundle of electrical wires coming out. "What is it?" she asked.

"How much?"

"I don't do the pricing. My dad does, and he's out on a buying trip; I expect him back tonight."

"Can I leave a deposit?"

"Well, sure, I guess." She worked her way back out from

under the table, and blushed the color of her hair when she saw Mac standing behind her, beside the counter.

"I'm with him," Mac said as if to apologize for standing where he was.

She pulled an old tattered receipt book out from under a stack of mail and removed the rubber band that held it together. "How much do you want to leave?"

"How's twenty sound?" Jake asked, wiping his hands on his pants.

She took Jake's name and address, and filled out a deposit receipt. "What do I call it?"

Jake smiled. "That's the Color Ray Emanator for a Hemiodemagnitizer!"

In the car, Mac would not stop staring at Jake. "Here we are in a life and death chase, and you're poking around for junk."

"Mac, you know I've been looking for that for months. What a find. It looks perfect."

Sometimes it was easy to be made at Jake, Mac thought, *very easy.*

Bobbie was waiting for them on his porch. He met them, and got into Jake's van. "Bobbie, you remember Mac?"

"Yeah, how's it going?" Bobbie stuck out his huge hand. He was one of Jake's weightlifting friends.

"Where to?"

"Go straight. I'll tell you where to turn."

It occurred to Mac that there was a reason why they hadn't driven his Chevette. Bobbie wouldn't have fit.

"Dave's watching the office. A Mr. Totwald, the guy's a lawyer. I don't know if he knows anything, but he's one of the Judge's buddies."

"How'd you find him so quickly?" Mac asked shaking his head.

"We watch for guys like this. You get to know who's who after a while. When Jake called last night, it wasn't too hard to connect him and the Judge."

"Jake, this network of yours is something else." Mac couldn't get used to it. Time and again, Jake would turn to them, weightlifters all over the world. Somehow they would do anything for Jake, just for friendship.

They parked as close as they could, which was near the river. The office was in an upscale converted brick warehouse. Dave met them at the corner.

"Hey, Jake, how are you? He's still in there. You want company?"

"I'm fine. Why don't you and Bobbie wait outside? Mac and I'll go in . . . we don't need to be intimidating."

Mr. Totwald was in a meeting; the receptionist was reluctant to break in with a message. Jake convinced her that it would not be a problem.

"He said he'd be out in a few minutes," she told them.

They sat down in the dark green leather wingback chairs. Jake was poking through the magazines on the table, thinking that law offices always felt the same, when he jumped to his feet. He looked at the receptionist. "Where'd he go?"

"He's in his office, I just talked with him. What do you mean?"

"He's gone."

"I told you he—"

Jake squinted at her.

"I'll call."

She dialed his number; there was no answer. "He has a private door, but how . . . how'd you know?"

"Does Mr. Totwald own property, something commercial, a factory or a warehouse, like that? Close by?"

"Yes . . . a warehouse, on Twenty-third," looking at her address book, "729, Twenty-third."

"Anything else?"

"No, nothing on this side of town."

Jake turned to Mac. "Quick, let's go."

They ran outside. Bobbie and Dave were a little surprised to see them so quickly. "Dave, is your car close? Mine's down near the river."

"Around the corner. Why?"

"Let's go. Our Mr. Totwald split. 729 Twenty-third."

They found the address; it was one of a dozen factory buildings. They parked along the side. The building had been divided up and leased. The serpentine hallway wound around, in between, and through seventeen different companies. As they looked around, they asked for Mr. Totwald.

It took twenty minutes. Mr. Totwald had gone to the building manager's office, on the third floor. The secretary was startled to see four men barge into her suddenly very small office.

"We're looking for Mr. Totwald. I understand he's here." Jake stared.

"Yes, he was, but you missed him. He left fifteen minutes ago."

"Did he have anyone with him? A woman and a young boy?"

"Yes . . . his cousin from Chicago, I think he said, and her son. They weren't feeling well."

"What do you mean?"

"They didn't look good. Neither spoke."

"Where'd they go?"

"He didn't say."

They left. Mac wanted them to walk faster. "Come on."

"Slow down. We don't know where to go. It's back to the phone. Damn, we were close, weren't we?" Jake said.

"He's going to kill them."

"I think he's going to wait the week, or else he'd have done it already."

"I hope they're okay," Mac said and he whispered a silent prayer.

They drove back to Bobbie's house. To Mac's dismay, they talked weightlifting the whole way.

"Jake, there's a kid you've got to check out," Bobbie said. "He's in Massachusetts, someplace. You remember Dave?"

"Holyoke, I think."

"We heard about him at the Regionals. He's, I don't know, sixteen or seventeen. Weighs one twenty-three, and does double body weight."

"Double . . . where's he training?"

"He's been working out at the Y. Someone said that even Armand is thinking of working with the kid."

"I thought he's retired?"

Mac was about to interrupt them, to change the subject, when they stopped.

Bobbie's house was bare. He had been married, but his wife left him two years ago. She took the children and cleaned everything out while he was at work. Bobbie kept it empty.

Jake and Mac looked around. The only decoration was the mantel lined with trophies and awards. Fifteen years ago, Bobbie had been a contender for the Olympics, until he tore the quadriceps in his left leg during a meet. He still lifted, but not in competition. "You never did like furniture," Jake said.

Bobbie smiled; only Jake or Dave could get away with teasing. "Yeah, but at least I don't collect junk. Coffee?"

They sat around in the kitchen. Bobbie had bought a

cheap chrome and Formica kitchen set, with five matching chairs; they looked cheap, but they were sturdy.

"What can we do?" Mac asked.

"Everything we can," Jake said. "Bobbie, you've got friends in the police department. You get in touch. Give them a description, names, everything. Meanwhile, Dave will take us around to check things out, okay?"

Dave nodded.

"What the hell is going on? The Judge may have had some hidden agenda—whatever you call it—against Bonnie and Martin. But he's out of the picture. So why does this Totwald run? Why wouldn't he just release them?" Mac asked.

Bobbie didn't believe in sugar. "Poison, pure poison." And cream, of course was fattening. So Jake didn't ask for anything, and sipped it black. He, too, wondered about Totwald's intentions. Mac was right; it was odd. He felt himself shudder as he swallowed. "What is going on?"

***

Chemmg showed up in the morning. Jake was exhausted; the nightlong struggle had taken its toll. "I thought this was just fantasy?" Chemmg asked Jake as he untied him from the tree.

"I could have died."

"Yes, I know. That is the point. But you didn't, did you? Here, I brought your clothes. Get dressed; I'll help you down. We'll have some hot tea."

Chemmg led the way back down the mountain. It was cold and wet, although the only snow was above the tree line. The trail down to their camp was a mile and a half long. It took them forty minutes.

They had a new, four-man tent that they shared. It was

warm and roomy. Chemmg had already made tea, which he had put in a thermos.

"So, my American wise guy, what do you have to say?"

"What was it?"

"Evil."

Jake was trying not to think about it, yet he wanted to know more. "Where'd it come from?"

"You."

"That's too easy."

"You want me to give you an answer; an explanation for that which I don't think can be explained. Greater men than you or me have spent their lives trying to find an acceptable theory. What they say, and I, and someday you, is cloaked in mysticism, because there is no other way to describe it."

"Mysticism?"

"What would you have me say?" Chemmg said patiently. "It's a God? Or, Evil is a being? Or, perhaps you would prefer to hear that Evil is Nature? No. Evil is real. Evil is inside us."

Jake poured another cup of tea. "If it's from me, then what is it that you've devoted your life to fight? You're telling me that you're fighting Evil imagined by you?"

"Jake, for those born in Tibet, born in a world of great limitations, Gods and Demons walk the land. We've structured our theology within those limitations. I didn't even think to question my Master until I had studied with him for twenty years. You've been with me for five, and you question my every word. That is your culture, and that is you. But if you want an answer, one you can accept, I can't give it to you."

"So what do I do?"

"Forget the epistemology of Evil. It will find you. Just when you think that you've been victorious, it will strike back. It never dies."

"So what is it?"

"Evil is in us all, and Evil exists aside from man. But you won't have to worry much; it will never give you that much time."

***

"Jake, you don't have to drink it black. Bobbie said he bought some sugar and a small cream; although he said he likes watching you drink it straight . . . Jake?"

"Oh, yeah. Great." Jake sheepishly looked at Mac. "I was just thinking about your question."

Bobbie pushed a small box of sugar and the waxed cardboard box of cream towards Jake. "I just didn't want to hear you complain about the coffee. But what you don't use you take with you."

Jake started to mix the coffee, cream and sugar. Bobbie nudged Dave. "I love this. He'll get it screwed up and then tell us how good it is . . . every time."

Jake pretended to be mad at Bobbie. He tried to squint at him in the way he knew he did when he was mad. It looked as though he was imitating a Pekinese.

Jake stopped smiling and got serious. "Mac, maybe the Judge wasn't alone in wanting Bonnie and Martin. That would explain something; although I want to know why."

THIRTY

It was a long afternoon. Bobbie had left to meet with his police officer friends. Jake and Dave were out checking with some of their contacts. Mac had declined to go with Jake, saying that he needed some time alone. "Anyway, you'll want someone to answer the phone." But it meant that he had nothing to do.

Mac paced.

He found a stack of weightlifting magazines under a pile of folded brown paper bags next to the refrigerator. They were the only reading material in the house. One of them was from England. It had an editorial against drugs in lifting by J. Krajczynski.

"Damn him!" Mac yelled at the magazine, and sent it windmilling across the room. He resumed his pacing.

Dave and Jake arrived back half an hour later.

"You know, you've screwed it all up," Mac yelled at Jake. "You and your damn antiques."

Jake just stood in the doorway. He knew that his quirks bothered people sometimes, but he rationalized them by saying that they never hurt anyone—except this time.

"We wasted . . . twenty or thirty minutes, looking for God knows what. For what, Jake? Twenty minutes. That's how much we missed them by, twenty minutes."

"I—" Jake couldn't look at Mac. Rightly or not, he felt Mac had a point. "I've got to pee," Jake mumbled, and went upstairs to the bathroom.

"Jesus, Mac. You didn't have to come down on him like that. He feels real bad about all this," Dave whispered to Mac.

"Jake feels bad? I'm not the one who stopped at the antique store when we should have been looking for Bonnie and Martin."

"Think about it. You're being a real jerk. Totwald didn't bolt until you and Jake showed up at his office. It wouldn't have made any difference if you had been twenty minutes earlier or an hour later."

"But—"

Dave's stare made Mac stop and think.

"Sorry. It's me Gaelic temper," Mac apologized in his best brogue. "I've had all afternoon to get worked up."

"Don't tell me. Tell Jake."

Mac went into the kitchen and found three cans of beer in the refrigerator. He was just handing one to Dave when Jake came down. "Sorry," he said to Jake. "I wasn't thinking. It wasn't your fault. I shouldn't have yelled at you. . . . Here's a beer."

"Thanks. But I do feel bad about this anyway."

"No one called," Mac said, slurping the foam spilling up out of the can. "Did you two learn anything?"

"Nothing, but we've got people looking. If Totwald moves, we'll know about it."

They finished the beer.

"I found a case in the broom closet, but they're warm." Mac came out of the kitchen with three more cans.

It was dark outside when Bobbie got back. "I think there might be trouble." Bobbie smiled hopefully. "A few guys on bikes followed me."

"Did you try to lose them?" Mac asked.

"Why should I? You guys drinking my beer?"

Mac handed him the can he had just opened. "It's one of the warm ones; I—"

"You come into my house and rob me blind. You're almost as bad as my ex."

They heard the sound of motorcycles. Bobbie suggested they go out and meet their new friends. He walked across the street while Jake, Dave, and Mac looked on from the porch.

Parked opposite the house were four bikes. The riders were leaning against them.

"You following me?"

One of the bikers moved away from his bike, toward Bobbie. "Yeah. So what?"

"I don't like bikers," Bobbie said as he walked closer. "Guess I don't like bikes much either. The lawyer hire you?"

"Don't know what you mean."

Bobbie pretended to look disappointed. "And we were getting off to a good start," he said as he lifted the bike off the ground. "Looks like you got a bad kick stand." He swung the bike out into the street and let it go. "You can scratch the paint if you're not careful."

"You shouldn't have—"

Two of the others grabbed his arms. "Pete, let it go. He said, 'No trouble.' Anyway, he's paid us enough—"

"He who?" Jake asked, standing behind them. "Who're you working for?"

The one named Pete started to turn away, but froze, a tremor passed through him, as though he were struggling with something.

"Who?"

"Joe Totwald."

"Where is he?"

"I don't know."

"How do you contact him?"

"He's got a portable phone."

"The number? What's the number?"

"497-2225."

Pete's companions were staring at Jake. One of them took a swing at him. With surprising speed, Jake blocked the blow and grabbed the man's wrist. A slight twist and the man was on the ground. It was enough.

"Okay, we're gone," the biker said.

They collected themselves and their bikes and rode away. Bobbie was looking at Jake. "How do you do that? It gives me the willies every time I see it."

"How do you lift a bike?"

"That's easy. I. . . yeah . . . it's easy."

"We got a number," Bobbie said to Mac as they went into the house. "Totwald's private phone."

"What do we do? Call?" Mac was excited. "Let's give it to the police."

"No," Jake said. "We don't call, not now. Bobbie, you've got people out looking, right?"

Bobbie nodded.

"Good, get the number to them."

Mac was fidgeting. "At least, let's tell the police."

"Mac, calm down. They'd have no problem getting the number themselves, but they need to go to court to be able to tap the phone. We'll give Bobbie's people a chance first. And why don't we do some pizza? Then we'll get back into it in the morning."

Mac and Jake had sleeping bags in the living room. Bobbie slept in his bedroom; Dave had gone home. Jake didn't say anything to them, but he was uneasy. Totwald wasn't just operating on the Judge's behalf, although it may have started that way. Totwald was doing things on his own. He was a player.

Jake knew, as these things always repeated themselves, there would be another attack. He slept lightly for an hour. It was enough. Then he got up and moved to the corner. What worried him was that where the Judge had been skillful in the psychic world, Totwald seemed to depend on muscle. Jake could handle this one on one, but if these guys used guns the odds shifted.

He heard something outside the house: two men. They were quiet. Jake woke Mac, "Shhh . . . crawl over to the stairs . . . and get up them. Now. Don't come down until I call you," Jake whispered. He left the two sleeping bags plumped up.

Five minutes passed. One man opened the front door; the other came in through the kitchen. They were armed with pistols fitted with silencers. Together, they shot into the bags. By the time they realized the bags were empty, Jake had them.

***

They left San Francisco in Jake's Corvette. It was a great car. He had paid $500 for it—for a 1953 red 'vette. It was a preproduction model, serial number 00029. For someone like Jake, it was the most powerful, beautiful, car he would ever own. The white leather seats were comfortable and designed for driving. He could drive for hours without fatigue. Once, he took it to a Corvette Club meeting. Most of the members were into Stingrays, which to Jake epitomized everything wrong with Detroit. Even by '57, they had screwed up its design, adding more chrome and interrupting its smooth, round, lines.

A couple of men came over to look at it. They were upset with Jake; the lighter and doorknobs were not original. He mentioned that he was considering having it painted, but when he said that he didn't care about matching the original color they walked away.

Jake loved the car, although the convertible top's rear window had yellowed so much that he couldn't see through it.

When he lived in LA, he loved to drive through the canyons. On weekends, he would drive up the Coast Highway. But during the time he was in San Francisco, he hadn't driven much.

Chemmg didn't share Jake's love for the car. He didn't dislike it; he just didn't understand the American love affair with cars. They drove east, to Merced, where Chemmg was living. They pulled into a diner at noon. Jake didn't notice the beige LeSabre follow them in. Chemmg did.

Jake ordered a hamburger with the works; Chemmg had tea and a slice of apple pie. Two men were waiting for them in the parking lot. Jake never saw it coming. Chemmg spun, kicking the gun out of one man's hand and pinning the other against a car. Both men seemed to go blank—that's what it looked like to Jake—and collapsed to the ground.

Jake let out a moan. "Aw, look what they did. My car!"

Chemmg could see nothing out of the ordinary, nothing that should have upset Jake. "I don't see any—"

"The tires. Look, they cut all four. They can't be repaired."

"That is serious?"

"Don't you know anything? Jeez! All four."

"I know horses and oxen, not cars. Why don't we take theirs?"

"And leave this?"

"You said we can't afford new tires," Chemmg argued, "and these can't be repaired. What is left? Anyway, you won't need a car with me."

Jake somehow felt convinced. As they drove away in the Buick, Jake turned on the air conditioning. "At least that's something," he thought. He asked about the men.

"They don't want me to meet or work with you. They don't want me to pass on to you what I know."

Jake didn't ask who they were; he knew he didn't want to know.

"Why don't they just shoot you, or me?"

"They might. There is nothing that dictates their methods, other than their own preferences."

"We're targets?"

"We were in your bright red car." Chemmg laughed. "We'll be fine when we get to my apartment."

***

Mac waited upstairs for a few minutes. He had heard the muffled gunshots and some scuffling, but if Jake wanted him to stay out of the way, then that's what he was going to do. Bobbie, on the other hand, lived there, and he wasn't going to hide from anyone.

"Mac get down here. They're gone!"

Bobbie pushed one of the bags away. There were two quarter inch holes in the floor. He picked up the other bag. There were three more holes. "Shit, they've got Jake."

Mac shook his head. "I think he has them. He knew they were coming in, and, see, there's no blood."

"What do we do now?"

"Sleep, if we can. In the morning, we'll do what we were going to do anyway."

279

Mac didn't sleep, he shut his eyes, he lay still, but he didn't sleep. He thought about Bonnie and how his life was about to change—if they could find her. If Jake was okay.

When it was light, he got up and made coffee. Bobbie came down when he was pouring the first cup.

"You look like shit, didn't sleep?"

"A fine way to talk to a priest, and no, I didn't."

"Oh, sorry. You look like shit, Father."

Dave showed up half an hour later. They told him what had happened. They decided to stick together. First, they drove to a little, corner diner. "Let's get breakfast," Bobbie said as he got out of the car; then, as an aside to Mac, "Great food, and great prices."

"Hi, Bobbie," said the waitress behind the counter. "Dave. How you boys doin'?"

"Fine, Rose," Bobbie said. He led them to the booth in the corner. It had six place settings, and seemed too small.

"The usual?" Rose asked.

Bobbie and Dave nodded.

"Just toast." Mac said.

The usual was, as far as Mac could tell, everything on the menu.

"Cream?" Rose asked as she unloaded her tray onto the table.

"Come on, Rose," Bobbie said patting his stomach, "you know it's fattening."

They were almost through when two policemen came in and joined them. "This is Father Mac. Mac, this is Larry, and this is Sid. Mac works with Jake."

They all shook hands and made small talk for a while.

"Nothin' for us, Rosie," Larry said.

While she cleared the table, Bobbie told them about the

bikers, and that Jake had disappeared, leaving behind five bullet holes in his floor.

Larry pulled out a notebook. "This Totwald is slime. He's one of those lawyers who goes beyond what he has to in order to get his clients off. He defends hoods. Shit, there isn't a cop in the city, even the bad ones, who wouldn't love to see him go down. But we can't get a thing on him. He's got powerful friends. Let's see. . . . He's got a warehouse down near the river on Twenty-third and several houses in Mount Oliver. He has associations with the Mazetti's. . . . They own too much to list. Although, if you need it, I could get you a printout."

"You serious about kidnapping? You going to press charges?" Sidney asked.

"Jake was insistent that we not do anything like that, just check with you. He said he didn't trust Totwald's connections," Bobbie said.

"You want us to look for Jake?"

Bobbie, Dave and Mac looked at each other; they nodded. "Yes, nothing too obvious, if that's possible," Mac said. "I've worked with Jake long enough to know that he can handle himself, and sometimes needs to be left alone. But if you see him—you know what he looks like?"

"Oh yeah, I've met him. Bobbie introduced us, maybe a year ago. You don't forget someone like that," Larry said.

"We've got some errands to run, but if you find out anything give me a call." Bobbie motioned them up. He handed Mac the folded, grease stained, check. "Thanks, we appreciated breakfast."

Mac was afraid to look at it. "Thank God," he said; it was only $23 and change.

Mac lost track of everyone he was introduced to. They went to gyms and bars. Most people had nothing. Some knew a little. Two mentioned the Mazetti's. Was there a connection between the Mazetti's and the Judge?

Mac called Lt. Dombrosky in Cleveland.

"Mac, what's up?"

"Can you talk?"

"Sure, we're the good guys, remember?"

"What do you know about the Mazetti family in Pittsburgh? Do they have anything to do with Judge Forbs?"

"I'm not sure anyone does anymore, you heard what happened?"

"You mean the stroke?"

"Yeah. Hit the Captain hard, real hard. In spite of what may have been going on, he was popular down here. But the Mazetti's, they're bad. I've heard stories, you know. They've got some connections here. Let me check on it and get back to you. You with Jake?"

"Yes, but we're in Pittsburgh, and I don't know when we'll get back. I'll call you later."

In the car, driving between bars, Mac said to Bobbie, "The problem with you guys—I'm catching on—you've got all these contacts either at gyms or bars. That means I either get a friendly punch in the shoulder by a man who could knock out a water buffalo, or I drink enough beer to float the Titanic."

Bobbie turned to Dave. "Aw . . . he doesn't like our friends," he said in a whine, then laughed.

"How does Jake find you guys?"

It was almost five by the time they got back to the house. Mac didn't want to let on, but he was worried. It wasn't like Jake to just disappear, not without saying something to Mac.

"Hey, how about pasta?" Bobbie yelled from the kitchen.

"Sure," Mac said, thinking that he wasn't hungry. He had been nibbling all day, every time they stopped for a beer.

The police car pulled up just after dark. They all ran to the porch. Jake got out of the back, carrying a large cardboard box. He thanked the officers as he turned to go up the walk. They said something to him that Mac couldn't make out, and drove away.

"Hey, Mac, I got it. I got it," Jake said looking up to the porch.

"You found them? Where are they? Are they okay?"

Jake just smiled as he walked past them into the living room. Bobbie, Dave and Mac gathered around Jake as he put the box down. "You won't believe it."

Jake knelt to unwrap it. He removed the lid, and pulled it out. "What do you think? It's perfect!"

"What is it?" Dave asked.

"My missing Color Ray Emanator."

Jake stood up grinning. He couldn't have been happier.

"What about Bonnie and Martin?"

"Oh, yeah, I knew there was something." Jake feigned sheepishness. "They're all right."

"What do you mean, *all right*?"

"I've checked them into a motel. You can see them later. . . . Look at this. The bulbs are still good."

THIRTY-ONE

Bobbie yelled. The spaghetti was boiling over; the sauce needed stirring; the cheese needed grating; the table had to be set; the beer had to be taken out of the freezer. Amid the chaos, dinner was readied. With pasta twirling, Mac finally got through to Jake. "Okay, come on, tell us what happened."

Jake looked at Bobbie and Dave. "You mean how I got my Color Ray Emanator?"

Bobbie laughed so hard he started to choke on his food. Dave tried not to laugh. He liked Mac and knew the joke was on him, but as hard as he tried, he failed.

"Dammit, Jake." Mac fought to gain control. "You know what I meant. . . . Bobbie? . . . Dave? . . . Oh, shit."

It took another five minutes for things to calm down enough to try it again. "Jake? Come on, what happened?"

"Mac, I'm sorry. It's just that you can be so damn serious—makes you a good target. Let me get some coffee, and I'll tell you what happened."

Bobbie had made a pot. He got out cups and, of course, the cream and sugar for Jake.

"Our problem was in finding Totwald. Rather than wait, I decided that I had to take the initiative. I don't understand why all the trouble over Bonnie and Martin, but given that it happened, it was logical to anticipate another attack. The only thing I was worried about was shooting—"

"There was," Bobbie interrupted. "You see my floor?" He tried to sound angry. "Who's going to fix it?" He didn't want the floor fixed—he liked the bullet holes; he was proud of them, like his trophies. "You seen 'em?"

"I was right. That's why I wanted Mac out of the room." Jake sipped his coffee; it was close—too much cream—he paused to fuss over it.

"Our guests were two of Totwald's bikers. It wasn't hard to get them under control. I was afraid that they might not know where Bonnie and Martin were. But they did, and were quite willing to take me there."

Jake poured himself a little more coffee. "Good, perfect," he mumbled. "You wouldn't have any pastries? Something sweet?"

Bobbie patted his stomach. "Not in this house."

Jake decided to add extra sugar to his coffee.

"Ah . . . Totwald . . . he had them at a warehouse, owned by the Mazetti's for storing tires; I assume they're into wholesaling . . . must be good money in it. You should see their—"

"Jake? Bonnie and Martin?"

"Okay . . . there was a night-watchman. He was no problem. He'll probably be fired for sleeping on the job. I called the police. I couldn't know whether Bonnie would want to file charges; if she did, then it made sense to get the police involved. The police, by the way, really don't like Totwald. As soon as I mentioned his name, they said there'd be a car out in five minutes. Actually, it took three.

"Bonnie and Martin were being held in a small unused office on the second floor. I let the police go in first—they like that. Anyway, Bonnie and Martin are fine. I checked them out on the way to the station. Between their statements and the statements from the two bikers—I might have prodded them a little, but who's to know?—they'll get Totwald, and probably send him away for a long time, in spite of his connections."

Jake poured a little more coffee into his cup; he'd made it too sweet.

"We were through at the station by seven thirty. I got Bonnie and Martin checked into a motel. The police arranged to have a squad car in the parking lot to watch the room. I caught a nap on the sofa. When I got up, I realized I still had time to get to the antique shop. I told the officers my intentions, and they arranged that I get a police chauffeur. The rest, you know.

"Now, you can understand why I've been so excited over getting my Emanator. You know, Bonnie and Martin's rescue was somewhat anticlimactic."

"Will they be okay during the night, if you're not there?"

"Yes." Jake grinned. "Actually, I intended to have them brought here, unless Bobbie objects." Jake looked at his watch. "They'll be here in about fifteen minutes. They've had a chance to get some rest, which they won't get here."

Mac paced like a little kid waiting for Christmas.

The police brought Bonnie and Martin over at nine; they were mobbed. For a few minutes, Jake thought it was funny to watch Mac trying to get Bonnie alone; Bobbie and Dave wouldn't hear of it.

"Bobbie, let's get some beer, grab Dave and Martin and sit on the porch. Mac's going to go crazy if he doesn't get a chance to be alone with Bonnie."

"Yeah, but she's cute."

"No but's."

For all of Martin's previous cockiness, the kidnapping had made him unsure of himself and wary of being separated from his mother. But like most boys, he was easily distracted and impressed by athletes, particularly ones this strong. Martin knew very little about lifting. He confused power lifting with weightlifting, and, like most teenagers, he saw nothing wrong with steroids. Within minutes, there was no way that anyone was going to stop Bobbie or Dave, they had found a potential convert; Jake just sat back and enjoyed. No one missed Bonnie or Mac.

In the morning, they got ready to go. There was nothing to pack. Jake called the police to tell them their plans. Bobbie and Dave had gotten Jake's van.

"I owe you. Thanks," Jake said.

"We all do," Bonnie said, giving Bobbie and Dave each a kiss. "Thank you."

Bobbie blushed. "Just take care of Martin. Who knows? He might be a contender someday."

Bonnie and Mac rode in the back; Martin sat up front with Jake.

For most of the drive, Martin talked about weightlifting. "You know the real thing. It's neat, not body building or that power lifting stuff. You know, the real thing. . . ."

Jake smiled. It was hard not to appreciate the enthusiasm of youth.

They weren't too far out of Cleveland when Martin whispered to Jake. "Father McNamara seems to like mom. Can he do that? I mean, he's a priest."

"You're going to have to talk with them about that. But be kind and understanding."

"What do you mean? Why wouldn't I?"

"Martin, you're young. Youth is energy and excitement. Just go easy. Mac loves your mother, but the consequences of that love are terrifying. He feels too strongly about his vows to just break them."

"So he made some promises. Who'd tell?"

"That's just it. It's obvious to you, but it isn't to him. Mac would never break them even if he knew that no one would ever know. That's not what vows are about."

"Okay."

"Also, right now you're not jealous or angry with him. You will be, and you'll be tempted to say things. Think twice, please. Mac will need your help when you're least willing to give it. Can you promise?"

Martin looked confused.

"Promise?"

"Will you take me to a lifting meet?"

"That's blackmail, but yes, I will."

"I promise. . . . Last night, you mentioned a guy named Norm something. He's special, huh? Tell me about him."

"His name is Norb Schemansky. And I'll tell you about him, if you'll stop picking at the cracks in my dashboard."

THIRTY-TWO

They were fifteen minutes away from Bonnie's house when they stopped for lunch at Brio, Bonnie's favorite restaurant.

Jake suggested they share two of the mozzarella and grilled vegetable appetizers.

"Martin chew your food," Bonnie whispered harshly to Martin.

"But . . . Jake . . . I—"

"I can't tell Jake how to eat, but I can tell you. Chew—"

Mac's laugh interrupted her. He was staring at Jake who had taken the opportunity to finish both servings and was wiping clean the plates with a piece of French bread.

"I give up!" Bonnie said. "You're an impossible influence."

Jake pretended to pout. "I'm no good for either of you, am I?"

"We love you, Jacob Krajczynski." Bonnie gave him a kiss on his cheek. "But I would have liked some of the mozzarella."

Bonnie, Mac, and Jake ordered pasta. Martin was of an age when lunch meant a hamburger. Brio's concession to the American passion for hamburgers wasn't what he expected. Theirs was prepared *au poivre:* hamburger drenched in freshly ground black and green peppercorns, and allspice, fried in a hot skillet on lightly browned salt, and served with a sauce made of the juices, Worcestershire sauce, butter, lemon juice, Scotch, and a teaspoonful of jalapeno vinegar. It didn't need the ketchup, mustard, and mayonnaise, which Martin smothered it with.

Over dessert, Mac reminded Jake that he had wanted to talk about their adventure.

"It's easy to get caught up in the food. But we should talk. I think that you two are safe. Totwald's in jail and the Judge is incapacitated. Although I still haven't any idea what really started it all."

"It was the Judge's son and friends," Bonnie said as though Jake had overlooked the obvious.

"Well, yes . . . but why? Even if it were the merest of coincidences that they all came together, why go to all that trouble after Martin was first rescued? Why pursue things after the Judge was out of the picture?"

"Maybe the Judge's orders carried a certain momentum," Mac said, more as a question than a statement.

"Mac, I hope so. I really do. But I want to know what your plans are, just in case things aren't over."

"Always the optimist, aren't you?" Mac smiled at Bonnie. "We've talked about it. I'm going to quit the priesthood. We're going to get married." Mac's face reddened. "Martin, I'm sorry. I was going to ask you." Mac looked at Bonnie. "I meant to talk with Martin. I—"

"He's here. Talk with him."

In the taunt silence, Martin started to laugh.

Jake jabbed Martin in the ribs with his elbow. "The deal?" he whispered.

"What?" Mac asked.

"Just something between Martin and me. Go on."

"Martin I . . . I love your mother, and I have asked her

to marry me, but I want your acceptance. I know that I'm not your father, and I won't try to act like I am, but I would like your approval."

Martin nervously fished a pool of ketchup for his last two French fries, uncomfortable in the position of arbiter. Jake caught his eye and gave him a wink. "A . . . sure." Martin grinned. "Sounds good to me."

Mac squeezed Bonnie's hand. "Thanks."

Martin turned back to his quest for table scraps.

"I'll have to talk with my Bishop. I don't know how long things will take. And Mrs. Meyernik will be upset."

"Maybe you two would like live in help?"

"No, she's dedicated to the church and the community. She'll never leave; maybe if I ask, though, it'll soften the blow."

"I expect to be invited to the wedding." Jake smiled, and nudged Martin. "There will be one, won't there?"

***

When Jake opened The Bookstall, his neighbors from the health food store came over.

"You're going to have to hire someone to fill in for you. The Arcade's been busier than we remember it, even this long before Christmas. You could've sold a lot last week."

Jake was walking around opening the bookcases. It felt good to be back; he loved the smells of the store. "I intend to be here through the holidays. So you don't have to worry about me. But thanks."

Alone among his books he surveyed the store. He wondered if the Judge's collection would be for sale; there were some choice works in it. He'd have to talk Ed.

He had set the mail down on his desk next to his coffee

and a bag of warm scones from the bakery at the far end of the Arcade. If he could, he would put off going through it until afternoon. He intended to spend the morning notifying customers that their books had arrived.

"Christmas shopping, so soon!" he mumbled. Jake liked the holidays as long as he didn't have to remember his family. That's what made it hard—the memories.

Jake's father, Konrad, had come to the United States in 1947. He had spent part of the war fighting the Germans and the rest as a prisoner of war. He didn't like to talk about it. As a kid, Jake asked him to tell war stories, but he never did. Jake's mother would try to distract Jake. She knew that it had been a painful time for her husband, and the memories drifted like storm clouds, never far beyond the horizon. He had lost his entire family and most of his friends. As Jake grew older, he came to realize that his father was in continual pain from injuries suffered during his internment.

Konrad Krajczynski had just gotten his doctorate in philology when the Germans invaded Poland. His dream had been to get a position teaching at the University of Warsaw and to devote his life to the study of medieval Polish literature.

After the war, when he came to the United States, he found that there was no academic interest in Polish literature. He ended up in Chicago, working in a bookstore near the University. Although he had given up any hope of an academic career, he counted many professors from the University as his friends. They often got together to discuss literature and philosophy. They recognized Konrad's brilliance, even through the almost unintelligible accent that many thought was mostly affectation.

In Chicago, Konrad met Mai. She was attending the University on scholarship. Her mother was Taiwanese; her father was American, a Merchant Marine on the Great Lakes. All of Konrad's friends were infatuated with Mai. She was bright, witty, unfairly beautiful, and very much in love with Konrad.

She quit the University to raise their only son, Jacob, named after Konrad's father. After Konrad died in 1966, Jake asked his mother if she had had any regrets leaving the University before she had gotten her degree. She told him that one always has regrets, that was part of living; but her love for Konrad and Jake—seeing Jake grow into manhood—made her life full and happy.

Christmas had been special for Konrad when he was growing up. It was a time of deep religious feeling and glorious celebration. His family would take the train from Breslau to Cracow, where his grandparents lived on a large farm. Each year, they spent a week and a half, for Christmas and New Year's Day. In Breslau, he was the serious, young, scholar, but at his grandparents, with all of his uncles, aunts, and cousins he was, for a short time, a young boy with sleigh-rides, skating on the frozen run-off pond, snowball fights, Christmas breads, roast goose, and midnight Mass with several hundred candle flames washing the walls of the small, parish church. It was a miraculous time.

In the United States, celebrating Christmas was all that was left of Konrad's family.

Mai Krajczynski died in 1978. Since then, Jake had felt funny about Christmas. It had been so special during his childhood; he felt that he should continue their tradition, but without family of his own, it seemed hollow. As long as he kept busy and didn't think about them, he would get through it. Of course, he thought, it was his memory of his family that also made Christmas a special time.

It seemed to come earlier and earlier each year.

When he got home, he started to plan: this year he was going to have a real Christmas party, and he was going to send out Christmas cards, for sure.

***

The Bishop took Mac's decision to leave the priesthood hard. Mac was one of his favorites.

"Is there nothing I can do to dissuade you?"

"No. This wasn't an easy choice. I wish I could have had options."

"I don't think that we'll see that in this generation, or the next. Officially, I can't give you my blessing, but I also don't want to lose you as a friend."

"You won't. We'll send you an invitation."

Mrs. Meyernik was hurt and thrilled. She liked Father Mac. He had brought more excitement and fun into the parish than she could remember, and she would dearly miss Jake. Mac assured her that she would be an honored guest at the wedding.

Mac moved into Bonnie's house, but he slept in the guest room. He said that until they were married he felt funny about being closer. Martin had not only accepted him into the family, but, when his mother was not around, he teased Mac about their sleeping arrangements. Mac would never admit it to Martin, although he had told Bonnie, he thought the teasing was a good sign. It meant that Martin accepted Mac and the marriage.

Martin's sister, Julia, on the other hand, was cold to Mac. She came home to visit every other weekend, but she had not known Mac as Martin had. She saw him as an interloper. It bothered Mac. Bonnie explained that Julia had been very close to her father and had taken his death hard. Mac would have to be patient. "She'll come around."

They planned to have the marriage ceremony the Friday after Thanksgiving. Although they couldn't have a Catholic wedding, they decided that a High Episcopal service would be the closest thing. It surprised them how much work there was to get everything prepared, even though they didn't want too elaborate a service or reception.

Bonnie's parents were living in a retirement community in Florida. They were ecstatic that she was remarrying. Her mother was a little disturbed that they were leaving the Church, but times had changed and Bonnie's generation did things differently, she said. Her father wanted to pay for the whole thing. "You're my daughter."

"Pop, you're living on a fixed income. Anyway, you paid for my first marriage; this one's on me."

They fought over it every time they talked, at least three times a week. Mac finally convinced him. "It wasn't easy," he told Bonnie. "I had to promise that we'd have our honeymoon in Florida."

Jake came over once a week for dinner. Saturday nights were his.

"Ready to work at The Bookstall?" Jake asked Mac; it was Jake's regular joke.

"Ask me after the wedding."

These were good days, in spite of Mac's crisis of faith. Jake would get Bonnie alone and ask after Mac. He worried, knowing that Mac would never say anything. She assured him that everything was as good as it looked. Jake was happy to see that Martin was taking things so well. But it was obvious that Julia was hurt and would need time to adjust.

"When are you going to invite us over to your apartment?"

Bonnie asked one evening. Mac, sitting opposite her, made a show of trying to shut her up.

Jake couldn't help seeing. "Hey, what's so wrong with my apartment? I've had people over, parties, dinners—everything. No one's ever died, or even complained."

"Remember, I warned you," Mac said to Bonnie.

"And you'll cook?" she asked.

"Ah, you do know the way to a man's heart. Of course, I'll cook. Actually, I'm planning a Christmas party. You'll both come?"

"Hey?" Martin asked. "What about me?"

"Sorry, I expected you to come; it's these two who need coaxing. Oh, before I forget. Next weekend, there's The World Cup in Columbus. Want to go?"

"Jake! That's when we're getting married. How can you do this?" Bonnie asked, looking truly hurt.

"The meet's on Saturday. You don't want company the day after your wedding, do you?"

Mac looked at Jake. "I know you. If you could figure out a way to miss the wedding you would, especially over lifting. Not this time."

"Promise. Martin and I will go down on Saturday. We'll be here for the wedding on Friday. Anyway, I have to be here . . . I'm the best man."

THIRTY-THREE

In fact, Jake spent very little time at The Bookstall.

The week before the wedding was busy. Bonnie had Greve's Flowers take care of the bouquets, boutonnieres, and sprays. They would have everything delivered on Friday by noon, and an assistant would stay with Bonnie to help set things up. Bonnie asked that they feature lilies throughout; they were her favorite flower, and she thought that they would have a pleasant connotation for Mac.

Although Mac never asked for it, he needed Jake's attention. He was firm in his decision, of that he had no doubts, but as he kept saying to Jake, "You know, it's my age. It's time for a job change." He could make light of it, but Jake knew that it had been a difficult decision. So Jake tried to stay with Mac as much as possible without being in the way.

Because this was not the usual marriage they met with Dr. McMullin, their minister, four times; once at St. Paul's, the other three times at The Club. The Club was actually Night Town, a restaurant and bar that Jake went to often. The regulars called it The Club. It seemed that way to Mac.

The Club was the back room, beyond the bar. It had eleven tables of various sizes, the smallest for two, and the largest for six. The maître d' carefully steered nonregulars away from there. The walls were covered with photographs, most were portraits made no later than 1900, and a large lithograph of Sitting Bull's defiant victory over Custer. There was a jukebox at the far end, stocked with jazz classics.

The regulars included an author who sat at the corner table, under a black and white photograph of her taken in 1939. The maître d' said that she was working on an exposé. Her table was always covered with papers. A painter, a blonde woman in her thirties, took the center table; she kept brochures of her work with her. It seemed to Jake that she lived there, and he wondered when she found time to paint.

Jake's favorite was the "walrus man," a short, thin Albert Schweitzer in rumpled and worn clothes. He was a poet, although none of his work had ever been published. He lived with his sister's family; she took him in after he graduated from Princeton in 1954. He liked to talk economics.

Another of the regulars, the loudest of them, was a Brazilian photographer named Luiz. He always carried his Leica, and wore a light meter on his belt. Luiz was the only regular who put money in the jukebox; he never looked at what numbers he pushed. He said he liked to be surprised—sometimes he was. Jake thought he was hyperactive because he was always moving, perpetually dancing. The waitresses just said that he was Brazilian, as though that explained everything. Whenever he sold a few prints, everyone knew; he would buy several bottles of champagne for The Club.

The back table, next to the jukebox, was Dr. McMullen's; it was one of the larger tables, with more light than the rest. He usually had company. Jake and Mac joined him twice for lunch, and conferred with him there a third time.

Although Jake didn't eat there often enough to have his own table, they all knew him, and he got The Club treatment. Within a minute of sitting down, without saying anything to anyone, he was brought a Glenfiddich, neat, and a cup of coffee with cream and sugar on the side.

By their third lunch, the waitress brought Mac his drink

too; Bombay Sapphire Gin with two drops of Vermouth de Savoie and one ice cube.

"Try the Dublin Lawyer," Jake suggested. "It's lobster pieces in a spicy cream sauce with Irish whiskey served over rice."

"Fourteen bucks?"

"It's on me. How often do you get married?"

While they were eating, Mac asked Jake about his plans for the weekend.

"I know you don't trust me, but on this I'm firm, the meet in Columbus is scheduled for Saturday only. I'll pick up Martin at five o'clock in the morning—I haven't told him the time yet. We'll get there for the weigh in at nine. We'll be back late Saturday night. As for Friday night, you can count on me. I've even had my blue suit—"

"Your only suit."

"Yes, my only and blue, suit cleaned. I can't let that go to waste."

The hardest part of the week for Jake was trying to figure out what to get them as a wedding gift. During one of his brief stints at The Bookstall it came to him. He went to the CD store in the Arcade. He had them select a thousand dollars worth of early music CD's. "On original instruments only," he warned the clerk. It was extravagant, but Mac and Bonnie were worth it, and more.

Bonnie had arranged with Brio to have them cater the reception, which she was going to have at her house. Craig, one of the owners, said that he'd personally see to the arrangements.

Most of the week was filled with all the details that magically sorted themselves out. Her parents arrived on Wednesday. Of course, they stayed at Bonnie's house. Bonnie had invited her sister, JoAnne, to stay also, but she declined. She had three children and, with her husband, that made five. Although there was room, she said that by the second day of their stay, "You'll have a contract put out on us. Anyway, let's not test our fragile sibling alliance."

Bonnie was grateful for JoAnne's help. Their mother kept giving advice, which, though well meaning, wasn't helping control the relative chaos. JoAnne ran interference—Bonnie didn't know if she could ever thank her enough.

Mac's family flew in on Thursday. They stayed in the same motel as JoAnne and her family. By Friday afternoon, they were all fast friends. Mac's parents understood how hard his decision had been. They had lived through his going into the priesthood, which, although he had grown up wanting to be a priest, was also a hard time. They didn't bring it up, but they made it clear that he had their support. Supporting their son was made easier by their infatuation with Bonnie.

The wedding party was thirty people. The service was as simple as such things can be and still be High Episcopal. Jake, true to his word, was there, and well behaved. He knew that this was not the time for clowning around; although the night before he had sat up for several hours thinking up all sorts of funny things he could do.

The wedding was over at six thirty. Bonnie's house was three blocks away. When everyone got there, they found it overrun with flowers. Mac made sure that the photographer got plenty of pictures. Mrs. Meyernik helped the caterers. They loved her, and the food was great.

There was a fire in the fireplace, and candles everywhere. Mac staked out a place to the left of the mantel. For once at a party, he didn't feel he had to circulate amongst his guests. He was no longer a priest, even in his mind he was a newly married man. He basked in the attention. Early on, before most of the guests had arrived, Julia came over to him, and gave him a hug and a kiss.

"Does this mean we're friends?" Mac asked.

"I think so. Martin told me what happened. And it's hard not to see how much mom loves you, and you her. I guess I was angry and hurt. Anyway, I shouldn't keep her from being happy."

"Julia, I know that I can't replace your father, and I won't try. As long as you accept me as your mother's husband, that's all I—"

"Oh, there's Larry, my boyfriend." She took Mac's hand, and pulled him away from his post, guiding him across the room. "He had a recital or he'd have been here earlier. I want you to meet him."

"A recital?"

"Didn't mom tell you? He plays Baroque oboe."

Mac could barely control his excitement. "Baroque?"

"I thought you'd like that." She winked at Mac.

Mac spent the night trying to corner Larry. He wanted to discuss his theory about the physical characteristics of early instruments and how they effected both technique and performance style. But it was his wedding night and no one was going to let Mac hole-up in his world of early music.

"I've got to go in a few minutes." Jake cornered Mac.

"Leave? We haven't talked at all. It's early, not quite ten thirty."

"We've got that meet tomorrow."

"Okay, leave early. But . . . thanks."

"Hey, what are friends—"

"Don't kid. You know what I mean, and 'thanks' barely covers it."

"But, that is what friendship is about."

"You set with Martin?"

"Yeah, I gave him the bad news, he's to be up and ready by five."

"Five?" Mac groaned.

"Don't worry, I also told him to be quiet when he gets up—your wedding night and all."

By the front door, Jake found Bonnie in the middle of a large group. He pushed his way through, saying that he had to leave. "Jacob Krajczynski," she gave him a big hug, "thank you so much for everything. You've got Martin really excited. It's good to see him happy. Have fun tomorrow."

It had snowed while they were inside, not much, just enough to give the trees a white dusting. He pulled his collar up and stuck his hands in his coat pockets. The air was still. The streetlights sparkled through the branches making them look like giant, wet, spider webs.

As he walked to his van, he felt sad. At first he dismissed it as the holidays. Then he thought maybe it was because of Mac. He realized that it was. Mac had had to make a hard decision. His love for Bonnie was the real engine behind his leaving the priesthood. Mac had the option, Jake didn't. Jake could never enter that world; he hadn't signed a paper, nor joined a prohibitive society; he hadn't even taken vows. It went deeper.

Sometimes the price felt too high.

THIRTY-FOUR

There was a light on in the kitchen. Martin was up and ready when Jake pulled into the drive. Almost before he came to a stop, Martin was opening the passenger side door.

"I'm impressed," Jake said.

"This is going to be great. I could hardly sleep."

"Buckle up. I've got breakfast—sandwiches, and coffee—in the bag behind you. We'll eat when we get on the freeway."

They didn't talk much as they drove through the city. The streets were dark, empty and wet. The snow had already melted. Once on the freeway, and away from the city, Jake asked Martin to pour him a cup of coffee.

"So, how's the new family?"

"It feels good. Mom really loves Mac; they're happy."

"Remember that when you get mad at him."

"I won't get mad."

"Okay, but remember that anyway. How about a sandwich?"

Martin placed the bag on his lap. He sorted through it, hefting the wax paper wrapped sandwiches.

"They're all the same," Jake said. "Just give me one."

"Mmmm." Martin bit into his sandwich. "Will . . . will we see Bobbie and Dave?"

"We'll see everyone. This is a big event. What do you know about it?"

"Well . . . you know." Martin was caught by the question; his knowledge hadn't kept pace with his enthusiasm. "You all were excited about it. I mean . . . it sounded—"

"Exciting? It is. These meets are for fun. The World Cup is by invitation only. The world champions in each weight category compete. The host country can enter as many lifters as it wants. We'll probably enter two or three. They don't have a chance, but it's a nice gesture."

"How do you know who wins?"

"The prize goes to whoever lifts the greatest percentage of the world record in his weight class."

"That's neat. Everyone's equal."

"Everyone? . . . What's one percent of six hundred pounds?"

"Six pounds."

"And of three hundred pounds?"

"Three. Oh . . . the bigger guys still have to lift more weight."

"When you're lifting up near your limit, every pound counts, regardless of how big you are. But it's as fair as such things can ever be."

"Jake, why do you like lifting so much?"

For half an hour, Jake answered the question. He talked about the absoluteness of the weight, and the nature of limits. He talked about lifting as symbolic of man's perpetual fight against gravity, breaking one's limits, reaching for the heavens. And he talked about the inner rewards of a sport that held little recognition beyond its small cadre of devotees.

"And I love the competitors. They're all characters." Jake laughed. "It comes from all that squatting."

"Steroids—"

"Don't say it. I know many athletes use 'em. But that doesn't make it, or them, right."

Martin didn't see it that way, but he knew that on this Jake had no sense of humor.

"There's one guy here I want you to watch. He represents everything that's great about lifting and, more importantly, everything that's great about humanity. Suleymanoglu . . . Naim Suleymanoglu. You're lucky, he hasn't competed in the States for a while.

"He's Bulgarian. I don't know what they feed their chickens, but there's a lot of good lifters from Bulgaria. Anyway, he's a small guy. You'll see: in his sweats he's just a little guy. You tower over him. But don't get smug. He lifts triple body weight plus twenty pounds. . . . Think about it."

Jake sipped his coffee. "But that's not the only thing that makes him great. Suleymanoglu is of Turkish heritage. Some years ago, the Bulgarian government set about a purity campaign. To rid Bulgaria of cultural adulterants, one of their policies was that people's names were changed from Turkish to Bulgarian. Suleymanoglu lived a privileged life as a champion lifter. But when they took his name he knew he had to leave Bulgaria. At a meet in Australia he sneaked out a bathroom window and sought refuge in the Turkish embassy. The Turkish government was, of course, pleased with his defection. To enable him to compete in the '88 Olympics on the Turkish team, the President of Turkey adopted him and bribed Bulgaria to release any claim over him.

"But remember, all of his world records—he held three— were set while he was a Bulgarian, under his Bulgarian name. So he decided that for them to count, for himself, under his real name, he had to break each one of them. He did! He's a giant."

They found the gym facilities, on the Ohio State campus. Even at eight, parking was difficult. Martin saw license plates from California to Florida.

It took them thirty minutes to get in. Jake knew everyone. Martin shook more hands than a Senator running for reelection. They found Bobbie and Dave.

Bobbie grinned at Martin. "So, when will we see you up there?"

Martin blushed. It embarrassed him that they kidded him like that; he felt he wasn't good at anything. Bobbie sensed Martin's discomfort and backed off.

The actual meet was scheduled for after lunch. Jake took Martin backstage. It never occurred to Martin to be surprised that Jake really did know every one. In the warm up room, Jake got caught up in an argument over whether the Olympics should have suspended lifters for using diuretics. He forgot about Martin, who wandered around in awe. Having seen him with Jake, no one—not even the officials—questioned his being there.

Martin left the room for a cup of coffee. When he got back, the room was empty, except for Jake, who stood up in his odd way, as if pulled straight up onto his feet. This was the first time Martin had seen it, although Bonnie had told him about it. Martin started to say something to Jake, when he heard someone talking behind him. He turned around; Suleymanoglu was talking to a member of his entourage. The man looked at Martin, and translated. "Please, Mr. Suleymanoglu would like to know if you know the man Mr. Jake, he calls him."

"Oh yeah, we're friends, he brought me down here."

Suleymanoglu, who had to look up to Martin and everyone else around him, smiled. He spoke through his interpreter. "You are blessed to have such a friend."

Martin grinned, but was unsure of himself. "Thanks."

They walked away from Martin. Then they stopped

while one of them, the interpreter, walked back over, "Mr. Suleymanoglu would like to say that Mr. Jake is also favored to have a friend like you."

Jake walked over, smiling. "I see you've met Suleymanoglu. What do you think?"

"He's . . . small."

"Yeah. Bobbie and Dave like the big, fat, guys; sure they're impressive in their way, but you just stood next to an impossibility."

The meet was over at quarter after four. Martin couldn't believe how fast the day had gone. Jake's good-byes took a while; they got on the road after five. The trip back was slow; it had snowed.

Martin fell asleep.

It wasn't too late by the time they pulled into Bonnie's drive. Mac met them at the door. "Good meet?"

"Great," Martin said, pushing his way past Mac for a clear shot at the bathroom.

"How's married life?" Jake asked as he closed the front door behind him.

Mac had been sitting with Bonnie in the living room, a fire in the fireplace, and listening to their new CDs. "Jake, this is fantastic. Where did you find all these? You must've spent a fortune."

"The CD store in the Arcade is most obliging. You should go there. And how much I spent is none of your business. Is there anything to eat? We didn't stop."

Mac accompanied Jake into the kitchen. Martin was already half into the refrigerator, fishing out leftovers.

"Oh, I almost forgot," Mac said to Martin as he reemerged, "a man called for you. He asked where you were and said something about SAT's. I said you'd be in tomorrow."

"That's weird. I never took them. Why should somebody call?"

"Maybe that's why, you probably should," Mac suggested. "He'll call you back."

Jake started to think about all this, but the sight of Martin standing with a plate of cold roast beef in one hand and a bowl of left over mashed potatoes in the other was too much. "Keep it move'n, keep it move'n." Turning to Mac, he said, "Is there some bread?"

Mac steered Jake in the right direction. Then he returned to Bonnie in the living room. "I don't think they'll destroy the kitchen, not completely, but I couldn't stay to watch the carnage."

She looked at Mac and laughed.

THIRTY-FIVE

He's gone!" Those were the first words that Jake heard after he answered the telephone.

"Mac? What time is it?"

"It's six thirty. I heard some noises. I checked his room—Martin's gone."

"Give me five minutes. I'll be there. Meanwhile, call the police."

Jake was wide-awake. He was angry; he knew that somehow he had gotten careless. "It won't happen again," Jake vowed, as he silently closed his back door.

It was cold and dark as he drove to Bonnie's house. Jake was calm when he got there, too calm. Mac had seen him like this before; it gave him chills.

"Come in. Let's keep it quiet. Bonnie's still asleep, I hope."

"What more can you tell me?"

"Jake, that's just it, nothing. I feel like shit. I was here; I've let Bonnie down. I—"

"Enough. Did you call the police?"

"Yes."

"Well?"

"What can they say now?"

"Okay, you're right. Go back to bed. I don't care if you can't sleep. Stay with Bonnie and stay here. I'll call when I know something. If you talk to the police again, fine, tell them whatever they need to know. But stay here."

Jake drove to Bratenahl. It was light—flat, overcast gray—by the time he got to the Judge's. He had to ring for five minutes before Ed answered.

"Where is he?" Jake asked when Ed opened the door.

"Who?"

"Martin. He's gone . . . kidnapped. What do you know?"

Ed pulled an old, brown and orange Cleveland Brown's robe tighter around his upper chest. "Come in . . . I've got to have a cup of coffee, you?"

"Sure."

In the kitchen, Jake started again. "I know you didn't do it, but Martin's gone—you must know something, anything."

"Nothing." Ed hesitated, uncomfortable with the word, "Dad's . . . been in bed; he's recovering, that's what the doctors say, but he's not involved in anything, not anymore."

"Think. Has anyone tried to contact him?"

"Well, yeah. Last Thursday. A guy called. He knew Dad was sick. He just said that I should give him a message. He said something like, 'Tell 'em we're takin' 'em.' I asked who it was, but he said to give my father the message; he'd know. I didn't think anything of it. He kind of laughed, made it sound like a joke."

"What did he sound like?"

"I remember thinking at the time the guy sounded like a gangster in a movie. Does that help?"

"Yes, it does." Jake sounded far away, lost in thought. "May I see your father?"

"Now? It's early."

Jake squinted at Ed.

"Well . . . sure. He sleeps most of the time, except when the therapist is here. I guess it shouldn't make much difference."

There was one live-in nurse on duty. She told them to be

quiet, and to let the Judge sleep, but she didn't try to keep them out of his room.

The Judge had lost weight. His pale skin was loose on his face and hands. The pillow was moist from spittle dripping from his mouth. The room smelled of medicine and urine.

"He's better than you think . . . than he looks." Ed whispered to Jake. "He can talk a little and he recognizes me."

Jake had known that he wouldn't learn a thing from the Judge, but he felt he had to see him anyway. "Okay, let's let him sleep."

On the stairs, Ed stopped and turned to Jake. "Did you have anything to do with what happened? I know this may sound strange, but with his stroke?"

Jake looked at Ed.

"I've spent most of my life hating and fearing him. I've wished he'd die. But seeing him helpless like that, I feel . . ." Ed stared back at Jake. The sun broke through the clouds and, for a second, refracted by the beveled, leaded window over the door, cast a slender rainbow across Ed's hand on the banister. "I love him."

"Ed, you love him because he's your father. You may have a tough time sorting things out; even healthy father-son relationships are difficult. Just don't feel guilty about loving him; he needs it. Don't hold back."

"I know it'll be hard. But you didn't answer my question. Did you have anything to do with his stroke?"

"Ed, I . . . yes and no. I don't know. We were in another world . . . dreamsharing . . . we were fighting, and we were losing. It was Mart—" Jake caught himself. He had meant to say Stel. Or had he? He wondered, as the chill of adrenaline rushed through him. "Martin?"

Jake drove back to his apartment, dazed at the revelation.

He had been so blind. He had asked himself repeatedly, why Martin? Now, it made sense; everything pointed in this direction. Why Martin? Because Martin had a potential like Jake's.

The Judge had tried to turn him, and failing at that, to kill him. They didn't want Martin alive, but moreover, he would do anything to get Martin back; that would give them a chance to get Jake too.

Suleymanoglu, he had seen it in Martin; that was what he'd meant when he had said that Jake was lucky to have Martin as a friend.

Jake had found his disciple, but was it too late?

***

Chemmg Tse Lu was twenty-five when his Master, Ka, sent him away. "You need time alone. I want you to go, to explore the world, to meet Evil, to see Good, to feel man's duplicity."

"Where? When?"

"Tomorrow. I want you to leave. I don't care what direction you take. I want you gone."

"For how long?"

"You'll know."

Chemmg left at first light. He was full of mixed emotions: fear, pride, anger, and love. He had expected Ka to be awake, to see him off. Instead, Ka slept, oblivious to Chemmg's leave taking. Chemmg had packed the night before: a spare robe, a bowl, a tea pot, and several ancient scrolls of prayers and vows, a gift two years earlier from Ka. He made a fire and prepared tea before he left. He tried to make enough noise, but there was no waking the old man. As he left camp, walking down the mountain path towards the flood plane and the village of his birth, he didn't see Ka wipe the tears from his eyes.

For months, Chemmg walked through the mountains from village to village, stopping at every monastery, claiming his right to hospitality. He was welcomed in some places; doors slammed in his face elsewhere. He had the sick, the lepers, and the deformed beg for his aid. Arrogant headmen consulted him as to the best way for them to be reborn as nobility—as if he could show them the way.

He saw peasants struggling to keep alive and the rich getting richer at the expense of the poor. Chemmg met travelers from the other side of the world: men seeking adventure, and men seeking spiritual growth. Bandits twice attacked him.

The weather changed. Winter approached. Without any conscious effort, he went south into India. He met many holy men and many fakeers. He studied the Hindu origins of his Buddhist beliefs, and he learned and practiced the Indian schools of yoga that most closely matched his.

Five years later, he felt the need to return to Tibet. It was late summer when he found Ka. A young boy of twelve was fussing over the fire, preparing their supper. Chemmg saw himself in the boy.

"Ah, we have company," said Ka to the boy. "I would like you to meet Master Chemmg Tse Lu." It was the first time that Chemmg had been called that by Ka. "He will be staying with us for a while. I'm sure he's got many stories to tell . . . and there is much for me yet to teach him, now that he's seen the world."

***

Jake had some suspicions as to who might have taken Martin.

As he drove by his apartment building, he felt there was

something wrong. He parked down the street, not in his garage. He took ten minutes to walk around the block and approach his building from the opposite end, sneaking through the driveways, hopping walls between adjacent garage complexes. He crept up the metal stairs. At the top, he cautiously looked into the kitchen. A man with a gun was waiting for him.

Jake matched his breathing with the man's breathing. It wasn't hard to get him under control. Jake sensed that there was another man in the front of the apartment, but he had time. He opened the door carefully. Lightly, he stepped in. "Where's the boy?" he whispered into the man's ear.

"I . . . don't . . ."

"Where?"

"He's . . . he's . . ."

Jake heard the other man walking towards the kitchen. Jake stood beside the doorway, wedged between his old, GE icebox and the wall.

Inches away from Jake, the man stopped at the doorway, he smelled of stale coffee and cigarettes. The man saw his partner standing awkwardly motionless. He drew his gun from his shoulder holster and stepped into the kitchen.

In the space of a blink, Jake faced him.

The man was a killer, Jake sensed, one who enjoyed killing, especially when one did it slowly.

Jake's right hand struck out at the man's throat. His fingers tore through the flesh and crushed the windpipe. He hesitated before he finished. Pressure applied to the man's neck ended the agony. Jake turned to the first man, who had dropped his gun to the floor.

The man reeked—sour and pungent—from fear. He was sickly pale. Vomit trickled from his mouth and ran down his white polo shirt.

"Where's the boy?" Jake asked.

"In the mills. Youngstown."

"How many are you?"

"Ten." The man couldn't take his eyes off his buddy. He shit his pants. "Everybody . . . from . . . Pittsburgh."

Jake called the police. They told him to stay; they would have a car there in five minutes. Jake tied the man up and unlocked the front door before he left. He didn't want the police to break the door down trying to get in. He was several blocks away when the police got to his apartment.

Jake had been through the old steel mills in Youngstown with a photographer friend. They were deserted, a valley of giant, rust covered monuments to the forgotten dreams of a nation growing too fast. Jake wondered about the incompetence and mismanagement that had brought them to this condition. On the south side of the valley, closer to the roads, the mills were being torn down. The plants on the north side were farther from the roads, and were still intact; Jake assumed that was where they'd have Martin.

If he drove in, they would see him coming five minutes before he got there. He parked at a diner a quarter mile from the old plant entrance. From the table in the corner he could see if anyone drove in or out of the parking lot. He studied the area.

Jake decided that he could get in at the far end by climbing down through several ruined buildings. He left his VW in the parking lot and started out.

Unshaven, in his dirty parka, he was just another unemployed steel worker. He didn't look around; it was a depressing neighborhood. At one time, it had been busy. When the mills were working, people made money. In the last fifteen years, with the plant closings, people despaired and destroyed their houses. Every other home had been burned to the ground. Only the poorest stayed. He could only guess how the bars stayed open.

No one noticed him as he ducked through a cut in the rusted, link fence. It started to snow as he worked his way down to the valley floor. Not enough to make it treacherous, but enough to provide some cover. He had to cross the slag heaps before he would get to the mill itself. There was a main building, two stories high, lined with tracks for overhead cranes, pits, and old machinery. Around it were maintenance and supply buildings, the furnaces, and railroad tracks. The main offices had been at the far end, closer to the diner.

Jake sensed that there were two men, twenty yards ahead of him. In another few feet, he would be visible to them. He stopped. With his help, they dreamed of summer and the beach. They dropped their guns. Jake appeared before them as just another vacationer out for a stroll. When he got within arms' reach, he knocked out one then the other, quickly and quietly.

Jake looked around, hidden by the gray-black mounds and brick wall. He had to work his way west, along the tracks to the offices half a mile away.

Jake crept down the cement stairs that led through an archway to the deserted work yard. Acres of frozen, red-brown equipment and tracks merely hinted at the activity that once existed here. He walked through a forest of black steel chemical tanks and pipes, with small, single room, red brick buildings scattered about. He chose not to go through the mill. It was too confined and too dangerous.

Jake sensed the presence of more men. He passed two in the mill. They never knew he was nearby. They were trapped in their hiding place and posed little threat.

Ahead of him, in one of the smaller brick buildings, was

another pair. He moved closer. One he saw by a window the other was hidden from his sight. Jake held the one he could see as he walked through the door. Just as he was about to probe for confirmation about where people were stationed, the other, thirty feet away, jumped up from behind an old generator and shot through his partner, killing him and wounding Jake in his left shoulder. He fell, and rolled behind a low brick wall that surrounded a pit. He had to get his pain under control before the man with the gun got closer—there wasn't much time.

It took a few seconds. Once the pain was gone, he slowed the bleeding. The man fired his gun again, and again. Each shot was just distracting enough to keep Jake from getting control over the man. His best chance, he thought, was to go for him while he was reloading. If he could see the man, his concentration would be better and the control would come quicker.

Jake heard the click. He jumped up and looked toward where the shots had come from. The man was fast. He was sliding a new clip into this pistol. Jake concentrated. The man's arm was already rising. Jake knew that he couldn't gain control fast enough, so he blurred the man's vision and dove back behind the wall. The gun went off, missing Jake by inches. The bullet threw chips of brick into the air, but Jake had him . . . there was no second shot.

Jake approached him slowly. The man was haughty, even captive as he was. Jake decided not to knock him out or kill him. Instead, he gave the man a dream; it was a bad dream, as though he drifted on LSD. Jake took the gun and threw it away. The man's own arrogance would be his undoing, Jake thought, as he left him huddled, shivering in a corner of fear.

Jake wondered what the response to the gunshots would

be. There were probably four more men, with at least two of them standing guard over Martin, so two would probably come after him. He got out of the building. He couldn't afford to be trapped. Above him, was a metal catwalk connecting several tanks and following the piping. He found a set of metal stairs, behind a large tank. He climbed up.

Jake was lucky. Ahead of him, on the catwalk, was one of the men. Jake probed, luring him closer. He hid behind a large loop of pipe, not from this man, but from his partner who he hadn't located. The man came forward. Jake grabbed him and pulled him out of sight.

"How many with the boy?" Jake whispered in the man's ear.

"Two."

"You're with the Mazetti's?"

"Yeah, Tom Mazetti has the kid."

"Where?"

"In the first building, second floor."

Jake grabbed the man's neck. He pressed. He didn't kill him, but the man would be unconscious for a while.

Jake felt around, sensing for the second man. He heard him almost before he sensed him. "Jerr . . . Jerr . . . Where are you?"

Before he could do anything, there was a thud. Jake had missed the third man, the one he had left hallucinating. That man had attacked his own comrade with a pipe. Two men were left guarding Martin.

Jake got to the office building. He rested just outside the door. The wound was distracting. He couldn't afford to be careless, if he didn't want to lose Martin. Jake stood motionless for five minutes, preparing himself.

He sent out a net, searching for the two men. He found

them and Martin. Jake got control of one man, but the second was difficult; he had some skill.

It was hard to hold one and fight the other. Jake felt himself weakening. The fighter would soon break free if Jake could not manage him. The man's attention wandered for a second, he didn't know why, but it was enough.

Jake took the upper hand. He entered the building and walked up the stairs. The first man was at the top.

Jake pinched his neck, knocking him out.

The second floor was a maze of hallways and offices. Broken glass was everywhere. It was odd, Jake thought, that he hadn't seen any beer cans; no one came here to get drunk, as though the building were somehow sacred, or haunted.

Martin and his captor were in the far office, overlooking the driveway. Jake sensed a sporadic energy from Martin: Martin was the distraction. Jake walked over to Mazetti.

"No! Jake don't kill him!"

Martin had sensed Jake's intent. "Okay, I won't. And it's good to see you too." He pressed carefully on the man's neck. Mazetti fell, unconscious, to the floor.

"He'll be out for a few hours," Jake said, grinning at Martin with his odd squint.

Martin laughed. "It sure took you long enough to find me. You're getting old."

Jake roared with laughter as he untied Martin. "Cocky, smart-ass kid."

"You're hurt?" Martin said, pointing to the large red stain on Jake's parka.

"I'm okay, for the time."

In spite of the wound, Jake hugged Martin. With his good arm locked around Martin's shoulder, Jake led him back to the diner.

THIRTY-SIX

At the diner, Martin ordered two cups of coffee while Jake called Mac, then the police. After they had finished their coffee, they drove to the hospital. The police met Jake there. At the mill, they had found two dead, five unconscious, including Tom Mazetti, and one lunatic. There were signs of one or two others, but they had escaped. The inspector interviewed Jake while the doctor finished tending his wound.

Mac and Bonnie showed up. Mac confirmed Jake's story. ". . . And, of course, the police departments in Pittsburgh, Cleveland, and Cleveland Heights can corroborate much of this."

The inspector said that he didn't think the DA would want any charges brought against Jake. "Anyway, you've done us a service; Mazetti had his hand in things here."

It was almost four by the time they left the hospital. The inspector walked them out to their cars. "Listen, Jake, I like you, and as I said, I appreciate what you did. But, please, don't come back. It'll take me a week to do all the paper work."

***

It was late spring, and the sun was hot in the thin cold air.

A small stream ran through the valley ahead of him. A few scraggly trees hung onto life along its trail. Chemmg was on an errand from his Abbot. He was bringing a scroll to the monastery in the next village.

Chemmg had been honored by the Abbot when he was chosen. In his remarkable naiveté, he didn't see the petty jealousies and pranks played against him by the others his age, at least he didn't react to them. The Abbot, however, wanted to give Chemmg a chance to be away from all that for a few days.

He walked along the narrow path through the new spring grasses. He could smell their growth in the air. He was happy.

As he came around a rock outcropping, he first heard, and then saw, a clan of bandits attacking a lone monk. Without thinking, Chemmg put the scroll down and ran into the fray. He jumped on one of the men. He had no idea what happened next. He was struck on the head, and came to some time later. The monk was wiping his forehead with a damp cloth.

"You're a foolish young man."

Chemmg looked around him. The bandits were gone, except for three bodies that had been dragged off the trail.

"You risked a lot to help a frail old man. But," the old man laughed, "as you can see, I really didn't need much help."

Chemmg felt embarrassed. For once, he was unable to think of anything to say.

"You'll be all right. You have an errand. When you're through, when you pass by here, look for me. We will talk."

It took Chemmg a day and a half to get to the other monastery. The Abbot there insisted that he stay the night. Chemmg couldn't get the monk out of his mind, and wanted to find him, but there was no way for him to excuse himself without insulting his host.

In the middle of the fifth day after the incident, Chemmg

was back in the valley. The bodies had been buried beneath a small mound of rocks. Some animal had already dug away one corner, and had eaten all the flesh off a leg. Food was too scarce to let such bounty go. He looked around. He called out for the old man. There was no answer. Then he felt a tweak; he needed to follow the path into the mountain, away from his village.

He walked for an hour along the mountain stream. The path worked its way up into the rocks. There was no shade and he was getting hot. Around a large rocky crag the path crossed over to the other side of the chasm by means of a rope bridge. Chemmg hesitated, but the feeling got stronger. He crossed.

Around the far side sat the monk, his legs folded under him, his hands locked in his lap, his body straight. He was meditating. Chemmg sat down and waited. He thought he heard laughter, but the monk had been quiet. Startled, he realized that the laughter came from inside his head. And there was something about it that made him want to laugh too. He held it in, trying not to disturb the monk. The harder he fought the harder it got. Suddenly, it burst out.

With a smile on his face the monk looked at Chemmg. "Why do you laugh?"

Chemmg understood that he had been led there and that the monk had somehow gotten into his head and made him laugh, yet it seemed absurd.

"You . . . made me."

"And how could I do that?"

"You," Chemmg paused, he had no idea how, and he didn't understand why he was being asked to explain.

"Ah, you'll come to my rescue, but you won't answer a simple question."

Chemmg was confused and challenged. He had never met anyone like this before. He stood up to leave.

"Wait. I have to come with you. Your Abbot won't understand that you want to study with me. I must meet him, and talk with him, to explain. . . . My name is Ka."

It made sense to Chemmg that he should study with him.

***

Jake suggested that Martin drive him back. They followed Bonnie and Mac. They were quiet, as Martin got used to driving Jake's VW.

"Thanks for saving me," Martin said, finally breaking the silence.

"Hey, no problem. It's what I do."

"Why do I feel like you have something to say that I don't want to hear?"

Jake smiled. "Because I do."

Martin felt uneasy. "You going to tell me, or just sit and grin?"

"Why do you think this happened? All of it?"

"I just got mixed up with some bad people. You know how that is? I mean, you know, it just happened."

"No. It didn't just happen. You're special. How did you know that I was going to kill that man? How did you help distract him? In fact, how did you keep from really joining the Judge's boys? Why should all these people make such a fuss over you?"

"I don't know. I don't understand. Did I do anything that someone else wouldn't have done?"

"It's not that someone else wouldn't have done it, it's that someone else couldn't have done it." Jake smiled. "What I'm saying is that you're special, untrained and unskilled, but you have potential . . . to be . . . like me."

Martin stared at Jake, and drove off onto the shoulder. Jake quickly matched his breathing to Martin's and calmed him down. He let Martin feel his presence, but not enough to startle him.

"Jake?" Martin whispered.

"What do you think?"

"I don't know. I mean I'm just a kid, and now you're telling me that I could be a . . . a . . ."

"Mystic?"

"Yeah. A Mystic. What's that mean?"

They talked for the hour it took them to get home. When they got there, Martin was unusually quiet.

"You two okay?" Mac asked.

"We're fine. Listen, Bonnie, what would you say if Martin helped me out at the store during his Christmas break? He said he could use the money, and I could use the help."

"Martin asked you about working?"

"Yeah."

"Is he okay?"

"Oh, yes. He's fine." Jake smiled.

***

For the next two weeks, until Martin went on Christmas vacation, Jake kept normal hours at The Bookstall. It took him most of that time to catch-up. Because the door remained shut, the store looked closed. The Christmas rush had little effect on his business. Jake liked that.

Martin showed up for work the week before Christmas. Jake had him straighten up the tables, getting familiar with where various books were, and packaging orders to be mailed out. Martin enjoyed working. Jake wasn't hard to work for. He kept things low key.

Early in the afternoon, Martin's first day, Jake put the "CLOSED" sign in the window. He wanted to talk with Martin without being interrupted.

Had Jake's friends at the health food store seen the sign in the window they would have gotten angry with him. They didn't, and they were pleased to know that Jake had taken their advice and hired someone.

"Did you bring lunch?" Jake asked Martin.

"I thought, you know, we're downtown, I'd eat out. No?"

"Did you bring any money?"

"How?" Martin said foolishly. "You haven't paid me yet, all I've got is bus fare."

"Tell you what, just for today, here's fifteen bucks, go to the sandwich shop, just above here, and get four of whatever you want . . . we'll do lunch." Jake laughed.

It was when Martin got back that Jake locked the door and put out the "CLOSED" sign.

"I may not have had a job before," Martin had a quizzical look, "but you don't seem to encourage people to buy from you."

"Well, that's not entirely true. People who want books, who love books, are always welcome, but otherwise . . . you're right."

"How do you make money?"

"Look at me. Do I look like a rich guy? What kind of sandwiches did you get?"

For a few minutes, they were quiet, enjoying their lunch. When Jake finished his first sandwich, he asked Martin if he had thought over what they had talked about the other night.

"You mean studying with you?"

"Yes. I know that you're not sure what's involved, and in a few hours of talk there's no way I can tell you."

"It sounds fun. It'd be neat to know all that stuff you can do."

"Martin, it's not fun; it's hard work. It's giving up a lot of things."

"How'd you get into it?"

Jake took his second sandwich. He thought about Chemmg, who never got to see this moment. Then, between bites, he told Martin about Tai Chi, about studying with Dr. Pak in San Francisco, and about his first meeting with Chemmg Tse Lu.

Jake talked for an hour. "Okay, now you have some idea. It's time for me to reopen. But first, I want you to try something."

Jake led Martin to the alcove under the stairs. He fished around in a couple of boxes, producing two cushions and a mat. Jake placed them on the floor. "I want you to try meditating."

Martin looked around in distress. "What if someone comes in? What if someone sees me?"

"I'll close this curtain. No one will see you back there. Okay?"

"Yeah. What do I do?"

"Good. I want you to sit on the cushions." Martin took off his shoes and sat down. "No, put this leg like this." Jake helped him assume the correct position.

"Well, that's close enough for now. We'll have to work on it. Stare at the wall; let your eyelids close a little. No, no, you're leaning to the right. Try to remember exactly how this feels." Jake held him upright with his finger tips. "Yes, that's it. Good. Here's the hard part. I want you to count each exhalation. Just breathe deeply. Try it."

"Breathing?"

"Yes." Jake watched him. He placed his hand on Martin's

stomach. "Bring the air down here. Good. Push my hand out as you breathe in. Feel it?" Martin nodded. "Good. Now Exhale and whisper 'one' as you exhale, but don't make it audible. Okay, that's it, 'two.'"

Martin looked up at Jake. "That's it? That's meditating?"

"Easy?"

"Yeah."

"Okay, I'll make you a bet. I'll make it even easier for you. You count ten exhalations and then start over, counting another ten, and so on. You do that for fifteen minutes, no, let's make that ten. If you can, and believe me I'll know if you lie, I'll buy lunch every day for the next three weeks."

"No sweat." Martin looked down at the cushion for a second. "There's a catch? Isn't there? You'll distract me, right?"

"No, I won't do a thing. I won't have to; you'll do it to yourself. So, is it a bet?"

"What if I lose? . . . although that's impossible."

"I'll let you decide my prize."

"Can I pick the restaurants?"

"If you can do it, you can have lunch anywhere you want."

"Start timing."

"It's one thirty-five." Jake closed the curtain, and sat down.

***

Jake couldn't help being just a little cocky. After all, he thought, he had been studying Tai Chi for a year, and he was smart.

"Mr. Krajczynski, we'll play a game. I don't stress the physical, not as much as I do the psychological, but you seem so sure of yourself, and I'm such a little man compared to you. What do you say?"

They were in Chemmg's apartment. It was empty, except for his terra cotta tea pot, three cups, a one quart pan, three robes, and several neatly folded blankets. The austerity frightened Jake, but he felt that he wouldn't be asked to live like this, not forever.

"So, what's the game?"

"Pushing. You just push me."

Jake knew what would happen. If Chemmg Tse Lu was good—and Jake didn't doubt it—he'd end up on the floor. He had played that sort of game before.

"Ah, you are . . . fowl, as you would say. I'll give you an advantage. Tie my hands together behind my back and blindfold me. All right?"

Jake smiled: Chemmg had given away too much. "It's chicken."

"Chicken?"

"Not fowl, and you're on."

He used his belt to tie Chemmg's hands, and Chemmg's sash to blindfold him. He gave the old man a shove, but his hand slid off him. Jake barely caught himself.

"I will make it still easier. You can come at me from any side. You can run or stand. Take off your shoes, you'll be quieter."

For fifteen minutes, Jake tried to best Chemmg. "You're doing something to my mind, making me trip. Right?"

"I could do that, but I haven't. I give you my word; this is merely a game of physical skills. I don't cheat."

Jake was wet and exhausted when he leaned over by the window trying to catch his breath. "Okay, you win. How'd you do it?"

"If you have patience, and do what I ask of you, someday you'll have your answer."

***

Five minutes had passed. Jake heard Martin, who was trying to deal with the prickling in his legs. "Not bad for the first time," Jake thought. He waited to see if Martin would give up.

Martin struggled to stay still for the full ten minutes. Jake pulled the curtain aside. "Well, what do you say?"

"My legs hurt."

"How'd you do counting?"

Martin looked sheepish. He thought about lying, but he knew Jake; he would never get away with it. "I was okay for two or three times, but after that I kept getting lost. How long can you do it?"

Jake grinned. "When you're good, you'll be able to do it for twenty-four hours, no problem. Don't try to stand, just straighten you legs and rub them. You'll be fine."

"So I lost. What do I owe you?"

"What do you think?"

Martin sat there on the floor, wondering if his legs would ever stop hurting. It came to him, just as he realized that the prickling had stopped. "I should practice meditating, huh?"

"Everyday. Here. Just like this."

Martin groaned.

THIRTY-SEVEN

Martin learned fast. Jake was impressed, but he didn't let on. Martin's legs still hurt him, but every day he could go a little longer before his mind wandered. By the end of the week, Jake could tell that Martin was willing to sit there for as long as Jake let him. He monitored Martin, not wanting him to over do it. He broke up the meditation sessions into four fifteen to thirty minute periods. Between them, they talked.

At the end of the week, on Saturday, the day before Jake's Christmas Eve party, Martin asked him about the Judge.

"You've never really talked about what happened with the Judge. Will you tell me?"

Martin couldn't help noticing Jake's smile slide off his face. "Lock the door and put up the 'CLOSED' sign."

"Jake, it's the last shopping day. You don't want to lose that much business."

"Do it."

Something in Jake's manner told Martin that this was a big moment. He felt some foreboding and a sense of excitement. He locked the door, put the sign in the window, and pulled down the shade on the door.

"Martin, sit here; get comfortable." Jake sat in his chair by the table. Martin chose to sit on his cushions, but with his knees drawn up against his chest, leaning against the wall. He glanced at the clock on the desk. *He's crazy. It's 1:12, look at the people shopping*, Martin thought.

"My Master kept this from me for several years, and I was much more advanced than you when I started studying with him. But I realize that it's the student who sets the pace, not the Master. Don't get cocky. There's a lot more for you to learn than you can imagine. We'll need years together.

"You've been through a lot, never understanding why, well, this will be your Christmas present. I'll take you there, where it happened. Just relax."

"What do you mean, 'take me there?'"

"Dreamsharing. We will dreamshare. I'll explain later, if you still have questions. Now, relax."

***

The air was cool, in spite of the bright sun. It was late fall. The leaves had turned bright crimson, yellow, and gold. The sweet smell of campfires and roasting meat wafted through the air, as the bargemen made breakfast along the T'ng.

Jake was sitting against a tree, smiling at Martin as Martin sat up, looking around confused.

"What? Where are—"

"We're in the land of the neeZeen."

"This is a dream?" Martin grabbed a handful of dry leaves. He held them close to his nose as he crumpled them. "A dream?"

"Well sort of—you can also live or die here—it's a dream, and it's real."

"Was the Judge here?"

"Yes. If you're okay, let's walk and I'll tell you about it as we go."

They walked towards the river. Jake said they would take a barge as far as the Coast Road. He told Martin about the Judge, *Vritrk*, as he was called by the neeZeeners. He told him about the band of seven and their quest to save the world from Evil, and of *Vritrk's* Changelings.

It took them an hour to find a barge that had room for them.

It impressed Martin that people acknowledged Jake as though they knew him, but they stared at him as though they were seeing a ghost. Jake noticed it too, although he was too distracted by the flood of memories to think much about it.

The barge arrived at T'ng'qrt in the evening. Jake had no money, at least none that would work there. When he suggested that High Priest Molezeen would reimburse him, the bargeman looked hurt. "But it is my honor to have helped you."

The innkeeper said the same thing, staring at Martin.

They shared a bedroom. "Jake, I don't understand. This is so real. How can this be a dream?"

"Go to sleep." Jake didn't have an answer to Martin's question. He knew that where they were was not a dream; that explaining it as dreamsharing barely answered anything. But where were they? "We'll talk about it later."

"What about your Christmas party tomorrow?"

"Don't worry about that. Trust me and go to sleep. If we can get horses, we have a long ride ahead of us."

"Horses?" Martin moaned. He had never ridden a horse in his life, and he knew he'd be sore if he did.

The next morning, after a breakfast of warmed *troan* and smoked fish—Martin was pleased with himself that he'd been able to drink something alcoholic without having to plead—Jake asked the innkeeper about getting horses.

"Go to the stables across from here; they're owned by my brother-in-law. Tell him I sent you. He'll take care of everything."

"I'm sure that the High Priest will reimburse—"

"Don't talk of money. It's our honor." The innkeeper seemed to bow to them.

The stable master's son rode with them, south to Zot'qrt, so that he could return the horses. It was a pleasant ride. It warmed as they rode; the trees near the capital were only beginning to turn color. Outside the North Gate, the boy took his leave as Martin and Jake entered Zot'qrt.

Jake wanted to find the inn he and d'Solteen had stayed in, the one with batter, the neeZeen version of pinball. They got lost in the maze of outdoor bazaars and alleyways.

It struck Martin as funny that for all of Jake's self-assurance, they seemed to be getting farther and farther away from any place that Jake truly recognized. Martin kept suggesting that they ask someone, but that offended Jake's sense of pride. "I'll find it. . . . This is familiar, over here. It's got to be down here."

Towards dusk, Martin was getting worried. Knowing Jake, they could keep walking all night. Then he heard horses, coming closer to them down the narrow streets. Around the corner ahead of them were a carriage and four horsemen—warriors by their looks—stopped, waiting for them. Jake let out a howl. "Jho! You old rascal. How are you?"

Their leader, taller and older than the rest, swung his right leg across the horse's neck and slid off. He embraced Jake. They slapped each other's backs. Jho broke Jake's grasp and looked closely at him. "I see that you've gained back all your weight." Jake's laugh echoed through the bazaars making people think that nGin was playing some prank.

Martin rocked back and forth, embarrassed by the intensity of their reunion. Jho stopped laughing and stared at him. Jake put hands on each of their shoulders. "Jho, this is Martin, he's from my world. Martin this is Jho, I told you about him."

Martin offered his hand; Jho hesitated taking it, still staring at him.

"Jho, you all right?" Jake asked.

"You don't see it?"

"What?"

"Never mind. Get in the carriage. We're expected at the temple."

They rode through the labyrinth of streets. Martin felt more at ease; he did not know where he was, but they weren't lost anymore. "Well, one way or another, we'll eat and rest tonight. I was getting worried."

Jake slapped Martin's knee. "You just don't trust me do you? I'd have found it. It was just a block down that street. Just a block, we were almost there." Even in the carriage at dusk, he could see the twinkle in Jake's eye.

The temple impressed Martin. It seemed like a Hollywood set for Camelot. The temple sprawled over a large area, a small city in itself. They went past the public section, down a long cloister. Cast in shadows, the inner courtyard was mysterious, tranquil, and beguiling. At the far end, they entered a series of offices. Just off the third was a large waiting room. Jho knocked on the heavy, wooden door. It opened. There, in a dark blue robe with silver piping around its edges, the cowl pulled back away from his head, stood Molezeen. "I had heard that it might be you. Although I never thought I'd see you again, my friend."

They embraced. Unlike the meeting with Jho, there was no outpouring of laughter. There was a solemnity to the reunion, inspired not so much because of Molezeen's position as High Priest, but due to the depth of their feelings for each other. "It would be an understatement to say that your departure from us was startling."

Jake gave a shrug and a sheepish smile. "Well, it was over, and it was time." He patted Molezeen's back, "Truth be known, I was startled too." Jake's laugh flooded the room.

Molezeen turned towards Martin. "Jake, your manners have not improved. This is?"

Jake put his arm around Martin and led him over to Molezeen. "Molezeen, this is Martin, my student; Martin, this is the High Priest of the neeZeen, Molezeen."

Molezeen embraced Martin, which made Martin uneasy. Molezeen sensed his discomfort and let go. "It is our custom." He turned to Jake. "I'm no longer the High Priest, however. Please, follow me. There's someone I want you to see."

Molezeen led them through his quarters, down a maze of narrow corridors and stairs. They walked through the large library, into the dining hall. He stopped and turned to Jake. "I've not forgotten you, my friend. We'll have dinner brought to us. I'm sure we have enough to satisfy even your legendary appetite."

Molezeen led them through a door off the side of the great hall. Down another corridor, at the end, was a closed door, protected by two of the temple guards. They saluted Molezeen and stood aside as he knocked.

The door opened. Martin gasped. He was looking at his twin. Molezeen smiled. "Stel, surely you remember Jake, and this is his student, Martin." Jake and Stel hugged, although Stel's eyes never left Martin. Jake held Stel away so that he could compare him with Martin. "You know, I never saw it, never. You two could be twins."

Martin and Stel shook hands. They felt comfortable with each other, like brothers. Molezeen said something to one of the guards, then ushered them into Stel's chambers. While they waited for dinner, Molezeen, Jho, and Jake stood around the fireplace talking about their adventures and catching up. Stel and Martin walked away from the others. Stel was excited. This was the first time in months that he could talk to someone his own age, and not about leadership responsibilities or continuing his education. Martin, too, valued his new friendship. Although their only commonality lay in Jake, as they talked about his eccentricities they discovered more and more what they shared with one another. They never knew that the others had stopped to listen to them.

A guard knocked on the door then wheeled a dinner cart in. They all took turns teasing Jake about his weight and the quantity of food available to him. Martin and Stel were the most ruthless. Jake shook his head at the two. "Double teamed, and by them! That's loyalty."

While they ate, Molezeen kept getting up and checking with the guards. Jake's curiosity got the better of him. "What's up? You keep pacing like an expectant father."

"When we heard that you might be coming to the capital, I sent word to d'Solteen and Llo. I've been expecting their arrival anytime."

"They're together?"

Stel looked at Molezeen, he wondered if he should tell Jake, or let him be surprised. Molezeen nodded. "They're married," Stel said.

Dinner was good. They ate and chatted. Molezeen had to send out twice for more wine. Stel and Martin sat apart from the rest. There were several conversations going at a time.

They'd begun to slow down, even Jake, when the door opened. D'Solteen and Llo walked in. They were radiant in their love for each other and in their excitement over the reunion. More food was ordered, against Llo's protestations. The chambers had not seen such merriment for generations.

Jake caught Llo with his odd stare, "You know, I think you're—"

"With child." Llo grinned. "Yes. He's due just after the Second Half Moon."

"He?"

"Of course, it's a boy." Llo looked at d'Solteen, then back to Jake. "Guess his name?"

"Oh, come on, how? I give up."

Llo laughed. "It's Jake."

THIRTY-EIGHT

When Jake got up in the morning, Martin was gone. For a moment, he was worried, but he realized that in the temple Martin would be safe. Jake dressed and sniffed his way to the dining hall. Molezeen, Jho, and Soan, were there.

"I'm sorry that I missed you last night. I was away on business and just got back," Soan said as they embraced. "Join us. You look . . . starved."

"I don't deserve this ridicule. I really don't."

Jho smiled at Jake. "They'll clear the table if you don't sit and eat."

"Where are Martin and Stel?"

Molezeen shrugged. "I don't know. I heard that they got up early and went out together." Jake looked worried. "They'll be fine."

D'Solteen and Llo joined them ten minutes later.

"It's so beautiful outside, could we eat out? Is that permissible?"

"It's not done, but there's no rule against it. We may be setting a new standard." Molezeen talked with one of the servers. "Let's go. They'll bring everything out to us."

They went to the courtyard.

"Cousin," Llo said, "this is truly splendid. Why do you keep it secret?"

The courtyard was a series of interconnected formal and

informal gardens, separated by large, full hedges, or walls, with fountains and ponds. A small stream meandered through. The path crossed it many times using a variety of bridges and stepping-stones. Even if he sighted along the cloisters, Jake could barely make out the far side.

Molezeen led them to a poet's garden. At the base of a small, man-made waterfall was a fish pond, half shadowed by a hedgerow of balsamic pines, and bordered by a moss garden. In the sun, on the far side of the pond, were several tables with chairs. Breakfast came out a few minutes later.

"This is beautiful. Thank you." Llo was enchanted with the garden.

"If this catches on, we may never get people back to work." Molezeen smiled. He actually thought that this would be good for morale, and wondered why no one had thought of it before.

***

Martin and Stel had become, in an instant, best friends. Although Stel held the title of High Priest, Molezeen acted as regent until Stel's training was complete. Of course, Martin too had been in training, although for a shorter time. They shared a common purpose in life.

They were the same age, and they shared a love of youthful fun. People recognized Stel; his likeness had been printed and circulated widely. But seeing two of them, twins, that shocked people. If one looked closely, it wasn't impossible to see that they weren't identical; the set of their eyes, the shape of their jaws, the folds of their ears, were all different enough. At a glance, or in profile, however, they could be reflections of each other. They were not cruel about it. They didn't tease people, but they did enjoy the confusion.

Stel told Martin about *Vritrk*, more than Jake had. Where Jake had played down the Changelings, Stel reveled in describing them in the minutest, gory, detail. High Priest or not, the fun was in the details. By halfday, they found themselves at the mouth of the Zot in a park, with a cypress forest of great age and size. "This is my favorite place to go. I can get away from the temple here. Sometimes I don't know how my cousin takes it there."

Stel led Martin to his hiding place, a small clearing, set in the rocks, thirty feet above the ocean.

"Will you and Jake be here long?"

"I don't know. He brought me here. He called it dreamsharing, but I'm confused." Martin sat, mindlessly picking up little pebbles and tossing them over the edge into the ocean. "Is this a dream?"

"No, it's no dream. Certainly not Jake's or yours," Stel argued. "I can tell you everything that's happened since he left, what, twenty halfmoons ago. And, if it was his dream, how are you able to be here with me now?"

"I don't understand. The, how do you say it, *Vritrk*? "

Stel laughed at Martin's attempt. "Go on, you'll never be able to say it right. Jake couldn't either."

Martin blushed, but he knew that the teasing was innocent. "He's a Judge from our world." He picked up a handful of pebbles and threw them. "I kind of liked him, for a while. Jake says the Judge was trying to turn me away from my destiny. He had a stroke after he and Jake came here."

"Well, I can tell you that I killed him, dead. . . . If you won't tell, I'll show you the Staff when we get back. You got to promise you won't tell."

"I promise."

They walked around the park, talking about their dreams,

the ones that could be and the ones that couldn't. There was great comfort for each of them knowing that the other also would have to make sacrifices. They lost track of time. It was dusk when they realized that they would be missed if they didn't get back soon.

Stel looked at Martin. "Let's race."

"How? I don't know the way."

"All right, let's race to the gate; just follow this path."

They raced to the gate. Martin won, but it was close. They picked another landmark, one they could see, and raced again. All the way back to the temple, they ran. Martin won half the races. When they got to the temple, they were soaked. Kidding, pushing, and boasting, they walked to Stel's suite. Molezeen and Jake were waiting for them.

"We were about to send the guard out for you," Molezeen kidded Stel. Although he would not admit it to Stel, he and Jake had begun to worry.

"We need to get cleaned up. We raced all the way back from Cypress Park."

"I won most."

"Did not. I—"

"Get out of here. You two have set back my life-long efforts to make the High Priesthood a position of dignity."

Stel and Martin seemed unsure if Molezeen was serious or not. Then Molezeen nudged Jake. "Take your baths and clean up. At least, I can insist that you don't stink for dinner." He laughed.

As the door closed behind them, Molezeen looked at Jake. "It's going to break his heart when you and Martin leave. You know that?"

"Yes, but we can't stay forever. My being here, our being here, affects your world, for good and for bad."

"Let's walk," Molezeen said, taking Jake's arm. "It'll take them a while to get ready. . . . We've talked about that, your effect here. You came into our world, you were good, but the Judge was also from your world. You sent him here . . . no?"

"I don't know. I certainly had a lot to do with it, but—you must have felt it—there was something behind *Vritrk*." Jake's voice dropped to a whisper, "There was laughter in the thunder that night."

"Yes, I heard it; Kendt did also. He was worried about it. I still do."

"He did die, didn't he?"

"His body was found two months after you left. They found it in the mountains. He died where he felt most at home. We had his body brought here. I should have shown you this morning. He's buried in the courtyard. It's a place of joy. Kendt would have liked that. I'll show you tomorrow."

"Tell me something. I thought you were High Priest for life?"

"According to our tradition, High Priest for life, yes, but this is my belief: *Vritrk* was a pawn and so were you—we all were. If I truly thought that you had sent *Vritrk* to us, to wreak his style of death upon us for several years, I'm afraid that your reception now would have been quite different."

Jake nodded his head.

"I am afraid for our future. If something were to happen to me before selecting the next High Priest, the choice would fall on our Senate. The politics would make the selection unsure. Stel returned with us a hero. He has the potential; he may develop far more than any of us ever could. I have made sure that his future is as secure as possible, although that's not to say safe. I'd have never gotten it through except that, as I said, Stel's a hero and I suggested that I remain on as regent. What could anyone say?"

Molezeen winked. Jake admired the genius of this maneuver.

"I've missed you, my friend," Jake said as he put his arm around Molezeen's shoulder. "Let's check on Martin and Stel. I'm hungry."

***

Again the next day, they awoke to find that Stel and Martin had gotten up before everyone else. They had eaten and disappeared by the time the rest showed up for breakfast.

Stel was going to show Martin the Staff he had used to kill *Vritrk*. He knew that Molezeen would disapprove unless everyone was present, but Stel wanted the moment to be his, a secret shared only with Martin.

They had to sneak through the library. At the far end, there was a small door, almost hidden between two sets of bookshelves. Behind it, down a narrow, spiral flight of stairs, was a storage vault for the use of the High Priest where he could keep his private papers and memorabilia. In the corner of the vault were the three Staves of Li. Stel closed the upper door behind them.

"Shit, it's dark," Martin whispered. "Where are—"

Stel bumped into Martin. "Don't move. There's a flight of stairs behind you." In the total blackness, he searched his pockets for a match. "Can you feel for the lantern? It's on the back of the door."

"Got it," Martin said. There was a fshshsh sound as Stel's match caught in a sulfurous cloud.

Stel held the lit lantern up. "Look."

Martin turned; the steep, stone steps started two inches from his right foot. "No problem," Martin said in a flat voice, which acknowledged how close he had been to disaster.

"Follow me."

With the lantern in hand, they made their way down the twenty, winding, narrow, stairs. At the bottom, the storage room was to the left.

Stel put the lantern down on the large table in the center of the room. "Here, sit down. I'll get it."

"Stel, what did you feel? You know, you thought you were going to die, didn't you?"

Stel sat down opposite Martin. "Yeah. It's kind of hard to describe it. Jake said that I was in a trance when I did it, and I almost died."

Martin was confused. "I thought that the Staff can't kill you?"

"It can't. But I didn't know that then. I was so prepared to die, that when *Vritrk* turned towards me and tried to ward me off, my mind had shut down. A kind of shock had set in. I'm not sure I understand it. You know Jake saved my life?"

"No. What did he do?"

"It was afterwards. I don't know what he did, but he cared for me for several days until I was all right. Molezeen said that had Jake not been with us, there was nothing anyone could have done for me."

"Have you used the Staff since then?"

"No."

Even in the dull yellow light, Martin could see Stel flush. It didn't sound true; Martin couldn't imagine not using it if he could. "No?"

"You can't tell anyone. Promise?"

"Of course."

"I've come down here a lot. No one knows."

Stel got up and walked over to the Staves. He picked up his. "Watch."

He turned down the lantern. There was a slight glow coming from the head of the Staff in his hand. It got brighter. The room was awash in a flickering white light.

"Huh?" Stel couldn't hide his grin. "Neat? It's taken me a while to figure it out."

Martin was impressed and not a little jealous. "Let me try?"

"No way. I told you, it'll kill you."

Martin shivered in the cold, feeling hurt at Stel's rejection.

Stel sensed Martin's hurt. "Hey, cold? Here, I just learned this."

Heat, not much, but enough to chase the chill away, filled the room. The light flickered more.

"It's kind of hard to do both. What do you think?"

Martin knew Stel was trying to make him feel better. But he couldn't help his feelings; they were always close to the surface. *Anyway,* he thought, *Stel and I are like brothers, and I'm special too, Jake said so. . . . Why can't I use the Staff?* Before Stel could do anything, Martin jumped up and grabbed one of the Staves from the corner.

"See, I can do it too!"

Stel gasped in shock and surprise. His adrenaline surged. "The Gods!" He knew Martin should be dead, charred black on the floor. "You really scared me," he said, gasping for air.

Martin laughed. "Yeah, but I can do it too."

Stel got his breath and laughed too. Their secret had just gotten bigger.

Martin grabbed the edge of the table with his other hand as a wave of vertigo hit him. "Whoa! I'm—"

"Sit down."

"I'm dizzy, like being stoned."

"Stoned?" Stel asked.

"Stoned, you know high or drunk."

"It'll pass. Breathe slowly."

"Okay, I'm fine. But my hand is tingling," Martin said. "It feels . . . good. I don't want to let it go."

"Yeah. I know. Sometimes I come down here just to be with them. Hey, try to make light."

"How?"

"You have to see, in your mind, the light coming from the Staff, really see it. Try."

Martin tried. A faint glow appeared. Not much, but it was new to him. Stel whistled. "Not bad, it took me longer to get that much. Imagine it brighter. . . ."

***

At breakfast, Llo didn't have to ask that they eat in the garden again. Molezeen suggested it, and led them to the site of Kendt's grave. There was a small, in-ground monument, tastefully inscribed to him. Jake was touched by the simplicity and elegance, befitting his memory of Kendt.

Out came the food and drinks. Molezeen suggested that they drink a toast to Kendt. "I've asked that we be brought a pitcher of warm *troan*. There's wine for you," he said to Llo. "Let's drink to Kendt. But, I insist, in joyous memory. He lived a full life, the life he chose, and he died when and where he wanted. Most of us never get those choices."

They drank to Kendt. It was hard for them not to feel sadness over his death, but that didn't last long. Jho was serving from the cart. He handed Jake a platter piled high with food. It broke the spell.

Llo asked Molezeen about Stel. "He's around, isn't he?"

"Yes. But he and Martin have become fast friends. They've

been running all over the place. I've gotten strange reports from the town . . . nothing serious. Just mischief. I don't think we can expect to see either of them until they get hungry."

Everyone looked at Jake, huddled over his platter. He looked up sheepishly. "You don't think I returned just for the food, do you?"

***

Stel and Martin spent as much time as they could in the vault, without raising suspicions. They shared a feeling of deep obligation and need to perfect their control over the Staves. Martin was almost as good as Stel in some things, and better in others. They goaded each other on in friendly competition.

They found that working a Staff was interactive. With a certain mind-set, it gave back to them. While holding the Staves, they discovered, they could sometimes communicate by thinking. It was tricky. Neither wanted to just open up everything to the other, but they felt their way along, developing control. After a few weeks, it seemed that they were able to communicate without the Staves as though that skill was transferable from the Staves to them.

At night, sharing Stel's chambers, they speculated on the true power and purpose of the Staves of Li. Stel showed Martin his copies of the *Koth'seen* and the *nQert'seen*. Martin looked at the illustrations as Stel read the story.

"Do you think nGin is still around?" Martin asked.

"I don't know. I mean, these were just children's stories for me until, you know, until *Vritrk* and the Staves."

"What about the other Staves?"

"No one knows. They were all supposedly destroyed in the battle against Evil."

"But we've got three."

"I know. Maybe the rest can be found."

They knew that what they were learning would impress both Jake and Molezeen, but they still had not told them. They took pleasure in their secrecy.

"What if Evil isn't dead? Maybe *Vritrk* was like a general. Maybe there's someone, something bigger?"

Stel nodded. He and Molezeen had thought as much. "We think so. That's why it's great that we've learned as much about these as we have."

"Yeah, but I'm not going to stay here forever."

"You could come back, couldn't you?"

"I don't know. I don't know how Jake got me here. I don't understand it. And how would I know if you needed me?"

"Maybe I could come to your world?"

"That would be great. I could show you some great stuff. I've got a great record collection, and now Mac has a CD player, it's—"

"Record? CD?"

"They're . . ." Martin knew he couldn't really explain, "You'll just have to visit." Martin looked worried. "But who will teach you how?"

They were excited at the prospects. At the same time, they shivered with the shared thought that maybe the Staves could help.

***

One day at lunch, Jake asked Molezeen about Stel and Martin. "Do they seem quieter? Different somehow?"

"I hadn't thought about it until now that you mention it, but yes, they are. I don't think it's bad. Do you?"

"No. But it'll make our leave taking still harder, and that's got to be soon. I brought Martin here to help him understand, not just what happened, but what life holds for him if he accepts and honors his potentials."

"Why soon?"

"I love you all. But it would be too easy to get lost here, and we have a world of our own. Besides, it could be dangerous to be away too long."

"Is that true?"

"I'm not sure, but I don't want to take chances."

"Have you decided when?"

"I think tomorrow. Please don't say or do anything for us. It's best if we just disappear. I'll send Martin back without his knowing. Otherwise, well, it'll be worse if he knows about it and has to say good-bye, although he'll probably hate me for it, for a while."

The next morning, Martin and Stel tried to get to the vault, but there was always someone in the library. Finally, during lunch, it was empty.

"What if we take the Staves back to your suite?" Martin asked. "No one would know, and we could work with them anytime we wanted."

"I guess we could, but we'd have to be careful. I've got a trunk they'll fit in. We could hide them there. All right?"

"Let's do it now."

Stel hid their two Staves under his robe. They made him walk funny. Martin started to giggle. It was contagious. Somehow, they made it to Stel's suite. Martin closed the door behind them. They slid to the floor, red faced, teary-eyed, and convulsing with laughter.

"I thought the priest was going to call for a doctor. I mean, he kept asking, 'You all right? . . . you all right?' The way you were walking."

"That was close. You hungry or do you want to practice?"

"Let's practice."

After lunch, Jake told Molezeen that it was time. "Let's find them."

They asked around, hoping that someone had seen Martin and Stel. In the hallway off the great room, leading to Stel's suite, they asked a priest, who was repainting a stained section of wall, if he had seen Stel or Martin.

"I think they're in there. They went down there about half an hour ago. They were acting strangely. But—"

"Thank you," Molezeen cut him off.

Jake turned to Molezeen in front of Stel's door, "I'll send him back quickly, then I'll go." He gave Molezeen a hug. "Let's get this over with."

They walked into the suite. Stel's back was towards the door; Martin had his back to Jake. In that instant, Martin disappeared. Jake looked at Stel, who had a stunned look on his face. "I'm sorry. This is rude, but I think it is best. We . . . a . . . good-bye."

Jake vanished.

THIRTY-NINE

Martin felt his head. There was a bump where he had hit it back against the wall. He looked around. Jake was sitting in his chair, motionless, neither awake nor asleep. But his eyes were open. Martin felt strange. Other than Jake, everything looked normal. Then he saw his Staff. "Oh shit!"

Martin jumped to his feet and picked it up. "Please don't let him see it, please . . ." he prayed. He didn't think there was much time, and he didn't want Jake to know he had it. He looked around; there in the back of the alcove was a deep shadow along the bottom edge of the wall. It was dark enough that the Staff would be invisible. Since Martin had started meditating, Jake never went beyond the curtain behind his desk.

He reached for the Staff.

"Well?" Jake asked, stretching his arms. "Merry Christmas."

Do not let him see it; do not let him see it, he thought. "Thanks, it was great. Will we go back?"

Martin watched Jake. He shook his head, as if waking up, and looked around. He seemed to look right at the Staff, but he did not say anything. Was it invisible?

"I don't think so."

"What?"

"Go back. I don't think so. Our interference, as little as it was, could change a lot. It could be risky."

Martin wanted to argue, but decided against it. He would

learn how to do it, he thought. If Jake didn't take him back there, he'd go by himself, even if it took several years to figure out how.

"What would you say if we called it a day?" Jake asked.

Martin looked at the clock. It was 1:12. "What day is this? Saturday? It is? Isn't it?"

"Yes. Let's close up."

Jake locked the door, and put the key in his pocket. The Arcade was crowded and festive.

"Damn," Martin said when they were halfway across. "Can I have the key? I left my gloves inside."

"I'll come in with you."

"No, you get the van, I'll meet you."

Martin closed the door behind him. He looked out the window, watching Jake work his way through the crowd. "Christ," Martin sighed.

The Staff was lying on the floor, where he had left it, three feet in front of Jake's chair. Jake never saw it. Never.

Martin put it in the back of the alcove, in the shadow. He turned Jake's desk light on. Even with the curtain open, it was impossible to see it.

What the hell am I going to do with it? He wondered.

Martin ran to the door. "My gloves!"

He ran back, found them, and then left The Bookstall.

Jake had just started the van when Martin climbed in.

"Got 'em? Good. Come on I'll buy you a beer."

"How? I'm too young, remember?"

"We'll go to my place; anyway you've never been there. You'll love it."

***

Jake hung up their coats. "Look around. I'll get the beer."

The apartment was the perfect counterpoise to his time with Stel. He felt that there was an aptness about the mess, and when he tried to imagine Jake living amid anything else, he could not. Martin sat in one of the barber chairs, slowly spinning around in circles.

Jake returned from the kitchen with two bottles of Samuel Adams Tandy Stout on a tray with two small, round glasses and an assortment of crackers and cheeses. "Well?"

"I like it. You're quite a . . . character."

Jake grinned; he took perverse pleasure in his world of collections. "Love me, love my eccentricities."

Jake handed him one of the small glasses, filled with beer. "It's not *troan*. Help yourself."

"Kinda generous with your beer." Martin turned the small glass around in his hand as if the two ounces were supposed to be precious.

"Smart ass kid. You don't know anything. This way, by keeping most of the beer in the bottle, it stays colder longer and keeps its carbonation. Why am I always explaining these things to you?"

For the two bottles of beer, they sat in silence, but it was far from empty. Jake had dreamshared with Martin; there was camaraderie between them. For his part, Martin now knew what Jake expected of him not, of course, in every detail, but in terms of his overall direction and obligation. Even in the one hour since returning, he was seeing things differently. He found himself evaluating things, feeling for their intrinsic nature, their good or their evil. That is not to say he was obsessed. Rather, it was as though he had been color blind before, and now he was not. It felt natural.

Although Martin felt comfortable teasing Jake like an equal, he also knew the tremendous gap between them as Master and student. He thought about his mother and Mac. He recalled talking with Jake about Mac's turmoil over marrying, and now understood something of Jake's concern. Martin reflected on how close he'd come to falling into the Judge's domain, and how much he owed to the love of those around him.

He didn't think about the Staff.

Jake sipped his beer. Things had taken an odd turn. He had never intended to dreamshare with Martin, not for several years, and why he would have taken him there he had no idea. Yet, there was rightness about it. Martin, he could feel, had matured. Curious, he probed, discretely. Jake hid his shock. Martin had more than matured. Jake sensed a mastery of skills that should have taken years to learn. How much, he couldn't be sure without alerting Martin to the intrusion.

How? Jake wondered. Was there that much that he didn't know? He wished that Chemmg were alive. There was much he wanted to ask. Having a disciple was a lot like having a child. In spite of what he had experienced, he found himself unsure of exactly how to proceed. "We learn from our mistakes, so that we can repeat them exactly," Jake mumbled.

"What?" Martin asked.

"Oh, just thinking. More beer?"

Martin took his beer and walked around. He reminded Jake of Chemmg in the way he looked at things. Martin loved the apartment. He sat down on the floor in the porch. To make room for the Christmas tree, Jake had stacked a lot of odds and ends in there.

"Do you mind?" Holding one of Jake's glass covered boxes, Martin asked Jake.

"No. Go ahead. Just don't mix things up." Jake laughed. Having Martin there filled a need he hadn't known he had. Until now, he hadn't understood Chemmg's sadness over Jake's not having a disciple.

Martin spent hours pouring over the collection on the porch. He was particularly attracted to the netsuke. He didn't know what they had been created for, but that wasn't important. He loved the subtlety and humor of the small figures. There were four boxes of them. Some were wood. Smudges and shiny spots suggested years of wear. Some were ivory or ceramic. A few were metal, greenish-bronze with feathered gold highlights. One by one, Martin took them out. He grinned at the monkeys and demons, felt the pathos of the poor, hunched holy men, and marveled at the implied detail on the birds.

Before the dreamsharing, had he known the value of just this collection he would have been stunned; now, it wouldn't have meant much. Nonetheless, he was stunned: each piece held a life and a spirit to him.

It got dark. Jake turned on a few lights. Martin put the boxes back. He stood up and stretched. Jake was puttering around.

"I should probably get home soon."

"Could I talk you into helping me get ready for the party? There's not a lot to do, but the help would be welcome."

"Okay, where's your phone?"

Jake pointed to an old-fashioned wall phone. It was black and heavy, with a separate box for the wiring and the bell. Martin called home.

"It's all right. Mom said you're supposed to feed me and get me back before she goes to bed."

"Dinner, huh? What would you say to huevos rancheros?" Jake asked, getting excited over the thought of dinner.

"I don't know what it is."

"You will. Come on, we'll talk in the kitchen. Unless you want to look around more?"

The kitchen had a wrought iron loop attached to the ceiling; fourteen old, beat-up, tin-lined, copper pans and skillets hung from it. In the corner was a ten-gallon copper stockpot. "Only for making chili," Jake said. Large clay cooking pots and bags of chili peppers—dried chipotle, pasilla, sweet New Mexico, ascondo, and chilitepina pods—filled one cabinet. Jake said that the true secret to authentic Mexican cooking was the cookware and the chilies.

The stove was a 1923 Tinnerman, standing on four, white, enameled legs, with the oven and broiler on the left. When Jake bought it, the oven and broiler had been on the right, but it had been easy to change around when he restored it. Across the top was a metal shelf, used to keep things warm.

Martin helped Jake. He chopped the onions and peppers. Jake explored the GE cabbage-head refrigerator, looking for left over sauce, eggs, and a small batch of frijoles. "I make my own," Jake said, as he put everything down on the counter.

The refrigerator was old and small and packed like Martin's closet. "Why don't you get a new one? You'd like it, they can hold more food."

"And give up such a beauty?"

Martin wasn't sure what frijoles were, but he had liked Jake's Spanish omelet, so he was certain he would like them.

Jake whistled while he cooked. Cooking made him happy. Even Mac couldn't deny that, as much as they disagreed over what was good food.

Jake assembled the huevos rancheros, with a sprinkling of shredded Jack cheese. He put the plates under the boiler. "All right, look in the cabinet to your right. Get out the Mescal."

"The what?"

"Tequila."

Martin liked dinner. He didn't know that Mac thought Jake's huevos rancheros were an abomination. Jake had made them for Mac once, a few years ago. Mac had stomach cramps all night and diarrhea the next day, and even though he had actually liked eating them, the mere thought of them was enough to put him off his food for a day. Jake insisted that it was just that Mac wasn't used to chilitepina, which he always used for huevos rancheros.

Jake showed Martin how to drink tequila, with a lime and salt.

For dessert, Jake brought out ice cream and liqueur. "I just hope you can hold your liquor. Your mother would have my hide if she saw all this . . . and Mac would finish me off."

Martin laughed. "The secret is safe with me."

"We seem to be full of secrets these days." Martin didn't see Jake's squint.

After the ice cream, Martin and Jake worked on the apartment. Jake had invited eight people, which, for him, was a lot. They moved most of the small stacks of boxes into the back room. They put up strings of lights and moved the chairs and table around.

"What about the tree? Do you want help with it?"

"No. That is my business. I want it to be a surprise for everyone, including you."

Martin felt sure it would be.

FORTY

Jake had a dream.

Jake heard someone knocking very softly on his door. "I'm coming, I'm coming," he said as he walked down the bare wood floor. The knocking, still soft, continued.

"What do you—" he said, but stopped. It was Chemmg.

It was winter, and Chemmg wore a green down-filled parka over his dark red robe. In spite of the snow, he had sandals with socks on, no boots. "I've heard the news," he said to Jake, walking past him into the apartment.

"Where've you been? I thought you were—"

"No, no. I've been away. I may be old, but I've still got some time left. And there's work to do, always."

Chemmg took one of the chairs from the dining room into the living room. He hated the barber chairs. Jake hung up his parka.

"So, it's good to see you. But, what news?"

"You have a disciple, of course."

"You heard about Martin?"

"And why wouldn't I?"

"You would. I'll call him. If he's home, he can get here in a few minutes."

Martin came over.

"Martin there is someone I would like you to meet . . . Chemmg, this is Martin, my disciple." Jake grinned. "Martin, this is my Master, Chemmg Tse Lu."

"Jake, don't you have something to cook?" Chemmg asked.

Jake looked at his old master and his young disciple, and his eyes began to water. He turned his back, mumbling, "Tea. Some snacks. Maybe something sweet."

"Good," Chemmg said as Jake walked to the kitchen

Jake fussed in the kitchen, giving them at least a little time alone.

When the tea was ready, Jake carried it and a tray of cookies back to the living room. "Chemmg, it's good . . . where is he?" Chemmg was gone.

"He had to leave. He wanted me to tell you that he approves of my being your disciple."

"That's it?" Jake felt hot tears running down his face. He put the tray down and turned away from Martin. He didn't want Martin to see him cry.

"Jake? He's happy. I think he'll rest now."

Jake woke up. His pillow was wet; he wiped the tears from his eyes. "Damn, I miss him," he said as he looked at the clock. It was early, but he figured he wouldn't sleep well if he tried, so he got up and worked on the apartment.

***

Martin had a dream.

It was a late winter's afternoon. Martin got a phone call from Jake, asking Martin to come over.

Martin went to Jake's apartment.

"Martin there is someone I would like you to meet . . . Chemmg, this is Martin, my disciple." Jake grinned. "Martin, this is my Master, Chemmg Tse Lu."

"Jake, don't you have something to cook?" Chemmg asked.

Jake looked at his old master and his young disciple, and his eyes began to water. He turned his back, mumbling, "Tea. Some snacks. Maybe something sweet."

"Good," Chemmg said as Jake walked to the kitchen. He turned to Martin. "I am deeply pleased that Jake has finally taken a disciple. And I am happy that it should be you."

Martin blushed. "I'm just a kid. I—"

"No, you are more. You are special. Someday, when you have learned enough to be on your own, you will feel a need to pass on to someone else what you know. It will burn at your soul until you do. In Tibet, where this sort of thing is more common, it isn't too hard to find students, and one or two will become your disciples. But here, in this world of things," Chemmg gestured to the clutter of Jake's apartment, "it's difficult. That doesn't lessen the need. Jake has suffered; I can tell."

Martin felt something, a gentle touch like the gossamer stroke of a feather, in his head. He knew that it was Chemmg. He welcomed him. And Chemmg, too, welcomed Martin. Together they shared their memories, their fears, and their aspirations. There was too much for Martin to absorb in a few minutes.

Chemmg was surprised. Martin had developed far more than he should have in such a short time. Chemmg broke contact.

"Jake is right. You are special."

"Will you stay here a while? There's a lot I can learn from you, and I'd like to get to know you."

"No. You've learned too much. Jake is your teacher, and he can take you further than I ever could, believe me."

Chemmg stood up. He touched Martin's cheek. "I must leave. I didn't really have much time. Tell my disciple, and good friend, Jake, that I heartily approve of his student. I love him and I love you, Martin Winslow. Good-bye."

Chemmg left quietly. Martin sat for a while, thinking about

Chemmg Tse Lu. In those few minutes, he had learned a lot from him, about him, about Jake, and about their purpose in life.

Jake came in carrying a tray of cookies and a pot of tea. "Chemmg, it's good . . . where is he?"

"He had to leave. He wanted me to tell you that he approves of my being your disciple."

"That's it?" Jake put the tray down and turned away from Martin.

"Jake? He's happy. I think he'll rest now."

Martin woke up. He was smiling with joy.

***

The invitation had said, "No presents," but Mac told Bonnie that they should get him something. "Even if he gets mad, we owe him."

They searched the antique shops, hoping that something would catch their attention. The West Side of Cleveland was full of small antique shops, from secondhand stores to antique emporiums. Every time Bonnie found something, Mac said that Jake had something just like it, but better.

After almost a week, they were ready to give up. They had had fun shopping together, but their goal seemed as far away as possible. "Why don't we just get him a toaster oven?" Bonnie suggested as they sipped on hot chocolate.

"That's it!" Mac grinned. "We've been looking for something that would fit one of his collections. And only Jake knows what that is. Let's get him a coffee set with a creamer and a sugar bowl. Huh? What do you think?"

They found a beautiful ceramic set. It had a contemporary Southwest Indian feel. Each piece was low and round, unglazed gray and glazed black. There was a coffee pot, a creamer, a sugar bowl, four small mugs, and a tray. It was pricey. The store gift-wrapped it for them. On the tag, it said it was from Bonnie, Mac, Julia, and Martin.

The party was to start at six-thirty. Bonnie wanted them to get dressed up. Julia and Martin didn't want to. Mac came to their rescue. "Bonnie, Jake's going to look like he always does and he's not going to care one way or the other if we get dressed up for this. Let Martin and Julia go the way they want."

Bonnie relented. "But I am going to get dressed up and so are you."

They were a little late by the time they arrived. Roy was there, with a tall red head, who he introduced as Catrina; she was another of his regulars. Mac recognized one of the health food store owners with a man he assumed was her husband. "Make yourselves at home; you know everyone," Jake said. "I've got to get back to the kitchen, things'll burn."

The place looked wonderful. They all loved the tree. It was in the corner of the living room. Jake had moved the jukebox out of the way. The tree had strands of silver tinsel, with snow sprayed from above so that it piled up as though it had snowed. Scattered carefully throughout the tree were twenty-three little stuffed songbirds; the empty glass bell jar that had held them was safely tucked into his bedroom closet. The tree was bathed in the colored lights from the Color Ray Emanator that he had found in Pittsburgh; no other lights were on in the living room, except the jukebox to the left of the fireplace. Under the tree, were a dozen boxes, all beautifully wrapped. Jake said that they were empties. "That way, if the tree stays up past Christmas it still looks festive."

Martin showed Bonnie and Julia around. Julia loved it. Bonnie was overwhelmed. Mac fixed himself a drink and got caught up with Roy.

Jake brought out trays of food. There was more than they'd

ever be able to finish: chili con queso, with home made chips, tamalitos filled with cheese and green chili, chicken tacos with a chipotle sauce, green corn tamales, cheese enchiladas, and for dessert, natilla, a creamy custard with a drizzle of caramelized sauce. "Help yourselves. I can't do everything," Jake yelled as he ran back into the kitchen for a pitcher of batitas that he had just mixed.

Bonnie whispered to Mac, "You've warned me; is this going to be okay?"

Mac smiled. "When he has the time to prepare, and there are this many people, I'd say it'll be spectacular, if you like Mexican."

Martin and Julia sat on the floor. Mac joined them but Bonnie refused.

The conversation was light and full of true holiday cheer. Jake's enthusiasm was contagious.

Roy started to sort quietly through the boxes under the tree. "Nothing for me? I can't find anything with my name on it."

"I told you, no presents. Come on, stop, you're going to mess it all up. Sorry, but there's nothing there for anyone." Jake looked around a little sheepishly, as though he suddenly felt that he should have had real presents. "I didn't think—"

"Jake, I know what your invitation said, but we do have something for you." Mac got up and brought the present out from where he had hidden it on the porch. "It's from the whole gang."

Jake started to put it under the tree. "No you don't; you open it. Here and now," Bonnie chided.

Jake was embarrassed. He hated this sort of thing; it was hard for him to receive. He tore off the wrapping and opened the box. On the floor in front of him, he placed the coffee set.

Everyone clapped and laughed. They had all had coffee with him one time or another.

Roy pulled a package out of Catrina's handbag. "I was going to leave this here as we left, but I hate seeing you like this. Take it like a man." He grinned as he handed it to Jake. "Of course it's from both of us."

Jake opened his present; copies of Roy's three books. "And they're paperbacks!" Roy said.

"You're not going to ask me to read them, are you?"

"Yes."

"I guess I probably should after all these years." Jake squeezed Roy's shoulder. "Thank you. It'll be my pleasure."

By midnight, all the guests had departed, with the exception of Mac and his new family. Bonnie and Julia insisted on cleaning up.

"Please, it's my party; I intend to clean up, not my guests."

"No, we're going to," Bonnie said. "You two look like you need to talk alone. So talk."

Mac watched Bonnie and Julia walk down the hall. "Okay Jake, what's up?"

"What?"

"With Martin."

Jake winked at Martin. "Mac, maybe I should've said something to you before, but . . . I've finally got a disciple."

Mac looked at Martin; suddenly it became clear to him why everything had happened as it had. "Martin? Do you know what you're getting into?"

"Yes, I do."

"Why don't you help your mother for a minute or two, I want to talk with Jake, alone."

Mac waited for Martin to leave. "Are you sure? Martin?"

"Mac, have you noticed anything different about him?"

Mac thought for a minute. "Well, he's better mannered, quiet, and polite. He doesn't argue as much."

"That's just a small part of it. Don't you feel that he's confident and determined, not out of the bravado of youth, but from experience? Forget that he's Martin Winslow."

Mac slowly nodded. "You're right. Why?"

"Because that's what he is. Martin is really special. He's progressed so far in the last couple of weeks, more than I did in a couple of years, it's a little frightening."

"You'll be careful with him? We've all been through a lot to get him back."

"Don't worry. We won't lose him again." Jake got up and poured a glass of eggnog. "Want some?"

Mac looked at his watch. "Sure."

Martin joined them. "They kicked me out of the kitchen."

It was nearly one o'clock by the time Bonnie and Julia quit. "We ran out of space to hide things. Tomorrow, you're on your own. . . . Look at the time. We should go soon." Bonnie looked at Mac; he would stay another hour or two if she didn't start campaigning.

"One more round of eggnog," Jake suggested. "Then you can go out into the cold night."

Bonnie fell asleep after half an hour, but it took Mac another fifteen minutes to know that it was really time to leave. Jake got their coats.

Jake was just closing the door as they started down the stairs when Martin turned and ran back. "Jake, wait a second."

Martin stood in front of Jake, the cold air from the stairwell rushing into the apartment. "I . . ."

"What? It's cold." Jake grinned.

"I just wanted to tell you . . . I like Chemmg Tse Lu." Martin turned and ran back downstairs and outside, skating down the snow covered sidewalk.